Sweet nothings, Long, Tall Texan style!

"Don't fight what you're feeling," he whispered roughly.

Meredith heard Rey's words as if through a fog, but her body obeyed him as he began to increase the teasing pressure of his mouth. She followed his lips and relaxed into the curve of his powerful body with a little shiver.

He devoured her mouth, tempting her until her mouth followed his, returning the arousing pressure. She could see the glitter grow in his narrow eyes, feel the grip of his lean hands as he pushed her hips against the sudden hardness of him. She gasped with embarrassment and then lost all sense of it as his mouth opened and pushed down hard against her parted lips, drowning her in passion.

It was like flying, she thought dazedly. He hesitated for an instant and her eyes opened, drowsy and curious. Her mouth was swollen, soft, tremulous. She looked at him with fascination, utterly helpless in his embrace.

"Why did you do that?" she asked huskily.

One dark eyebrow rose. He didn't smile. "Why did you let me?" he shot back.

He may not be silver-tongued, but the man is surely a devil...

"That shouldn't have happened," Leo said harshly.

"It's like the flu," Janie said, dazed, staring up at him. "It makes you...ache."

He shook her gently. "You're too young to have aches, and I'm old enough to know better."

Of course he hadn't meant to kiss her. He'd made his opinion of her clear for years, and even if he liked kissing her, it didn't mean that he was ready to rush out and buy a ring. Quite the opposite.

She stepped away from him, her face still flushed, her eyes full of dreams. "No—no harm done," she stammered. She cleared her throat and fought for inspiration. It came unexpectedly. Her eyes began to twinkle wickedly and she smiled. "I have to take lessons when they're offered."

His eyebrows shot up. Had he heard her say that, or was he delusional?

She was pretty when she smiled like that, he thought, observing her. "Do I get invited to supper?" he drawled, lost in that soft, hungry look she was giving him. "If you say yes, I might consider giving you a few more lessons...."

DIANA PALMER

THE HART BROTHERS
REY & LEO

HQN™

ISBN 0-373-77089-8

THE HART BROTHERS: REY & LEO

Copyright © 2005 by Harlequin Books S.A.

The publisher acknowledges the copyright holders
of the individual works as follows:

A MAN OF MEANS
Copyright © 1999 by Diana Palmer

LIONHEARTED
Copyright © 1999 by Susan Kyle

This edition published by arrangement with Harlequin Books S.A.

® and TM are trademarks of the publisher. Trademarks indicated with
® are registered in the United States Patent and Trademark Office, the
Canadian Trade Marks Office and in other countries.

www.HQNBooks.com

Printed in U.S.A.

CONTENTS

For Cissy at Writerspace, Sara, Jill and Celeste, and all the wonderful readers, many of whom I was privileged to meet in Atlanta in 2001 at our author tea, who visit me online there at my Web site. Love you all. DP

A MAN OF MEANS

Chapter One

Meredith Johns glanced around her worriedly at the out-of-control Halloween party-goers in their colorful costumes. Meredith was wearing an outfit left over from college days. She made a good salary at her job, but there was no money for little luxuries like Halloween costumes. She had to budget just to be able to pay the utility bill in the house she shared with her father.

The past few months had been traumatic, and the wear was telling on her. She needed to get out of the house, Jill, one of her colleagues, had said firmly—especially after her most agonizing experience at home. Meredith was reluctant. Her father was only just back at their house after three days. But Jill was insistent. So she'd put on the only costume she had, a bad choice in many ways, and walked the three blocks to her friend's downtown apartment. She grimaced at her surroundings. What an idiot she'd been to come to this wild party.

But it really had been a tumultuous week for Meredith and she'd wanted to get her mind off her troubles. Her father's violent behavior at the house they shared was unnerving. They were both still grieving, but her father had taken the tragedy much harder. He felt responsible. That was why a scholarly, conservative college professor had suddenly retired from his job and turned into an alcoholic. Meredith had tried everything she could think of to get him into treatment, but he refused to go on his own accord and the treatment facilities which would have taken him wouldn't unless he went voluntarily. Only a violent episode that had landed him in jail had temporarily spared her of this saddening experience. But he was out three days later and he had a new bottle of whiskey. She still had to go home after the party. He'd warned her not to be late. Not that she ever was.

Her grey eyes were sad as she sipped her soft drink. She had no head for alcohol, and she was as out of place here as a cup of tea. Not only that, her costume was drawing unwanted attention from the men. So was her long blond hair. It had been a bad costume choice, but it was the only thing she had to wear on the spur of the moment. Going to a Halloween party in her street clothes would have made her stand out, too.

She moved away from a slightly tipsy colleague who wanted to show her around Jill's bedroom and unobtrusively put her glass on a table. She found Jill, pleaded a headache, thanked her for a "good" time and headed out the front door as fast as she could. Once on the sidewalk, she drew in a long, sweet breath of fresh air.

What a bunch of wild people! She coughed delicately, remembering the unmistakable smell of that smoke that had been thick enough to obstruct clear vision inside. She'd thought it would be fun to go to a party. She might even meet a man who would be willing to take her out and cope with her father. And cows might fly, she told herself. She hadn't been out on a date in months. She'd invited one prospective date to her home for supper. But after a good look at her father, who was mean when he drank, the prospective suitor took off. Her heart wasn't in it, anyway. Recently she'd given up trying to attract anyone. She had her hands full already. Her grief was still fresh, too.

An odd noise attracted her attention as she started back toward her own house. She felt self-conscious in her getup, and remembering the lewd remarks she'd drawn from a man who was normally very polite and gentlemanly, she was sorry she hadn't had a coat to wear. Her clothes were mostly old, because by the time she made the mortgage payment and took care of the bills, there wasn't much left over. Her father couldn't work and wouldn't get help, and she loved him too much to desert him. It was becoming a costly proposition.

She wrapped her arms around herself and hoped she was covering up enough skin to discourage stalkers. But her skirt was very short and tight, and she was wearing fishnet hose, very high heels, a low-cut blouse and a flaming pink feather boa. Her blond hair was loose around her shoulders and she was wearing enough makeup to do justice to a ballet recital. She winced, hoping she hadn't been noticed. She'd gone to the party as a burlesque dancer. Sadly she looked more like a professional hooker in her garb.

She rounded a corner and saw two shadowy figures bending over what looked like a man on the ground.

"Hey! What do you think you're doing there?!" she yelled, making as much noise as possible. Then she started running toward them and waving her arms, yelling threats as she went.

As she expected, the surprise of her aggressive presence shocked them into retreat. They jumped up and ran away, without even looking back. The best defense, she thought with faint amusement, was always a good offense. It was a calculated bluff, but she'd seen it work for women smaller in stature than she was.

She ran to the downed man and examined him the best she could in the dim glow of the streetlights.

Concussion, she thought, feeling his head and encountering a metallic smelling wetness. Blood. He'd been hit on the head by his assailants, and probably robbed as well. She felt around under the jacket he was wearing and her hand touched something small and square on his belt. She pulled it out.

"Aha," she said with a triumphant grin. A man dressed as well as he was could be expected to have a cell phone. She dialed 911 and gave the operator her location and the condition of her patient, staying on the line while the dispatcher got an ambulance en route.

While she waited for it, she sat down on the pavement beside the man and held his hand.

He groaned and tried to move.

"Don't do that," she said firmly. "You'll be okay. You mustn't move until the EMTs get here. I haven't got anything to treat you with."

"Head...hurts."

"I imagine it does. You've got a heck of a bump. Just lie still. Feel sick, sleepy...?"

"Sick," he managed weakly.

"Lie still." She lifted her head to listen for the ambulance, and sure enough, a siren sounded nearby. The hospital was less than two blocks from her home, maybe four from here. Lucky for this guy, whoever he was. Head injuries could be fatal.

"My...brothers," the man was whispering brokenly. "Hart...Ranch. Jacobsville, Texas."

"I'll make sure they're contacted," she promised.

He gripped her hand, hard, as he fought not to lose consciousness. "Don't...leave me," he ground out.

"I won't. I promise."

"Angel," he whispered. He took a long, shaky breath, and went back into the oblivion he'd left so briefly. That wasn't a good sign.

The ambulance rounded the corner, and the headlights spilled out onto Meredith and her patient. She got to her feet as two EMTs, one male and one female, piled out the doors and rushed to the downed man.

"Head wound," she told them. "Pulse is slow, but steady. He's coherent, some nausea, his skin is cold and clammy. Blunt force trauma, probably mild concussion…"

"Don't I know you?" the female EMT asked. Her face brightened. "Got you! You're Johns!"

"That's me," Meredith said with a grin. "I must be famous!"

"Sorry, not you—your dad." She winced at the look on Meredith's face.

Meredith sighed. "Yes, he spends a lot of time on ambulances these days."

"What happened here?" the woman asked quickly, changing the subject. "Did you see anything?"

"I yelled and scared off two guys who were bending over him," she volunteered. "I don't know if they were the ones who hit him or not. What do you think?" she added as the woman gave him a professional once-over.

"Concussion, definitely," she agreed. "Nothing broken, but he's got a lump the size of the national debt here on his head. We'll transport him. Coming along?"

"I guess I should," Meredith said, waiting until they loaded him onto the gurney. He was still unconscious. "But I'm not exactly dressed for visiting a hospital."

The EMT gave her a speaking glance. "Should I ask why you're dressed like that? And does your boss know you're moonlighting?" she added wickedly.

"Jill Baxley had a Halloween party. She thought I should come."

The other woman's eyebrows levered up. "Jill's parties are

notorious for getting out of control. I've never even seen you take a drink."

"My father drinks enough for both of us," came the reply. "I don't drink or use drugs, and I need my head examined for going to that party. I escaped early, which is how I found this guy."

"Lucky for him," the woman murmured as they loaded him into the back of the ambulance. "Judging by his condition, he could have died if he hadn't been found in time."

Meredith climbed up into the back and sat down on the bench while the driver got in under the wheel and the female EMT called the hospital emergency room for orders. It was going to be a long night, Meredith thought worriedly, and her father was going to be very upset when she got home. He and her mother had been really close, but her mother had been fond of going to parties and staying out until the early morning; sometimes with other men. Recent events had made him dwell on that behavior. Her father seemed to have transferred that old contempt to her. It made her uneasy to think of arriving home in the wee hours. Anything could happen. On the other hand, how could she leave this man? She was the only person who knew who to contact for him. She'd promised to stay with him. She couldn't let him down.

He was examined by the resident on duty in the emergency room, who diagnosed concussion. He'd been unconscious most of the way to the hospital, but he'd come out of it just once to look up at Meredith and smile, tightening his big hand around the fingers that were holding it.

His family had to be notified, and Meredith was coaxed into making the call to Jacobsville for the harassed and overworked emergency room staff.

She was given a phone and a telephone directory which

also listed Jacobs County, of which Jacobsville was the county seat. She looked through it until she found a listing for Hart Ranch Properties, Inc. That had to be it.

She dialed the number and waited. A deep, drawling voice answered, "Hart Ranch."

"Uh, I'm calling for a Mr. Leo Hart," she said, having found his driver's license in the wallet his assailants hadn't had time to steal. "He's at Houston General…"

"What happened?" the voice asked impatiently. "Is he all right?"

"He was mugged. He has a concussion," she added. "He can't give the staff any medical information…"

"Who are you?"

"I'm Meredith Johns. I work…"

"Who found him?"

"I did, actually. I called the ambulance on his cell phone. He said to call his brothers and he told me where they were…"

"It's two o'clock in the morning!" the voice pointed out angrily.

"Yes, I am aware of that," she began. "It only happened a little while ago. I was walking down the street when I saw him on the sidewalk. He needs his family—"

"I'm his brother, Rey. I'll be there in thirty minutes."

"Sir, it's a long way to Houston from where you are. If you drive that fast…!" she said at once.

"We have an airplane. I'll get the pilot out of bed right now. Thanks." He added that last word as if it hurt him, and hung up.

Meredith went back to the waiting room. Ten minutes later, she was admitted to the room where the victim had been examined.

"He's conscious," the attending physician told her. "I'm

going to admit him overnight, just to be sure. Any luck with his family?"

"His brother is on the way, in his own plane, apparently," she said. "I didn't get a thing out of him. Sorry."

"People get upset and they don't think," the resident said with a weary smile. "How about staying with him? We're understaffed because of that respiratory virus that's going around, and he shouldn't be alone."

"I'll stay," she said with a grin. "It's not as if I have a hectic social life."

The resident pursed his lips and smirked at her outfit.

"Halloween party," she said, grimacing. "And next time I get invited, I'll have a broken leg, I swear it!"

Forty-five minutes later, there was a problem. It was six feet tall, had black hair and dark eyes and it erupted into the hospital cubicle like an F-5 tornado, dressed in jeans and boots and a fringed rawhide jacket thrown carelessly over what looked like a beige silk shirt. The wide-brimmed hat slanted over those threatening eyes was a Stetson, one of the most expensive made, with its distinctive feathered logo pin on the hatband. He looked impressively rich, and excessively angry.

The man was livid when he saw his big brother, still drifting in and out of consciousness, on the examining table. He gave Meredith a scrutiny that could have peeled paint off old furniture, his eyes narrowing contemptuously on her costume.

"Well, that explains why you were on the street at two in the morning," he snarled angrily. "What happened? Did you feel guilty and call for help after you tried to roll him?" he added sarcastically.

"Look here," she began, rising.

"Save it." He turned to the big man on the table and laid a lean, strong hand on his brother's broad chest. "Leo. Leo, it's Rey! Can you hear me?" he asked in a tone that combined affection with concern.

The big man's eyes blinked and opened. He stared blankly up at the leaner man. "Rey?"

"What happened to you?" Rey Hart demanded gently.

Leo grinned wearily. "I was thinking about new forage grasses and wasn't paying attention to my surroundings," he murmured drowsily. "Something hit me in the head and I went down like a brick. Didn't see a thing." He winced and felt clumsily in his pockets. "Damn! My wallet's gone. So's my cell phone."

Meredith started to tell him that she had the phone and wallet in her purse for safekeeping, but before she could speak, Rey Hart gave her a furious, speaking glance and walked out of the cubicle like a man hunting a fight.

His brother drifted off again. Meredith stood beside him, wondering what to do. Five minutes later, Rey Hart walked back in accompanied by a tall man in a police uniform. He looked familiar, but Meredith couldn't quite place him. She knew she'd seen him before.

"That's her," Rey told the policeman, indicating Meredith. "I'll sign anything necessary as soon as I see that my brother's going to be okay. But get her out of here."

"Don't worry. I'll handle it," the policeman said quietly. He handcuffed Meredith with easy efficiency and pulled her out of the cubicle before she could protest.

"I'm being arrested?" she exclaimed, stunned. "But, why? I haven't done anything!"

"Yes, I know, I've heard it all before," the officer told her in a bored tone when she tried to explain what had happened. "Nobody's ever guilty. Honest to God, dressed like that, out on the streets alone after midnight, you were bound to be up to no good. What did you do with his cell phone and his wallet?"

"They're in my pocketbook," she began.

He confiscated it from her shoulder and propelled her out of the building. "You're going to be in a lot of trouble. You picked the wrong man to rob."

"See here, I didn't mug him! It was two men. I didn't see their faces, but they were bending over him as I came down the sidewalk."

"Soliciting is a felony," he pointed out.

"I wasn't soliciting anything! I'd just come from a Halloween party dressed as a burlesque dancer!" she raged, furious that she was being punished for having done someone a good turn. She read his name tag. "Officer Sanders, you have to believe me!"

He didn't say a word. He drew her with him, firmly but gently, and put her into the back seat of the police car.

"Wait," she told him before he could close the door. "You get my wallet out of my purse and look in it. Right now," she insisted.

He gave her an impatient look, but he did what she asked. He looked through the plastic inserts in her wallet and glanced at her with a changed expression. "I thought you looked familiar, Johns," he murmured, using her last name, as most people she knew at work did.

"I didn't mug Mr. Hart," she continued. "And I can prove where I was when he was being mugged." She gave him her friend Jill's address.

He gave in. He drove to Jill's apartment, went to the door, spoke to an obviously intoxicated and amused Jill, and came back to the squad car. He let Meredith out of the back of the squad car and took off the handcuffs. It was cool in the night air, and Meredith felt self-conscious and uncomfortable in her garb, even though the police officer knew the truth now.

"I'm really sorry," he told her with a grimace as he met her grey eyes. "I didn't recognize you. All I knew was what Mr. Hart told me, and he was too upset to think straight. You have to admit, you don't look very professional tonight."

"I do realize that. Mr. Hart cares about his brother, and he doesn't know what happened," she pointed out. "He walked in and saw his brother on the table and me dressed like this," she indicated her clothing, "and his brother said his wallet and cell phone were missing. He doesn't know me from a stump. You can't blame him for thinking the worst. But those two men who hit him would have gotten his wallet if I hadn't come along, and they're still on the loose."

"Can you show me where you found him?" he asked.

"Of course. It was just down the sidewalk, that way."

She led and he followed her, with his big wide-angle flashlight sweeping the sidewalk and the grass as they walked. She pointed to an area of flattened grass. He left her on the sidewalk and gave the area a thorough scrutiny, looking for clues. He found a candy wrapper and a cigarette butt.

"I don't guess you know if Mr. Hart smokes or likes candy?" he asked.

She shook her head. "Sorry. All he told me was his brothers' name and where they lived. I don't know anything more about him."

He stood up. "I'll ask his brother later. Wait here while I call for one of the technicians to bag this evidence," he told her.

"Okay," she said agreeably, drawing the feather boa closer. It was getting cold standing around briefly clad, waiting for crime scene investigators. "Somebody's going to love being turned out of bed to come look at a cigarette butt and a candy wrapper," she stated with helpless amusement.

"You'd be surprised at what excites those guys," he chuckled. "Catching crooks isn't exactly a chore to them. It's high drama."

"I hope they catch these two," she said firmly. "Nobody should have to be afraid to walk down the streets at night. Even after dark, dressed like this, alone," she added pointedly, indicating her clothes.

"Good point," he was fair enough to admit.

He called in his location and requested crime scene technicians. Meredith was ready to go home, but she couldn't leave until she'd given the policeman a statement for his report. She sat in his car, with the overhead lights on, writing out what she knew of the attack on Leo Hart. It didn't take long, because she didn't know much.

She handed it back to him. "Can I go home now?" she asked. "I live with my father and he's going to be upset because I'm coming home so late. I can walk. It's only about three blocks from here."

He frowned. "Your father is Alan Johns, isn't he?" he asked. His expression changed. "Do you want me to go with you?"

She didn't usually flinch at facing her irate parent. She was gutsy, and she could handle herself. But tonight, she'd been through a lot. "Would you?" she asked, uneasy because her fear was visible.

"No problem. Get in."

He drove her to her house and went to the door with her. The house was dark and there was no movement inside. She let out a sigh of relief. "It's okay. If he was awake, the lights would be on. Thanks, anyway," she said with a smile.

"If you need us, call," he said. "I'm afraid I'll be in touch again about this. Rey Hart already reminded me that his brother is our state attorney general. He's not going to let this case go until it's solved."

"I don't blame him. Those guys are a menace and they're probably still running around looking for easy targets to rob. Take care."

"You, too. And I'm sorry about the handcuffs," he added, with the first smile she'd seen on his lean face since her ordeal began.

She smiled back. "My fault, for wearing a costume like this on the streets," she admitted. "I won't do it again. Thanks for the ride."

Back at the hospital, Rey Hart sat by his brother's bedside until dawn, in the private room he'd obtained for him. He was worried. Leo was the hardiest one of the lot, and the most cautious as a rule. He was the prankster, always playing jokes, cheering them up in bad times. Now, he lay still and quiet and Rey realized how much his sibling meant to him.

It infuriated him that that woman had thought nothing of robbing his brother while he was sick and weak and helpless. He wondered what she'd hit him with. She wasn't a big woman. Odd, that she'd been able to reach as high as Leo's head with some blunt object. He recalled with distaste the way she'd been dressed. He was no prude, but in his early twenties he'd had a fling with a woman he later found out was a private call girl. He'd been infatuated with her, and thought she loved him. When he learned her profession and that she'd recognized him at once and knew how wealthy he was, it had soured him on women. Like his married brothers had been, and Leo still was, he was wary of females. If he could find a man who could bake biscuits, he told himself, he'd never let even an old woman into the house ever again.

He recalled their latest acquisition with sorrow. He and Leo had found a retired pastry chef who'd moved in with them—the last of the Hart bachelors—to bake their beloved biscuits. She'd become ill and they'd rushed to the drugstore to get her prescriptions, along with candy and chocolates and a bundle of flowers. But her condition had worsened and she'd told them, sadly, that the job was just too much in her frail state of health. She had to quit. It was going to be hard to replace her. There weren't a lot of people who wanted to live on an isolated ranch and bake biscuits at all hours of the day and night. Even want ads with offers of a princely salary hadn't attracted anyone just yet. It was depressing; like having Leo lying there under white sheets, so still and quiet in that faded striped hospital gown.

Rey dozed for a few hours in the deep night, used to sleeping in all sorts of odd positions and places. Cattle ranchers could sleep in the saddle when they had to, he thought amusedly, especially when calving was underway or there was a storm or they were cutting out and branding calves and doing inventory of the various herds.

But he came awake quickly when Sanders, the police officer who'd arrested that woman last night, came into the room with a murmured apology.

"I'm just going off shift," Officer Sanders told Rey. "I thought I'd stop by and tell you that we've gone over the scene of the attack and we have some trace evidence. The detectives will start looking for other witnesses this morning. We'll get the people responsible for the attack on your brother."

Rey frowned. "Get 'them?'" he queried. "You've already got her. You arrested her!"

Officer Sanders averted his eyes. "Had to turn her loose," he said uneasily. "She had an alibi, which was confirmed. She gave me a statement and I took her home."

Rey stood up, unfolding his intimidating length, and glared at the officer. "You let her go," he said coldly. "Where's my brother's cell phone?" he added as an afterthought.

The policeman grimaced. "In her purse, along with his wallet," he said apologetically. "I forgot to ask her for them when I left. Tell you what, I'll swing by her house and get them on my way home…"

"I'll go with you," he said curtly. "I still think she's guilty. She's probably in cahoots with the guys who attacked Leo. And she could have paid someone to lie and give her an alibi."

"She's not that sort of woman," the policeman began.

Rey cut him off angrily. "I don't want to hear another word about her! Let's go," he said, grabbing his hat, with a last, worried glance at his sleeping brother. He wondered how the policeman could make such a statement about a woman he'd just met, but he didn't really care. He wanted her in jail.

He drove his rental car, with the off-duty policeman beside him, to Meredith's home, following the directions Officer Sanders gave him. It was in a run-down neighborhood, and the house was in poor condition. It only intensified Rey's suspicions about her. She was obviously poor. What better way to get money than to rob somebody?

He went to the door, accompanied by the policeman, and knocked. Hard.

He had to do it three times, each with more force and impatience, before someone answered the door.

Meredith Johns was disheveled and white-faced. She was clutching a bulky washcloth to her face and wearing a robe over the clothes she'd had on the night before.

"What do you want now?" she asked huskily, her voice slurred and jerky.

"Been drinking, have you?" Rey Hart asked in a blistering tone.

She flinched.

Officer Sanders knew what was going on. He read the situation immediately. He stepped past Rey, grim and silent, grimacing when he saw Meredith's face. He went by her and into the living room and began looking around.

"Hard night, I gather? It must be a continual risk, in your profession," Rey said insinuatingly, with a speaking glance at her dress in the opening of the old, worn robe. "Do your marks make a habit of beating you up?" he added with cold contempt.

She didn't answer him. It was hard to talk and her face hurt.

Officer Sanders had gone into the bedroom. He came back two minutes later with a tall, disheveled but oddly dignified-looking man in handcuffs. The man, who'd been quiet before, was now cursing furiously, accusing Meredith of everything from prostitution to murder in a voice that rose until he was yelling. Rey Hart looked at him with obvious surprise. His eyes went to Meredith Johns, who was stiff as a poker and wincing every time the man yelled at her. The policeman picked up the telephone and called for a squad car.

"Please, don't," Meredith pleaded, still clutching the ice-filled cloth to her face. "He's only just got out…"

"He isn't staying. This time, he's going to be in jail for longer than three days," the officer said firmly. "You get to the hospital and let one of the residents look at you, Miss Johns. How bad is it? Come on, show me," he demanded, moving closer.

Rey stood by, silent and confused, watching as Meredith winced and moved the bulky cloth away from her face. His breath was audible when he saw the swelling and the growing purple and violet discoloration around her eye, cheek and jaw.

"God Almighty," Rey said harshly. "What did he hit you with?"

"His fist," the policeman replied coldly. "And it isn't the first time. You have to face facts, Miss Johns," he told her. "He isn't the man he used to be. When he drinks, he doesn't know what he's doing. He'll kill you one night when he's like this, and he won't even remember doing it!"

"I won't press charges," she said miserably. "How can I? He's my father! He's the only family I have left in the world…."

The policeman looked at her with compassion. "You don't have to press charges," he told her. "I'll provide them myself. You'd better phone your boss and tell him you won't be in for a few weeks. He'll have kittens if you walk into the office looking like that."

"I suppose he would." Tears ran down her pale cheeks, all the more eloquent for being silent. She looked at her raging, cursing father and sadness claimed her features. "He wasn't like this before, honest he wasn't," she told them. "He was a kind, loving, caring man."

"Not anymore," Officer Sanders replied grimly. "Get to the hospital and have your face seen about, Miss Johns. I'll take your father outside until the unit comes…."

"No," she groaned. "Please, spare us that! I can't bear to have the whole neighborhood watching, hearing him…like that, again!"

He hesitated. "Okay. I'll watch for them out the window. The unit can drop you by the hospital, since it's going there first…."

"I'll take her," Rey said at once, without wondering why he should do such an about-face. He didn't trust the woman, or even totally believe her story. But she did look so pitiful. He couldn't bear to leave her in that condition to get to the hospital. Besides, whatever her motives, she had gotten help for Leo. He could have died if he hadn't been cared for.

"But…" she began.

"If," he added coldly, "you change clothes first. I am *not* being seen in public with you in that rig!"

Chapter Two

Meredith wished she felt up to a fight. Her long blond hair was down in her face, her grey eyes were sparking fire. But she was sick to her stomach and bruised. She would rather have gone to bed if these stubborn men would just have let her alone. But her face could have broken or shattered bones. She knew that. She grimaced, hoping her insurance would cover a second "accident" in as many months.

When the unit arrived, Meredith turned away from the sight of her raging father being carried off and closed the door. Probably it wasn't surprising to the neighbors anymore, it happened so often. But she hated having everyone know.

"I'll get dressed," she said in a subdued tone.

Rey watched her go and then shoved his hands into his pockets and looked around the room. It was shabby. The only bright things in it were books—hundreds of them, in bookcases and boxes and stacked on tables and chairs. Odd, he thought. They were apparently short of cash, judging by the worn old furniture and bare floor. There was only a very small television and a portable stereo. He glanced at the CD case and was surprised to find classical music dominating the discs. What a peculiar family. Why have so many books and so little else? He wondered where the woman's mother was. Had she left the father, and was that why he drank? It would have explained a lot. He knew about missing parents, especially missing mothers—his had left the family while the five Hart boys were young, without a backward glance.

Minutes later, Meredith came back, and except for the bruised face, he might not have recognized her. She was wearing a beige sweater set, with a tweed coat over it. Her blond hair was in a neat bun and her face devoid of makeup. She wore flat-heeled shoes and carried a purse that looked new.

"Here's your brother's cell phone and his wallet," she said, handing it to him. "I forgot to give them to Officer Sanders."

He glared at them and put them in his pocket. He wondered if she'd have given them back at all if he hadn't come here. He didn't trust her, regardless of what the policeman had said. "Let's go," he said stiffly. "The car's outside."

She hesitated, but only for a minute. She wasn't going to be able to avoid a checkup. She knew the problems that negligence could cause. Even a relatively minor problem could become major.

Unexpectedly Rey opened the car door for her. She slid in, surprised to find herself in a new luxury car. She fastened her seat belt. His brother, Simon Hart, was state attorney general. Rey owned a ranch. She remembered how his injured brother, Leo, had been dressed last night, and her eyes went to Rey's expensive hat and boots and silk shirt. Of course, they were a wealthy family. Considering her state of dress—or undress—the night before, she could understand his misgivings about her character.

She sat wearily beside him, the ice-filled cloth still in her hand. She held it to the side of her face that was bruised and hoped that it would spare her some of the swelling. She didn't need a doctor to tell her that it was a bad blow. The pain was almost unbearable.

"I took a hit to the face a few years ago in a brawl," he

volunteered in his deep, slow drawl. "It hurt like hell. I imagine your face does, too."

She swallowed, touched by the faint concern. Tears threatened, but she never cried now. It was a weakness she couldn't afford.

He glanced at her, puzzled. "Nothing to say?"

She managed to get her voice under control. "Thank you for taking me to the hospital," she said huskily.

"Do you usually dress like that when you go out at night?" he asked belatedly.

"I told you. There was…a Halloween party," she said. It hurt to talk. "It was the only costume I had."

"Do you like parties?" he asked sarcastically.

"My first one…in almost four years," she managed to say. "Please…hurts…to talk."

He glanced at her and then was quiet. He didn't like her. He didn't trust her. Why was he taking care of her? There was something unexpectedly vulnerable about her. But she had spirit.

He walked her into the emergency room. She filled out forms and was ushered back into a treatment cubicle while Rey sat in the waiting room between a squalling toddler and a man coughing his head off. He wasn't used to illness. He'd never seen much of it, and he didn't know how to cope with it. Accidents, sure, he was a good hand in an emergency, and there were plenty on a ranch. But he hated hospitals.

Meredith came back a good thirty minutes later with a prescription and a frown.

"What did he say?" he asked conversationally.

She shrugged. "He gave me something…for pain," she said, waving the prescription.

"They sent me to a plastic surgeon," he volunteered as they went through the automatic door.

She didn't speak.

"I had a shattered bone in my cheek that they couldn't repair," he persisted.

"I'm not…going…to any damned…plastic surgeon!"

His eyebrows arched. "Your face could be distorted."

"So what?" she muttered, wincing because it really did hurt to speak. "It's not…much of a face, anyway."

He scowled. She wasn't pretty, but her face had attractive features. Her nose was straight and elegant, she had high cheekbones. Her mouth was like a little bow, perfect. Her eyes, big and grey, fascinated him.

"You should go," he said.

She ignored him. "Can you…drive me by the pharmacy?"

"Sure."

She gave him directions and he waited while she had the prescription filled. He drove her back to her house and left her there reluctantly.

"I'll be at the hospital with Leo if you need anything," he said as if it pained him to say it.

"I don't need any help. Thanks," she added stiffly.

His eyebrows arched. "You remind me of me," he murmured, and a thin smile touched his lips—a kind one. "Proud as Lucifer."

"I get by. I really am…sorry about your brother. Will he be all right?" she asked at her door.

He nodded. "They want to keep him for two or three days. He'll want to thank you."

"No need. I would have done it for anyone."

He sighed. She was going to look bad for a long time, with her face in that condition. She'd been beaten and he felt responsible, God knew why. He took a breath. "I'm sorry I had you arrested," he said reluctantly.

She pursed her lips. "I'll bet…that hurt."

"What?"

"You don't apologize much, do you?" she asked, as if she knew.

He scowled down at her, puzzled.

She turned away. "No sweat. I'll live. So long."

She went in and closed the door. Rey, who'd done without companionship for a number of years, suddenly felt alone. He didn't like the feeling, so he shoved it out of his mind and drove back to the hospital. He wouldn't see her again, anyway.

Leo came back to himself with a vengeance late that afternoon. He had Rey lever the head of his bed up and he ate dinner with pure enjoyment.

"It's not bad," Leo murmured between mouthfuls. "But I wish I had a biscuit."

"Me, too," Rey said on a sigh. "I guess we could buy a restaurant, as a last resort," he added dejectedly. "One that serves breakfast."

"Who was that woman who came in with me?" he asked Rey.

"You remember her?" Rey was surprised.

"She looked like an angel," he mused, smiling. "Blond and big-eyed and all heart. She held my hand and sat down on the sidewalk in the cold and talked to me until the ambulance got there."

"You were unconscious."

"Not all the time. She even came in with me on the ambulance," he said. "She kept telling me I was going to be all right. I remember her voice." He smiled. "Her name was Meredith."

Rey's heart jumped. He felt uneasy. Leo usually didn't pay much attention to strange women. "Meredith Johns," he agreed.

"Is she married?" Leo asked at once.

Rey felt threatened; it irritated him. "I don't know," he said.

"Do you think you could find somebody who knows how to get in touch with her?" his brother persisted. "I want to thank her for saving me."

Rey got up from the chair where he'd been sitting and walked to the darkened window, peering out through the blinds while he played for time. "She lives near the place where you were attacked," he said finally, unable to lie.

"What does she do for a living?"

"I don't know," Rey said, feeling uncomfortable. He couldn't get her father's accusing remarks out of his mind. She'd said she was dressed up for a party, she'd even found someone to give her an alibi, but Rey didn't completely believe her. What if that whole defense was a lie? What if she was some sort of prostitute? He didn't want his brother getting mixed up with a woman like that. He didn't trust women, especially strange women. Then he remembered her poor, bruised face and he felt bad about his suspicions.

"I'll ask one of the nurses," Leo said abruptly.

"No need," Rey told him. He turned back around with his hands in his pockets. "If you're determined, I'll go get her in the morning and bring her in to see you."

"Why not tonight?"

Rey let out an impatient breath. "Her father roughed her up because she got home late last night. I took her to the emergency room this morning before I came back here."

Leo's eyes narrowed and went cold. "Her father beat her? And you took her back home to him?" he said angrily.

"He wasn't there. They took him off to jail," he said. His face hardened even more. "She'll have a hell of a bruise. They said she couldn't go back to work for a few weeks." He moved one shoulder restlessly. "Considering the way they live, I don't know how she'll manage," he added reluctantly. "They don't seem to have much. Apparently the old man doesn't work and she's the only one bringing home any money." He didn't volunteer his opinion of how she made it.

Leo leaned back against the pillows. His big frame was without its usual vibrance. His dark eyes were dull, and his lean face was drawn. His blond-streaked brown hair was unkempt, and looked odd in the back where they'd had to shave it to put stitches in. It was a reminder of how tricky head wounds were. Leo was very lucky not to have brain damage. Rey thought about the assailants and his eyes blazed.

"I'm going to phone Simon tonight," he told Leo. "I'm sure the local police will do all they can to catch the guys who waylaid you, but they'll work even harder if they get a call from the state attorney general."

"There you go again, pulling strings," Leo mused.

"It's for a good cause."

"Did you find my wallet and my cell phone?" Leo asked.

"The woman had them. They're in my pocket."

"Good. I didn't think she had anything to do with mugging me. Don't forget your promise to bring Meredith here in the morning," he said.

Now it was "Meredith." Rey didn't like the whole idea of having Leo around the woman, but he didn't have a legitimate reason for keeping her from Leo's side. It would sound even more suspicious if Rey started throwing out sarcastic remarks about her. Leo did love to pull his chain.

"Okay," he said reluctantly.

"Good man," Leo replied with a wan grin. "Nothing like family to look after you."

"Next time, watch your back instead of daydreaming

about forage grasses," Rey said firmly. Then he leaned forward in the chair. "So, tell me what sort of grasses the Cattleman's Association is advocating."

Rey got a hotel room near the hospital, so that he could have a bath and get some rest. The night staff had the phone number, so they could call him immediately if he was needed.

He phoned Simon before he went to bed.

"Leo's been mugged?" Simon exclaimed. "And you didn't call me last night?"

That tone was still intimidating, even though Rey was thirty-one. Simon was the eldest of the five brothers, and the bossiest, next to Cag.

"I was too upset to phone anybody," Rey returned, "and too busy trying to handle…another problem that cropped up. He's all right. Honest. I didn't find out until the early hours of the morning, and it's been a long day. He was already out of danger before it occurred to me that I needed to let you know."

"All right," Simon said, sounding as if he was more relaxed. "Do they have a suspect?"

"No. I thought we did, but it turned out to be a dead end," he added, without going into details about Meredith Johns. "There were two of them, and they haven't been caught. It's a miracle he wasn't killed, and that they were stopped in time before they robbed him. You might give the local police chief a call. Just to let him know we're all interested in solving the case."

"You want me to use my influence for personal gain?" Simon drawled.

"Hell, yes, I do!" Rey shot back. "This is our brother, for God's sake! If a big, strong man like Leo can get mugged in a residential neighborhood, so can anybody else! It doesn't say a lot for the security in this area."

"No, it doesn't," Simon agreed. "I'll point that out to the police commissioner, first thing tomorrow. Then I'll run down to Jacobsville and get Cag and Corrigan and we'll be right up to see about Leo."

Rey chuckled. It was the first bit of humor he'd felt so far. The five brothers rarely went so far as to gang up on people, but considering the size and reputation of them, they got results when they did. This was an emergency, anyway. They could have lost a brother. The perpetrators had to be caught.

"They should be home by now," Rey replied. "I couldn't phone them because they were showing those Japanese businessmen around the ranch and the town."

"I'll see how much luck they had. Japan is very careful about its import beef. The fact that we run organically raised cattle will certainly go in our favor," Simon said.

"Yes, it will. Get some sleep. And don't worry about Leo. He's fine. I'd never have left the hospital if I'd had one doubt about that."

"I'll stop worrying."

"Give my love to Tira and the boys," Rey added.

"I'll do that. See you tomorrow."

Rey hung up, thinking about Simon and his family. Tira was redheaded and gorgeous, and the boys favored both of them, although they had Simon's dark eyes and hair. Corrigan and Dorie had a boy and a girl. Cag and Tess had just a boy, but they were talking about how nice a daughter would be. Meanwhile, Rey and Leo enjoyed being uncles, but had no interest in joining the ranks of the married.

If it wasn't for those biscuits, Rey thought miserably. It was going to be expensive to have the local café make biscuits for them every day until they employed a new biscuit maker, but if they got desperate enough, and offered enough of an incentive, they could probably manage it.

Turning his attention elsewhere, Rey gave a thought to poor Leo with his stitches and his headache, and another to Meredith Johns's bruised face. Tomorrow, he'd have to deal with Leo's request to see her, and he wasn't looking forward to it. He wished he knew why.

Rey went to Meredith Johns's house the next morning after he'd had breakfast. It took her a minute or two to answer the door, and for an instant, he thought that perhaps she might not be in any condition to answer it. She'd been badly bruised.

But she opened the door and peered up at him bravely, even though she looked like a refugee from a bar brawl. Her left eye was swollen shut completely now.

"Leo wants to see you," he said easily, noticing how the top of her blond head only came to his shoulder. She wasn't tall. Even bruised, her face had a beautiful complexion. Her mouth was pretty. He shook himself mentally. "He wants to thank you for what you did. He remembers that you rode in on the ambulance with him. You didn't tell me that," he added with faint accusation.

"I wasn't thinking," she said. "I was worried about what would happen when I came home late."

"Have you heard any more about your father this morning?" he asked grimly.

"They're going to charge him with simple battery," she said heavily. "I can't afford a lawyer. He'll have a public defender and he'll probably have to stay in jail for a few weeks." She looked up at him. "It will be a godsend, you know, because he'll dry out completely."

He hated the compassion he felt. "Did your mother leave him?" he asked.

She averted her face. She couldn't bear to talk about it

yet. "In a way," she said huskily. "Are you going to drive me?" she added, glancing at him over her shoulder. "The bus doesn't run for another thirty minutes."

"Sure," he agreed.

"Then I'll get my jacket and purse."

She went into another room and came back quickly, leading the way out the door. "Is he conscious now?"

"Very," he murmured dryly. "When I left him, he was telling a nurse what she could do with the wash basin, and how far."

She chuckled. "He didn't seem like that kind of man," she murmured. "I had him figured for a gentleman, not a renegade."

"We're all that kind of man," he replied.

"All?"

He led her to the car and put her into the passenger seat. "There are five of us. The other three are coming up this morning to have a talk with the police."

"I remember. You said that your brother was the attorney general."

"He is," he replied. "We tend to stick together."

Her eyes went to his hands on the steering wheel. He had nice hands, very lean and strong with neat, clean fingernails. He was a tough-looking man, like a cowboy.

"How's your face?" he asked unexpectedly.

She shrugged. "It still hurts. It will for a while, but I'll be fine."

"You should see that plastic surgeon."

"Why?" she asked heavily. "My insurance won't pay for cosmetic surgery, and there's not much chance that they can do any major repair on tiny shattered bones."

"You're not a doctor. Stop giving yourself medical advice."

She stared at him for a long moment and started to speak, then lost the opportunity when he pulled up in the hospital parking lot, cut off the engine, and got out.

Rey waited for her and led her up to the floor where his brother's room was located.

Leo wasn't alone. Three other men were with him, one big and dark and missing an arm, the other lean and light-eyed and handsome, and a third big one with black eyes and a threatening face towering over both the others.

"That's Cag," Rey indicated the black-eyed man. "Corrigan," he nodded toward the light-eyed man, "and that's Simon," he finished, smiling at the one-armed man. "This is Meredith Johns. She rescued Leo."

"Nice to see you and know who you are," Leo said, alert now and interested as his dark eyes swept over the neat woman just inside the door. "Miss Johns, I presume?"

She smiled self-consciously, because everybody was looking at her bruised face. "Yes," she said.

Simon Hart frowned when he got a good look at her. "What the hell happened to you?" he demanded.

"Her father," Rey said for her. "She got in late and he beat her up."

Leo looked suddenly as intimidating as the other three. "Where is he?" he asked.

"In jail," Meredith said heavily. "For several weeks, at least, and he'll have time to dry out."

"Good." Leo looked toward Simon. "Maybe you can find a way to get him into rehab before he gets out."

"I'll look into it," Simon said at once.

"And some counseling wouldn't come amiss," Rey put his two cents worth in.

"I'll see about that, too," Simon replied. "Nice to meet you, Miss Johns. We're all grateful for what you did for Leo."

"You're all very welcome," she replied. She clutched her purse, intimidated by the group of brothers.

"Come here," Leo said, holding out his hand. "They're big and they look tough, but they're really marshmallows. You don't have to feel threatened. I'll protect you."

"She doesn't need protecting from us!" Rey snapped.

The others gaped at him. It wasn't like Rey to act that way.

He cleared his throat. He didn't want them asking themselves embarrassing questions about his attitude. He shoved his hands into his pockets. "Sorry. I didn't sleep much last night," he explained.

Meredith went to stand beside Leo, who took one of her small, cold hands in his and looked up at her with interest.

"Have you seen a doctor?" he asked.

"Your brother took me to the emergency room yesterday," she said.

"Rey. His name's Reynard, but he's called Rey," Leo informed her.

She smiled. "You look much better today. Head hurt?"

"A bit, but my vision's clear and I'm not disoriented," he said, quoting the doctor. "I have a good prognosis."

"That's nice to hear. You were in pretty bad shape."

"I'd have been in a lot worse shape, but for you," Leo said. "I hear that you can't work out in public for a while, until your face heals," he added. "Can you cook?"

She blinked. "Of course," she said at once.

"Can you make bread?"

She frowned. "Bread?"

"More specifically, biscuits," he added, and had the oddest expression on his face.

She shifted her purse in the hand he wasn't holding. "Well, yes, those and rolls and loaf bread," she said, as if everybody could do it.

Leo shot a glance at Rey, who was just staring at him without daring to say a word. He knew what was coming, and he couldn't decide how he felt about it. He didn't want to think about it.

"How would you like a brief stay in Jacobsville, Texas, in a big sprawling ranch house where your only job would be to make biscuits every morning?" Leo asked with his best smile.

Rey and the other brothers were staring at her, waiting. She wondered why. And Rey was frowning, as if he didn't like the idea at all. Probably he still secretly thought she was a hooker. He couldn't seem to credit her with any sense of decency.

She thought about his attitude for a few seconds, and decided that it wouldn't be a bad idea to take the job, and show him that you really couldn't judge a book by its cover. It wouldn't hurt that arrogant cowboy to be taken down a step or two, and she was just the girl who could do it.

She smiled. It hurt her face, but what was a little pain for a good cause? She turned back to Leo. "Mr. Hart, I think I'd like that job very much!"

Chapter Three

"Good for you!" Leo exclaimed, animated and smiling. "You won't be sorry, Meredith. Honest."

She smiled back at him. He was nice, like a big brother. She liked him already. "I can do housekeeping, too," she told him. "I'll earn my keep."

"You'll go on salary, of course," he insisted. "It won't be a holiday."

"Nothing is a holiday with those two," Simon murmured dryly. "They aren't kidding about biscuits. They'll run you crazy baking them."

Rey and Leo gave their brother a disgusted look.

Meredith grinned. "I don't mind," she assured Simon. "I love to cook."

"It won't be that hard," Leo promised, with another speaking glance at Simon. "We just love biscuits. But we'll make you feel right at home. Anything you need, you can have— a new stove…" he added mischievously.

She thought about her father and her job, and her smile faltered. "I have to wrap up a few loose ends first," she began.

"No problem," Leo assured her. "I can't get out of here for another day at least, or so that doctor said," he added with impatience.

"You'll stay until he lets you out," Rey said firmly. "Concussions are tricky. You know that."

Leo grimaced. "I guess so. I hate hospitals."

"I'm not too wild about them myself," Rey had to agree.

"It would be a very sad world without them," Meredith spoke up.

She seemed irritated, Rey thought, and wondered why. "I'll run you back home when you're ready," Rey told her. "We'll be in touch before we're ready to leave."

"All right." She held Leo's hand again and squeezed it gently, to the amusement of all the Harts except Rey. "You get better. I'll see you soon."

"Thanks again," Leo told her with genuine gratitude.

"It was nothing." She gave him another smile, tugged her hand free, and let Rey herd her out the door after a quick goodbye to the other brothers.

"I thought your brother was big until I saw all of you together. Goodness, you're all huge!" she exclaimed when they were outside in the parking lot. She gave him a long scrutiny. "And there doesn't seem to be an extra ounce of fat on any of you."

"We don't sit behind desks. We're ranchers, not office workers, and we work hard, right alongside our cowboys," he said. His dark eyes cut sideways. "Leo likes you."

She smiled. "I'm glad, because I like him, too."

That set him off and he tried not to let it show. He didn't want her to like Leo. He wished he knew why. He glanced at her as he wove skillfully through traffic toward her house. "Do you have family besides your father?" he asked.

"A cousin or two near Fort Worth," she said. She glanced out the window, absently rubbing the ring finger of her left hand, trying not to choke up over the question. "What is Jacobsville like?" she asked to divert him from any further questions.

"It's small," he said easily. "There are a lot of ranches in the area. We have good pasture and soil, and we get enough rain to manage healthy crops." He grinned. "A lot of us are heavily into organic cattle raising. And with the industry under threat right now, we'll probably keep our financial heads above water when some other ranchers are going under."

"I like organic food," she said. "It may have a few more blemishes and bug bites, but if it doesn't kill bugs, it won't kill me," she added with a grin.

He chuckled. "Good point. Do you like animals?"

"I love them. I'd like to have a cat, but it's not possible. Dad's allergic to them." She sighed wearily, leaning her head back against the headrest. Her bruises were still giving her a lot of pain. Her hand went to them and she winced.

"You should see that plastic surgeon," he reminded her.

She shook her head. "Can't afford it. Even if I could, I don't want to go through weeks of surgery."

He hesitated and then he shrugged. "Have it your way."

"I'll heal." She touched her cheek again self-consciously. "I'm not sure going to work for you is a good idea. I mean, people might think the five of you beat me up!"

He laughed wholeheartedly. "Nobody who knows us would ever think that. Especially," he added, "if you can bake. Simon was right. I'm afraid we're famous locally for our addiction to biscuits."

Actually they were famous a lot further out than Jacobsville, but he didn't want to make her think they were loopy.

She took the words at face value. "I like to cook."

He glanced at her again, taking in her very conservative way of dressing. "You don't look like the same woman I met just after Leo was assaulted."

"I almost never dress up," she confided. "And it really was

a costume," she pointed out. "I wasn't lying. I don't make my living on the streets."

"How old are you?"

Her eyebrows arched. "Old enough."

"Are you over twenty-one?" he persisted.

"I'm twenty-three, almost twenty-four," she replied.

"And not married?"

"I've had responsibilities for the past few years," she said distantly, staring out the windshield. "My father has become the largest of them. I've been afraid to leave him alone."

"He's obviously dangerous when he drinks."

She hesitated, fingering her purse. "He seemed to lose himself in the bottle overnight. I thought I could handle him, control him, break the cycle. I couldn't even get help for him. My father doesn't think he has a drinking problem, so nobody would take him." She looked over at him. "I'm very grateful to your brother for his help. As I mentioned the night he was arrested, my father has only been like this for the past few months. It's not a long-standing problem. But I couldn't solve it alone."

"You're going to work for us," Rey said. "And it's not that much of a problem for Simon. He's good at his job."

"Is it a big ranch?" she asked unexpectedly.

"Enormous," he replied, "and one of five ranches we own as a family. Things get hectic during roundup, as you'll find out if you're still there next Spring."

"I won't be," she said with some certainty. "When I heal, I have to get back to my job."

"What do you do?" he asked curiously. "Is it housecleaning or working as a cook in a restaurant?"

She almost bit her tongue at the demeaning comment. "You don't think I'm qualified to do anything else?"

He averted his eyes to the road. "I don't know you, Miss

Johns," he commented carelessly. "But you seem pretty domestic to me."

She didn't feel well enough to retaliate. But one day, she promised herself, she was going to make him eat those condescending words.

"I've made beds and done light cleaning," she said, talking around her actual profession.

"Aren't you ambitious?" he persisted, with a faint frown. "Most women are, these days."

"That sounded bitter," she commented. "Did you get thrown over by an ambitious woman?"

"By a couple of them," he said curtly, and his expression became hard.

She hadn't thought of him that way. They'd been adversaries from the first contact. But it occurred to her as she gave him a quick, covert scrutiny, that he was a sensuous man. He wasn't handsome—except for Corrigan Hart, the rest of the brothers seemed cursed by a lack of conventional good looks.

But Rey had a lithe, graceful stride, and a strong face. He had good hands, clean and long-fingered. She liked the blackness of his straight hair, the high cheekbones, the long, thin, chiseled mouth. He was the sort of man who could have attracted women, except for his personality. The Harts didn't strike her as particularly gregarious or good mixers from her brief acquaintance with them. Leo was the one with the warmest personality. He made her feel at ease. The man beside her made her uncomfortable, insecure, nervous. She wasn't usually so strung-out by a man's proximity. Not that she'd had a lot to do with men in very recent years. Her father's overprotective, possessive nature had seen to that. He'd been so certain that she was going to end up like her mother.

She closed her eyes briefly, hating the memories.

"If you want to go and see your father before we leave for Jacobsville, I'll ask Simon to arrange it."

She stiffened. "I don't want to see him again until he's sober," she replied. "We both need time to get over what happened."

"Is your face the only place he hit you?" he asked unexpectedly.

"He got me in the back and the side, too, but those were only bruises. The doctor checked me over thoroughly." She sighed wearily. "I'm so tired," she murmured absently.

"I'm not surprised. You can get some rest. I'll phone you tomorrow, when we'll know more about Leo's condition and when he'll be released."

"Okay."

He stopped in front of her house and parked the car, walking to the door with her. He looked down at her while she fumbled the key into the lock. She was, in some ways, the most vulnerable woman he'd ever met. But there was steel in her makeup. He sensed that she wasn't like this usually, that she was fiery and independent and determined.

"This isn't the first time your father's laid into you, is it?" he asked suddenly.

She glanced at him, surprised. "No. But until this happened, it was more humiliating than painful." She frowned. "How did you know?"

He seemed concerned. "When I was in school, I had a couple of friends whose fathers got violent during binges. There's an…attitude, a posture, that people get when they've been beaten. I can't explain it, but I recognize it when I see it."

"Do you want to know what it is?" she asked with a world-weary smile. "It's a feeling of futility, of knowing that no matter what you do, you can't hold out physically against a man who's enraged and bent on hurting you. Because you know if you fight back, it will be even worse, maybe fatally worse. I don't like it," she added, her pale eyes beginning to glow, "and he's never getting the chance to do this again. He's my father. I love him, and I feel sorry for him. But I'm nobody's victim. Not even his."

He pushed his hands into his slacks' pockets and smiled at her. Her face was bright with color, and her eyes were alive, like peridots in sunlit water. He remembered her long blond hair around her shoulders and he wondered what she'd look like in pink silk. The thought shocked him and he scowled.

"Did I glue my nose on upside down?" she asked, raising her eyebrows.

He let out a short laugh. "No. I had a wild thought. Do you need an advance on your salary? I mean, is there anything you have to get for the trip that you can't afford?"

"I don't have a car," she began, and hated remembering why.

He glared. "I didn't say you were going to have to get to Jacobsville on your own. You'll go with Leo and me. Simon drove my car up from Jacobsville."

"Do I get to ride in the car, or have you got me earmarked for the trunk?" she returned.

He pursed his lips. Odd feelings were kindling inside him. "Keep that up and you'll be riding on the back bumper."

She wrinkled her nose. "Nice. Real nice. I can see you're going to be a great boss."

"If you don't burn the biscuits, I will be," he said.

"I'll stick close to your brother," she promised. "He'll protect me."

He didn't like that, but he wasn't going to let it show. "Leo's a tease," he said flatly. "Don't get your hopes up. He's not a marrying man. Neither am I," he added deliberately.

Her eyes widened. "Well, gee whiz, that's a major disappointment! And to think, I was only willing to take the job because of the marriage prospects!"

His face shuttered. "Sarcasm doesn't get you any points with me. I'm just making the position clear. We need a cook, not a prospective soul mate."

"Speak for yourself," she told him, turning back to her door. "I think Leo likes me already."

"I just told you…!"

She opened the door and looked back at him with pure irreverence. "Your brother can speak for himself. You don't own him, and you don't own me. I'll do what I please."

"Damn it…!"

"With charm like that, it's no surprise to me that you're still single," she said as she walked into the house.

"I can be charming when I've got a reason to be," he said icily. "But that's something you'll never know!"

"Lucky me!"

He started to speak, closed his lips tight, and walked back to his car.

She closed the door quickly and leaned back against it, almost shivering with anger. Of all the conceited, infuriating men she'd ever met, that one took the cake!

The next day, Rey phoned her midmorning to tell her that he and Leo would pick her up at one for the drive down to Jacobsville.

She had her suitcase packed and the house closed up when the big luxury car pulled into the driveway. It was a late-model car, and it looked odd, sitting in front of the shabby little house.

As she walked to the car, Meredith saw curtains fluttering and knew that the neighbors were getting an eyeful.

They probably thought she was being carried off by the mob. That amused her and she smiled, glad that something diverted her mind from her father and her pain, and the misery of the past few months.

"We hadn't planned to ask you to help us move cattle," Rey drawled when he saw how she was dressed, in jeans and a striped shirt and boots.

"I haven't volunteered, either," she assured him. "But I didn't think you'd want me to do housework in a dress." She gave him a wry glance. "Those old black-and-white sitcoms weren't historically accurate, you know. I never saw a woman vacuum the carpet wearing a dress and high heels and pearls!"

"You can do housework in a suit for all I care, as long as you can bake me a pan of biscuits every morning," Rey said, taking the suitcase and putting it in the trunk.

"Good morning," Leo called from the open window of the front seat, grinning as Rey opened the back door and helped her inside.

"Good morning," she said brightly. "You look much better."

"I feel better, except for the headache." He gave her a long look. "You aren't in very good shape yourself. Face hurt?"

"Yes. I guess we're both like walking wounded, huh?" she asked with a grin as she leaned back into the warm leather seat.

"Maybe we should take a nurse with us," Rey muttered as he got in and started the car.

Meredith cleared her throat, but before she could speak, Leo turned to his brother. "I don't need nursing, thank you very much!" Leo said curtly.

"Neither do I!" Meredith agreed.

Rey glanced at them as he pulled out into the street. "I've

seen accident victims who looked better than the two of you."

"Don't let him insult you, Meredith," Leo told her. "I'll tell you all about his weak spots so that you can deal with him."

She wouldn't have expected Rey to have any of those, but she was keeping her mouth shut and her options open for the time being. Her new boss looked formidable, and even Leo seemed curious about his lack of warmth.

"Are you all from Jacobsville originally?" Meredith changed the subject.

"No, we're from San Antonio," Leo said. "We inherited the Jacobsville property and it needed a lot of work, so we made it our headquarters. It's convenient to Houston and San Antonio, and frankly, it's isolated and gives us some privacy. We don't like cities as a rule."

"Neither do I," she said, recalling her grandmother's beautiful flower garden at the old place near Fort Worth. She smiled. "I wish Dad hadn't taken the job in Houston in the first place."

"What does he do?" Leo asked.

"He's retired," she said, not wanting to go into specifics. It hurt to talk about her family. Her father was a sore spot just now, anyway.

"Simon talked to the authorities," Rey interrupted. "They're going to make sure he gets counseling and he won't be released until he's kicked the alcohol habit." He glanced over the seat at her, his dark eyes intent. "They think it will be better if you don't have any contact with him for a few weeks, until he's through the worst of the withdrawal symptoms."

"I know about withdrawal," she replied, absently smoothing her hand over her jeans. "Bad habits are hard to break, even new ones."

"You two must read a lot," Rey replied. "I never saw so many books in one place as I did at your house. Even our library isn't that stuffed, and we all read."

"I love reading," she agreed. "We have a television, but neither of us had much time to watch it. Until recently," she added reluctantly, and winced at the thoughts that went through her mind. "I hope they get those men who mugged you, Mr. Hart," she told Leo fervently.

"Leo," he corrected. "It's really Leopold, but nobody calls me that," he added with a grin. "We're pretty informal with our employees."

"Do you have a lot?" she asked curiously.

"A good many in Jacobsville," he replied. "Although we don't have a full-time vet, we do have several accountants, livestock managers, computer programmers, salesmen…you name it, we've got one. It's big business these days to run cattle. We even have a man who does nothing but keep up with legislation that may impact us."

"Do you have dogs and cats?" she asked.

"Always," Rey replied. "We have border collies that help us herd cattle, and we keep cats in the barn to help handle the rats."

"We had a cat in the house," Leo added, "but it was Cag and Tess's, and they took it with them when they moved into their new house. At least she won't have to cope with Herman," he told his brother, and laughed.

Rey smiled involuntarily. "You might not have wanted to work for us if we still had Herman."

"Who's Herman?" she wanted to know.

"He was Cag's albino python," he told her. "He weighed a hundred and ten pounds and lived in a cage in Cag's bedroom. He gave Herman up when he married Tess. He said it would be crazy to keep an animal that big and dangerous around their son. They're still over the moon about that little boy."

"Yes, but there are people who don't even consider things like that," Meredith murmured absently. "I remember a little girl who had to have plastic surgery because she was bitten in the face by her father's pet boa constrictor."

"Herman didn't bite, but Tess almost had a heart attack when she first came to work for us and found him in the washing machine."

"I can sympathize with her," Meredith said. "I haven't come across many snakes. I'm not sure I want to."

"We have rattlers and water moccasins around the place," Rey told her. "You have to watch where you walk, but we've only had one person bitten in recent years. Snakes are always going to be a hazard in open country. You can't be careless."

"I'll remember."

"We've got a big garage apartment," Leo told her. "It's got picture windows and a whirlpool bath. Tess lived there until she and Cag married. I think you'll like it."

"I don't mind where I stay," she said easily. "I'm grateful to have a job at all. I really couldn't go to work in Houston looking like this. It would have been embarrassing for my boss."

"You won't have people staring at you on the ranch," Leo assured her. "And it won't take too long for those bruises to heal."

"I'll be fine, but you'll have to take it easy for a few days still, I'm sure they told you that," she returned at once. "No violent exertion. Concussion is tricky."

"I know that," Leo told her. "We had a man who was kicked in the head by a horse. He dropped dead three days later while he was walking into the corral. It was a hard lesson about head injuries. None of us ever forgot it."

She averted her eyes. She didn't like thinking about head injuries just now.

"I've got to stop for gas," Rey said as they reached the outskirts of the city and he pulled into a self-service gas station. "Anybody want something to drink?"

"Coffee for me," Leo said. "Meredith?"

"I'd like a small coffee, black, please."

"I'll go get it after I fill the tank," Rey said. He got out and started pumping gas.

Leo leaned his arm over the back seat and looked at Meredith openly, his dark eyes quiet and gently affectionate.

"You're still having a hard time with Rey, aren't you?" he asked her.

"He doesn't really like me," she confessed with a wry smile. "And I have to admit, he puts my back up, too. He seems to want to think the worst of me. He was convinced that I mugged you."

He chuckled. "You aren't tall enough to have knocked me out," he said. "But Rey doesn't like women much. He had a bad time of it with a young woman who turned out to be a call girl," he added, noticing absently how stunned Meredith seemed to be at that remark. "He had the ring bought, the honeymoon spot picked out, and then he found out the truth about her. It took him years to get over it. He was crushed."

"I guess so," she said heavily. "Good Lord, no wonder he thought the worst when he saw how I was dressed."

Leo frowned. "I just barely remember the rig you had on. What was it, some sort of costume?"

"I'd been to a wild Halloween party and had just escaped when I saw those men bending over you," she told him. "I ran at them waving my arms and yelling, and frightened them off."

"That was taking a hell of a chance!" he exploded.

She shrugged. "I've done it before," she said. "I learned it from my…from my brother's best friend," she amended, forcing the words out. It was much too soon to try to talk about her tragedy. "He taught karate in the military. He said that sometimes all it needed was a yell and the element of surprise to spook an attacker and make him run. It works."

"Not all the time," Leo said darkly, "and not for women. I'm all for equality, but most men are bigger and stronger than most women, and in hand-to-hand, you'd lose. You can't count on a man running, loud noise or not."

"Well, it worked for you," she amended, and smiled at him. "I'm glad, because I couldn't have wrestled those guys down."

He nodded. "See that you remember it," he told her. "Don't take chances. Get help."

"Some help those partygoers would have been," she scoffed. "Half of them were drunk, and the other half probably wouldn't have walked across the street to save a grandmother from a mugging!"

"Then why were you at a party with them?" he asked reasonably.

She picked at a fingernail. "A girl I know from work said I needed a night off and insisted that I come. I wore an old costume, the only one I had, and thought I'd enjoy myself. I don't do drugs or drink, and one of the men made a blatant pass at me." She wrapped her arms around her body in a defensive posture that betrayed her fear. "I was anxious to get away from the whole mess, luckily for you," she added with a grin.

"I don't like parties much, either," he said. "Getting drunk isn't my idea of a good time."

She glanced out the window. Rey had finished pumping

gas and was inside the convenience store now. "Does he drink?" she asked.

"Very rarely. I've been known to, under provocation, but Rey's levelheaded and sober. He can be mean, and he's got the blackest temper of all of us, but he's a good man to have on your side when the chips are down."

"He doesn't like me," she repeated.

"He'll come around, give him time," Leo told her. "Meanwhile, you've got a job and a place to stay while your face heals. We all have hard times," he added gently. "But we get through them, even when we don't expect to. Give yourself time."

She smiled. "Thanks," she said huskily. "You really are a nice man."

"Nice, clean, sober, modest and incredibly handsome," he added with a wicked grin. "And I haven't even gotten to my best points yet!"

"Compared to your brothers," she began, "you—"

The door opened before she could hang herself, and Rey shoved a cup of coffee at her before he handed the second one to Leo.

"It's hot," he told them as he slid in and took the soft drink out of his jacket pocket and put it in the cup holder.

"Cold caffeine," Leo said, shuddering. "Why can't you drink coffee like a normal man?"

"I drink coffee at breakfast," Rey told him haughtily.

"So do I, but you don't have to have rules on when to drink it!"

Rey started the engine with a speaking glance.

"See that look?" Leo indicated it to Meredith. "When he looks like that, you've already lost whatever argument you're in the middle of. We call it 'the look.' I once saw him break up a fistfight with it."

"I don't plan to argue," Meredith promised.

Rey gave her "the look," and it lingered before his attention turned back to the windshield.

Meredith sat back against the leather seat and wondered suddenly if she wasn't making the biggest mistake of her life.

Chapter Four

The Hart Ranch was almost as Meredith had pictured it, with neat wooden fences concealing electrified fencing, improved pasture land and cattle everywhere. There were also pastures with horses, and there was a barn big enough to store a commercial jet. But she loved the house itself, with its graceful arches reminiscent of Spanish architecture, and the incredible number of small trees and shrubs around it. In the spring, it must be glorious. There were two ponds, a decorative one in the front of the house and a larger one behind the house in which a handful of ducks shivered in the November sun.

"Do you have goldfish in the pond?" she asked excitedly as Rey stopped the car in front of the house on an inlaid stone driveway.

"Goldfish and Koi," he answered, smiling reluctantly at her excitement. "We have a heater in the pond to keep them comfortable during the winter. There are water lilies in there, too, and a lotus plant."

"Does the other pond have goldfish, too, where the ducks are?" she wondered.

Leo chuckled. "The other one is because of the ducks. We had to net this pond to keep them out of it so we'd *have* some goldfish. The ducks were eating them."

"Oh, I see." She sighed. "It must be beautiful here in the

spring," she said dreamily, noting the gazebo and the rose garden and stone seats and shrubs around the goldfish pond.

"It's beautiful to us year-round," Leo told her with lazy affection. "We all love flowers. We've got some more roses in a big flower garden around the back of the house, near a stand of pecan trees. Tess is taking courses in horticulture and she works with hybrids."

"I love roses," Meredith said softly. "If I had time, I'd live in a flower garden."

"I suppose cleaning rooms is time-consuming," Rey murmured sarcastically as he got out of the car and went in the front door of the house.

Leo glanced at her curiously while Rey was out of earshot. "You clean rooms?"

"I don't," she told him with a sharp grin. "But I'm living down to your brother's image of my assets."

Leo pursed his lips. "Now, that's interesting. You sound like a woman with secrets."

"More than you'd guess," she told him heavily. "But none that I'm ashamed of," she added quickly, just in case he got the wrong idea.

"Rey doesn't like you, does he?" he murmured, almost to himself. "I wonder why? It's not like him to pick on sick people."

"I'm not sick," she assured him. "I'm just battered, but I'll heal."

"Sure you will," Leo promised, smiling. "You'll be safe here. The only real chore you'll have is baking. By the time you're completely back on your feet, your father will be sober and in counseling, and your home life will have changed drastically."

"I hope so," she said huskily.

He watched her eyes grow tragic and haunted. He frowned.

"Meredith," he said slowly. "If you need to talk, ever, I can listen without making judgments."

She met his clear dark eyes. "Thanks, Leo," she said with genuine gratitude. "But talking won't change a thing. It's a matter of learning to live with…things."

"Now I'm intrigued."

"Don't push," she said gently. "I'm not able to talk about my problems yet. They're too fresh. Too painful."

"And more than just your father, or I'm a dirt farmer," he drawled.

She shrugged. "Perhaps."

"Anyway, just take your time and let the world pass you by. You're going to love it here. I promise."

"Am I?" She watched Rey come back out of the house with an elderly lady in tow, wringing her hands on her apron.

"That's Mrs. Lewis," Leo told her. "We talked her into coming back to bake biscuits for us, even though she'd retired, but now we're losing her to arthritis. She's going to show you the ropes. But not right now," he added quickly.

"No time like the present," Meredith disagreed with a smile. "Busy hands make busy minds."

"I know how that works," Leo murmured drolly.

Rey opened the back door and helped Meredith out. "Mrs. Lewis, this is Meredith Johns, our new cook. Meredith, Annie Lewis. She's retiring. Again." He made it sound like a shooting offense.

"Oh, my, yes, I'm losing the use of my hands, I'm afraid," Mrs. Lewis said. "Glad to meet you, Miss Johns."

"Glad to meet you, too, Mrs. Lewis," Meredith replied.

"I'll take your bag to your room, while Mrs. Lewis shows you around the house," Rey added.

"She just got here," Leo protested.

"And there's no time like the present to show her the house," Rey replied.

"That's just what she said," Leo sighed.

Rey glanced at Meredith, who gave him a wicked grin and followed along behind Annie Lewis, who was making a valiant effort not to ask about the terrible bruises on Meredith's face.

"It's a big, sprawling house, and it takes a lot of cleaning," Mrs. Lewis said as she led Meredith down the long hall and opened doors to the very masculine bedrooms both with dark, heavy Mediterranean furniture and earth tones in the drapes and carpets. "The men aren't messy, thank God, but they track in all that mud and dust and animal fur! They had beige carpeting when I came here." She glanced at Meredith with a shake of her head. "Red mud just won't come *out* of beige carpet!"

"Or anything else," Meredith added on a soft laugh.

"They work hard, and they're away a lot. But the foreman lives in the bunkhouse with a couple of bachelor cowboys, and they'll look out for you."

"I don't know that I'll be here very long," Meredith replied quietly. "They offered me the job so that I can have time for these to heal." She touched her face, and looked straight at the older woman, who was struggling not to ask the question in her eyes.

"Nobody will hurt you here," Mrs. Lewis said firmly.

Meredith smiled gently. "My father got drunk and beat me up, Mrs. Lewis," she explained matter-of-factly. "He's a good and kind man, but we've had a terrible tragedy to work through. He hasn't been able to cope with it except by losing himself in a bottle, and now he's gone too far and he's in jail." She sighed. "I tried so hard to help him. But I couldn't."

Mrs. Lewis didn't say a word. She put her arms around Meredith and rocked her in them. The shock of it brought the tears that she'd held back for so long. She wept until her body shook with sobs.

Rey, looking for her, stopped dead in the doorway of his bedroom and met Mrs. Lewis's misty eyes over Meredith's bowed shoulders. It shocked him to see that feisty, strong woman collapsed in tears. It hurt him.

Mrs. Lewis made a gesture with her eyebrows and a severe look. Rey acknowledged it with a nod and a last glance at the younger woman as he walked back down the hall.

Supper was riotous. Meredith had made a huge pan of homemade biscuits and ferreted out all sorts of preserves to go with them. For an entrée, she made fajitas with lean beef and sliced vegetables, served with wild rice and a salad. Dessert was fresh fruit and fresh whipped cream, the only concession besides the biscuits that she made to fat calories. She'd also found some light margarine to set out.

"This is good," Rey commented as he glanced at her. "We usually have broiled or fried steak with lots of potatoes."

"Not bad once a week or so, but terrible for your cholesterol," she pointed out with a smile as she finished her salad. "Lean beef is okay for you, but not in massive doses."

"You sound like a dietician," Leo chuckled.

"Modern women have to keep up with health issues," she said evasively. "I'm responsible for your health while I'm working for you. I have to be food-conscious."

"That's fine," Rey told her flatly, "but don't put tofu and bean sprouts in front of me if you want to stay here."

Her eyebrows arched. "I hate tofu."

"Thank God," Leo sighed as he buttered another biscuit. "I got fed tofu salad the last time I went to Brewster's for supper," he added with absolute disgust. "I ate the olives and the cheese and left the rest."

"I can't say that I blame you," Meredith said, laughing because he looked so forlorn.

"Janie Brewster thinks tofu is good for him," Rey commented. "But she thinks he needs therapy more. He doesn't like fish. She says that has some sort of connection to his fear of deep water." He glanced at his brother with wicked affection. "She's a psychology major. She already has an associate degree from our local junior college."

"She's twenty," Leo said with a twist of his lower lip. "She knows everything."

"She just got her associate degree this spring," Rey added.

"Good. Maybe she'll get a job in New York," Leo said darkly.

"Why New York?" Meredith asked curiously.

"Well, it's about as far east as she can go and find her sort of work," Leo muttered. "And she'd be out of my hair!"

Rey gave him a covert glance and finished his fajitas.

Meredith finished her own meal and got up to refill coffee cups. She had a feeling that Leo was more interested in the nebulous Brewster girl than he wanted to admit.

"We need groceries," she told them when she'd served dessert and they were eating it. "Mrs. Lewis made me a list."

"You can use one of the ranch trucks to drive to town," Leo suggested carelessly.

Her fingers toyed with her fork. "I haven't driven in several months."

"You don't drive?" Rey exclaimed, shocked.

She couldn't meet his eyes. "I take buses." Cars made her feel guilty.

"Why?"

She remembered a day she should have driven. The memories were horrible…

"Meredith, it's all right," Leo said gently, sensing something traumatic about her behavior. "I'll drive you. Okay?"

"You won't," Rey replied. "You're in worse shape than she is. Which brings up another point. You don't need to be walking around town like that," he told her.

She wasn't offended; it was a relief. She even smiled. "No, I don't guess I do. Will you do the shopping?" she asked him, her wide, soft eyes steady on his.

He felt wild little thrills shooting through his body at the impact. It had been years since he'd been so shaken by eye contact alone. He didn't move. He just stared at her, his dark eyes unblinking, curious. His body rippled with vague hunger.

Leo, watching the eye contact, tried not to grin. He cleared his throat, and Rey seemed to remember that he had a forkful of fruit halfway to his mouth. He took it the rest of the way and chewed it carefully before he spoke.

"I'll get the groceries," Rey volunteered. He glared at both of them, noting the shaved place where Leo had stitches near the back of his head. "Obviously I'm the only one here who can walk around without drawing curious stares from bystanders!"

Leo buttered another biscuit. "That sounds like sour grapes to me. If you want attention, try walking around without your pants."

"I didn't say I wanted attention," Rey returned hotly.

"Good thing." He glanced at Meredith with a mischievous smile. "He looks like hell without his pants," he said conversationally. "Hairiest legs of the bunch."

"That's debatable," Rey shot back. "Yours aren't much better."

"What a good thing you two aren't Scottish," Meredith said demurely.

It took a minute for them to get it, then Leo burst out laughing, trying to picture his younger brother in a kilt. Rey lifted a corner of his thin mouth, but he wasn't in a smiling mood. It bothered him, that Meredith had been crying in Mrs. Lewis's arms, that she didn't drive, that she was so mysterious about her life. She was twenty-three, almost twenty-four. Most women by that age had been involved in a serious relationship, some more than one. Many had been married.

His heart skipped. Was that her secret? He remembered watching her rub her ring finger in the car. He glanced at it curiously. She didn't wear a ring, and there was no sign that she'd been wearing one there. She didn't act married. She hadn't talked about having a husband. She was single, apparently by choice. But had there been men in her past? He was still carrying scars from his one great love affair, from the deception he'd endured. Meredith had gone out walking to a party in a rig that made her look like a prostitute, and she'd been comfortable doing that. It wasn't something an innocent girl would have considered.

Knowing that, he looked at her in a different way, speculatively. She had a nice figure and she wasn't all flushing smiles like Janie Brewster when Leo was around. Meredith was oddly mature for her age, almost matronly. She seemed to be used to giving instructions, too. She was a puzzle that disturbed him. What if she was hiding something sordid in her past? He and Leo had taken her in on faith and pity, but now he wondered if they'd made a terrible mistake. If she were in league with the men who'd robbed Leo, they might have a dangerous situation developing. What if she'd planned the whole thing as a means to an end?

Basically Rey didn't trust her. He wasn't going to let down his guard, either, no matter if looking at her did raise his blood pressure. She wasn't going to know that she did. And he'd keep his eyes open, all the time, just in case.

* * *

The days turned to a week. Meredith's painful bruises faded slowly. She lost some of the brooding sadness that seemed to cling to her like the jeans she wore around the house when she was working. She found the slower, easier pace strange, and she missed the urgency of her daily routine. But as the days went by lazily, she realized that she hadn't really given herself time to think. She'd avoided it, ignored it, hoping that the past would vanish. Now she was face to face with it, forced to reflect on what had happened.

She sat beside the fishpond one sunny afternoon, between chores, and watched the goldfish under the surface of the dark water as they moved sluggishly. The water wasn't frozen, but it was cold. The pond heater only kept a small area heated, so the fish were limited in movement. She could imagine how it would be to sit here in the summer and watch them move around in their watery world, with flowers blooming all around.

She'd loved planting flowers. She missed her home, her bulbs and shrubs, the familiar things that she'd accumulated around her. Now it was all gone, sold without a second thought to make the memories bearable. It was too late, and she wished she'd been more sensible. There were things she should have kept. Mike's stupid baseball cap, the one he always wore on the rare occasions when he wasn't working, and when he went fishing. She missed her mother's collection of small silk Chinese boxes and her pretty evening gowns. She'd thrown all those things away. At the time, it had seemed reasonable to cut all the ties with the past. It didn't, now.

The sound of a truck pulling up to the front door caught her attention. Rey and Leo had been out of town for two days, attending another cattle convention, this time in Denver.

They climbed out of the cab of the big six-wheeled pickup truck and retrieved their suitcases from the back, waving as the ranch truck pulled right out again and took off down the road.

Meredith got up and went to join them.

"Want some coffee and pie?" she asked with a smile.

"That would really hit the spot," Leo said, returning the smile. "I hate commercial flights."

"You're the smart guy who said our jet needed to be overhauled," Rey reminded him.

"It did," Leo replied.

Rey was looking at Meredith openly. "The bruises are fading," he remarked. "You have more color, too."

"I've been getting out in the sunlight," she replied easily. "I like to watch the fish, even though they don't move much."

"We might put a big aquarium inside," Rey remarked, unaware of his brother's quick, curious glance. "I like fish myself."

"They've done studies," Meredith volunteered as they stood aside to let her enter the house first. "They say watching fish swim is calming. It helps relieve stress."

"God knows, we could use some of that," Leo chuckled. "Especially when cattle prices fall and feed prices go through the roof."

"Cattle raising must be a complex process," she remarked.

"Very complex," Rey said. He frowned as he watched her walk. "Hip sore?" he asked.

She laughed self-consciously. "Well, yes, it is. How did you know?"

"You've got a light limp on the right side. Barely noticeable."

She rubbed her hip self-consciously. "I fell on that side,

the night Dad hit me," she told him. "The floor's pretty hard."

"There's a whirlpool bath in your bedroom," Rey reminded her. "It'll help the soreness."

"I discovered that," she said, grinning. "What a luxury! We only have a shower at home, and it's temperamental."

Rey gave her a long look. "When we've had time to catch our breath, I'll see what I can find out about your father, if you'd like."

Her face brightened. "That would be nice."

He smiled slowly, liking the way her pale eyes seemed to glow when she was pleased. She wasn't bad-looking at all, and her figure was just about perfect. He wondered how she could have remained single for so long, with her homemaking skills, not to mention her sweet personality and that knockout body.

She was watching him with equal appreciation, and totally unaware of it. He had a lithe, powerful physique that made her think of rodeo. He walked with a unique sort of grace, and he didn't stoop or slouch, ever. She liked his eyes best of all. They were almost a liquid-brown, and they had black rims around the pupils. He was rugged and sensuous, and she looked at his wide thin mouth and wondered for the first time how it would feel to kiss it.

Her thoughts horrified her. She dragged her eyes away and excused herself in an absolute fluster to go make coffee.

Leo lifted both eyebrows and stared at his brother after she was out of earshot. "Well, well," he murmured. "You do seem to be making an impression on her."

"Cut it out," Rey said testily.

"And vice versa," came the irritating reply.

Rey made a rough sound in his throat and stomped off down the hall to his room. He put down his suitcase, took off his suit and dress shirt and got into jeans and a checked long-sleeved work shirt. He glanced at himself in the mirror as he buttoned it, his eyes blank as he recalled the wild flush on Meredith's cheeks. It shouldn't please him. He didn't trust her. She could be trying to play them all for suckers. But he smiled, just the same.

Meredith had coffee and cherry pie in saucers on the table by the time the brothers were changed and walking into the kitchen.

"Coffee's fresh," she said.

"Aren't you having any?" Rey asked.

"I have to get the clothes into the dryer," she excused herself with a quick smile. "Yell if you need anything."

She was gone in a flash.

Rey stared broodingly at his pie and frowned. She didn't want to have coffee with them. Why?

"You make her nervous," Leo said, answering the unspoken question. "She knows you don't trust her."

Rey frowned as he nibbled at his pie and sipped coffee. "I don't know her," he replied. He gave his brother a speaking glance. "We've always done background checks on employees," he added firmly. "I don't think we should make an exception of her, even though she's temporary."

"Translated, that means you want to know more about her than you do," Leo drawled, grinning.

"Maybe I do," Rey confessed. "But she's in a position to do a lot of damage if she isn't what she seems. You could have been killed, or suffered brain damage," he added quietly. "If she's in cahoots with the guys who mugged you…" He let the sentence trail off meaningfully.

Leo grimaced. "I don't like poking into peoples' private business," he replied. "But you're right. It's risky not to check her out."

"I'll get the agency on it first thing tomorrow," Rey said. He took another bite of the pie. "She's a hell of a good cook," he murmured.

"Makes good coffee, too," Leo commented.

They looked at each other and grimaced. It was going to upset Meredith if she found out what they were up to. But it was too much of a gamble not to find out what they could about her background and character. On the other hand, Leo promised himself, he was going to intercept that background check before Rey had a chance to see it. If Meredith had secrets she was hiding for a good reason, he wasn't going to give her away to Rey.

It took several days for the private detective to get to the case and send a report to the Harts.

Rey was out of town at a one-day seminar on a new spreadsheet computer program the brothers were using for herd records when the report arrived. Leo carried the report into his office and closed the door while he read it.

When he finished, he let out a harsh breath. So that was Meredith's secret. No wonder her father drank. No wonder she was so reticent and quiet about her past. He smiled as he considered her true profession, and he was determined that Rey wasn't going to know about it until disclosure was inevitable. Rey was too prone to conclusion-jumping and rushing to judgment. It was about time he had a set down, and Meredith was just the woman to give it to him. Meanwhile, he'd let Rey work on hanging himself. Obviously Meredith was enjoying her anonymity, and considering the high-powered pressures of her daily job, it wasn't surprising that she found mundane housekeeping a nice change. It wouldn't hurt to let her enjoy the vacation from stress, without probing into her feelings. No doubt she still felt the grief, even after several months.

He touched the report with idle fingers, frowning as he recognized one of the names on it. Mike had been a Houston policeman. He was also a friend of Colter Banks, a Texas Ranger and cousin of the Harts, who worked out of the Houston ranger office. It really was a small world. He wanted to tell Meredith that he remembered Mike, but he didn't want to blow her cover. He also didn't want her to know that they'd been checking up on her.

He put the file into the filing cabinet, deliberately putting it under the wrong letter of the alphabet. If Rey asked, he'd just tell him that the agency was working on it but had other, more urgent cases to assign agents to first.

Meredith was alone in the house when Rey came in, late that night, from his business trip. Leo had gone to dinner at the Brewsters' house again, presumably at the invitation of Janie's father, to talk about a new breeding bull the Brewsters were trying to sell him.

She'd just started the dishwasher and was ready to turn the lights off in the kitchen when she heard Rey come in.

He paused in the kitchen doorway, a black Stetson slanted over one dark eye, wearing a grey vested suit that clung lovingly to the hard, muscular lines of his tall body. Meredith felt ragged by comparison in her jeans and red T-shirt, and barefoot. Her hair was disheveled because she'd been scrubbing the floor with a brush, and she wasn't wearing makeup. She hadn't expected to see either of the brothers before she went to bed.

Rey's dark eyes went to her pretty feet and he smiled. "You don't like shoes, do you?"

She grimaced. "No, and it's not good to go without them. No arch support." She studied his lean face. He had dark circles under his eyes. "Would you like some coffee and something to eat?"

"I would," he said heavily. "They gave me peanuts on the plane," he added with absolute disgust.

She chuckled. The sound was pleasant, and Rey was surprised at how it touched him to hear her laugh.

"I'll make you a nice thick low-fat ham sandwich with sauce."

"Thanks," he said, sliding a chair out so that he could straddle it. He tossed his hat into the chair beside him and ran a hand through his thick dark hair. "Make the coffee first, Meredith. I've got paperwork that has to be done tonight before the accountant comes to do the books in the morning."

"Can't it wait?" she asked gently. "You look worn to a frazzle. You need an early night."

His eyes searched hers intently. "I don't need mothering," he said, angered out of all proportion.

She flushed and turned away. She didn't apologize or say another word, but her hands shook as she filled the coffeepot and started it brewing.

Rey cursed himself silently for snapping at her. It was unkind, especially after she'd volunteered to feed him. She'd been working hard, too, he could see the spotless floor and the brush and bucket she'd been using on it. She must have done it on her hands and knees. It was a big kitchen, too. He wasn't the only one who was tired.

He got up from the chair and moved to stand just behind her. His lean hands caught her small waist and pulled her back against him. "I'm sorry," he said, his voice deep and husky with sudden emotion.

Her cold fingers came to rest on his and her whole body went rigid as a flash of white-hot pleasure shot through it. She caught her breath. He heard it. His own body tautened and the hands around her waist suddenly grew possessive, rough, insistent, as they pulled her tight against him.

He could hear her breathing change. He could feel the faint tremor of her hands over his. Impulsively he bent his head and his mouth touched the side of her neck.

Chapter Five

Meredith knew her knees were shaking. She hoped she wasn't going to fall on the floor at his feet with sheer excitement. It had been years since a man had made her feel such a rush of pleasure, and even then, it had been one-sided. She'd been crazy about a man who only saw her as a sort of unrelated sister. But even that wasn't as powerful as what she was feeling with Rey Hart.

His mouth became insistent as it moved slowly up her neck. He began to turn her, in the silence that was suddenly alive with passion. His hard lips traveled to the hollow of her throat, where a tiny pulse hammered, and then up to her chin. His teeth nibbled her chin, moving on to her lower lip. He tugged it away from the top one and tasted it with his tongue. All the while, his lean, strong hands were sliding up and down at her waist, smoothing her body completely against him.

His teeth nipped at her top lip with a sensual approach that made her breath shiver in her throat. He was experienced, far more so than she was. For all her professional capability, in this way she was a novice, and it showed.

He noticed her lack of sensual response with absent curiosity. She was attracted to him, that was obvious, but it was as if she didn't know what to do.

He guided her hands to his vest and flicked open buttons

while his lips teased around hers. She fumbled and he laughed softly, his nose rubbing against hers as he moved her hands and unfastened the buttons on his vest and shirt with deft efficiency. He coaxed her hands inside, against thick hair and hard, warm muscle, while his mouth began to bite at hers, tempting her lips to part. She was stiff, trying not to respond, but her body was hungry.

"Like this," he whispered gently, teaching her mouth the lazy, sensual rhythm he wanted from it. "Taste my mouth, the way I'm tasting yours. Don't fight what you're feeling."

She heard the words as if through a fog. She didn't understand what he was saying, but her body obeyed him. She was in a sensual limbo, her hands flat against his chest, her head lifted, her eyes slitted and looking up into his as he began to increase the teasing pressure of his mouth. She followed his lips. She relaxed into the curve of his powerful body with a little shiver.

He devoured her mouth roughly, again and then again, tempting her until her mouth followed his, returning the arousing pressure. She could see the glitter grow in his narrow eyes, feel the grip of his lean hands as he pushed her hips against the sudden hardness of him. She gasped with embarrassment and then lost all sense of it as his mouth opened and pushed down hard against her parted lips, drowning her in passion.

It was like flying, she thought dazedly. He hesitated for an instant and her eyes opened, drowsy and curious. Her mouth was swollen, soft, tremulous. She looked at him with fascination, utterly helpless in his embrace. He felt an unfamiliar protectiveness toward her. It had been years since he'd kissed an innocent. Meredith's lack of experience was obvious. He was enjoying it.

"Yes," he murmured gruffly, and he bent again. His arms

enfolded her, tender arms that no longer forced her into intimacy. His mouth was tender, too, exploring hers with slow mastery, careful not to overwhelm her.

She sighed into his hard mouth, relaxing against him. Her hands moved restlessly on his broad, bare chest, and contracted in the thick mat of hair that covered him.

He lifted his head, staring down into her wide eyes with somber delight. His hands smoothed hers deeper into his thick hair and hard muscle. He traced the edges of her short nails with his thumbs. His breath was jerky. He didn't like having her see that he was vulnerable. There were too many things he still didn't know about her, and he didn't trust her. She seemed innocent, but he couldn't forget the dress she'd been wearing and the accusations her father had made about her. He didn't dare trust her on such short acquaintance. On the other hand, his body was singing with pleasure from the long, hot contact with hers. He couldn't force himself to let her go. Not just yet.

"Why did you do that?" she asked huskily.

One dark eyebrow lifted. He didn't smile. "Why did you let me?" he shot back.

She felt uncomfortable. Despite the effort it took, she moved away from him. He let her go with no show of reluctance. He watched her struggle for composure while he refastened buttons with easy confidence, concealing the effect she had on him. He didn't even look ruffled.

"The coffee must be done by now," he pointed out when she seemed unable to move.

She turned stiffly and went to fill cups and put them, along with cream and sugar, on the table.

While he fixed his coffee, she made him two thick ham sandwiches with hands that slowly lost their tremor. She was devastated by a kiss that didn't seem to have disturbed him at all. She remembered the sudden hardness of his body, but she knew all about anatomy. A man couldn't help that reaction to anything feminine, it was part of his makeup. It wasn't even personal.

Somehow, it made things worse to know that. She felt his eyes on her back, and she knew he was measuring her up. She had no idea why he'd kissed her, but she didn't trust his motives. He didn't like her. She couldn't afford to let her guard down. Rey Hart would be hell on a woman who loved him. She knew that instinctively.

By the time she had the sandwiches made, her hands were steady again and she was able to put them on the table with a cool smile.

"I have to tidy up the living room…" she began.

He caught her hand as she started past him. "Sit down, Meredith," he said quietly.

She sat. He sipped coffee and studied her for a long moment. "I talked to Simon while I was away," he said. "Your father has been released from jail and placed in an alcohol treatment center. It's early days yet, but the prognosis is good. It helps that he hasn't been drinking that heavily for a long time."

She looked relieved and anxiously waited to hear what else Rey had to say about her father.

He continued. "The therapist wouldn't reveal any intimate details to Simon, you understand, but he was able to say that your father had been unable to deal with a family tragedy. Now that he's sober, he's extremely upset about what he did to you." He looked grim. "He doesn't remember doing it, Meredith."

She averted her eyes to her coffee cup. For something to do, she lifted it and took a sip of blistering black coffee, almost burning her lip. "That's common in cases of alcohol or drug abuse," she murmured absently.

He studied her over the rim of his coffee cup. "You won't be allowed to communicate with him until he's through the treatment program, but he wanted you to know that he's desperately sorry for what he did."

She ground her teeth together. She knew that. Her father wasn't a bad man. Until he'd started abusing alcohol, he'd been one of the gentlest men alive. But, like all human beings, he had a breaking point which he reached when tragedy erupted into his life.

"He isn't a bad man," she said quietly. "Although I know it must have seemed like it."

"I've seen drunks before," Rey replied. "My brothers have gone on benders a time or two." He smiled faintly. "In fact, Leo holds the current record for damage at Shea's Bar, out on the Victoria road. He doesn't cut loose often, but when he does, people notice."

"He doesn't seem the sort of man who would do that," she remarked, surprised.

"We're all the sort of men who would do that, given the right provocation," he told her.

She smiled. "Do you get drunk and wreck bars?" she couldn't resist asking.

"I don't drink as a rule," he said simply. "A glass of wine rarely, nothing stronger. I don't like alcohol."

She smiled. "Neither do I."

He leaned back in his chair and studied her quietly. His hair was still faintly disheveled where her hands had caught in it when he was kissing her, and his lower lip was swollen from the pressure of her mouth. She knew she must look almost as bad. Her hand went unconsciously to her unruly hair.

"Take it down," he said abruptly.

"Wh…what?"

"Take your hair down," he said huskily. "I want to see it."

She'd just gotten her wild heart under control, and now it was galloping all over again from that sultry tone, from the dark, intent caress of his eyes on her face.

"Listen, I work for you," she began with a tremor in her voice.

He got up from the chair and moved toward her with a lazy, almost arrogant stride. He drew her up in front of him and started pulling out hairpins. Her hair, unbound, fell in soft waves down her back, almost concealing one eye.

"It's hard to manage when it's down," she said self-consciously.

"I love long hair." He tangled his lean hands in it and coaxed her face up to his. He searched her eyes at point-blank range. "I've kissed girls years younger than you who knew even more than I do. Why are you still a novice?"

She swallowed hard. He was making her knees weak again. She couldn't quite get a whole breath of air into her lungs. Her hands rested on his chest lightly and she felt her heart choking her with its rapid beat as she stared into his narrowed, dark eyes.

"What?" she asked, barely having heard much less understood the question.

His hands were exploring the cool length of her hair with fascination. "You're not bad-looking, Meredith. Surely you've dated."

"Yes," she said, disconcerted. "But I'm old-fashioned."

Both eyebrows went up over a cynical smile. "That's a pitiful excuse in this day and age."

"Why?" she asked, her clear grey eyes staring up into his with no thought of subterfuge. "The whole reason for the women's movement is so that women can have the freedom to do as they please. I'm not promiscuous. Why should I need an excuse?"

He blinked. She made his question sound unreasonable.

"I thought sexual liberation was the soul of the movement," he drawled.

"Being chaste is sexual liberation, in my book," she replied. "You'd be amazed how many women in my graduating class practiced abstinence."

"In high school, I gather," he said absently, tracing the length of her hair with his hands.

She almost corrected him, but then, she really mustn't destroy the illusions he had about her as a domestic. "Yes. In high school."

He moved closer to her, his lean body a sensual provocation that made her breath catch. He laughed softly. "Care to test the hypothesis?" he murmured softly.

"I work for you," she repeated, playing for time.

"So?"

"So it's not wise to mix business…"

"…with pleasure?" He caught her waist and drew her close. "It's been a while since I found a woman so desirable," he whispered, bending to her mouth. "Experience bores me. You," he bit off against her soft lips, "are a challenge."

"Thank you, but I don't want to be," she whispered, trying to pull away.

He lifted his head and searched her eyes. "No curiosity about the great unknown?" he taunted.

"No desire to treat it as a sophisticated game," she corrected abruptly.

He hesitated, but only for an instant. His lean hands contracted and then released her. He went back to his chair and sat down. "Touché," he said with a curious glance. "All right, Meredith, I'll sit here and eat my sandwiches and we'll pretend that we're still strangers physically."

"Good idea," she approved. She reached down for her half-empty coffee cup and put it in the sink.

He was halfway through a sandwich when she excused herself and went to fluff up the pillows in the living room and put magazines and books back in their places. Leo had left things strewn about before he'd gone to the Brewsters'. She was glad, because it gave her a valid reason not to sit next to Rey with her emotions in turmoil.

By the time she'd gone back to the kitchen, Rey had finished his sandwiches and coffee and was coming out the door.

"You're safe," he drawled. "I'm going to change and get to work in the study. Where's Leo?"

"Having supper at the Brewsters' house," she told him. "He said he'd be early."

"That means he'll be late," he mused. "Janie Brewster will have found twenty excuses to keep him talking to her father. She's one determined young lady, but Leo's equally determined. He doesn't want ties."

"Doesn't that sound familiar?" she murmured wickedly.

His eyes slid up and down her body in a silence that teemed with tension. "I never said I didn't want ties," he corrected. "I said I didn't want marriage. There's a difference."

"Don't look at me," she said carelessly. "I don't have time for relationships."

"Of course. All that cleaning must demand a lot of you," he said deliberately.

She flushed. He had no idea what her life was like on a daily basis, and she wanted very badly to tell him. But he was so almighty arrogant and condescending that he put her back up. She wasn't going to tell him a thing. He'd find out soon enough.

She put her hands on her hips and stared at him. "And what's wrong with being a housekeeper?" she demanded, going on the offensive. "Where would you and your brother be right now if there weren't women you could hire to bake and clean for you? I guess you'd have to get married then, or learn to cook, wouldn't you?"

He glared at her. "I could cook if I wanted to."

"You're the sort of man who makes a woman wish she didn't have a culinary skill to her name," she said icily. "You are so 'lord of the manor-ish', Mr. Hart!"

"It isn't a manor," he pointed out. "They have those in England. We call this a ranch."

She glared at him.

He grinned. "You really do rise to the bait beautifully," he murmured, and something flashed in his dark eyes. "The sandwiches were good," he added.

She looked surprised. "Nothing but ham and a home-made sauce," she faltered.

"You do that a lot with food," he remarked gently. "I like the way you experiment with dishes. I even like the way you garnish the plates. You make things look appetizing."

She didn't realize that he'd even noticed. "I learned that from a dietician," she said without thinking. "If food is decorative, sometimes it makes up for bulk."

He smiled quizzically. "You can't decorate biscuits," he teased. "But you make really good ones."

"Thanks." She smiled back. "I'll tidy up the kitchen if you're through."

"I am. Don't stay up too late," he added and his eyes were suddenly bright with mischief. "You need plenty of rest so that you can make biscuits for breakfast!"

"Okay. I'll get an early night." She laughed and went on past him to the kitchen.

He stared after her for several long seconds with an expression that he was glad she didn't see. He liked the taste of her. That hadn't been wise, kissing her that way. He was going to have to make sure it didn't happen again. He didn't need complications.

Nothing was the same between Meredith and Rey after that day. They were aware of each other. It wasn't blatant, but she could feel tingling in her spine when Rey was in a room. It was instinctive. Her eyes followed him like puppies, and she flushed wildly when he caught her at it and gave her that amused, worldly glance.

Leo noticed, too, and it worried him that Rey was encouraging Meredith. He knew Rey too well to think he'd had a change of heart toward his bachelor status.

"You're leading her on," Leo accused his brother one evening when they were alone in the study with the door closed. "Why?"

Rey gave him a surprised glance. "You make it sound like a crime to flirt with her."

"In your case, it is," his brother said flatly. "You're a rounder. She isn't."

Rey shrugged. "She's not exactly off limits," he told his brother. "Not at her age."

"And what do you have in mind? Seduction?" Leo persisted irritably. "She's already been damaged enough by what happened with her father. The bruises are barely healed, and the mental scars are still there. Don't play games with her."

"Aren't you self-righteous all of a sudden?" Rey shot back angrily. "You've been stringing Janie Brewster along for weeks, and we both know you don't have any intention in hell of getting serious about her. All you want is first chance at that damned seed bull they're thinking of selling! Does she know?" he added maliciously.

Leo's eyes began to glitter. "Janie is a child," he said furiously. "I pick at her, and not because of any damned bull. I'm certainly not hell-bent on seduction!"

"She's not a child," Rey countered. "You're leading her down a blind alley, when you know full well she's in love with you."

Leo looked shocked. "She's not in love with me! Maybe she's got a crush. That's all!"

"You don't see the way she looks at you, do you?" Rey replied solemnly.

Leo cleared his throat. "We're talking about Meredith," he said firmly.

Rey's eyes narrowed. "Meredith is an adult."

"And she works for us," Leo went on relentlessly. "I'm not going to stand by and let you make an amusement of her."

"Jealous?" his brother taunted.

Leo was very still. "Is that the draw?" he asked softly. "Are we competing for a woman again?"

Rey's eyes flashed. "I would never have known about Carlie if you hadn't started propositioning her in front of me. Do you think I can forget that?"

"I keep hoping you will someday. She would have taken you for the ride of your life," Leo said quietly. "You're my brother. I couldn't stand by and do nothing."

Rey turned away with a muttered curse. Leo was right; he had saved him from even worse heartache, but the memory was still raw enough to hurt.

"Don't try to take it out on Meredith," Leo told him firmly. "She's had enough tragedy. Let her do her job."

Rey glanced at him over his shoulder. "I would, if she'd remember why she's here," he said venomously. "It's not my fault that every time I turn around, she's drooling over me! A saint could be tempted by a woman whose eyes worship him like that. I'm only human!"

"Don't raise your voice," Leo cautioned.

"Why? Do you think she's standing outside the door eavesdropping?" Rey drawled sarcastically. "What if she did hear me? It's the truth. She wants me. A blind man could see it."

"That's no reason to take advantage of her. She's not like your usual women."

"No, she's not. She has no ambition, no intellect. Besides that, she's so inexperienced, it's unreal. I never thought kissing a woman could be boring, until she came along," Rey added coldly, trying not to let Leo see how attracted he was to their housekeeper. "She's so naive, it's nauseating."

Outside the door, Meredith stood poised like a statue with a cup of coffee in a saucer shaking in her hands. She'd come to offer it to Rey, and overheard words that had never been meant for her ears. She fought tears as she turned around and went quickly and silently back down the hall to the kitchen.

Hearts couldn't really break, she told herself firmly, as she dabbed at the tears with a paper towel. She was just feeling the aftereffects of her devastating experience at home. It wasn't as if she was really drooling over Rey Hart.

She felt like sinking through the floor when she realized that she did spend an inordinate amount of time staring at him. He was handsome, sensuous, attractive. She liked looking at him. And maybe she was infatuated, a little. That didn't give him the right to say such horrible things about her.

If she hadn't been listening, she'd never have known about them in the first place. She'd have gone right ahead, mooning over him and having him know it and be amused by it. Her pride felt tattered. She'd never been one to wear her heart on her sleeve, but Rey had kissed her as if he enjoyed it, and she'd built dreams on those kisses. She realized now how truly naive it had been. The first man who paid her any attention in years, and she fell head over heels for him. Seen in that context, perhaps it wasn't surprising after all. She'd heard Leo accuse him of being a rounder, and she had to admit that his experience ran rings around hers. Apparently he was accustomed to playing sensual games with women. That was all those devastating kisses that had brought her to her knees had meant to him—just a game. And she'd taken it seriously!

Well, she told herself firmly, he needn't worry that she'd throw herself at his feet again. From now on, she was going to be the perfect employee, polite and courteous and eager to please—but she'd never stare at him longingly again. Thank God she'd overheard what he said to Leo. It had spared her a terrible humiliation. A little hurt now was far better than being wrung out emotionally down the road because she'd been ignorant of the facts. Wasn't she herself always telling people that the truth, however brutal, was always best in the long run? It was time to take her own advice.

When Rey and Leo came in to breakfast the next morning, she put bacon and eggs and biscuits on the table with a cool, professional smile.

Rey was oddly subdued. He didn't give her the arrogant scrutiny that had become force of habit in recent days. In fact, he didn't look at her at all. Leo kept up a pleasant conversation about the day's chores. They were moving some sick cattle into a pasture near the house so the vet could examine them, and stock was being shifted into closer quarters as well, within easier reach of the hay barn.

"I thought you had those big round bales of hay?" Meredith asked curiously.

"We do," Leo agreed. "But we still bale it the old-fashioned way and stack it in the barn. You lose some of the round bales through weathering by sun and rain. The hay that's kept dry in the barn has less deterioration and better nutrition."

"But you feed more than hay?"

Leo chuckled. He buttered a second biscuit. "You are sharp. Yes, we have a man who mixes feeds for better nutrition. No animal proteins, either," he added. "We're reactionaries when it comes to ranching. No artificial hormones, no pesticides, nothing except natural methods of pest control and growth. We're marketing our beef under the Hart Ranch label, as well, certifying it organic. We've already got several chain supermarkets carrying our product, and we've just moved onto the Internet to extend our distribution."

"That's amazing," Meredith said with genuine interest. "It's like having custom beef," she added, nodding.

"It is custom beef," Leo told her. "We're capitalizing on the move toward healthier beef. Quick profit methods are going to fail producers in the long run, especially with the current attitude toward hormones and antibiotics and animal-product proteins for feed. We think that once organic beef catches on, the market will justify the added expense."

"Word of mouth will take you far, too," Meredith said. "Hospitals teach nutrition these days, not only to patients but to the community. Tailored beef will find a market among consumers with heart problems, who'll pay the extra cost for healthier cuts of meat grown organically."

Rey was listening. He finished his biscuit and poured himself another cup of coffee from the carafe on the table. "J.D. Langley pioneered that organic approach locally," he remarked. "He and the Tremayne boys got into terrific fights with other producers at seminars for a while. Then we saw the disasters overseas and suddenly everybody else was jumping on the bandwagon."

"They'll be glad they did, I think," Meredith said.

"Which reminds me," Leo said, eyeing her. "Mrs. Lewis said her larder hadn't been opened since you came here. So…what are you making these biscuits with?"

She gave them a wary glance. "Light olive oil," she said slowly.

Rey gaped at his biscuit as if it had suddenly sprouted hair. "Olive oil?!" he gasped.

"Listen," she said quickly, aware of horrified stares, "olive oil is so healthy that people who live on a Mediterranean diet have only a fraction of the vascular problems we have in abundance in this country. The fat content is still there, but it's a vegetable fat, and it's actually good for you. Until I told you, you didn't even know you'd given up great gobs of animal fat in those biscuits!"

The brothers looked at each other. "Well," Leo had to admit, "they taste just as good as the others did."

"That's true," Rey agreed reluctantly.

"And we're getting older," Leo continued. "We don't want clogged arteries giving us heart attacks and strokes."

"Or bypass surgery," Rey sighed.

"So I guess olive oil isn't so bad, after all," Leo concluded, with a grin at Meredith.

She grinned back. "Thank goodness. I had visions of being tarred and feathered," she confessed.

"I'm not giving up butter, though," Rey told her firmly, dipping his knife into the tub next to the biscuit basket. "Nothing tastes like real butter on a biscuit."

Meredith didn't look at him. She couldn't confess that what he was eating was not butter, but rather a light margarine that actually lowered cholesterol levels. She only smiled and poured herself another cup of coffee.

* * *

Leo and Rey had started moving bulls into the lower pasture, where new forage grasses were thriving even in autumn, when a mangy old longhorn bull suddenly jerked his head and hooked Leo in the shoulder.

Leo yelled and threw a kick at him, but the aggravating animal was already trotting nonchalantly into the new pasture without a backward glance.

"How bad is it?" Rey asked, leaving the cowboys to work the cattle alone while he looked at his brother's shoulder.

"Probably needs stitches," Leo said through his teeth. "Drive me to the house and let me change shirts, then you can take me to Lou Coltrain."

"Damned bull," Rey muttered as he put his brother into the ranch truck and took off home.

Meredith was sweeping off the back steps when they drove up. She gave Leo's bloodstained shirt a quick glance.

"Come on in here, let me have a look," she said gently.

Disconcerted, Leo let her remove the shirt from his shoulder and bathe the blood away with a clean cloth.

She probed around the edges of the cut and nodded. "You'll need stitches. Here. Hold this tight against the cut until you get to town."

"I need to change shirts," he began.

"You need to get to the doctor. Which one do you use?" she persisted, picking up the mobile phone she kept on the table.

"Dr. Lou Coltrain," he said.

"I'll phone and tell them you're on the way," she said firmly.

Rey gave her a curious glance, but he hustled Leo out the door and into the truck again.

When they got to the office, Dr. Lou Coltrain's nurse,

Betty, came right out to meet them and guide them back into a cubicle.

Lou walked in, took a professional look at the cut, and grinned. "Stitches," she said. "How about a tetanus jab?"

Leo grimaced. "Well…"

She patted him on the shoulder that wasn't injured. "We'll have you fixed up and out of here in no time."

He sighed, glancing at his brother. "I hate shots."

Rey shrugged. "You'd hate tetanus more," he told Leo. "Besides," he added, "I hear she gives sugarless gum to the good patients."

Leo made a face at him.

When Leo was stitched up and given his tetanus shot, Rey drove him back to the house, where Meredith made him a cup of coffee and cut him a slice of cherry pie, making sure he had a cushion for his back in the straight chair at the table.

Rey glared at the special treatment his brother was getting. "Maybe I should get gored," he commented drolly.

Meredith stared at him, and she didn't smile. "You'd get a vinegar dressing and a cup of cold coffee," she said.

He glared at her, too. He felt as if he'd been put in the corner without supper. It wasn't a feeling he liked. He gave them both a hard look and went back out the door, smoldering with bad temper.

Chapter Six

"I shouldn't have said that," Meredith said wryly when Rey was gone. "I set him off again."

"It won't hurt him to have one woman who doesn't fall all over herself when he's around," Leo told her flatly. "Sometimes too much success can ruin a good man."

She toyed with her coffee cup. "Women like him, I guess," she said.

He gave her a quick glance that she didn't see before he started on his pie. "He's had girlfriends since he was in grammar school. But there was only one serious one. She turned out to be a real loser," he added quietly. "She soured him on women."

She sipped coffee. "You can't judge an entire sex by one woman," she pointed out.

"Well, we had our mother as an example, too," he continued. "She left Dad with five young boys and never looked back. We haven't been overawed with sterling examples of womanhood, although Simon and Corrigan and Cag have made good marriages in spite of that."

She smiled absently as she looked at him. "I had a brother of my own," she said without thinking.

"Yes, I know," Leo replied, surprising her into silence. "His name was Michael Johns. He worked for Houston PD."

Her gasp was audible. "How…do you know about him?"

"Remember Colter Banks?"

"Yes. Colter was Mike's best friend."

"Well, Colter's our second cousin," he told her. "I knew Mike, too. I'm sorry."

She clenched one fist in her lap and tried not to give way to tears. "Do the others…know?"

"No, they don't," he replied. "They weren't that close to Colter, and they never met Mike. I haven't told them, and I'm not planning to."

She searched his dark eyes. "What else do you know about me, Leo?" she asked, because of the way he was watching her.

He shrugged. "Everything."

She let out a long breath. "And you haven't shared it with Rey."

"You wouldn't want me to," he murmured dryly. "He's having too much fun being condescending. When the time comes, he's got a few shocks coming, hasn't he?"

She laughed softly. "I hadn't meant to be cloak-and-daggerish. It's just that it still hurts too much to talk about," she said honestly.

"Colter told me the circumstances. It wasn't your fault," he replied. "Or your father's. I gather that he drinks because he feels responsible?"

She nodded. "We both dined out on 'what-if' just after it happened," she confessed. "I know that it probably wouldn't have made any difference, but you can't help wondering."

"It doesn't do any good to torment yourself over things that are history," Leo said gently.

"I don't do it intentionally," she murmured.

"The first step was getting your father into treatment," he said. "Getting you out of your rut was the second. You don't have any memories to contend with here. I've noticed the difference in you just in the past week." He smiled. "You're changing already."

"I suppose so." She smiled back. "I've never even been on a ranch before. I could love it here. It's such a change of pace."

"When you're back to normal, we've got plenty of opportunity around here for your sort of job," he pointed out.

She chuckled. "Don't rush me. It's far too soon to think about leaving Houston." She didn't add that she didn't want to be that close to Rey, considering his opinion of her at the moment. "I've only been down here a week."

"Okay. I'll let it drop, for now." He leaned back in his chair and winced, favoring the arm he'd had stitched. "Damned bull," he muttered.

"Did they give you something for the pain?"

"No, and I didn't ask for anything. I have over-the-counter painkillers if it gets really bad. So far, it hasn't."

"You know, of course, that statistically farm and ranch work have the highest ratio of accidents," she said.

"Any job can be dangerous," he said easily.

She pursed her lips and lifted her coffee cup to them. "Your brother's a walking job hazard," she said thoughtfully.

"Oh? In what way, exactly?" he asked.

She wouldn't have touched that line with a pole. She laughed. "He's abrasive. I don't think he wants me here."

"I've noticed his attitude. I hope you haven't let it get to you?"

"I haven't. Anyway, he'll mellow one of these days," she said.

"He could use some mellowing. He's a disillusioned man."

She smoothed the lip of the cup. "Did he love her very much?"

He knew she was talking about Carlie. He sighed. "He

thought he did. His pride suffered more than his heart." He hesitated. "I didn't help matters. I made a play for her deliberately, to show him what she was. That was a miscalculation. A bad one. He's never forgiven me for it. Now, if I pay any attention to a woman, he tries to compete with me…"

She noticed the way his voice trailed off, and she averted her eyes. "I get the picture," she said.

"It's not like that, not with you," he began.

She forced a smile. "He's not interested in me," she said bluntly. "And just in case you're worried that I might be falling all over him, there's no danger of that, either. I was outside the door when he was talking to you. I wasn't eavesdropping, but he was speaking rather loudly. I heard what he said. I'd have to be certifiable to lose my heart over a man like that."

He grimaced as he read the faint pain that lingered in her eyes. "I wouldn't have had you hear what he said for the world," he said deeply.

She managed a smile. "It's just as well. It will keep me from taking him seriously. Besides, I'm not really down here looking for a soul mate."

"Just as well, because Rey isn't any woman's idea of the perfect partner, not the way he is right now. I love him dearly, but I can afford to. It's another story for any woman who loses her heart to him." He studied her warily. "Just don't let him play you for a fool."

"I wouldn't dream of it," she said. "Even if I got the chance."

He nodded. He finished his pie and coffee and got to his feet. "I'd better change and get back to work. Thanks for running interference, by the way. You're a cool head in an emergency," he remarked with a smile.

"I've had lots of practice," she said modestly and grinned. "But try to stay away from horned things for a while."

"Especially my brother, the minor devil," he said, tongue-in-cheek, and grinned back when she got the reference and started laughing.

After Leo went back to work, Meredith went out to gather eggs. It seemed very straightforward. You walked into the henhouse, reached in the nest, and pulled out a dozen or so big brown eggs, some still warm from the chicken's feathered body.

But that wasn't what happened. She paused just inside the henhouse to let her eyes adjust to the reduced light, and when she moved toward the row of straw-laced nests, she saw something wrapped around one nest that wasn't feathered. It had scales and a flickering long tongue. It peered at her through the darkness and tightened its coils around its prey, three big brown eggs.

Meredith, a city girl with very little experience of scaly things, did something predictable. She screamed, threw the basket in the general direction of the snake, and left skid marks getting out of the fenced lot.

Annie Lewis, who was doing the laundry, came to the back door as fast as her arthritis would allow, to see what all the commotion was about.

"There's a…big black and white *snnnnnakkkkkke*…in there!" Meredith screamed, shaking all over from the close encounter.

"After the eggs, I reckon," Annie said with a sigh. She wiped her hands on her apron. "Let me get a stick and I'll deal with it."

"You can't go in there alone with the horrible thing and try to kill it! It must be five feet long!"

"It's a king snake, not a rattler," Annie said gently, recognizing the description. "And I'm not planning to kill it. I'm going to get it on a stick and put in the barn. It can eat its fill of rats and poisonous snakes and do some good out there."

"You aren't going to kill it?" Meredith exclaimed, horrified.

"It's a king snake, dear," came the gentle reply. "We don't like to kill them. They're very useful. They eat rattlesnakes, you know."

"I didn't know." Meredith shivered again. "I've never seen a snake except in a zoo, and it was a python."

"You'll see lots of them out here in the country. Just remember that if one rattles at you, it means business and it will strike. Rattlesnakes are venomous."

Meredith looked around as if she expected to be mobbed just at the mention of them.

"You can finish the washing," Annie said, trying not to grin. "I'll take care of the snake."

"Please be careful!"

"I will. After all, you get used to things like…"

Rey drove up and stopped the truck just short of the two women, exiting it with his usual graceful speed.

"What's going on?" he asked as he pulled a box of assorted bovine medicines out of the boot of the truck.

"There's a snake in the henhouse!" Meredith exclaimed.

He stopped with the supplies in his arms and stared at her curiously. "So?" he asked.

"I'm just going to move it for her, Rey," Mrs. Lewis said with a grin. "It sounds like a king snake. I thought I'd put him in the barn."

"I'll get him for you." He put the box on the hood of the truck. "Scared of snakes, are you?" he scoffed.

"I'd never seen one until a few minutes ago," she said huffily, and flushed. He was looking at her as if she were a child.

"There's a first time for everything," he said, and his eyes made a very explicit remark as they lingered on her breasts.

She gave him a glare hot enough to fry bacon, which he ignored. He walked right into the chicken lot and, then, into the henhouse.

Barely a minute later, he came back out with the snake coiled around one arm, its neck gently held in his other hand.

"Would you look at this, it's Bandit!" he exclaimed, showing it to a fascinated Mrs. Lewis. "See the scar on his back where he got caught in the corn sheller that time?"

"So it is!" she said. "Hello, old fella!" She actually petted the vile thing under the chin.

"How can you touch that thing?!" Meredith groaned. "It's a snake!"

Mrs. Lewis glanced at Rey. "Reckon we should tell her that he used to live in the house?"

"Probably not," Rey suggested, aware of her white face. "I'll just stick him up in the loft. Come on, Bandit, I'll put you in a safe place."

Meredith was holding both chill-bump laden arms with her hands and shivering.

"There, there," Annie said gently. "He wouldn't bite you unless you provoked him. He's very gentle."

"If you say so."

"I do. Now you go back in there and get the eggs. Don't let Rey see how frightened you are. Trust me, he'll take advantage of it. You'll find rubber snakes in the refrigerator, the blender, the washer…"

"No!" Meredith exclaimed, horrified.

"Just grit your teeth and go back in the henhouse," Annie suggested. "Quick, before he comes back out."

Meredith took a quick breath and gave Annie a miserable glance, but she did as she was told.

Her skin crawled when she had to pick up the basket and gather the eggs, especially the ones the snake had been curled around. Now, every time she went to the henhouse, she'd be shivering with apprehension.

You've looked at gunshot wounds, accident victims, every sort of horror known to human eyes, she told herself firmly. The snake wasn't even lacerated! So get it done and move on.

She did, walking back out into the sunlight with a full basket of eggs and a forced look of composure on her soft face.

Rey was waiting for her, leaning against the bumper of the truck with his arms crossed and his hat pulled low over his eyes.

She didn't dare look at him for long. In that indolent pose, his lean, muscular body was shown to its very best advantage. It made her tingle to think how it had felt to be held against every inch of that formidable frame, to be kissed by that long, hard mouth.

"You get thrown, you get right back on the horse," he said with approval. "I'm proud of you, Meredith. It would be hard for even a ranch-born girl to go back into a henhouse where a snake had been lurking."

She took a slow breath. "We don't face things by running away from them, I guess," she agreed.

His eyes narrowed under the wide brim of the hat. "What are you running away from, Meredith? What is your father running away from?"

She clutched the basket to her chest. "That's nothing that you need to concern yourself with," she said with quiet dignity.

"You work for me," he replied.

"Not for long," she pointed out. "In another week or so, I'll be a memory."

"Will you?" He lurched away from the bumper and went to stand just in front of her, a tall and sensual threat. His fingers touched her soft mouth lightly. "Those bruises still look pretty fresh," he pointed out. "And you did ask for a month's leave, or so you said. Did you?"

She grimaced. "Well, yes, but I don't have to stay here all that time."

"I think you do," he returned. He bent and drew his mouth slowly over hers, a whisper of a contact that made her breath catch. He smiled with faint arrogance as he stood up again. "Anything could happen," he drawled. "You might like ranch life."

"I don't like snakes already."

"That was a fluke. They're generally hibernating by November, but it's been unseasonably warm. Spring is generally when you have to watch where you put your hands. But you don't need to worry. I'll protect you from snakes. And other perils."

"Who'll protect me from you?" she asked huskily.

He raised any eyebrow. "Why would you need protection?" he asked. "You're well over the age of consent."

"I've lived a very sheltered life," she said flatly.

He pursed his lips as he studied her, examining the statement. "Maybe it's time you walked out of the cocoon."

"I'm not in the market for an affair."

"Neither am I." He smiled slowly. "But if you worked at it, you might change my mind."

"I don't think so," she said. Her eyes were cool as they met his. "I wouldn't want you to think I was 'drooling' over you," she added deliberately.

His face changed. He knew immediately that she'd overheard what he'd said to Leo. He was sorry, because it wasn't true. He'd been desperate to throw Leo off the track. He didn't want his brother to know how attracted he was to her.

"Eavesdroppers never hear anything good about themselves, don't they say?" he asked quietly.

"Never," she agreed. "Now, if you'll excuse me, I'll go wash the eggs."

"I said something else that you'll remember with sordid ease," he murmured as she started past him. He caught her by the shoulder and tugged her close, bending to drag his mouth roughly across hers. "But I didn't mean that, either," he whispered against her parted lips. "Your innocence makes my head spin. I lay awake at night thinking of all sorts of delicious ways to relieve you of it."

"You'd be lucky!" she exclaimed, shocked.

He laughed softly as he let her go. "So would you," he drawled. "I've been called 'sensual hell' in bed, and I can assure you it wasn't meant to be a derogatory remark."

"Rey Hart!" she burst out.

"But why take anyone else's word for it?" he teased. "I'll be glad to let you see for yourself, anytime you like."

"If you think…I have never…of all the…!"

"Yes, it does tend to make women flustered when I mention what a great lover I am," he said with a wicked grin.

She couldn't get one coherent sentence out. She stomped her foot hard, turned around, and stormed into the kitchen, almost knocking herself down with the door in the process. It didn't help that Rey stood out there laughing like a predator.

If she expected Rey to be apologetic about what he'd said, she was doomed to disappointment. He watched her with narrow, assessing eyes as she went about her household duties. He didn't harass her, or monopolize her. He just watched. The scrutiny made her so nervous that she fumbled constantly. Her heart ran wild at the attention from those dark, steady eyes.

"Why don't you want to do something else besides keep house?" Rey asked her one evening when she was putting supper on the table. Leo, as usual, was late getting in. Rey had volunteered to set the table while she fixed Mexican corn bread and chili.

"Keeping house has less stress than most outside jobs," she said, not looking at him.

"It pays lousy wages," he continued, "and you could get into a lot of trouble in some households, with men who'd see you as fair game."

"Do you see me that way?" she asked, wide-eyed.

He glowered at her. "No, I don't. The point is, some other man might. It isn't a safe career. In a profession, there are more laws to protect you."

"Most professional people have degrees and such. Besides, I'm too old."

"You're never too old to go back to school," he replied.

She shrugged. "Besides, I like cooking and cleaning."

He eyed her curiously. "You're very good at handling injured people," he said suddenly. "And you're remarkably calm in an emergency."

"It's good practice for when I have kids," she said.

He drew in a short breath. "You like being mysterious, don't you?"

"While it lasts, it's fun," she agreed.

His eyes narrowed. "What dark secrets are you keeping, Meredith?" he asked quietly.

"None that should bother you, even if you found them

out," she assured him. She smiled at him from the stove. "Meanwhile, you're getting fresh biscuits every day."

"Yes, we are," he had to agree. "And you're a good cook. But I don't like mysteries."

She pursed her lips and gave him a teasing glance over her shoulder. "Too bad."

He put the last place setting on the table and sat down at his place, just staring at her, without speaking. "You know," he said after a minute, frowning, "there's something familiar about your last name. I can't quite place it, but I know I've heard it somewhere."

That wasn't good, she thought. He might remember Leo talking about her brother. She didn't want to have to face the past, not just yet, when she was still broken and bruised and uncomfortable. When she was back on her feet and well again, there would be time to come to grips with it once and for all—as her poor father was already doing.

"Think so?" she asked with forced nonchalance.

He shrugged. "Well, it may come back to me one day."

Fortunately Leo came in and stopped his train of thought. Meredith put supper on the table and sat down to eat it with the brothers.

The next morning, Rey came out to the kitchen with a bright silver metal gun case. He set it down beside the counter, out of the way, before he started eating his breakfast.

"Going hunting?" Meredith asked impishly.

He gave her a wary glance. "Skeet shooting," he corrected. "The season's over, but I practice year-round."

"He won two medals at the World championships in San Antonio, this year," Leo told her with a grin. "He's an 'A' class shooter."

"Which gauge?" she asked without thinking.

Rey's face became suspicious. "All of them. What do you know about shotguns?"

"I used to skeet-shoot," she volunteered. "My brother taught me how to handle a shotgun, and then he got me into competition shooting. I wasn't able to keep it up after I grad…after high school," she improvised quickly. She didn't dare tell him she gave it up after she finished college. That would be giving away far too much.

He watched her sip coffee. "You can shoot, can you?" he asked, looking as if he were humoring her. He didn't seem to believe what she claimed.

"Yes, I can," she said deliberately.

He smiled. "Like to come down to the range with me?" he asked. "I've got a nice little .28 gauge I can bring along for you."

By offering her his lowest caliber shotgun, he was assuming that she couldn't handle anything heavier.

"What's in the case?" she asked.

"My twelve gauge," he said.

She gave him a speaking glance. "I'll just shoot that, if you don't mind sharing it. Uh, it doesn't have a kick or anything…?" she added, and had to bite her tongue to keep from grinning at her innocent pose.

He cleared his throat. He didn't dare look at Leo. "No," he said carelessly. "Of course it doesn't have a kick."

In truth, it would kick worse than any other of the four gauges, but Rey was planning to call her bluff. She was putting on an act for his benefit. He was going to make her sorry she tried it.

"Then I'll be just fine with that gun," she said. "More apple butter?" She offered him an open jar and spoon.

"Thanks," he replied smugly, accepting the jar. He put it

down and buttered another biscuit before he spooned the apple butter into it. "Don't mind if I do. Leo, want to come along?" he asked his brother.

Leo was also trying not to grin. "I think I will, this time," he told his brother. This was one shooting contest he wasn't about to miss. He knew that Mike Johns was a champion shooter. If he'd been the one who taught his sister, Meredith would shock Rey speechless when she got that shotgun in her arms. He was going along. He didn't want to miss the fun.

"The more the merrier, I always say," Rey chuckled.

"Funny thing, that's just what I was thinking," Leo replied, tongue-in-cheek.

Meredith didn't say another word. She finished her breakfast, waited until they finished theirs, and put the dishes in the dishwasher. Then she dressed in jeans, boots, and a long-sleeved flannel shirt with a down-filled vest and a bib cap, and went off to let Rey show her how to shoot a shotgun.

The target range was unusually busy for a lazy Friday afternoon in November. It was a cool day, with a nice nip in the air. Meredith felt good in the down vest. It was one she'd often worn when she went to the firing range with Mike in cold weather. Coats were cumbersome and often got in the way of a good, quick aim.

Rey and Leo stopped to pass the time of day with two elderly shooters, both of whom gave Meredith a warm welcome.

"This is Jack, and that's Billy Joe," Rey introduced the white-haired men, one of whom was tall and spare, the other overweight and short. The short one had walked briskly the short distance from the red pickup truck parked at the clubhouse, and he was out of breath already. "We all go to district, state and national shoots as a team from our club."

"But we get honorable mention, and Rey wins the medals," Billy Joe, the shorter man, chuckled, still trying to catch his breath. "We don't mind. We're just happy that somebody from our club breaks records!"

"Amen to that," Jack agreed, smiling.

"All right, let's get to shooting," Billy Joe said, turning back to his truck. "Stay where you are, Jack. I'll bring your gun, too!"

He turned back toward the truck, rushing and still breathless. Meredith frowned. His cheeks were unnaturally pink, and it wasn't that cold. His complexion was almost white. He was sweating. She knew the symptoms. She'd seen them all too often.

"You might go with him," Meredith said abruptly, interrupting Jack's banter with Rey.

"Excuse me?" Jack asked.

Just at that moment, Billy Joe stopped, stood very still for a minute, and then buckled and fell forward into a crumpled heap at the door of his truck.

Meredith took off at a dead run. "Somebody get me a cell phone!" she called as she ran.

Leo fumbled his out of the holder on his belt and passed it to her as she knelt beside Billy Joe.

"Get his feet elevated. Find something to cover him with," she shot at the other men. She was dialing while she spoke. She loosened the man's shirt, propping the phone against her ear—the worst way to hold it, but there was no other way at the moment—and felt down Billy Joe's chest for his diaphragm. "Get his wallet and read me his weight and age from his driver's license," she added with a sharp glance in Leo's direction.

Leo dug out the wallet and started calling out information, while Rey and Jack stood beside the fallen man and watched with silent concern.

"I want the resident on duty in the emergency room, stat," she said. "This is Meredith Johns. I have a patient, sixty years of age, one hundred and eighty pounds, who collapsed without warning. Early signs indicate a possible myocardial infarction. Pulse is thready," she murmured, checking the second hand of her watch as she took his pulse with her fingertips, "forty beats a minute, breathing shallow and labored, grey complexion, profuse sweating. I need EMTs en route, I am initiating cardiopulmonary resuscitation now."

There was a long pause, and a male voice came over the line. With her voice calm and steady, Meredith gave the information again, and then handed the phone to Leo as she bent over the elderly man and did the spaced compressions over his breastbone, followed by mouth-to-mouth breathing.

Rey was watching, spellbound at her proficiency, at the easy and quite professional manner in which she'd taken charge of a life-or-death emergency. Within five minutes, the ambulance was screaming up the graveled road that led to the Jacobsville Gun Club, and Billy Joe was holding his own.

The EMTs listened to Meredith's terse summary of events as they called the same resident Meredith had been talking to.

"Doc says to give you a pat on the back," the female EMT grinned at Meredith as they loaded Billy Joe onto the ambulance. "You sure knew what to do."

"Yes," Rey agreed, finding his tongue at last. "You've obviously had first-aid training."

He probably meant it as praise, but it hit Meredith in the gut. She glared at him. "What I've had," she emphasized, "is five years of college. I have a master's degree in nursing science, and I'm a card-carrying nurse practitioner!"

Chapter Seven

Rey stared at his new cook as if she'd suddenly sprouted feathers on her head. His summation of her abilities was suddenly smoke. She was someone he didn't even know. She was a health care professional, not a flighty cook, and certainly not the sort of woman to streetwalk as a sideline.

She nodded solemnly. "I figured it would come as a shock," she told him. She turned her attention back to the EMTs. "Thanks for being so prompt. Think he'll be okay?"

The female EMT smiled. "I think so. His heartbeat's stronger, his breathing is regular, and he's regaining consciousness. Good job!"

She grinned. "You, too."

They waved and took off, lights flashing, but without turning on the sirens.

"Why aren't the sirens going?" Rey wanted to know. "He's not out of danger yet, surely?"

"They don't like to run the sirens unless they have to," Meredith told him. "Some people actually run off the road and wreck their cars because the sirens rattle them. They use the lights, but they only turn on the sirens if they hit heavy traffic and have to force their way through it. Those EMTs," she added with a smile, "they're the real heroes and heroines. They do the hardest job of all."

"You saved Billy Joe's life," Jack said huskily, shaking her hand hard. "He's the best friend I got. Thank you."

She smiled gently and returned the handshake. "It goes with the job description. Don't try to keep up with the ambulance," she cautioned when he went toward Billy Joe's truck, which still had the key in the ignition. The two men had come together.

"I'll be careful," the older man promised.

"Whew!" Leo let out the breath he'd almost been holding, and put up his cell phone. "You're one cool lady under fire, Meredith."

She smiled sadly. "I've had to be," she replied. She glanced at Rey, who looked cold and angry as it occurred to him, belatedly, that she'd played him for a fool. "I can see what you're thinking, but I didn't actually lie to you. You never asked me exactly what I did for a living. Of course, you thought you already knew," she added with faint sarcasm.

He didn't reply. He gave her a long, contemptuous look and turned away. "I've lost my taste for practice," he said quietly. "I want to go on to the hospital and see about Billy Joe."

"Me, too," Leo added. "Meredith…?"

"I'll go along," she said. "I'd like to meet that resident I spoke with. He's very good."

Rey glanced toward her. "You'll get along. He keeps secrets, too," he said bitterly, and got behind the wheel.

Leo made a face at Meredith, opening the third door of the big double cabbed truck so that she could sit in back. He put the gun cases in the boot, in a locked area, and climbed in beside Rey.

The resident turned out to be a former mercenary named Micah Steele. He was married to a local girl, and he'd gone back to school to finish his course of study for his medical license.

"I couldn't very well carry a wife and child around the jungles with me," Micah told her with a grin. He was tall and big, and not at all bad-looking. She could picture him with a rifle in one arm. But now, in a white lab coat with a stethoscope thrown carelessly around his neck, he seemed equally at home.

"When's Callie due?" Leo asked.

"Any minute," he said, tongue-in-cheek. "Can't you see me shaking? I'm the soul of self-confidence around here, but one little pregnant woman makes me a basket case!"

"Callie's quite a girl," Rey agreed, smiling at the big man.

Micah gave him a look. "Yes, and isn't it lucky for me that you hardly ever went into her boss Kemp's office for legal advice, while she was still single?"

Rey pursed his lips. "Kemp eats scorpions for breakfast, I hear. I like my lawyers less caustic."

"Last I heard, the local bar association had you down as a contagious plague and was warning its members to avoid you at all costs," Micah replied wickedly.

"I never hit any local lawyers." Rey looked uncomfortable. "It was that Victoria lawyer, Matherson," he muttered. "And I didn't even hit him that hard. Hell, he's lucky I wasn't sober at the time! Otherwise, he'd have had twice the number of stitches!"

Meredith listened to the repartee with wide, fascinated eyes, but Rey wouldn't meet her eyes and Micah, too, cleared his throat and didn't pursue the subject.

"Matherson took a client who accused us of assault," Leo volunteered. "Cag had hit him, several times, after he got drunk and assaulted Tess, who's now Cag's wife. But the bounder swore that he was the injured party, that we falsely accused him and all took turns pounding him. He convinced a jury to award him damages. Not a lot of money," Leo added solemnly, "but the principle was what set Rey off. He was in a bad mood already and he had a few too many drinks at Shea's Bar, out on the Victoria road. To make a long story short," he added with a chuckle, "Matherson was having a quiet beer when Rey accused him of handling the ex-employee's case for spite because he lost an argument with us over Tess when he was handling her inheritance. Matherson took exception to Rey's remarks, and the two of them set about wrecking the pretty stained-glass window that used to overlook the parking lot."

"Used to?" Meredith fished, sensing something ominous.

"Yes, well, Matherson made a rather large hole in it when Rey helped him into the parking lot the hard way," Leo concluded.

Micah Steele looked as if it was killing him not to burst out laughing.

"He," Leo jerked his thumb toward Steele, "had to remove quite a number of glass particles from Matherson's rear end. *And* we got sued again, for that!"

"But the jury, after hearing Kemp's masterful summation of our grievances," Rey interrupted, "decided that Matherson was only entitled to the cost of the repair job on his butt. Shea had insurance that replaced the stained-glass window with one of comparable age and exclusivity." Rey smiled smugly. "And the judge said that if she'd been sitting on the first case, the rat Matherson was representing would have gotten a jail sentence."

Leo chuckled. "Only because Kemp put Tess on the stand and had her testify about what really happened the night Matherson's client took her on a date. The jury felt that Rey was justifiably incensed by the former verdict." He glanced at Meredith wryly.

"Yes, but I understand that Shea's two bouncers meet Rey at the door these days and won't let him in if he's not smiling," Micah contributed.

Rey shrugged. "I never get drunk anymore. I've learned to handle aggression in a nonphysical manner."

The other two men actually walked down the hall. Meredith noticed their shoulders vibrating.

Rey took a step toward Meredith, half irritated by the character assassination job his brother and Micah Steele had just done on him, and even more put out by Meredith's unmasking.

"You knew I had no idea about your education," Rey accused Meredith. "Why didn't you say something at the outset, when Leo first went to the hospital?" he demanded in a low, deep tone. "I may have jumped to conclusions, but you provided the springs, didn't you?"

She grimaced. "I guess so. But it was only a little jump from telling you about my job to talking about the reason Daddy started drinking. It's...still very fresh in my mind," she added huskily. "It's only been six months. The memories are—" she swallowed and looked away "—bad."

Unexpectedly he reached out and caught her fingers in his, tugging her closer. The hall was deserted. In the background there were muted bell-tones and announcements and the sound of lunch trays being distributed. "Tell me," he said gently.

She bit her lower lip hard and lifted her tormented eyes to his curious ones. "Not...yet," she whispered tightly. "One day, but...not yet. I can't."

"Okay," he said after a minute. "But I'd like to know how you learned to shoot."

"My brother, Mike, taught me," she said reluctantly, staring at his broad chest. She wanted to lay her head on it and cry out her pain. There hadn't been anyone to hold her, not when it happened, not afterward. Her father withdrew into his own mind and started drinking to excess at once. Her job was all that had kept Meredith sane. She hadn't been able to let out her grief in any normal way.

Rey's mind was working overtime. He stared down at her, still holding her fingers entwined tightly with his own, and he frowned as bits and pieces of memory began fitting themselves together.

"Mike. Mike Johns." His eyes narrowed. "Our cousin Colter's best friend, and one of Leo's acquaintances. He was killed…!"

She tried to tug her fingers away. He wouldn't let her. He pulled her into his arms, holding her there even when she struggled. But a few seconds of resistance were all she had. She laid her flushed cheek against his broad chest and let the tears flow.

Rey's arms contracted roughly. He smoothed his hand over her nape, caressing, soothing. "There was a bank robbery in Houston," he recalled quietly. "Mike was a cop. He was at the bank with your mother. It was Saturday. He was off duty, but he had his service revolver under his jacket." His arms tightened as her sobs grew painful to hear. "He drew and fired automatically, and one of the robbers sprayed fire from one of those damned little automatic rifles in his general direction. He and your mother died instantly…"

Meredith's fingers dug into his wide back. He rocked her, barely aware of curious glances from passersby.

"Both men were caught. You don't kill a cop and get away with it in Texas," he added softly. "They were arraigned and treated to a speedy trial just a month ago. You and your father testified. That was when your father really went off the deep end, wasn't it, when he had to see the autopsy photos…"

Micah and Leo came back down the hall, frowning when they saw the condition Meredith was in. Even as they watched, her eyes rolled back and she would have fallen to the floor except for Rey's strong arms lifting her.

Later, she wouldn't recall much except that she was hustled into a cubicle and revived. But when she started sobbing hysterically, they'd given her a shot of something that put her out like a light. She came to back at the ranch, in her own little garage apartment.

She opened her eyes, and there was Rey, sitting by the bed, still wearing the same jeans and shirt and boots he'd worn to the shooting range. Meredith was aware of the bedspread covering her up to her waist. Her boots were off, but she was also wearing the same clothes she'd started out in that morning.

"What time is it?" she asked in a husky, slightly disoriented tone.

"Five hours past the time you flaked out on me," he said, smiling gently. "Micah knocked you out. He thought some sleep might help." The smile faded into quiet concern. "You don't sleep much, do you, Meredith?" he asked surprisingly.

She sighed, brushed back her disheveled blond hair, and shook her head. "When I go to sleep, I have nightmares. I wake up in a cold sweat, and I see them, lying there on the floor, just the way they looked in those vivid crime scene photos." She closed her eyes and shivered. "People look so fragile like that, they look like big dolls, sprawled in pitiful disarray on the floor. Everybody stares at them…"

He brushed back her hair with a lean, gentle hand. "They got the guys who did it," he reminded her. "Including the trigger man. He'll serve life without any hope of parole. He'll pay for it."

Her pale eyes were tormented as they met his. "Yes, but it won't bring them back, will it?" she asked. "And do you know why they said they did it? For a bet. For a stupid bet, they killed two innocent people!"

"They also ruined their own lives," he reminded her, "and the lives of their own families."

She looked at him blankly, scowling.

"Don't you ever think about that?" he asked softly. "Criminals have families, too. Most of them have loving, decent parents who took care of them and disciplined them and blame themselves for what their children do. It must be pure hell, to have your child kill someone, and feel responsible for it."

"I haven't considered that," she admitted.

He continued. "When I was in high school, one of my best friends was arrested for murder. He killed the old man next door in the process of stealing his wallet. He wanted to buy his girl a diamond necklace she liked, and he didn't have any money. He figured the man was old and didn't need money anyway, so he might as well take it. He was sorry about it, but he never figured on killing the man or getting caught."

"Was he a good friend?" she asked.

He looked at their linked fingers. He nodded. "We were pals since grammar school. He wasn't quite as bright as some of the other boys, but he had a gentle nature. Or so we thought." He met her eyes. "His mom and dad always had a houseful of other peoples' kids. They were everybody's mom and dad. It shattered them when Joey went to prison. Even the children of the old man felt sorry for them."

"Funny," she mused. "I never even thought of how it would feel to have a child or a parent or a sibling who broke the law in some terrible way." She met his eyes. "I guess I'd feel guilty, too."

"Most kids are raised right. But some of them have a wild streak that nobody can tame, others have poor impulse control. Many are handicapped. Nobody goes to jail because he wants to."

"I never thought of you as a sensitive man," she blurted out, and then flushed at the insult.

His eyebrows lifted. "Who, me? I stop to pick worms out of the highway so my tires won't bruise their little bodies, and you think I'm insensitive?"

It took a minute for the words to make sense, and then she burst out laughing.

"That's better," he said. He smiled and squeezed her fingers. "You're going to be okay. You've had a lot of traumatic experiences just lately. No wonder you caved in."

"Lucky for you," she shot back.

"Me? Why?"

"Because if we'd unpacked those shotguns, I'd have destroyed your ego," she said with a smug smile. "At Mike's gun club, they used to call me 'dead-eye.'"

"Oh, they did, did they?" he challenged. "Well, we'll see about that when you step up to my gun range."

She studied his lean face. He wasn't handsome, but he had strong, stubborn features. He was familiar to her now, almost necessary. She thought about going back to Houston with real panic.

He touched her cheek where the bruises were a mixture of purple and yellow, much less vivid now. "He really knocked you around," he said, and his face hardened visibly. "I don't care if a man is drunk, there's no excuse for hitting a woman."

"Shades of primitive man," she chided with a smile.

"Women are the cradles of life," he said simply. "What sort of man tries to break a cradle?"

"You have a unique way of putting things."

"We had Spanish ancestors," he told her. "They were old-world men, conquerors, adventurers. One of them made his way to Texas and was given a huge tract of land under a Spanish land grant, for services to the crown of Spain." He noticed a start of surprise on her face. "Do you know the legend of the Cid?"

"Yes!" she exclaimed. "He was a great Spanish hero. Cid is for the Arabic 'Sidi' which means Lord."

"Well, our ancestor wasn't El Cid," he said on a chuckle. "But he fought his way through hostile neighbors to claim his land, and he held it as long as he lived. Our family still holds it, through our late uncle, who left us this ranch."

"This is the original grant?" she exclaimed.

He nodded. "It isn't nearly as big as it was a couple of hundred years ago, but it's no weekend farm, either. Didn't you notice the antique silver service in the dining room?"

"Yes, I've been afraid to touch it. It looks very old."

He smiled. "It came from Madrid. It's over two hundred years old."

"An heirloom!" she breathed.

"Yes. Like the ranch itself." He tilted his head and studied her for a long time. "Now I understand. Your father wasn't violent until the killer's trial, was he?"

"No, he wasn't." She looked down at Rey's big, warm hand wrapped around her own. It made her feel safe. "He told Mike to drive Mama to the bank," she added reluctantly. "He had papers to grade. He couldn't spare the time, he said, and he snapped at her when she protested that Mike was spending his day off, carting her all over Houston." She glanced at him. "I was called in to work at a clinic my boss holds in the Hispanic community every Saturday. There's a regular nurse, but she was at home with a sick child. I went to stand in for her." Her eyes fell to his broad chest. "I could have asked someone to go in my place. I didn't. So he and I both have our guilt."

"Because you lived and they didn't," Rey said bluntly.

She gasped. "No, that's not true!"

"It is true." His black eyes held hers relentlessly. "The same thing happens to people who survive airplane crashes, automobile wrecks, sinking ships. It's a normal, human reaction to surviving when other people don't. It's worse when the victims include close relatives or friends."

"Where did you learn that?" she asked.

"From Janie Brewster," he said.

She frowned. "That name sounds familiar."

"We've mentioned her to you. She's the daughter of a neighboring cattleman," he related. "She got her associate degree in psychology from our community college, and now she's studying it in Houston," he added with a grin. "She's almost twenty. They let her take college courses while she was still in high school, so she's ahead."

"Oh."

"She's not hard on the eyes, either," he murmured, avoiding her eyes. "She and her father live alone. Leo and I have a standing dinner invitation, any time we care to show up."

She started to say "oh" again, and realized how juvenile she was behaving. She straightened her shoulders against the pillow that was propping her up, and tugged at the hand Rey still held. "Then if she can bake biscuits, you're saved when I leave, aren't you?" she asked coolly.

"Well, she can't exactly bake stuff," Rey had to admit.

"Why?"

"She has no sense of time. She sets the timer and it goes off, and she never hears it. So the chicken bounces, the heat-and-serve rolls usually come out black, and I won't even mention what happens to vegetables she tries to cook on *top* of the stove." He gave her a sad look. "She did try to make us a pan of biscuits once." He actually shuddered.

"Not a successful try?" she fished.

"We had to take the damned things home, or her father would never have let us near the Salers heifers he was offering for sale." He glanced at her. "Leo just bought us a big Salers bull, and we needed purebred heifers to breed to him. Purebred breeding stock brings a big price, especially if you show cattle and win ribbons." He shrugged. "So we took the biscuits home."

"Did you eat them?" she persisted.

He shook his head and he shuddered again.

"Then what did you do with them?" she asked, thinking he probably fed them to the cattle dogs or some livestock.

"Well, actually, we took them out to the skeet field and used them for clay pigeons," he confessed with a grin. "They were the best damned targets we ever had, but we didn't dare say where we got them!"

She put her face in her hands and burst out laughing. "Oh, the poor girl!" she chuckled.

"Don't worry, we'd never tell her," he promised. "But we did ask her for another pan of biscuits, without telling her why." He sighed. "That woman has a ready-made profession as a target maker, and we haven't got the guts to tell her so. Hell of a shame!"

She brushed at her eyes with the hem of her blouse. Poor Janie. And she'd been jealous.

"What does she look like?" she asked, curious.

"She comes up to my shoulder. She's got light brown hair, longer than yours, and her eyes are green. If she didn't know everything, and tell you so every time you saw her, she might get married one day."

"You don't want to marry her?" she teased. "Not even for an inexhaustible supply of skeet targets?"

"I don't want to marry anybody," he said bluntly, and he looked her straight in the eye when he said it. "I love my freedom."

She sighed and smiled. "So do I," she confessed. "I don't think I could ever settle for diapers and dishes. Not with my background."

"You were a science major, weren't you?" he asked abruptly.

"Yes. Chemistry and biology, genetics—stuff like that. I made good grades, but it was hard work. Then I went right to work for my boss, straight out of college. I need to be two people, just to catch up. I run my legs off. The stress is pretty bad sometimes."

"No wonder keeping house and baking biscuits seemed like a holiday to you," he said to himself.

"It's been fun," she agreed. "I love to cook. I do it a lot, at home. I used to when Mama was alive," she recalled. "She hated housework and cooking. I came home from work and did it all."

"I've read about the sort of work you do," he commented, recalling articles he'd seen in the daily newspaper. "You're second only to a physician in authority. The only thing you can't do is write a prescription without his supervision."

"That's true." She smiled.

He studied her slender body, her exquisite figure nicely outlined by the garments she was wearing. "All those years, nothing but textbooks and exams and, then, a hectic career. No men?" he added, with a calculating stare.

"I dated," she replied. "I just couldn't afford to get serious about anybody. My father scraped and begged and borrowed to get the money to finance my nursing education," she told him. "Even Mike…contributed to it." She drew in a steadying breath and locked her fingers together on her lap. "It would have been so petty of me to throw all that up, just so I could go to parties and get drunk with the other students."

"Surely there wasn't much of that, at a community college?"

She laughed. "You'd be surprised. There was all too much, for my taste. But I didn't live on campus. I lived at home and commuted." She met his searching gaze. "That party I was at, when Leo was attacked—the woman who gave it was a college classmate who works for a doctor in our practice. I knew she sort of had a reputation. I guess I should have realized how wild things would get, but I was so depressed that I let her pressure me into going to the party. It was a mistake."

"A lucky mistake, for my brother," Rey said gently. "He might have been killed, if you hadn't come along when you did." He scowled. "You said, you ran at the attackers, waving your arms."

She nodded. "Mike taught me about shock tactics," she said sadly. "I was afraid it wouldn't work, but I had no weapon, no other way of stopping them. So I took the risk."

"I'm grateful that you did." He shook his head slowly. "But it was an act of lunacy, Meredith. You could have been lying on the grass next to Leo."

"But I wasn't." She hunched her shoulders as if she felt a chill. "I think there might be a force behind every single chain of events," she said thoughtfully. "I don't believe in chaos," she elaborated. "The body is such a messy, beautiful miracle. A single cell has chemical processes that are so complex, so meticulously crafted, that I can't believe life is an accident. If it isn't accidental, it has to be planned." She shrugged. "That's simple logic. That's why I don't think God is a myth."

They were silent for a moment. "You're the most intriguing woman I've ever met," he murmured, and his dark eyes fell to her soft, full mouth.

"Surely not?" she asked demurely. "I don't have any secrets left."

"That's what you think," he said in a soft, low tone.

She looked up and he moved toward her, one hand catching the wooden headboard as he levered his hard mouth down against her soft one.

Her hands instinctively went to his chest, but its muscular warmth was fascinating. She'd never done anything really intimate with her infrequent dates, having been completely turned off by men with fast reputations. She preferred gentlemen to rounders. She knew that Rey had been a rounder. She wanted to draw away. She really did.

But Rey Hart was completely out of her experience. He wasn't aggressive and insistent, as one of Meredith's rare dates had been. He didn't rush at her. He didn't insist. He wasn't insulting with the speed of his advances. He simply bent and kissed her, slowly and gently, with nothing more intimate than his hard, tender lips touching hers. He nibbled her upper lip and lifted his mouth slowly.

"You're doing a surfboard imitation," he murmured. "There's no need. I'm too good a cattleman to rush my fences."

She was trying to understand the slow, sensuous speech when his lips came down on hers again and caressed her upper lip. Her hands pressed flat against his muscular chest. She liked the way he felt. She could feel the quick, strong pulse of his heart under her palms. She could feel the growing rise and fall of his breathing.

His teeth nibbled her lips again, tenderly, and she found her hands moving under his arms and around him. She wanted to be held close, tight. She wanted him to envelop her against him. She wanted something more than this torturous teasing of his mouth on hers.

She made a husky, high-pitched little cry into his mouth and her nails bit into the solid muscles of his back.

"What do you want?" he whispered just above her lips.

"Kiss me," she moaned huskily.

"Kisses are dangerous, didn't you know?" he murmured, smiling against her responsive mouth. "They can be very addictive."

She was following his lips mindlessly. Her body was on fire. She'd never felt such headlong desire. Belatedly she realized that his hands were at her rib cage. Whether by accident or design, they were moving slowly up and down, up and down, so that his long fingers just lightly brushed the underswell of her breasts. It was extremely provocative. It was arousing.

She caught her breath as they moved ever closer to entrapment, and her eyes locked into his.

"Don't you like it this way?" he asked at her lips, brushing his mouth against them.

"Like...it?" she murmured mindlessly. Her body was reaching up toward those tormenting hands. She was shivering with every pulsating motion of her body, trembling with new and exciting surges of pleasure.

He laughed softly, sensuously. "Never mind." He lifted a hand to her hair and tugged out the hairpins, so that her beautiful long hair fell down around her shoulders. He tugged aside the top she was wearing, so that her shoulder was bare. Then he bent to it with his mouth, and she felt the warm, moist press of his lips right in the hollow of her shoulder.

Her nails dug into him. She lifted toward his mouth with a hoarse moan as she felt the slow tracing of his tongue against skin that had never known a man's touch. She was on fire. She was going to go up in flames right here. She didn't want to think, see, hear anything. She only wanted Rey to keep on touching her, to keep on holding her, to never, never stop...!

Chapter Eight

Just when the world was spinning away in a warm, pleasurable oblivion, the sound of loud, urgent footsteps echoed down the hall and brought Rey upright.

He looked at her with narrow, blank eyes as the sound grew louder. He cursed under his breath and got to his feet, keeping his back to her as he moved to the window, gripped the curtains and stared out at the pasture beyond.

Meredith dragged the bedspread up under her arms, over her clothes, and tried to steady her breathing. When she remembered what she and Rey had been doing, she blushed.

The door, ajar, was pushed completely open, and Leo came in with a tray. On it were a china cup and saucer, with a silver coffeepot, a silver cream and sugar service and a napkin and spoon. On a china plate were some dainty little chicken salad sandwiches.

"I thought you might be hungry," Leo said with a gentle smile as he put the tray on her lap. It had legs, so it would stand alone over her lap. "Mrs. Lewis came over to fix supper, and I had her make you these."

"Thank you!" she exclaimed. "And thank Mrs. Lewis, too. I was just starting to feel empty!"

Rey made an odd sound and she reached for a tiny sandwich very quickly, not daring to glance at him after the enthusiastic and unwise remark she'd just made.

Leo turned his eyes toward his brother. "Something wrong with you?" he asked curiously.

"Stomach cramp," Rey said without turning. "I had chili and salsa for lunch. Heartburn's killing me!"

"You should go and take an antacid tablet," Leo advised. "And drink some milk."

"I guess I'd better." Rey took a long breath and turned around, feeling more normal, finally. He glanced at Meredith. "I'm glad you're okay."

"I'll be fine. Thanks for the conversation," she said, and wouldn't meet his eyes. But she smiled shyly.

He just looked at her. Suddenly his dark eyes began to burn. He studied her intently, as if something had just happened that shocked him.

"Are you all right?" she asked impulsively.

He took a slow breath. He was still staring at her, to his brother's covert amusement. With her hair around her shoulders like that, sitting up in bed, smiling at him, he felt as if his whole life had just shifted five degrees. She was uncommonly pretty with her hair down. She had a warm, kind heart. She'd put her life on the line for a total stranger. Why hadn't that occurred to him in Houston, when they first told him that she'd saved his brother from attackers?

"Leo probably owes you his life," Rey said carefully. "But it bothers me that you risked your own to save him."

"Wouldn't you have done that same thing, even for a total stranger?" she mused.

He hesitated. "Yes," he said after deliberating for a few seconds. "I suppose I would have."

"See? You have all sorts of potential as a prospective husband," she added with a wicked smile, which got wider when he reacted. "You're sexy, you're rich, you drive a nice car, and besides all that, you like animals." She began nodding her head. "Definite potential."

His high cheekbones flushed and he glared at her. "I don't want to get married."

"Don't worry about it," she said soothingly. "It's perfectly natural for a bachelor to resist matrimony. But you'll come around." She wiggled both eyebrows. "If you get me a ring, I'll let you see my collection of used chewing gum wrappers and bottle caps."

He was still glaring.

Leo chuckled. "I'd love to see your used chewing gum wrappers, Meredith," he said enthusiastically. "In fact, I may start collecting right now!"

Rey stared a hole through his brother while, inside him, something froze.

"I'll even consider marrying you," Leo added wickedly.

She laughed, not taking him seriously. "Sorry. It's Rey or nobody. My heart's set on him." She frowned. "Pity I couldn't trade you something for him," she murmured to Leo.

Rey was getting angrier by the second, and uncomfortable at the idea that Leo was trying to cut him out.

"Make me an offer," Leo told her. "But he can't cook, and he has a temper worse than a sunburned rattler. Besides that, you can't domesticate him. He wears his spurs to the dinner table."

"So do you!" Rey accused.

"I sit more daintily than you do," Leo said imperturbably.

Rey rammed his hands into the pockets of his jeans and glared at Meredith again. "You can't give people away."

"I'm not trying to give you away," Leo said calmly. "I want to make a profit." He scowled suddenly and his eyes widened as he looked at his brother's boots.

Meredith was staring at them, too. She pursed her lips and exchanged a look with Leo.

Rey glared back at them belligerently. "What?" he demanded hotly.

Both Leo's eyebrows went up, along with both hands, palms out. "I didn't say a word!"

"Neither did I," Meredith assured him.

Rey looked from one to the other and finally looked down. There, on one of his feet, was a dainty little foot sock with a tassel on it, covering the steel toe of his brown cowboy boot. He'd unknowingly picked it up under Meredith's bed while he was kissing her.

Rey jerked it off, cursed royally, shot a furious glance at Meredith and his brother, who were trying valiantly not to look at him, and stomped out.

Helpless laughter erupted from the two people left in Meredith's room, and the sound of it infuriated Rey.

Leo was obviously ready to set up shop with their recently disclosed nurse, and Rey didn't like it. Leo was the plague of housekeepers everywhere, but he was also easier on the eyes than the other brothers, and he was charming. Rey had never learned how to use charm. He always looked uncomfortable when he smiled. Especially with women like Meredith, who was painfully shy and naive. He wasn't used to such women. But what made it so much worse was the dropping sensation in his stomach that he'd experienced when he'd stared at Meredith. He hadn't had anything like that since Carlie, who made his pulse race almost as fast as Meredith did when he kissed her.

He could still taste Meredith on his mouth. She didn't know much, but she made up for her lack of knowledge with enthusiasm and curiosity. He thought about carrying the lessons much farther, about baring her to the waist. His heart began to slam into his throat as he tried to imagine what she looked like under her blouse. He already knew that the skin

of her shoulder was warm and soft, like silk. He remembered
her husky moan when he'd kissed her there, the way her fingers had bitten into his back like little sharp pegs.

He'd been away from women for a long time, but he still
knew what to do with one, and his imagination was working overtime just now. Meredith had attracted him when she
was just his cook. Now that he knew about the intelligent,
capable woman underneath the flighty camouflage, he was
fascinated with her. She was everything a man could wish
for.

Not that she wanted him, oh, no. She'd made it plain. But
that teasing speech about marriage had unnerved him. His
freedom was like a religion. He didn't want to get married.
Of course he didn't!

But it was natural to think of Meredith with children. He
could picture her baking biscuits for him every morning and
holding a child in her arms at night while they watched
television. He could picture her playing catch with a little
boy out in back, or picking wildflowers with a little girl at
her skirts. She was kind and sweet. She'd make a wonderful
mother.

There was her job, of course. He knew something about
her profession, that it was supposed to be high pressure. She'd
be called upon to make life and death decisions, to comfort
the sick and grieving, to make herself involved in the daily
lives of her patients so that she should counsel them on how
to maintain good health. Besides all that, she had a college
degree.

Rey was college educated, too, with a degree in management and a minor in marketing. He was the mind behind the
business decisions, the coordinator of the labor pool, and the
director of marketing for the brothers' cattle cooperative. He
was good at what he did. He enjoyed conversations with

other educated people, and he'd convinced himself that Meredith wouldn't know Degas from Dali, Domingo from Dwight Yoakum, Hemingway from Dr. Seuss. Now he knew better, and his respect for her increased.

She'd saved Billy Joe's life at the gun club. He recalled that she must have known what to do for Leo as well, when she'd found him after he was mugged. Leo really did owe her his life. She was competent, confident, and she wasn't hard on the eyes, either. She had wonderful qualities.

But he didn't want to marry her. He wasn't sure about Leo. His eyes narrowed as he recalled the way Leo conspired with her. Leo had known all about her already. Obviously they'd been talking together since her arrival at the ranch, because Leo hadn't been a bit surprised when she rushed over to manage Billy Joe's heart attack.

Why hadn't he noticed that? Leo had called for Meredith when he was in the hospital. He was obviously fond of her. Maybe he was interested in her romantically, too. He'd been interested in Tess, before Cag had walked off with her, but Tess hadn't realized it. Or if she had, she'd ignored it. Leo wasn't hard on the eyes, either, and when it came to charm, he had his share and Rey's as well.

As he walked down to the barn to talk to one of his men, Rey had a terrible premonition that Leo had been serious when he joked about being willing to marry Meredith. Would she be desperate enough, lonely enough, frightened enough, to marry Leo and give up her job and living with her father? Her father had beaten her badly. She might be looking for a way out of the torment, and there was Leo, successful and handsome and charming, just ready to take her in and protect her.

Rey felt himself choke on dread. He couldn't imagine living in a house with Meredith if she was married to his brother. He'd rather throw himself headfirst into a cement mixer!

But, then, Leo had been teasing. Leo was always teasing. Rey forced himself to breathe normally and at least give the appearance of someone who was relaxed. Sure, it was just a joke. He didn't have to worry about the competition. There wasn't any. He pulled his hat lower over his eyes and walked on down the aisle to the man who was doctoring a heifer.

Several days later, Meredith received a huge bouquet of assorted roses from Billy Joe, now out of the hospital and back on the shooting range. She put them in water in the kitchen, along with the card, which the brothers blatantly read.

"He'd marry you," Rey drawled with pure acid in his tone as he dragged out a chair and sat down to lunch. "He's been widowed twenty years."

Meredith gave Leo a mischievous glance and fiddled with putting biscuits in a linen-lined basket. "He's not bad-looking for a man his age, and it wouldn't hurt him to have a nurse under his roof." She glanced at Rey's eloquent back. "But can he cook?"

Rey sipped coffee noisily.

"And does he slurp his coffee?" she added without missing a beat.

"That was done deliberately, to show you that I don't give a damn about manners!" Rey growled.

"All right, just don't expect me to take you to any nice restaurants while we're courting," she said easily, setting the basket of biscuits on the table.

"Lady, you aren't taking me as far as the mailbox," he said curtly.

He looked ferocious. That black temper was already kindling. Meredith studied his bent head curiously. You never knew about men. She'd seen some very mild-mannered ones come to the emergency room with wives who'd been beaten within an inch of their lives. It didn't hurt to see how far a man would go when he got mad. Especially after her experience with her father.

"You'll have to learn to scrape the mud off those enormous boots, too," she went on in a conversational tone. "And not slurp your soup. Your hair could use a good trim…"

"Damn it!"

He shot to his feet, eyes blazing in a rigid face, with a dusky flush creeping along his high cheekbones with all the warning color of a poisonous reptile.

Meredith stood her ground, watching him clench those big fists at his side.

"Rey," Leo cautioned abruptly, and started to get to his feet.

Meredith went right up to Rey, looking him in the eyes, quiet, still—waiting.

Rey was breathing through his nostrils. His jaw was clenched with fury. But intelligence won easily over bad temper. His chin raised slowly. "You're testing me," he said out of the blue. "You want to know if I'll hit you."

"It's something a woman needs to know about a man," she said very quietly. "And she needs to find it out where she can get help if she needs it." She didn't look at Leo, but Rey knew that was what she meant. She smiled gently. "No, you don't hit," she said in a soft, quizzical tone. "You do have a temper, but it's not a physical one."

He was still breathing through his nose. "If you were a man, it might be," he told her bluntly.

"But I'm not a man," she replied.

Her eyes were almost glowing with feeling. He got lost in those soft, warm, grey eyes. He hated the way he felt when he was near her. He'd been fighting it ever since he carried her up to her garage apartment after she'd fainted at the hospital. He liked the feel of her in his arms. He liked kissing her. He liked the way she picked at him and teased him. No woman had ever done that before. As his older brothers had been before they married, he was taciturn and uncommunicative most of the time. His very attitude put most women off.

It didn't put Meredith off. She wasn't afraid of his temper, either. She made him into a different person. It wasn't something he could easily explain. He felt comfortable with her, even while she was stirring him to passion. He could imagine just sitting in front of the television with her and holding hands, late at night.

The image intimidated him. He sat back down, ignoring Meredith, and started putting butter and strawberry preserves on four biscuits.

Leo gave him a measuring look. "Don't eat all the biscuits."

"I'm only getting my share. She," he jerked his thumb towards Meredith, "didn't make but eight this morning. That's one for her, four for me, and three for you."

"And why do you get four?" Leo asked belligerently.

"Because she proposed to me," he said with pure smug arrogance, and a look that made Leo's teeth snap together.

"I did not," Meredith said haughtily, sitting down across from him. "I said I was thinking of you as a marriage prospect, not that I actually wanted to go through with a ceremony." She cleared her throat. "I'll have to see how you work out."

Rey smiled faintly. "That sounds interesting."

He didn't necessarily mean what it sounded like he meant. She mustn't jump to any conclusions here. But her cheeks were getting very rosy.

He noticed that. It was a devilish game they were play-ing, and he could do it better. He stared pointedly at her soft mouth as he put a cube of fresh pear into his mouth, slowly and deliberately.

She felt very uncomfortable in odd places when he did that. She ate her beef and gravy and tried to ignore him.

"I like having fresh fruit," Rey said with a slow smile. He speared a grape with his fork and eased it slowly between his lips.

She moved restlessly in her chair. "It's healthy stuff."

"No wonder you were trying to get us to eat right," Leo said, trying to break the growing spell Rey was casting on her. "You teach nutrition, I suppose."

"In a way. I'm supposed to counsel patients on changing bad habits and making lifestyle changes when they're war-ranted," she explained. If only her hand didn't shake while she was holding the stupid fork. Rey saw it and knew why, and she hated that damned smug smile on his lean face!

He picked up a piece of perfectly cooked asparagus spear and slowly sucked it into his mouth, using his tongue mean-ingfully.

"I have to fix dessert," Meredith choked, jumping to her feet so quickly that she knocked her chair winding and had to right it.

"I saw that chair jump right out and trip you, Meredith," Rey commented dryly. "You ought to hit it with a stick."

"I ought to hit *you* with a stick instead!" she raged at him, flushed and flustered and out of patience.

"Me?" Both eyebrows arched. "What did I do?"

She pictured hitting him across the jaw with the biggest frying pan she had. It was very satisfying. Pity she couldn't do it for real.

She went to the cupboard and drew out the ingredients

for an instant reduced fat pudding. She had some low-fat whipped cream in the freezer that she could top it with. Meanwhile, Rey would finish his meal and stop using fruits and vegetables to torment her with. She could have kicked him.

Behind her, Rey was talking comfortably to Leo about some new equipment they were ordering, and about routine chores that had to be completed before Thanksgiving this month and the Christmas holidays next month. Most of the ranch hands would have Thanksgiving, the day after, and that weekend free. Next month, they'd have Christmas Eve and Christmas Day free, along with four days before or after, depending on the schedule. Some of the men had families in far-flung locations and they had to travel a distance for the holidays. The Harts made a practice of giving the men time off to go home during the holiday season by staggering work schedules, so that there was an adequate crew here to work when days off were assigned.

Then they moved on, naturally, to a discussion about Thanksgiving dinner.

"You're going to stay until after Thanksgiving, aren't you?" Rey asked Meredith.

She had her back to them. "Yes, I'd like to," she said, because she'd already been planning special menus and light, noncaloric desserts for it. "Unless you're planning to go away for it," she added quickly.

"The family has a Christmas party, when we all get together. We sort of save Thanksgiving for just us, so the others can have the day with their wives and kids," Leo told her. "It's been sort of hit and miss since Mrs. Lewis has been plagued with arthritis. As you know, we got her to come back to work just briefly, but her hands won't hold out to make bread and do any scrubbing with them, despite medicine. She has her children up from Corpus Christi for the holidays and cooks for them. We sort of got leftovers."

She grimaced. "Well, I'll make sure you have a big Thanksgiving dinner this year," she said gently. "With all the trimmings. Including biscuits," she added when they both looked her way.

She finished whipping the pudding, and put it in bowls in the refrigerator to chill before she sat back down. "That will make us a nice dessert tonight," she commented. "I don't suppose you want it any sooner?"

They shook their heads. "I've got a meeting with our marketing staff in half an hour," Rey said, checking his multifunction watch.

"And I've got to go over the new equipment list with our mechanic and see if we've got everything ready to order," Leo added.

"How about a nice Greek salad for supper?" Meredith asked. "I make it with Feta cheese and black olives and eggs. I bought the ingredients yesterday at the store. Except for the eggs, of course. I'll get those out of the henhouse."

"Sounds nice," Leo said with a grin.

"Watch where you put your hands," Rey murmured without looking right at her. "I haven't seen my pet snake in the barn lately."

She gave him a cold look. "If I see him, I'll get him on a stick and put him right back in the barn," she said with pure bravado.

Rey glanced at her with dancing dark eyes. "I'd pay real money to see you do that," he chided.

So would I, she thought, but she didn't say it. She just smiled smugly.

The brothers finished their last swallows of coffee and went out the door still talking business.

Later, Meredith went out to the henhouse to gather the eggs, with her straw basket on her arm. Rey had unnerved her with his comment about the damned snake. Now she was sure it was in there, waiting for a gullible victim to frighten.

She took a deep breath and walked carefully into the dim confines of the henhouse. She bit her lower lip and approached the nest slowly. She stopped dead. There was actually a snake in there. He was wrapped around the eggs. He was licking his snaky lips.

She shivered with fear, but she wasn't going to let the stupid thing make her a laughingstock twice.

She saw a long, thick stick on the straw-covered floor. She put her basket down, still watching the snake, and picked up the stick.

"It's okay, old fellow," she said to the snake. "It's okay. I'm just going to ease you out of the nest. Don't get mad, now. I won't hurt you. It's okay."

While she was talking, softly, she eased the stick under its coils and very carefully lifted it. It was very still, not moving its head except to hiss. So far, so good. She had it up on the stick. It was heavy.

As she pulled it out of the nest, she noticed that it was really quite long. It really didn't look much like that black and white one Rey had put in the barn. This one had a pretty brown pattern on its back and had a white underbelly. But, then, it wasn't striking at her or anything, so she wasn't worried.

She held it far out in front of her and stepped carefully out of the henhouse into the bright light. As she did, the snake hung from the stick, looking rather bored by the whole thing.

She carried it through the yard and out toward the barn. One of the men was standing by a truck, watching her progress. His jaw fell. She wondered what was wrong with him. Maybe he'd never seen a woman carry a snake around before.

"Nice day," she called to him.

He didn't answer. She shrugged and kept walking.

The barn was empty, except for the bales of hay that were stacked neatly on the bottom and the loft of the huge structure. Over against one wall there was a corn crib with stacks and stacks of dried corn, and a machine that shelled them.

"Here we go, old fellow," she told the snake. She eased him over the wooden box and slid him down into the piles of unshelled corn.

He drew back in a threatening pose and hissed at her again.

Odd, the shape of his head, she thought, frowning as she studied him. It looked like an arrowhead. That other snake's head had been rounded.

Well, it might be some other species of king snake, she supposed. Weren't there several?

She walked back out of the barn into the daylight, whistling softly to herself as she started back to the henhouse. She was so proud of herself. She'd gotten the snake on the stick all by herself, without screaming once, and she'd carried him all the way to the barn and put him in the corn crib. She wasn't afraid of the snake anymore. As Rey had said, they were beneficial. It wasn't right to kill something just because you were afraid of it, she told herself.

The man who'd been standing by the truck was nowhere in sight, but the truck was still running and the driver's door was standing wide-open. She wondered where the driver had gone. He must have been in a hurry for some reason.

Meredith went back to the henhouse, put the stick down, picked up her basket and went to gather eggs. There were no more snakes, but there were plenty of eggs. She could boil several to go in her nice Greek salad. The spinach she'd bought to make it with was crisp and cold and almost blemishless. The brothers would love a salad if it had enough eggs and cheese and dressing.

She got the last egg into the basket and walked back out again, pausing to reach down and pet one of the big red hens who came right up to her and cocked its head curiously toward her face.

"Aren't you a pretty girl?" she said, smiling. She liked the way the chicken felt. Its feathers were very smooth and silky, and the chicken made the sweetest little noises when she petted it. She'd never been around farm creatures. She found that she enjoyed the chickens and the cattle dogs and the endless cats that hung around outside begging for handouts.

Two other hens came up to her, curious about the tall creature in jeans and tank top. She petted them, too, laughing as they crowded close. But then one started to peck the eggs, and she stood up again.

She turned back toward the house, her mind on the snake and her bravery. She'd have to remember to tell Rey and Leo about it…

"Meredith!"

The loud, urgent deep voice sent her spinning around. Rey was running toward her, bare-headed, with the cowhand who'd been next to the running pickup truck at his heels.

"Hi, Rey," she said hesitantly. "What's wrong?"

He stopped just in front of her. He caught her a little roughly by the arms and took the basket away from her, setting it aside, while he looked at every inch of her bare arms and hands. He was breathing rapidly. He seemed unnaturally pale and tight-lipped.

"It didn't bite you?" he demanded.

"What?"

"The snake! It didn't bite you?" he snapped.

"No, of course not," she stammered. "I just got it on a stick, like you did, and put it in the corn crib."

"Get my Winchester," Rey told the other man in a harsh tone. "Load it and bring it back here. Hurry!"

"I don't understand," Meredith said with noticeable confusion. "What's wrong with you? Why do you need a gun?"

"Oh, baby," he whispered hoarsely. He pulled her against him and bent to kiss her in view of the whole outfit, his mouth hard and rough against hers. "Baby!"

She had no idea what was wrong, but she loved the faint tremor in his hard arms as they crushed her against his body. And she loved the way he was kissing her, as if he couldn't get enough of her mouth. He'd called her "baby…"

She held on and moaned under the crush of his lips.

He drew back. "I'm sorry. It was such a shock. I was scared out of my wits, I didn't even stop to grab my hat when Whit came into the office…!"

Her mouth was pleasantly swollen. She looked up at him dreamily and smiled.

"You don't have a clue, do you?" he asked huskily, searching her soft grey eyes.

"Mmm. About what?" she murmured, only half hearing him.

The other man came out with a rifle. He handed it to Rey. "Safety's on," the man advised.

"Thanks, Whit."

He moved back from Meredith. "I'll go kill it."

"Kill it?" Meredith exclaimed. "You can't! It will eat the rats, it's harmless…!"

"Sweetheart," he said very gently, "you were carrying a copperhead moccasin."

"Yes?" She stared at him blankly.

"It's one of the most poisonous snakes in Texas!"

She stood looking after him with her mouth open and her heartbeat choking her. She'd been carrying the damned thing on a stick, with it hissing at her. She felt the blood leave her head. Seconds later, she was lying on the hard ground. Fortunately she missed the basket of eggs on the way down.

Chapter Nine

"You're making a habit of this lately," Rey murmured as he carried Meredith up the stairs to the garage apartment. "I never figured you for a fainter, Meredith," he added dryly.

He was still bare-headed, but he wasn't grim now. He was smiling.

"Of course I fainted! I picked up a poisonous snake!" she gasped, still in shock.

"Well, you've got guts, woman, I'll give you that," he said with a slow smile, shifting her a little closer. "Picked up a poisonous snake with a stick and carried it all the way to the barn, and it didn't bite you. Now I've heard everything."

"It did hiss a little," she recalled, shivering.

"It had eaten three eggs," he murmured. "Probably it was too busy digesting to care where it went at the time. Lucky for you."

She laid her cheek against his broad, strong shoulder and held on tight. She had a sudden thought. "It didn't bite you?" she asked worriedly.

"It didn't get the chance. Didn't you hear the shot? I got it as it was crawling down from the corn bin onto the floor." He chuckled. "If I hadn't gotten it, though, Bandit would have. King snakes are natural enemies of any poisonous snake. They eat them. I hate to kill even a copperhead, but we can't have poisonous snakes around the livestock, or the men. Or, especially," he added with a warm glance at her, "in the henhouse. At the very least, a bite from one can put a man in the hospital."

She shivered, and her arms tightened around Rey's neck. "I was so proud of myself," she murmured. "I had no idea I was taking my life in my hands. It didn't look exactly like the other snake, but the patterns were sort of similar. I know about snake bites because I've helped treat them, but I don't know one snake from another unless I see pictures of them!" she added defensively.

"You'll learn." He kissed her forehead with breathless tenderness. "My brave girl," he whispered. "You'll never know how scared I was when Whit came running to tell me what you were doing."

It made soft little ripples of pleasure run through her body when he said that. He was being protective about her. She closed her eyes and drank in the warm nearness of him, the easy strength of his arms as he carried her. She felt safe as she'd never felt in her whole life. It was nice to lean on somebody strong, just for a little while.

He felt the vulnerability. He told himself that he wouldn't take advantage of it, but who was he kidding? She was soft and cuddly like this, and it was almost an involuntary action when his mouth slowly moved over hers as he reached her door.

The pressure was light, comforting. She sighed under the warmth and delight of it, and her lips parted, just the least little bit.

His whole body contracted with desire at that faint response. He looked down into her half-closed, misty eyes with growing hunger.

The look was as new as the tenderness. She couldn't tear her eyes away from that dark hunger in his. She forgot the snake, the scare, the people outside in the yard, everything. He bent back to her, and she met his mouth hungrily with her own, her arms clinging fiercely to his shoulders.

He groaned aloud. It was too soon, but he didn't care. He managed to open the door and close it behind them, making a beeline for the neatly made-up bed. He barely took time to put her down on the coverlet before his body slid against and over her own, his arms under her, taking his weight while his mouth made new, insistent demands on her innocence.

He lifted his head a torturous few seconds later, and his eyes blazed into her own. One lean hand slid deliberately under the hem of her tank top. At the same time, one long, powerful leg eased between both of hers and his hard mouth began to tease around the corners of hers.

"Danger will do it every time," he murmured deeply.

"Will...do what?" she asked, burning with new longings as his hand began to move up her rib cage toward the lacy little bra she was wearing under the top.

"This." His mouth opened on hers and became quickly insistent. While he kissed her, his fingers found the catch on her bra and flicked it open. She jumped when she felt his hand on flesh that had never known a man's touch before. He lifted his head and looked into her eyes. "I know. It's new territory," he said gently. His fingers stroked the delicate, warm flesh as lightly as a breeze. "Try to think of it as a rite of passage."

She felt strange new sensations. There was a tightening, a swelling, in her breasts as he touched them. She lifted involuntarily, and her eyes mirrored her surprise.

"Innocence is a rare, rare thing these days," he said at her lips. "I respect it. And you'd better thank your lucky stars that I do," he added as his mouth bit hungrily at hers. "Because with an experienced woman, I'd lock the door and I wouldn't hesitate a minute."

She felt the words like the caress of his hands on her body. She moaned huskily under the demanding crush of his mouth. She felt his tongue tracing her lips, teasing under them, darting and touching and withdrawing. She felt his teeth, too, in a sensual caress that only intensified the new sensations he was teaching her to feel.

She felt her back arch again as he traced around the curves of her breast without ever touching the hard, taut nipple. She wanted him to touch it. Her body ached to have him touch it. She didn't understand why it should be such a violent, aching need…!

He laughed in a soft, sexy way against her lips. "Is this what you want?"

He caught the nipple between his thumb and forefinger and she lifted off the bed with a sharp cry. Heat spread over her, through her. Her short nails dug into his back fiercely and she gasped with pleasure.

"Baby," he groaned roughly, aroused by her unexpectedly ardent response. "Baby, you turn me on so hard…!"

The top was suddenly around her collarbone and his mouth—his mouth!—was right on her nipple, suckling her while his tongue tasted the hardness with a subtle caress that made her shiver. Her hands caught in the thick strands of his dark hair and held him to her body while he explored it with his mouth. She'd never imagined that she was capable of so much passion, and so unexpectedly swift. He could do anything to her, and she didn't have the willpower to stop him. Even a simple "no" was beyond her now. She wanted more. She wanted his eyes on her, his hands on her. She wanted his body closer.

As if he knew that, both lean hands smoothed up from

her waist and onto her soft breasts. His fingers were rough from hard work, but their touch was pure heaven. She caressed his nape, moving rhythmically with each slow brush of his fingers, lost in pleasure.

He lifted his head to look at what he'd uncovered. She was beautiful, not too big or too small. She was just right. He loved the way her body moved when he touched it. He loved knowing how innocent she was. He'd never been with an innocent. Making love to one was a whole new experience, with levels of pleasure he'd never tasted. Her soft little moans excited him as much as those enthusiastic fingers caressing his back.

She felt his eyes and she opened hers, looking up at him. "Am I doing it right?" she whispered breathlessly.

His body tautened even more. "Yes," he whispered. "Just right."

He bent and drew his mouth gently over hers with a soft, cherishing pressure. He felt it open under his, felt her arms pulling at him. It wasn't a good idea to let this go any farther than it already had. While he was thinking it, he was moving slowly between her long legs until his body rested in the fork of hers. He eased down against her, letting her feel the slow burgeoning of his body against her belly.

She caught her breath.

He heard it, and lifted his head. His eyes were smoldering with desire, his body was rigid with it. He was getting little surges of insistent pleasure that ran the length of his spine. Her hips moved as if they were responding helplessly to the touch of him. She was making him ache like hell.

His hand moved to her hip and bit into the soft flesh, stilling the faint motion of her hips instantly while he rested on the elbow of his other arm. "Meredith," he said softly. "That will get you seduced. Right now."

She felt hot all over. Her mind seemed barely under her control. She searched his dark eyes with wonder. Her hands were against his shirt, right on the buttons. She felt him against the lower part of her body, and it felt right. It felt wonderful. She wanted to writhe under him and tempt him into intimacy.

His hand contracted and he gave her a wise, challenging stare as he read the look on her face. "Don't do it," he said huskily. "I'm years ahead of you in experience, but I can still lose my head. You don't want me to do that. Not really."

She pulled at a stabilizing breath. Her heart was still whacking around at the walls of her chest, as if she'd been running a race. "Are you sure I don't want you to do that? I mean, if you get pregnant, I'll marry you," she said breathlessly, and with deathbed humor. "Honest!"

He looked at her as if he couldn't believe his ears. The passion drained out of him, replaced by howling amusement. He started laughing. "Damn you, that wasn't fair!" he accused.

"Well, I like that! You're laughing, and here I've made you a solemn promise," she persisted, eyes twinkling.

"Hell!" He rolled away from her and sat up on the edge of the bed to run a lean hand through his disheveled hair. He glared down at her. "Now you've got fingerprints and lipstick and perfume all over me. The men will laugh themselves sick if I go to work smelling like a flower garden."

She tugged down her top and gave him an impish grin. "We could rush into my bathroom and shower it off, together," she offered wickedly.

He laughed again. He'd never laughed as much in his life as he did with her. Was this the way she'd been, before the tragedies of the past year that had marred her life? She'd said she didn't date much, but how in the world could men ignore a sweet, pretty little woman like that?

"I can't believe you spend your weekends watching television with your father," he murmured.

"I don't. I work."

He frowned. "On the weekends?"

She sat up, reaching under her blouse to refasten the bra he'd unsnapped. She wondered why she didn't feel embarrassed. "Seven days a week, for the past six months," she said honestly. "Before that, six days a week, and I had to rest on Sunday. I usually work ten-hour days, sometimes longer if we have an emergency."

He didn't like that. "You don't have any free time, do you?"

She shook her head. "I've been dedicated to the job since I got out of college."

"And no men," he murmured with a speculative glance.

She grimaced. "Well, there was one I liked very much. We went out together for four months, and I was very nearly in love with him. But he never touched me. I thought he was building up to it, or something." She sighed. "Then I saw him, with another man." She shrugged. "He thought of me as a friend. I thought of him as a boyfriend. I sort of lost confidence in myself after that."

"It happens, in the modern world," he replied quietly.

"Before that, I had crushes on boys who never noticed me, except to ask me to help them with math or chemistry." She searched his eyes. "Of course, I didn't exactly look like this until last year."

"How did you look?" he asked curiously.

She got off the bed, went to get her purse, and took out a plastic insert. She pulled a photo from behind a credit card and handed it to him.

His eyes widened. "Good heavens!"

She winced. "I was sixty pounds overweight, and I

couldn't lose it at all. I guess I tried every diet known to man. Then I took nutrition classes and learned how to get it off the sensible way. That's why I know so much about low-fat cooking."

He looked from the photo to her face and smiled. "You were pretty before, too," he said slowly. "You know, Meredith, it's not the outside that attracts people. It's what you are, how you treat other people, that makes friends of them. You risked your life to save my brother, then you stayed with him until his family came. I wasn't very flattering to you when we first met, but I've had a lot of time to think about what you did. You're good people. Really good people."

She flushed and cleared her throat. "Thanks." She gave him a mischievous look. "So, would you like to get married Friday, or is Monday better for you?" she added with a grin.

He chuckled. "Sorry, I have to wash my dogs."

She sighed. "Rejected again."

He pursed his lips and let his eyes run over her slowly. "You could lie back down and we could discuss it again."

"Absolutely not. I only have so much willpower. You shouldn't throw yourself at women that way unless you're asking to be seduced. It's unfair."

"You're not bad yourself, kid," he murmured with a warm smile. He got up. "I've got to go back to work. Come here."

She went to him. "Changed your mind?" she asked. "I can get a ring today…"

He put a finger over her mouth. "How do I smell?"

"Is that all you want?!" she exclaimed. "Good Lord, you got me all the way over here to *smell* you?"

He bent and kissed her hungrily, pulling her so close that she could feel him against every cell of her body. But before she could cling, he put her away. "How do I smell?" he persisted.

She sniffed him. "You smell like aftershave."

He bent and sniffed her, and frowned. "You're not wearing perfume, are you?"

She shook her head. "I'm allergic to most strong fragrances."

"You smell like flowers."

She smiled. "Herbal shampoo. Flowers don't bother me. Well, real ones do sometimes, but not flowery scent. I can use scented shampoos and wear one or two colognes, but no perfumes. They're too strong."

"At least I don't smell womanly," he said with mocking relief. "I'd never live that down."

She cocked her head and stared up at him. "There goes the shower," she sighed.

He tapped her nose. "Now, cut that out." His fingers traced the fading bruises on her cheek and jaw and his eyes narrowed. "He'll never touch you again, I swear he won't," he said in a low, dangerous tone.

Her heart lifted at the look on his face. "Oh, my, aren't we getting possessive?" she teased.

He didn't smile. "Careful," he told her quietly. "I'm not teasing."

Her eyes widened with something like wonder.

"Hasn't anyone ever stood up for you?" he asked curiously.

"Just my brother. But he never had to protect me from Daddy. I know it looks really bad, but my father was the most gentle man on earth until we lost Mama and Mike. He goes crazy when he drinks, and he never remembers what he did." Her eyes fell to his chest. She toyed with his shirt buttons, wondering absently how it would feel to smooth her fingers over his bare chest. "I miss my brother terribly," she added simply.

"I'm sure you do. And your mother."

She grimaced. "She and I weren't really very close," she confessed. She searched his eyes. "You see, what Daddy yelled about her that night you were at the house was pretty much true. She was a very attractive woman, and she had lovers." She winced. "I hated knowing that. You can't imagine what it did to Daddy. She even bragged about them."

"She doesn't sound like much of a wife," he murmured.

"She didn't act like one, either. She did love to spend money, though. That's why she picked rich lovers." Her face clouded. "I was so ashamed of her. I guess she saw herself as a modern woman. I'm not. There's a big difference between sleeping with someone you truly love, and jumping into bed with anyone who has some money."

He nodded and touched her soft, swollen mouth. "She's soured you on men, hasn't she?"

"Sort of. Until you came along, at least," she admitted, without looking at him. She stared at his shirt button. "Bad temper and all, you've got some wonderful qualities."

He gave her a wry look. "I'll have to tell my brothers. They didn't know."

She chuckled. "Thanks for letting me come here to heal, anyway."

He felt uneasy. "That sounds like goodbye, Meredith."

She sighed. Her fingers stilled on his buttons. "I can't stay much longer," she said sadly. "Even though I'd like to. My boss is shorthanded as it is, and the woman filling in for me doesn't like leaving her kids in day care. She retired when she had the second one."

"Retired?"

"Yes. She said keeping two kids in day care ate up her whole paycheck." She lifted her eyes to his. "Since her husband got a raise, it was actually cheaper for her to stay home with the kids than it was to work. She loves it."

There was a strange look on his face. He rubbed his fingertips over her short fingernails absently. "Would you want to stay home with your kids?"

She stared up at him, transfixed. "Yes, I would. Those first few years are so important. If I could find any way to do it, I would, even if I had to sacrifice some little luxuries."

"That would be tricky. You're a highly trained professional."

"One of my friends was a highly trained doctor," she replied. "She gave up her job and stayed home with her little boy until he was in kindergarten. Even then, she arranged her schedule so that she'd be there when he got home in the afternoons."

He was frowning, and his fingers were still smoothing over hers. He wanted to ask if she thought she could get used to ranch life and snakes. He was afraid to say it. The act of commitment was still very new to him. He couldn't rush her.

He sighed, troubled. "What does your father do, by the way?" he asked suddenly.

"Oh, he teaches in the veterinary department of his college in Houston."

His hand stilled on hers. "He's a veterinarian?"

"He has a doctorate in veterinary medicine, yes. Why?"

Wheels were turning in his head. He stared at her thoughtfully. "Will he have a job to go back to, after all the trouble he's had with the law?"

"You're very perceptive," she said after a minute. "Actually, no, he won't. The college phoned before his last bender and told him not to come back. You can't blame them, either," she added sadly. "What would it do to the college's image, to have an alcoholic on staff with a dangerous temper?"

"Not much," he had to admit. "Did he drink before the shooting?"

"Never. Not even a beer," she replied. "But he's set records in the past six months. I couldn't get him near a treatment center. At least he's in one, now."

"Not only in it, but improving by the day," Rey said unexpectedly. "He'd like you to come see him. I can run you up there Sunday, if you'd like to go."

That was surprising. "You've spoken to him?" she asked.

He nodded. "I had Leo phone Colter. He has contacts who helped arrange it." He drew in a deep breath. "Your father seems pretty rational right now. Of course, he isn't drinking, either." His eyes darkened. "I meant exactly what I said. He'll never touch you again in anger."

"When he's sober, he never would. I can't believe…he really wants to see me?" she asked haltingly.

He brushed his hand against her cheek. "He loves you. I'm sure you love him, too. You don't throw people away because they make a mistake—even a bad one. You get help for them."

"I tried."

"Sure you did. But it's better this way. When he comes home, we'll decide where to go from there. For now, I'll drive you to Houston on Sunday to see him. Want to go?"

"Oh, yes," she said. Her expression was soft, wondering. "You'd do that, for me?"

He smiled. "Anything you want, kiddo," he murmured. "It's the least I can do for the only woman who's ever proposed to me."

She pursed her lips and gave him an impish look. "We could lie down and talk about it."

"No, we couldn't," he told her firmly, and chuckled as he removed her hands from his shirt. "I have to get back to work.

I was in the middle of a meeting when you did your snake charmer routine. I left twelve employees sitting in the board-room with glasses of water and no ashtrays. At least six of them smoke, despite all the regulations. I expect they've at-tacked the other six with chairs by now, or vice versa. I've got to get back. Quick."

"I'd love to go Sunday," she said.

"Fine. I'll run you up there Sunday afternoon. We can go to church first."

Her eyebrows lifted. "I'm Methodist."

He grinned. "So are we. It's a date." He opened the door. Before he went out it, he glanced back over his shoulder. "And stay out of the henhouse for the rest of the day, will you?"

"Anything for my prospective fiancé," she said with a theatrical gesture of her arm.

He shook his head and walked out, still chuckling.

Later, she wondered what he'd meant, about making de-cisions when her father got out of rehab. She didn't dare think too hard about it. But it sounded very much as if he wanted to go on looking out for her.

She was a modern woman. She could look out for herself. But it was kind of nice to have a man act protective and pos-sessive, especially one like Rey, who didn't seem the sort to do it habitually. She remembered the hunger in his lean body when he held her, when he kissed her. She remembered the strange tenderness he reserved for her. It was an adven-ture, just being around him. They'd known each other such a short time, really, but she felt as if she'd known him all her life. The thought of going back to Houston without him was suddenly frightening.

She did the routine things until Sunday, except that when

she gathered eggs, she was overly cautious about going into the henhouse. She'd learned from Rey that snakes often traveled in pairs, so she was careful to look before she stepped anywhere that the ground was covered.

She'd become something of a legend among the Hart ranch hands already. They removed their hats when she walked by, and they spoke to her in respectful tones.

"It's really strange," she remarked at the dinner table on Saturday evening, glancing from Leo to Rey. "The men seem sort of in awe of me."

Rey chuckled and exchanged an amused look with his brother. "They are. None of them has ever picked up a copperhead on a stick."

"It let me," she reminded him.

"That's the awesome thing," Leo remarked. "You see, Meredith, copperheads have a nasty reputation for attacking without provocation. It's kind of mystic, what you did." He pursed his lips and gave her a teasing glance over his buttered biscuit. "Any snake charmers in your family?"

"No, but Mike had a pet boa for a while, until it ate one of the neighbor's rabbits," she sighed.

"*Yuccch!*" Rey said, and shivered.

"It was an accident," Meredith insisted. "It escaped out the window and was gone for three weeks. We figured it was starving, because it hadn't been fed in so long. Besides that," she added, "the rabbit was vicious. It attacked everybody who opened the cage."

"Why did the neighbor keep rabbits?"

"He sold them for meat to a specialty grocery store."

Rey chuckled. "Maybe the boa was a reincarnated tastetester," he mused.

Leo made a face. "I wouldn't eat a rabbit if I was starving. On the other hand, snake's not so bad. Remember when we were in Arizona on that hunting trip, camping out, and our guide caught that big, juicy rattler?"

"Sure do," Rey agreed, nodding. "Tasted just like chicken!"

Obviously that was a private joke, because the brothers looked at each other and burst out laughing.

"What became of the boa?" Leo asked, interested.

"Mike had just sold it to a breeder," she recalled sadly. "He was engaged to the sweetest, kindest girl I ever knew. It devastated her when he was killed. They had to sedate her for two days, and she couldn't even go to the funeral." She shook her head. "I felt as sorry for her as I did for Dad and me."

"What happened to her?" Leo asked.

She finished her coffee. "She became a missionary and went to South America with a group of them." She winced. "She had the worst luck…it was that plane that was mistaken for drug smugglers and shot down. I think she was one of the survivors, but she didn't come back to America with the others."

"Poor kid," Rey said.

"Colter was upset over the shooting for a long time, too," Leo recalled. "Just between you and me, he was sweet on Mike's girl, but too much a gentleman to do anything about it. He thought the sun rose and set on Mike."

"I never knew," Meredith said softly.

"Neither did Mike. Or the girl," Leo added with a smile. "Colter's a clam. He never talks."

"Is he still with the Texas Rangers?" Meredith asked.

Leo nodded. "Got promoted to lieutenant just recently. He's good at his job."

She pushed back from the table. "If you two are through, I'll just wash up. Rey's going to drive me up to see my dad tomorrow."

"What a sweet guy!" Leo exclaimed with a wide-eyed look at his brother.

"He's being nice to me, because I'm the only woman who ever proposed to him," Meredith volunteered with a wicked grin. "He feels guilty because he turned me down."

"Good. I'll marry you, Meredith," Leo volunteered at once. "You just name the time and place, and I'll buy a new suit…!"

"Shut the hell up!" Rey said curtly, and hit his brother with his Stetson.

Leo protected his shoulder. "Meredith, he's picking on me!" he wailed.

"Do you want biscuits for breakfast?" she asked Rey.

He stopped flogging his brother. "All right. But only for biscuits," Rey said. He got up and deliberately bent and kissed Meredith, right in front of Leo. "Don't stay up too late. Leo and I have to check the livestock in the barn."

"Okay. Wear a jacket," she said, smiling up at him.

He bent and brushed his mouth against hers one more time. "It's not cold."

"It is. Wear a jacket," she insisted.

He sighed and made a face, but he picked up his light-weight denim jacket from the hat stand by the back door as he went out.

Leo followed him, but with a new expression on his face. He'd seen something he hadn't expected during that teasing exchange. He wondered if Rey realized that he was in love with that sweet little biscuit-making woman. And unless he missed his guess, it was mutual.

Chapter Ten

The next morning, Meredith sat next to Rey in church and felt his hand holding hers almost all the way through the service. She felt different with him than she'd ever felt with anyone else. Rey made her feel as if she could do anything. He made her feel strong and confident and safe.

She glanced up at him while they shared a hymnal and he forgot what he was singing. They searched each other's eyes slowly, until they realized that everybody else had stopped singing and were sitting down. Smiling sheepishly, Rey sat down and tugged her down beside him.

After the service, they got amused, affectionate looks from bystanders who knew Rey and had heard about his new cook.

But he didn't seem to be the least bit embarrassed by the attention. In fact, he made a point of introducing Meredith to several people, adding the little known information that she was a licensed nurse practitioner as well as a great biscuit chef.

Meredith flushed, because it sounded as if he were very proud of her, especially when he related how her quick thinking had probably saved Billy Joe's life at the target range. Billy Joe was well-known and liked locally, so that brought even more smiles. She clung to his hand with unashamed delight when they left.

"See, you're already a local celebrity," he teased. "And I didn't even get around to mentioning the snake."

"We should forget the snake," she said quickly.

He chuckled. "No, we shouldn't. It wins me points if I have a...cook who isn't even afraid of poisonous snakes."

She heard that hesitation before "cook," as if he wanted to say something else instead. It made her tingle all over. She couldn't stop smiling, all the way to the Jaguar convertible he drove when he wasn't working.

"This is a very flashy car," she commented as he put her in on the passenger side.

"I like sports cars," he said with a grin.

"So do I," she confessed. She didn't even put on a scarf. In fact, she pulled the pins out of her hair and let it fall around her shoulders.

"Won't it tangle in the wind?" he asked when they were seat-belted in place.

"I don't care." She looked at him and smiled warmly. "I like to feel the wind."

"Me, too."

He started the car, put it in gear, and pulled out onto the highway. When they were on the interstate, heading toward Houston, he let the powerful car do its best.

"Now this is a HORSE!" he called over the roar of the wind.

She laughed with pure delight. It was the most wonderful day of her life. She even forgot where they were going in the excitement of being with him in the elegant vehicle.

But all too soon, they were pulling up at an impressive brick building with its function discreetly labeled on a metal plate near the door. It was a substance abuse rehabilitation center, three stories tall, and staffed impressively with psychologists, psychiatrists, and health professionals, including physicians.

Rey held her hand to the information desk and then up to the second floor waiting room, where her father would be brought to visit with them.

"They don't like visitors the first week," Rey explained to her. "You probably knew that," he added, remembering her profession.

"I've never had anybody in here," she said quietly. She was nervous and she looked it.

He caught her fingers in his again and held them tight. "It's going to be all right," he said firmly.

She met his eyes and took a deep breath. "Okay," she said after a minute, and her body lost some of its rigidity.

There were footsteps and muffled voices. A minute later, her father came in the door, wearing slacks and a knit shirt, and behind him was a uniformed woman with a clipboard.

"Miss Johns? I'm Gladys Bartlett," the woman introduced herself with a firm handshake. "I'm the staff psychologist on your father's case."

"Hello, Merry," her father said hesitantly. He winced when he noticed the faded bruises on her face. "I'm sorry, my dear," he choked.

Meredith let go of Rey's hand and went forward to hug her father warmly. Mr. Johns closed his eyes and hugged her back, hard. His lips trembled as he forced them together, but tears ran down his lean, pale cheeks. "I'm so sorry," he sobbed.

She patted him on the back and tears fell hotly from her own eyes. "It's okay, Daddy," she whispered brokenly, comforting him the way he'd once comforted her and Mike when they were little, and something had hurt them. He'd been a wonderful father. "It's okay," she said again. "You're going to be fine. We both are."

"My son. My boy!" He shook all over. "I said I was too busy to take her to the bank. I asked him…I *asked* Mike…to go instead. He'd be alive, but for me!"

"Now, Mr. Johns," the counselor said gently, "we've been over this several times already. You can't assume blame for the lawless acts of other people. Ninety-nine times out of a hundred, nothing would have happened if you'd asked your son to go to the bank on your behalf."

"But this was the one out of a hundred," he husked. "And I can't live with the guilt!"

"I've had my own problems with it," Meredith confessed. "I could have refused to go in to work that day and taken her instead."

"And you'd be lying dead instead of Mike," her father replied curtly. "And I'd be just as eaten up with guilt!"

"You're both missing the point," Rey said, standing up. "You can't control life. Nobody can."

They all looked at him. He stood quietly, his hands deep in his slacks pockets, and stared back. "Einstein said that God didn't play dice with the universe, and he was right. Even in seeming chaos, there's an order to things, a chain of events that leads inevitably to conclusions. People are links in the chain, but people don't control the events. Life has a pattern, even if we don't see it."

"You've studied philosophy," Mr. Johns said quietly.

Rey nodded. "Yes, I have."

The older man, with thinning hair and glasses and a faintly stooped posture, moved away from Meredith and smiled. "I took several courses in it, myself. You have a degree, haven't you?"

"I do, in business. A master's, from Harvard," Rey volunteered, something that Meredith hadn't even known.

"Mine is in medicine. Veterinary medicine. I'm…"

"I know. You're Dr. Alan Johns," Rey said, shaking hands. "Your daughter is staying with us on the ranch in Jacobsville, baking biscuits, while she recovers."

Dr. Johns winced and flushed. "They told me what I did to you," he said, glancing shamefaced at his daughter. "I swear before God, I'll never take another drink as long as I live!"

"You won't get the chance," Rey said. "I intend to watch you like a red-tailed hawk."

"Excuse me?" Dr. Johns stammered.

Rey studied his boots. "We don't have a vet on staff. We have to call one down from Victoria, because our vets are overworked to death. It would be nice to have our own vet. We pay competitive salaries and you'd have your own house."

Dr. Johns sat down quickly. "Young man, I...!"

Rey lifted his head and stared him in the eyes. "You made a mistake. People do. That's why they put erasers on pencils. You can work for us. We'll keep you straight, and you won't have to take some sort of menial job in Houston just to make ends meet. You'll like the ranch," he added. "We have a good crew."

"Someone might know what I did," Dr. Johns stammered.

"Everybody knows already," Rey said, and shrugged. "It's no big deal to us. We've got one man who came back from cocaine addiction—let me tell you, that was a story and a half—and another one who was a habitual DWI for six years until we hired him and helped him get straight." He smiled. "We don't hold a man's past against him, as long as he's willing to stay straight and work hard."

Dr. Johns was having a hard time keeping control of himself, and it was obvious. "Young man, I'll work without a salary, if that's what it takes. And I promise, you'll never have cause to regret giving me a job."

"Not unless you keep calling me 'young man,'" Rey said with a grin. "I'm Reynard Hart, but everybody calls me Rey."

"Glad to meet you," the older man said. "Rey."

Rey nodded. "How much longer will they keep you?" he asked, and glanced at the woman with the clipboard.

"Another week should do it," she said with a big smile. "And how nice, to see him with a settled environment to look forward to the day he leaves! I believe in minor miracles, but I don't see many. This is certainly one."

Rey gave her a complacent smile. "Miracles only happen for people who believe in them," he said, chuckling.

"Thanks, Rey," Meredith said huskily.

He only shrugged. "How could I ignore the father of the only woman who ever proposed to me?" he said, matter-of-factly, and with a smile that made her blush.

"You proposed to him?" her father asked with raised eyebrows.

"Several times," she said with mock disgust. "But he has to wash his dogs, so he can't marry me."

Dr. Johns laughed heartily.

The counselor relaxed. This was going to work out. Dr. Johns was never going to end up in rehab again, she was certain of it. She only wished she could say the same for more of her poor patients.

On the drive back to Jacobsville, Meredith was on top of the world. "Not only does he get a new job, but one doing what he always loved best, working around large animals."

"He likes cattle, does he?" Rey asked absently, enjoying Meredith's animated company.

"He grew up on a cattle ranch in Montana," she explained. "He was even in rodeo for six or seven years before he went to college."

Rey expelled a breath. This was going to work out even better than he'd dreamed. Amazing, he thought, how a single act of kindness could expand like ripples around a rock dropped into a pond.

"He's not much good on a horse anymore," she continued chattily, "but he really knows veterinary medicine."

"He might go back to teaching one day. Not in Houston," he added gently. "But Texas is a big state, and when he's been away from alcohol a couple of years, who knows?"

"The ranch will be good for him. You did mean it, didn't you?" she added quickly. "It wasn't something you said to help him want to get better?"

"I very rarely say things I don't mean, Meredith," he replied. "Well," he added with a frown, "I wasn't exactly telling the truth about washing the dogs."

"Excuses, excuses." She toyed with her purse. "Rey, thank you for giving him a second chance."

He laughed gently. "I've got an ulterior motive," he murmured dryly. "When you come to the ranch to visit him, you can make me a pan of biscuits."

"Just you? Not one to share with Leo?"

He shifted behind the wheel. "He can go find someone to make him biscuits," he said. "Surely, somewhere in Texas, there's a woman who'd do it just for him."

"Your other brothers, do their wives bake?"

"Dorie and Tess do," he said. "But Tira hasn't got a clue how to," he added on a sigh. "Simon doesn't mind. They have a cook who can. Although he's really not much on biscuits, so it doesn't matter." He grinned. "You should see him with his sons. Two of them now. They're still toddlers, and he's a whiz at fatherhood. Dorie and Corrigan have a boy and a girl and Cag and Tess have a son. That makes me an uncle five times over! Christmas is going to be a real treat this year."

She thought about Christmas. It was going to be a lonely one for her, with her father down here on the ranch.

He saw the look on her face and reached out to catch her hand in his. "Hey," he said softly, "you're invited for Christmas, you know. We'll pack up the kids and go over to the annual Christmas party at the Doctors Coltrain. They have huge layouts of Lionel trains that they run every year, especially with a little boy of their own who'll be big enough to play with them in a couple of years. Draws a big crowd. Do you like train sets?"

She smiled. "I do." It lifted her heart to know that she was going to be included in the family get-together. She loved children. It would make the season less traumatic for her and her father, because they were missing two members of their immediate family.

"We'll make it a happy Christmas," he said softly.

She tangled her fingers into his. "I'll have that to look forward to, when I go back."

"It's premature right now, but if you decide to move down here, too, I'd bet good money that Micah Steele would offer you work."

She looked at his big, warm hand holding hers. "I like Jacobsville."

His fingers grew possessive. "I like you."

"Thanks. I like you, too, and if you'll loan me your cell phone, I'll call the minister right now and we can set a date," she added with wicked haste.

He chuckled. "Hold on, tiger, I may have been lying about washing the dogs, but marriage is a big step. You have to look out for me. I know you can tame snakes and handle heart attacks, and you bake good biscuits. But how do you look in a suit, and can you dance?"

"I look great in a suit," she said firmly, "and I can do Latin dances."

He grimaced. "I can't. How about a nice, slow two-step?"

"I can do that, too!"

He glanced at her. "What do you like to read?" he asked. The next few minutes were spent in gleeful harmony, going over things they had in common. They liked the same basic forms of relaxation, and they even thought alike on politics and child-raising. It was a very good start. Meredith had seen far too many relationships start out with nothing more than sex for a foundation, and they didn't last. It took common interests, common beliefs, friendship, to make a lasting marriage.

Marriage. That word, once so warily approached, now seemed as natural as letting Rey hold her hand all the way back to Jacobsville. She wondered where they were going together in the future, and hoped it was someplace nice.

She had to go back to work the following week. Friday morning she had her suitcase packed. She was wearing her tailored beige suit with her blond hair in a neat ponytail when she followed Rey out the front door. He carried her suitcase to his car and put it in the trunk.

"I'll be back late this afternoon," he told Leo. "If you need me, I'll be on my cell phone." He patted the cell phone carrier on his belt.

"Oh, I think I can cope," Leo drawled with a wink at Meredith. "Don't be a stranger, Meredith," he added. "We'll miss you. But thanks for making us all those pans of frozen biscuits!"

"It's a good thing you have a walk-in freezer, is all I can say," she mused, chuckling. "But don't forget the directions on how to cook them," she added. "They're only dough until then."

"I'll have it all down pat in no time," Leo promised.

"Meanwhile," he added, rubbing his big hands together with visible delight, "there are still six biscuits left over from breakfast!"

"No use asking you to save me a couple, is there?" Rey asked on a sigh.

"Blood is thicker than water, except where biscuits are involved," Leo shot back. "Sorry."

Rey got in the car and started the engine without another word.

Meredith was quiet most of the way to Houston. She was oddly reluctant to go back to work, although she loved her job. She was going to miss Rey and Leo and Mrs. Lewis. She was even going to miss the chickens.

"You can come down anytime you want to," Rey reminded her, when he noticed that she was brooding. It had been hard, but he'd kept his hands to himself for the duration of her stay at the ranch. He was planning a frontal assault in the near future. This wasn't the time, though.

"I know." She stared out the window at the bare trees and chilly flat landscape. "Thanksgiving comes along pretty soon."

"Your father will be working for us by then. You can come and spend a few days while you're off."

"I might still be on call," she worried.

He was grim and silent himself, after she said that. The rest of the way to Houston, he had the radio on, letting it fill the cool silence.

He dropped her off at her father's house. It looked cold and unwelcoming as she unlocked the front door so that he could sit her suitcase inside.

She turned back to him, her grey eyes wide and sad as they met his dark ones. He hadn't removed his hat, and it was hard to see his face in the shadow of it.

"Well, thanks for everything," she began.

He stared down at her with a sense of loss. After their ride up to Houston to visit her father, there seemed to be a curtain between them. They'd been very close that Sunday. But he'd gotten cold feet, he admitted to himself, and he'd drawn back. He felt the threat of her in his heart and he was trying to run from it. Suddenly it was like trying to run from himself.

"You'll be here alone," he said quietly. "Make sure you keep your door locked. We haven't had any reports that they caught the guys who rolled Leo. Just in case, don't let your guard down."

"I'll be fine," she promised him.

She looked so small and vulnerable standing there. He hated leaving her.

"You wear your jacket when it's cold like this," she told him firmly, noticing that he was standing in the cold wind in just the shirtsleeves of his chambray shirt.

"And my raincoat when it's raining," he said with a mocking smile. "You wear yours, too."

She hesitated. "Well, goodbye," she said after a minute.

"You and I won't ever say goodbye, Meredith," he replied. "It's 'so long.'"

She forced a smile to her lips. "So long, then."

He was still hesitating. His face was absolutely grim.

"I know where a jeweler's is open this early," she said suddenly, with mischievous enthusiasm.

It warmed him to hear her tease, to see that wonderful smile. "Do you, really?"

She nodded. "You can even have a diamond. But it would have to be a small one."

His dark eyes twinkled. "You just hold that thought," he said gently. "One of these days we might talk about this marriage hang-up of yours. Meanwhile, I've got to…"

"If you say 'wash the dogs,'" she interrupted, "I'll slug you!"

He chuckled. "I wasn't going to say that. I've got to get back and finish my marketing strategy for the next year before we have our year-end board meeting."

"I guess that's pretty complicated."

"No more than treating diseases and plotting nutrition," he replied. He studied her quietly. "I'll miss you. Don't stay away too long."

"Why?" she prodded.

"You have to save me from attacks on my virtue from hordes of amorous, sex-crazed women," he said without cracking a smile. "Who knows when I might weaken and give in to one of them, and then where would we be?"

"I've got my heart set on a virgin," she informed him.

He laughed helplessly. "Sorry, honey, you missed the boat by a decade or so."

She snapped her fingers. "Damn!"

"On the other hand, I didn't," he said in a deep, soft voice, and moved closer. He framed her face in his lean hands and studied it hungrily for several seconds. "You make me ache every time I touch you," he whispered, bending. "I'll starve to death before you get back."

"Starve...?" She wasn't thinking. She was watching his long, hard mouth come closer. She held her breath until it settled, ever so softly, on her parted lips. And then she didn't think at all for several long, tempestuous seconds.

Too soon, he caught her by the arms and pushed her away. "You stop that," he muttered breathlessly. "I refuse to be seduced on the front lawn."

She was trying to catch her own breath. "No problem. There's a nice soft carpet just five steps this way," she indicated the hall.

"I'm not that kind of man," he said haughtily.

She made a face at him.

He chuckled and kissed her one last time, teasingly, before he pulled back and started toward his car. "I'll call you."

"That's what they all say!" she cried after him.

"Then you call me, honey," he said in that deep, sexy voice that made her melt. "You've got my number, even if you don't know it yet." He winked and went on to the car. He didn't look back, even as he drove away. Meredith's eyes followed the car until it was out of sight. She didn't cry until she was inside, behind the closed door.

She was back at work and going crazy in no time, overrun by people with everything from stomach viruses to the flu. She had a good immune system, and she didn't catch any of the ailments, but she missed Rey terribly.

Three days before Thanksgiving, her father telephoned her from the ranch, full of excitement about his new job. He seemed like a different person. He told her he was still going to therapy sessions, but in Jacobsville with a psychologist. He was doing much better, and he was going to make everything up to his daughter, he swore it. And wasn't she coming for Thanksgiving?

It took real nerve to tell him the truth, that she hadn't been able to get off because of the time she'd already missed. There was simply nobody available to replace her. She'd have Thanksgiving Day, but nothing more.

She'd tried to beg the time off to have a long weekend, but her boss hadn't been pleased and he refused. He wanted her on call that weekend, and she couldn't be and go to Jacobsville. The office held a huge clinic for the local immigrant population on Saturdays, as well as Sunday afternoons, and Meredith was competently bilingual in medical terms.

It made her indispensable. Not that she minded. These people were desperately in need of even the most basic health care, and Meredith was a whiz at preventive medicine. She counseled them, advised them on nutrition and wellness, and tried not to let her heart break at the sight of little children with rotting teeth and poor vision and a dozen other ailments that money could have corrected easily. The disparity between the rich and the poor was never more evident than in minority communities.

But the fact was, she had one day off for Thanksgiving and no real time for herself. It was a reminder of just how pressured her job really was, and how demanding. She loved what she did, but she hated being made to feel guilty when she asked for time off—something she hadn't done since her brother's and mother's untimely deaths. Actually it had been a battle royal to get time off for bereavement leave, and the funerals, and she'd had to go right back to work the day after the burials. It had been too soon, but she'd thought work would be good medicine.

Perhaps it had been, but she was living on nerves. The weeks at the Hart ranch had given her a taste of a whole other life. It was one she recalled with joy and missed every day. Most of all, she missed Rey. Now she wouldn't even see him. Her father said that he'd ask someone to loan him a vehicle, and he'd come to have Thanksgiving with her. That cheered her up a little, but it would mean she wouldn't see Rey. It was a bad blow. She told her father that she'd make dinner, which cheered him up as well.

Thanksgiving Day came, and Meredith got up before daylight to start cooking. She was determined that she and her father were going to have the best Thanksgiving dinner she could manage. She'd bought a turkey and a small ham, and raw ingredients to make dressing and sweet potato soufflé, green beans, ambrosia, homemade rolls and cherry and pumpkin pies.

She'd just taken the last pie out of the oven when she heard a car pull up in front of the house. She didn't stop to take off her apron or run a brush through her disheveled hair. She ran to the front door and opened it, just in time to see her father and Rey come up on the porch.

"Happy Thanksgiving, Merry," her father said, and hugged her warmly.

Rey grinned. "We thought you might like company to help you eat all that food," he told her.

"I didn't make any biscuits," she said worriedly. "Just homemade rolls."

"I love rolls." He held out his arms. "Well, come on," he chided when she hesitated. "You can't treat a red-hot matrimonial prospect like me to the cold shoulder! You'll never get me to say 'yes' from arm's length!"

Her father coughed. "I'll just, uh, check on the turkey," he said with an impish smile and went into the kitchen.

Rey nudged Meredith back inside the house, closed the door, and kissed her to within an inch of her life. He barely stopped to breathe before he was kissing her again, enfolding her in a bearish embrace while he made up for what seemed like years of abstinence.

"You'll smother me," she complained weakly.

"Stop complaining and kiss me," he murmured against her swollen lips. He kissed her ever harder.

"I'm not…complaining!" she gasped when he finally stopped.

He bit her lower lip ardently. "I am," he groaned. "Come on, woman, ravish me!"

"Here?" she exclaimed, wide-eyed.

"Well, give your father a quarter and send him to the store for cigarettes!" he asked with comical desperation between kisses.

"Nobody here smokes," she pointed out.

"Excuses, excuses," he murmured against her lips, using her own favorite complaint. His arms tightened and he only stopped when he had to breathe. "What a long, dry spell it's been, Merry," he whispered huskily. "Come back here…"

She kissed him and kissed him with no thought of the future. It was wonderful to be held and cuddled and wanted. She thought she'd never felt so much joy in her whole life as she did here, in Rey's hard arms.

"There's that carpet you mentioned when I left here last time," he said breathlessly, indicating the floor. He wiggled both eyebrows. "We can lock your father in the kitchen and you can ravish me, right here!"

"Not on your life." She linked her arms around his neck. "I won't ravish you until you agree to marry me," she managed unsteadily.

"Is that a proposal?" he murmured huskily.

"Sure. You can have a ring. I think there's a ten-year-old cigar around here somewhere with a band on it…"

He was still kissing her between words. "I'll phone the minister first thing tomorrow. You can have a blood test at work. I already had Micah Steele do one on me. He said he'd love to have a nurse practitioner of his very own, by the way, if you're interested. We can have a Christmas wedding in Jacobsville."

Her mind was spinning. She couldn't quite understand what he was saying. Of course, he was kissing her and she could hardly think at all. "Blood test…work for Micah… Christmas wedding?" she murmured.

"Mmm-hmm," he whispered, kissing her again. "You can

get me a ring whenever you like, but I got you one already."
He fumbled in his jacket pocket and pulled out a velvet-covered jeweler's box. He opened it and showed it to her. Inside was a glorious emerald solitaire, and a diamond and emerald wedding band. "If you don't like it, we can throw it in the fishpond and go buy you something else…"

"I love it!" she exclaimed, flustered by the sudden turn of events.

"Good. Here." He took out the engagement ring, pocketed the box and slid it gently onto her ring finger. "Now it's official. We're engaged. Remember what you just promised," he added with a wicked grin. "The minute your father leaves, I'll let you ravish me on the carpet!"

Chapter Eleven

"But, Rey, Daddy won't leave," she whispered. "There's a turkey in the kitchen!"

"He can take it with him," he said generously.

She laughed and hugged him very hard. "I can't believe this."

"Neither can I," he said, nuzzling his cheek against hers. His arms tightened. "Even when I was suspicious of you, I couldn't bear you out of my sight. I still can't. This past week has been endless. I thought we could cool it for a few weeks, while I got things into perspective. But the only thing I got into perspective was how lonely I was without you." He lifted his head and looked down into her wide, rapt eyes. "I love my freedom. But not as much as I love you."

"And I love you, Rey," she said huskily. "I was lonely, too. I feel as if I've known you for centuries."

"Same here," he replied. "We're going to make a good marriage."

"A very good marriage," she agreed, and lifted her face so that he could kiss her again. He did, at length and very nicely, until her father came out of the kitchen with a turkey leg in one hand and asked if there were plans to take the dressing out of the oven before it got any blacker. Rey told him their news while Meredith took off at a dead run to rescue dinner.

* * *

Meredith worked out a two-week notice and gave up her job, to the dismay and regret of her boss, who hadn't wanted to lose her. He did see that she couldn't have a husband in Jacobsville and a job in Houston, however, and he made them a wedding present of a beautiful faceted crystal bowl.

Micah Steele offered her a job at his office, which she accepted with pleasure, on the understanding that she could work three days a week instead of six. Micah understood being a newlywed, since he and his Callie were still newlyweds as well, even with a baby on the way.

The only hitch was that all Rey's brothers got together and took over the wedding plans, to his dismay and Meredith's horror.

"It's going to be a humdinger of a wedding," Leo promised with relish, rubbing his hands together. "Cag had this great idea for entertainment."

"I don't want to hear it," Rey said firmly.

"You'll love this," Leo continued, unabashed. "He's got this great hard-rock band from Montana coming down to play their new hit record. They just had a hit single about getting married," he added with a rakish grin. "And they're having a caterer from San Antonio bring down the buffet lunch. The wedding gown is coming from one of the couture houses in Paris…"

"But you don't even know my size!" Meredith protested breathlessly.

"We looked in your dresses," he said imperturbably. "Got your shoe size, too, and we also looked in your drawers and got the, ahem, other sizes." He grinned sheepishly. "Everything is couture, and silk. Only the best for our new sister-in-law," he added sweepingly.

Meredith didn't know whether to laugh or scream.

"We booked you a room at a five-star hotel for your honeymoon," he continued, glancing at Rey. "You still speak French, don't you?"

"French?" Meredith gasped.

"Well, your rooms are in Nice," he said. "The French Riviera. You've got a suite, overlooking the beach. Monaco is just on down the beach from there."

Rey whistled. "Not bad, for a rush job."

"We try to be efficient," Leo said, and his eyes twinkled. "We even ordered her a trousseau with formal gowns and casual clothes. Lots of pinks and blues and soft beige colors. We thought pastels would suit her."

Her mouth was open. She was trying to take it all in without fainting. She was only beginning to realize that the horror stories she'd heard from Tess about weddings and the brothers were true.

"You did kidnap Dorie and tie her in a sack with ribbon and carry her home to Corrigan!" she gasped.

"He didn't have a Christmas present," Leo explained patiently. "We gave him one. Look how well it worked out!"

"You hooligans!"

"Our hearts are all in the right place," Leo protested. "Besides, Dorie could bake. Which brings us to Tess, who could also bake…"

"You blackmailed Callaghan into marrying her, I heard!" Meredith was getting her second wind now.

"He's very happy. So is Tess."

"And poor Tira," she continued, unabashed. "You arranged her wedding and she didn't even get to choose her own gown, either!"

"She was pregnant. We had to hurry, there was no time," Leo explained matter-of-factly.

"I am not pregnant!" she exclaimed, red-faced.

Leo gave Rey a quick, speculative glance. "Yet," he replied. He grinned.

"If you would just give me a little time to organize my own

wedding," she began, exasperated, and thought, I'm being nibbled to death by ducks…!

Leo checked his watch. "Sorry, I'm running late. The printer is waiting for me to check the proofs."

"Of what?" she burst out.

"Oh, just the wedding invitations. We're overnighting them to the people we invited. The governor's coming, so is the lieutenant governor. The vice president wanted to come, but he has to be in Singapore…" He frowned and checked his back pocket. "There they are! I almost forgot the interview questions. Here." He handed Rey two folded sheets of paper. "You'll have time to look them over before the camera crews move in."

Meredith and Rey exchanged wide glances. "What camera crews?" she asked.

"Just a few reporters," Leo waved them away with a lean hand. "You know, CNN, Fox, the international press…got to run!"

"International press!" Meredith choked.

"We've just signed an important export deal with Japan, didn't I mention it?" Leo called back. "They love organic beef, and we've got some. I mentioned it to our public relations people and they called the news people for us. Your father's writing the statement we're giving them. He's sure got a way with words, hasn't he?"

He waved again, climbed into his truck, and sped off.

"Invitations," Meredith said haltingly. "Clothes. Honeymoons. Reporters."

"Now, now," he said, pulling her into his arms. "Just think of all the work they've saved you. You'll have nothing to do but dress and say yes, and fly off to the Riviera with your brand-new husband!"

"But, but," she blurted.

"I want to marry you right away," he added. "You're a qualified health professional, and I have a terrible pain that you can cure in only one night."

She got the idea, belatedly, and hit him.

He chuckled, bending to kiss her gently. "It's no use trying to stop them," he said. "Besides, they're very good at it. I used to be, too." He scowled. "Somehow, it's not as much fun being on the receiving end, though."

She just shook her head.

The wedding was beautiful, despite her misgivings. Meredith wore the most gorgeous gown she'd ever seen, with yards and yards of exquisite lace over satin, with a long veil made of the same lace and a bouquet of pure white roses. Her father gave her away, and all four of Rey's brothers were best men. Tess, Cag's wife, stood with Meredith as her matron of honor. In a very short time, the two women had become close friends.

Most of Jacobsville turned out for the affair, but Meredith had eyes only for her handsome husband, who was dressed to the hilt as well. They exchanged rings and Rey lifted the veil very slowly. He'd been romantic and gentle and teasing over the days before the wedding. But when he looked at her now, his eyes were quiet and loving and very solemn. He bent and kissed her with such tenderness that she knew she'd remember the moment for the rest of her life.

They clasped hands and ran down the aisle and out of the church together, laughing gaily as they were pelted with rice and rose petals. At the waiting limousine, Meredith turned and tossed her bouquet. Surprisingly it was caught by Janie Brewster, notorious locally for her rubber chicken dinners and trying to catch Leo Hart's eye. She blushed vividly and clutched the bouquet, her eyes on it and not on anyone nearby. Which was as well, because Leo looked suddenly homicidal as the ranch foreman elbowed him and grinned.

The newlyweds waved and dived into the limousine, already packed and ready to take them to the airport. They'd already announced that the reception would have to go on without them, to the brothers' shock and dismay.

"I hated for us to miss it," Rey told her on the way to the airport, "but I know my brothers. They'd have found some way to embarrass us."

She chuckled, snuggling close to him. "Well, we're safe now."

The flight to France was long and boring. They held hands and couldn't sleep as the little computers above the seats marked the long trail on a map, showing the progress of the flight. When the jumbo jet finally landed, they walked like zombies into the airport to go through passport control and then on to wait for their luggage so that they could get through customs and to the waiting car that would take them to their hotel. The driver, holding a sign that read Hart Newlyweds had met them at the gate and arranged to meet them at customs. Meredith was yawning visibly when they found the driver and followed him and the wheeled luggage out the door. He and Rey exchanged comments that went right over Meredith's head.

"I don't speak French," she said worriedly when they were in the car. "I took a double minor in German and Spanish."

"No Latin?" he teased.

"There's a special course of it for nursing students," she replied with a smile. "Fortunately you don't have to learn the whole language anymore, although I wouldn't have minded. I'm so tired!"

"We'll have a nice long rest when we get to the hotel." He pulled her close. "I could use a little sleep myself!"

The car pulled up under the covered entrance and a bellboy came out to get the luggage. Rey paid the driver and made arrangements to contact him when they were ready to go sightseeing in a day or two.

Meredith followed Rey and the luggage to the desk clerk and waited while he got the key to their suite.

It didn't take long. Rey unlocked the door and opened it. And the bellhop burst into helpless laughter.

There, on the bed, very obviously courtesy of the Hart boys, were two life-size blow-up dolls, a blond female and a dark-haired male, in the midst of a garden of thornless roses of every color known to man. They were obviously engaged in a notorious newlywed ritual.

Rey tipped the bellhop and opened the door himself, waving the man out while he tried not to bend over double laughing.

When he closed the door again, Meredith was removing the dolls and roses with tears of mirth running down her cheeks.

"Just wait until they break something, anything," she threatened. "We can have them put in body casts for a sprained ankle…!"

He came up behind her and caught her around the waist. "And I'll help you. But, later, sweetheart," he added in a soft, hungry tone as he turned her into his arms. "Much, much… later!"

She was a professional health care worker. She knew all the mechanics of marriage. In fact, she counseled young wives in them. This was totally out of her experience.

Rey undressed her with slow precision, while he kissed every soft inch of skin as he uncovered it. He never rushed. He seemed to have committed the whole night to her arousal, and he went about it like a soldier with a battle plan.

She was teased, caressed, kissed until she felt as if there wasn't a bed under her at all. The roses were scattered over the carpet by now, along with half the bed linen. She was under him and then over him as he increased the insistence of his hands and mouth on her body. She heard high-pitched little cries of pleasure and barely realized that they were coming from her own throat.

One particularly enthusiastic embrace landed them on the carpet, cushioned by the sheet and blanket and, under them, the thick comforter.

"The bed," she whispered, trembling with unsatisfied hunger.

"It will still be there when we're finished," he replied breathlessly as his mouth bent again to her taut, arching breasts. "Yes, do that again, sweetheart!" he added when she pulled his head down to her.

He guided her hands along his lean, fit body to his hips and pressed them there as he suddenly shifted between her soft legs and his mouth ground into hers with intent.

The abrupt shift in intensity took her by surprise and lessened the sharp pain of his possession of her. His hard mouth absorbed the tiny cry that pulsed out of her tight throat, and his hands moved under her hips to caress her.

After a few seconds, she began to relax. He shifted again and found the place, and the pressure, that made her lift toward him instead of trying to escape the downward rhythm of his hips.

She clung to his damp shoulders as the little bites of pleasure became great, shivering waves. She could feel him in every cell of her body, and she wanted to look at him, to see his face, but she was intent on some distant goal of pleasure that grew by the second. Her mouth opened against the hollow of his shoulder and she moaned, her eyes closed, her body following the lead of his own as the heated minutes lengthened.

Her nails suddenly stabbed into his back and she gasped.

"Yes," he groaned at her ear. "Now, baby, now, now…!"

As if her body had given him some secret signal, his hips became insistent and the rhythm increased to madness. She reached, reached…reached…until the pleasure exploded inside her and began to spread in racking hot waves from her head to her toes. She rippled with him, sobbed against his skin, as the ecstasy she'd never known flamed through her with hurricane force.

"Rey!" She cried out pitifully as the wave peaked, and she felt her body go incandescent with joy.

His hands gripped her hips as he riveted her to his insistent hips. She heard his breathing become raspy and hoarse and then stop as he groaned endlessly against her throat and his entire body convulsed over her.

She felt him shake as the madness began to drift away.

"Are you all right?" she whispered urgently.

"I'm...dying," he choked.

"Rey!"

She held him close until the harsh contractions of his body slowed and then stopped. He collapsed on her with his whole weight, his breathing as labored as his heartbeat. His mouth burrowed into her throat hungrily.

"Never like that, Mrs. Hart," he whispered huskily. "You just made me a whole man!"

"Did I, really?" she whispered with a silly giggle.

He laughed, too. "That's what it felt like." He sighed heavily and lifted his head to look at her. His hair was as damp as hers, and he looked exhausted. He brushed loose blond strands away from her cheeks. "I'm glad we waited. I hope you are."

"Yes." Filled with wonder, she touched his hard mouth, which was swollen from its long contact with hers. "I think I swallowed the sun," she whispered. "It was...glorious!" She hid her face in his throat, still shy of him, especially now.

He laughed again, lazily brushing his mouth over her closed eyes. "Glorious," he agreed with a long sigh. He rolled away from her gently, onto his back, and pulled her against him. "We fell off the bed," he remarked after a minute.

"I thought we were thrown off it," she murmured sleepily. "You know, by the hurricane."

"Hurricane." He kissed her forehead gently. "That's what it felt like."

"I'm sleepy. Is it normal?"

"Yes, it is, and it does worlds for my masculinity," he drawled. "Feel free to tell anyone you like that you ravished me to such an extent that I fell out of bed in my excitement, and you went to sleep from the tidal wave of pleasure!"

She managed one tired little chuckle. "I'll take out an ad in a magazine," she promised. She wrapped her arms and one leg around him, completely uninhibited now. "I love you, but I have to go to sleep now."

"Suit yourself, but I hope you're not throwing in the towel. I'm a brand-new bridegroom, remember, you can't just roll over and go to sleep once you've had your way with me... Meredith? Meredith!"

It was no use. She was sound asleep, worn-out by the pace of the wedding and her first passion. He lay watching her sleep, his eyes quiet and tender and loving. It had already been, he mused, one hell of a wedding night, even if they hadn't waited for it to get dark.

When she woke up, she was wearing a nightgown and lying on the bed, under the covers. Rey was sipping coffee and sniffing freshly cooked food under silver lids. He glanced up as Meredith sat up in bed and blinked her eyes sleepily.

"Supper?" she asked.

He grinned. "Supper. Come and eat something."

She pulled herself out of bed, feeling a little uncomfortable and grinning as she realized why. She sat down beside Rey, who was wearing a pair of blue silk pajama bottoms and nothing else, and looked under lids.

"Seafood," she sighed, smiling. "My favorite."

"Mine, too. Dig in, honey." He reached over and kissed her softly and gave her a wicked grin. "It's going to be a long, lovely night!"

And it was.

They came back to the ranch after several magical, wonderful days together to find the house deserted. There was a note propped up on the kitchen table, obviously left by Leo, because his name was signed to it.

"Goodbye, cruel world," it read. "Have run out of biscuits.

No relief in sight. Can't go on. Have gone into Jacobsville to kidnap a cook or beg door-to-door for biscuits. If I fail, drag the river. P.S. Congratulations Meredith and Rey. Hope you liked the wedding present. Love, Leo."

"He wouldn't really kidnap a cook," Meredith said.

"Of course not," Rey agreed. But he had a very odd look on his face.

"Or beg door-to-door for a biscuit."

"Of course not," Rey repeated.

Meredith went to the telephone. "I'll call Dad."

He waited while she dialed the cottage her father occupied and tapped his foot while it rang and rang.

"Dad?" she asked suddenly. "Have you seen Leo?"

There was a pause, while Rey gestured with his hands for her to tell him something. She flapped a hand at him while she listened and nodded.

"Okay, Dad, thanks! Yes, we had a lovely honeymoon! We'll have you up for supper tomorrow. Love you, too!"

She hung up and sighed. "Well, Leo's gone to San Antonio."

"What the hell for?" he exclaimed.

"Apparently he walked out of Barbara's café with a cook in his arms and put him in the ranch truck…"

"Him?" Rey exclaimed.

"Him." She sighed. "The cook escaped out the other door and ran to get Chet Blake."

"The chief of police?" Rey looked horrified.

"Chet was laughing so hard that he didn't get to the café before Leo took off in a cloud of dust, barely escaping public disgrace. He tried to hire the little man to bake him some biscuits, but the cook refused, so Leo took harsh measures." She chuckled. "Dad said he phoned halfway to San Antonio and said he'd be back in a few days. He thinks he'll go to that genetics workshop until the heat dies down here."

"We'll never live that story down," Rey sighed, shaking his head.

"There is a solution," she remarked. "We can find him a nice wife."

He laughed even harder. "Leo's the one of us who'll have to be dragged to the altar behind a big horse," he told her. "For all that Janie Brewster is desperate to marry him, he's as elusive as smoke."

"Janie's pretty," she recalled, because the girl caught her bridal bouquet at the wedding.

"She's a doll, but she can't boil water," Rey told her. "He'd never get a biscuit if he married Janie. Besides, she's not mature enough for him."

"She could change."

"So could he, sweetheart," he drawled, pulling her close to kiss her. "But I wouldn't hold my breath in either case. Now here we are, at home, and all alone, and I'll give you one guess what I'd like you to do next," he whispered suggestively.

She smiled under his lips. "Would it have something to do with flour and olive oil and skim milk and a hot oven?" she whispered back.

He actually gasped. "Darling!" he exclaimed, and kissed her even harder.

She linked her arms around his neck. "So," she whispered, moving closer, "Just how badly do you want that pan of biscuits, sweetheart?" she teased.

Chuckling, he bent and lifted her clear of the floor and turned down the hall. "Let me show you!"

Eventually he got a pan of fresh biscuits and a whole jar of fresh apple butter to go on them—along with a nice pat of low-fat margarine. And he didn't even complain!

* * * * *

LIONHEARTED

Prologue

Leo Hart felt alone in the world. The last of his bachelor brothers, Rey, had gotten married and moved out of the house almost a year ago. That left Leo, alone, with an arthritic housekeeper who came in two days a week and threatened to retire every day. If she did, Leo would be left without a biscuit to his name, or even a hope of getting another one unless he went to a restaurant every morning for breakfast. Considering his work schedule, that was impractical.

He leaned back in the swivel chair at his desk in the office he now shared with no one. He was happy for his brothers. Most of them had families now, except newly married Rey. Simon and Tira had two little boys. Cag and Tess had a boy. Corrigan and Dorie had a boy and a baby girl. When he looked back, Leo realized that women had been a missing commodity in his life of late. It was late September. Roundup was just over, and there had been so much going on at the ranch, with business, that he'd hardly had time for a night out. He was feeling it.

Even as he considered his loneliness, the phone rang.

"Why don't you come over for supper?" Rey asked when he picked up the receiver.

"Listen," Leo drawled, grinning, "you don't invite your brother over to dinner on your honeymoon."

"We got married after Christmas last year," Rey pointed out.

"Like I said, you're still on your honeymoon," came the amused reply. "Thanks. But I've got too much to do."

"Work doesn't make up for a love life."

"You'd know," Leo chuckled.

"Okay. But the invitation's open, whenever you want to accept it."

"Thanks. I mean it."

"Sure."

The line went dead. Leo put the receiver down and stretched hugely, bunching the hard muscles in his upper arms. He was the boss as much as his brothers on their five ranch properties, but he did a lot of the daily physical labor that went with cattle raising, and his tall, powerful body was evidence of it. He wondered sometimes if he didn't work that hard to keep deep-buried needs at bay. In his younger days, women had flocked around him, and he hadn't been slow to accept sensual invitations. But he was in his thirties now, and casual interludes were no longer satisfying.

He'd planned to have a quiet weekend at home, but Marilee Morgan, a close friend of Janie Brewster's, had cajoled him into taking her up to Houston for dinner and to see a ballet she had tickets for. He was partial to ballet, and Marilee explained that she couldn't drive herself because her car was in the shop. She was easy on the eyes, and she was sophisticated. Not that Leo was tempted to let himself be finagled into any sort of intimacy with her. He didn't want her carrying tales of his private life to Janie, who had an obvious and uncomfortable crush on him.

He knew that Marilee would never have asked him to take her any place in Jacobsville, Texas, because it was a small town and news of the date would inevitably get back to Janie. It might help show the girl that Leo was a free agent, but it wouldn't help his friendship with Fred Brewster to know that

Leo was playing fast and loose with Janie's best friend. Some best friend, he thought privately.

But taking Marilee out would have one really good consequence—it would get him out of a dinner date at the Brewsters' house. He and Fred Brewster were friends and business associates, and he enjoyed the time he spent with the older man. Well, except for two members of his family, he amended darkly. He didn't like Fred's sister, Lydia. She was a busybody who had highfalutin ideas. Fortunately, she was hardly ever around and she didn't live with Fred. He had mixed feelings about Fred's daughter Janie, who was twenty-one and bristling with psychology advice after her graduation from a junior college in that subject. She'd made Cag furious with her analyses of his food preferences, and Leo was becoming adept at avoiding invitations that would put him in her line of fire.

Not that she was bad looking. She had long, thick light brown hair and a neat little figure. But she also had a crush on Leo, which was very visible. He considered her totally unacceptable as a playmate for a man his age, and he knocked back her attempts at flirting with lazy skill. He'd known her since she was ten and wearing braces on her teeth. It was hard to get that image out of his mind.

Besides, she couldn't cook. Her rubber chicken dinners were infamous locally, and her biscuits could be classified as lethal weapons.

Thinking about those biscuits made him pick up the phone and dial Marilee.

She was curt when she picked up the phone, but the minute he spoke, her voice softened.

"Well, hello, Leo," she said huskily.

"What time do you want me to pick you up Saturday night?"

There was a faint hesitation. "You won't, uh, mention this to Janie?"

"I have as little contact with Janie as I can. You know that," he said impatiently.

"Just checking," she teased, but she sounded worried. "I'll be ready to leave about six."

"Suppose I pick you up at five and we'll have supper in Houston before the ballet?"

"Wonderful! I'll look forward to it. See you then."

"See you."

He hung up, but picked up the receiver again and dialed the Brewsters' number.

As luck would have it, Janie answered.

"Hi, Janie," he said pleasantly.

"Hi, Leo," she replied breathlessly. "Want to talk to Dad?"

"You'll do," he replied. "I have to cancel for dinner Saturday. I've got a date."

There was the faintest pause. It was almost imperceptible. "I see."

"Sorry, but it's a long-standing one," he lied. "I can't get out of it. I forgot when I accepted your dad's invitation. Can you give him my apologies?"

"Of course," she told him. "Have a good time."

She sounded strange. He hesitated. "Something wrong?" he asked.

"Nothing at all! Nice talking to you, Leo. Bye."

Janie Brewster hung up and closed her eyes, sick with disappointment. She'd planned a perfect menu. She'd practiced all week on a special chicken dish that was tender and succulent. She'd practiced an exquisite crème brûlée as well, which was Leo's favorite dessert. She could even use the little tool to caramelize the sugar topping, which had taken a while to perfect. All that work, and for nothing. She'd have been willing to bet that Leo hadn't had a date for that night already. He'd made one deliberately, to get out of the engagement.

She sat down beside the hall table, her apron almost stiff with flour, her face white with dustings of it, her hair disheveled. She was anything but the picture of a perfect date. And wasn't it just her luck? For the past year, she'd mounted a real campaign to get Leo to notice her. She'd flirted with him shamelessly at Micah Steele's wedding to Callie Kirby, until a stabbing scowl had turned her shy. It had angered him that she'd caught the bouquet Callie had thrown. It had embarrassed her that he glared so angrily at her. Months later, she'd tried, shyly, every wile she had on him, with no success. She couldn't cook and she was not much more than a fashion plate, according to her best friend, Marilee, who was trying to help her catch Leo. Marilee had plenty of advice, things Leo had mentioned that he didn't like about Janie, and Janie was trying her best to improve in the areas he'd mentioned. She was even out on the ranch for the first time in her life, trying to get used to horses and cattle and dust and dirt. But if she couldn't get Leo to the house to show him her new skills, she didn't have a lot of hope.

"Who was that on the phone?" Hettie, their housekeeper, called from the staircase. "Was it Mr. Fred?"

"No. It was Leo. He can't come Saturday night. He's got a date."

"Oh." Hettie smiled sympathetically. "There will be other dinners, darlin'."

"Of course there will," Janie said and smiled back. She got out of the chair. "Well, I'll just make it for you and me and Dad," she said, with disappointment plain in her voice.

"It isn't as if Leo has any obligation to spend his weekends with us, just because he does a lot of business with Mr. Fred," Hettie reminded her gently. "He's a good man. A little old for you, though," she added hesitantly.

Janie didn't answer her. She just smiled and walked back into the kitchen.

* * *

Leo showered, shaved, dressed to the hilt and got into the new black Lincoln sports car he'd just bought. Next year's model, and fast as lightning. He was due for a night on the town. And missing Janie's famous rubber chicken wasn't going to disappoint him one bit.

His conscience did nag him, though, oddly. Maybe it was just hearing Janie's friend, Marilee, harp on the girl all the time. In the past week, she'd started telling him some disturbing things that Janie had said about him. He was going to have to be more careful around Janie. He didn't want her to get the wrong idea. He had no interest in her at all. She was just a kid.

He glanced in the lighted mirror over the steering wheel before he left the sprawling Hart Ranch. He had thick blond-streaked brown hair, a broad forehead, a slightly crooked nose and high cheekbones. But his teeth were good and strong, and he had a square jaw and a nice wide mouth. He wasn't all that handsome, but compared to most of his brothers, he was a hunk. He chuckled at that rare conceit and closed the mirror. He was rich enough that his looks didn't matter.

He didn't fool himself that Marilee would have found him all that attractive without his bankroll. But she was pretty and he didn't mind taking her to Houston and showing her off, like the fishing trophies he displayed on the walls of his study. A man had to have his little vanities, he told himself. But he thought about Janie's disappointment when he didn't show up for supper, her pain if she ever found out her best friend was stabbing her in the back, and he hated the guilt he felt.

He put on his seat belt, put the car in gear, and took off down the long driveway. He didn't have any reason to feel guilty, he told himself firmly. He was a bachelor, and he'd never done one single thing to give Janie Brewster the impression that he wanted to be the man in her life. Besides, he'd been on his own too long. A cultural evening in Houston was just the thing to cure the blues.

Chapter One

Leo Hart was half out of humor. It had been a long week as it was, and now he was faced with trying to comfort his neighbor, Fred Brewster, who'd just lost the prize young Salers bull that Leo had wanted to buy. The bull was the offspring of a grand champion whose purchase had figured largely in Leo's improved cross-breeding program. He felt as sad as Fred seemed to.

"He was fine yesterday," Fred said heavily, wiping sweat off his narrow brow as the two men surveyed the bull in the pasture. The huge creature was lying dead on its side, not a mark on it. "I'm not the only rancher who's ever lost a prize bull, but these are damned suspicious circumstances."

"They are," Leo agreed grimly, his dark eyes surveying the bull. "It's just a thought, but you haven't had a problem with an employee, have you? Christabel Gaines said they just had a bull die of unknown causes. This happened after they fired a man named Jack Clark a couple of weeks ago. He's working for Duke Wright now, driving a cattle truck."

"Judd Dunn said it wasn't unknown causes that killed the bull, it was bloat. Judd's a Texas Ranger," Fred reminded him. "If there was sabotage on the ranch he co-owns with Christabel, I think he'd know it. No, Christabel had that young bull in a pasture with a lot of clover and she hadn't primed him on hay or tannin-containing forage beforehand. She won't use antibiotics, either, which would have helped prevent trouble. Even so, you can treat bloat if you catch it in time. It was bad luck that they didn't check that pasture, but Christabel's shorthanded and she's back at the vocational school full-time, too. Not much time to check on livestock."

"They had four other bulls that were still alive," Leo pointed out, scowling.

Fred shrugged. "Maybe they didn't like clover, or weren't in the same pasture." He shook his head. "I'm fairly sure their bull died of bloat. That's what Judd thinks, anyway. He says Christabel's unsettled by having those movie people coming next month to work out a shooting schedule on the ranch and she's the only one who thinks there was foul play." Fred rubbed a hand through his silver hair. "But to answer your question— yes, I did wonder about a disgruntled ex-employee, but I haven't fired anybody in over two years. So you can count out vengeance. And it wasn't bloat. My stock gets antibiotics."

"Don't say that out loud," Leo chuckled. "If the Tremaynes hear you, there'll be a fight."

"It's my ranch. I run it my way." Fred looked sadly toward the bull again. He was having financial woes the likes of which he'd never faced. He was too proud to tell Leo the extent of it. "This bull is a hell of a loss right now, too, with my breeding program under way. He wasn't insured, so I can't afford to replace him. Well, not just yet," he amended, because he didn't want Leo to think he was nearly broke.

"That's one problem we can solve," Leo replied. "I've got that beautiful Salers bull I bought two years ago, but it's time I replaced him. I'd have loved to have had yours, but while I'm looking for a replacement, you can borrow mine for your breeding season."

"Leo, I can't let you do that," Fred began, overwhelmed by the offer. He knew very well what that bull's services cost.

Leo held up a big hand and grinned. "Sure you can. I've got an angle. I get first pick of your young bulls next spring."

"You devil, you," Fred said, chuckling. "All right, all right. On that condition, I'll take him and be much obliged. But I'd feel better if there was a man sitting up with him at night to guard him."

Leo stretched sore muscles, pushing his Stetson back over his blond-streaked brown hair. It was late September, but still very hot in Jacobsville, which was in southeastern Texas. He'd been helping move bulls all morning, and he was tired. "We can take care of security for him," Leo said easily. "I've got two cowboys banged up in accidents who can't work cattle. They're still on my payroll, so they can sit over here and guard my bull while they recuperate."

"And we'll feed them," Fred said.

Leo chuckled. "Now that's what I call a real nice solution. One of them," he confided, "eats for three men."

"I won't mind." His eyes went back to the still bull one more time. "He was the best bull, Leo. I had so many hopes for him."

"I know. But there are other champion-sired Salers bulls," Leo said.

"Sure. But not one like that one," he gestured toward the animal. "He had such beautiful conformation—" He broke off as a movement to one side caught his attention. He turned, leaned forward and then gaped at his approaching daughter. "Janie?" he asked, as if he wasn't sure of her identity.

Janie Brewster had light brown hair and green eyes. She'd tried going blond once, but these days her hair was its natural color. Straight, thick and sleek, it hung to her waist. She had a nice figure, a little on the slender side, and pretty little pert breasts. She even had nice legs. But anyone looking at her right now could be forgiven for mistaking her for a young bull rider.

She was covered with mud from head to toe. Even her hair

was caked with it. She had a saddle over one thin shoulder, leaning forward to take its weight. The separation between her boots and jeans was imperceptible. Her blouse and arms were likewise. Only her eyes were visible, her eyebrows streaked where the mud had been haphazardly wiped away.

"Hi, Daddy," she muttered as she walked past them with a forced smile. "Hi, Leo. Nice day."

Leo's dark eyes were wide-open, like Fred's. He couldn't even manage words. He nodded, and kept gaping at the mud doll walking past.

"What have you been doing?" Fred shouted after his only child.

"Just riding around," she said gaily.

"Riding around," Fred murmured to himself as she trailed mud onto the porch and stopped there, calling for their housekeeper. "I can't remember the last time I saw her on a horse," he added.

"Neither can I," Leo was forced to admit.

Fred shook his head. "She has these spells lately," he said absently. "First it was baling hay. She went out with four of the hands and came home covered in dust and thorns. Then she took up dipping cattle." He cleared his throat. "Better to forget that altogether. Now it's riding. I don't know what the hell's got into her. She was all geared up to transfer to a four-year college and get on with her psychology degree. Then all of a sudden, she announces that she's going to learn ranching." He threw up his hands. "I'll never understand children. Will you?" he asked Leo.

Leo chuckled. "Don't ask me. Fatherhood is one role in life I have no desire to play. Listen, about my bull," he continued. "I'll have him trucked right over, and the men will come with him. If you have any more problems, you just let me know."

Fred was relieved. The Harts owned five ranches. Nobody had more clout than they did, politically and financially. The loan of that bull would help him recoup his losses and get back on his feet. Leo was a gentleman. "I'm damned grateful, Leo. We've been having hard times lately."

Leo only smiled. He knew that the Brewsters were having a bad time financially. He and Fred had swapped and traded bulls for years—although less expensive ones than Fred's dead Salers bull—and they frequently did business together. He was glad he could help.

He did wonder about Janie's odd behavior. She'd spent weeks trying to vamp him with low-cut blouses and dresses. She was always around when he came to see Fred on business, waiting in the living room in a seductive pose. Not that Janie even knew how to be seductive, he told himself amusedly. She was twenty-one, but hardly in the class with her friend Marilee Morgan, who was only four years older than Janie but could give Mata Hari lessons in seduction.

He wondered if Marilee had been coaching her in tomboyish antics. That would be amusing, because lately Marilee had been using Janie's tactics on him. The former tomboy-turned-debutante had even finagled him into taking her out to eat in Houston. He wondered if Janie knew. Sometimes friends could become your worst enemy, he thought. Luckily Janie only had a crush on him, which would wear itself out all the faster once she knew he had gone out with her best friend. Janie was far too young for him, and not only in age. The sooner she realized it, the better. Besides, he didn't like her new competitive spirit. Why was she trying to compete with her father in ranch management all of a sudden? Was it a liberation thing? She'd never shown any such inclination before, and her new appearance was appalling. The one thing Leo had admired about her was the elegance and sophistication with which she dressed. Janie in muddy jeans was a complete turnoff.

He left Fred at the pasture and drove back to the ranch,

his mind already on ways and means to find out what had caused that healthy bull's sudden demise.

Janie was listening to their housekeeper's tirade through the bathroom door.

"I'll clean it all up, Hettie," she promised. "It's just dirt. It will come out."

"It's red mud! It will never come out!" Hettie was grumbling. "You'll be red from head to toe forever! People will mistake you for that nineteenth-century Kiowa, Satanta, who painted everything he owned red, even his horse!"

Janie laughed as she stripped off the rest of her clothes and stepped into the shower. Besides being a keen student of Western history, Hettie was all fire and wind, and she'd blow out soon. She was such a sweetheart. Janie's mother had died years ago, leaving behind Janie and her father and Hettie—and Aunt Lydia who lived in Jacobsville. Fortunately, Aunt Lydia only visited infrequently. She was so very house-proud, so clothes conscious, so debutante! She was just like Janie's late mother, in fact, who had raised Janie to be a little flower blossom in a world of independent, strong women. She spared a thought for her mother's horror if she could have lived long enough to see what her daughter had worn at college. There, where she could be herself, Janie didn't wear designer dresses and hang out with the right social group. Janie studied anthropology, as well as the psychology her aunt Lydia had insisted on—and felt free to insist, since she helped pay Janie's tuition. But Janie spent most of her weekends and afternoons buried in mud, learning how to dig out fragile pieces of ancient pottery and projectile points.

But she'd gone on with the pretense when she was home—when Aunt Lydia was visiting, of course—proving her worth at psychology. Sadly, it had gone awry when she psychoanalyzed Leo's brother Callaghan last year over the asparagus. She'd gone to her room howling with laughter after Aunt Lydia had hung on every word approvingly. She was sorry she'd embarrassed Cag, but the impulse had been irresistible. Her aunt was *so* gullible. She'd felt guilty afterward, though, for not telling Aunt Lydia her true interests.

She finished her shower, dried off, and changed into new clothes so that she could start cleaning up the floors where she'd tracked mud. Despite her complaints, Hettie would help. She didn't really mind housework. Neither did Janie, although her late mother would be horrified if she could see her only child on the floor with a scrub brush alongside Hettie's ample figure.

Janie helped with everything, except cooking. Her expertise in the kitchen was, to put it mildly, nonexistent. But, she thought, brightening, that was the next thing on her list of projects. She was undergoing a major self-improvement. First she was going to learn ranching—even if it killed her—and then she was going to learn to cook.

She wished this transformation had been her idea, but actually, it had been Marilee's. The other girl had told her, in confidence, that she'd been talking to Leo and Leo had told her flatly that the reason he didn't notice Janie was that she didn't know anything about ranching. She was too well-dressed, too chic, too sophisticated. And the worst thing was that she didn't know anything about cooking, either, Marilee claimed. So if Janie wanted to land that big, hunky fish, she was going to have to make some major changes.

It sounded like a good plan, and Marilee had been her friend since grammar school, when the Morgan family had moved next door. So Janie accepted Marilee's advice with great pleasure, knowing that her best friend would never steer her wrong. She was going to stay home—not go back to college—and she was going to show Leo Hart that she could be the sort of woman who appealed to him. She'd work so hard at it, she'd have to succeed!

Not that her attempts at riding a horse were anything to write home about, she had to admit as she mopped her way down the long wooden floor of the hall. But she was a rancher's daughter. She'd get better with practice.

She did keep trying. A week later, she was making biscuits in the kitchen—or trying to learn how—when she dropped the paper flour bag hard on the counter and was dusted from head to toe with the white substance.

It would have to be just that minute that her father came in the back door with Leo in tow.

"Janie?" her father exclaimed, wide-eyed.

"Hi, Dad!" she said with a big grin. "Hi, Leo."

"What in blazes are you doing?" her father demanded.

"Putting the flour in a canister," she lied, still smiling.

"Where's Hettie?" he asked.

Their housekeeper was hiding in the bedroom, supposedly making beds, and trying not to howl at Janie's pitiful efforts. "Cleaning, I believe," she said.

"Aunt Lydia not around?"

"Playing bridge with the Harrisons," she said.

"Bridge!" her father scoffed. "If it isn't bridge, it's golf. If it isn't golf, it's tennis… Is she coming over today to go over those stocks with me or not?" he persisted, because they jointly owned some of his late wife's shares and couldn't sell them without Lydia's permission. If he could ever find the blasted woman!

"She said she wasn't coming over until Saturday, Dad," Janie reminded him.

He let out an angry sigh. "Well, come on, Leo, I'll show you the ones I want to sell and let you advise me. They're in my desk…damn bridge! I can't do a thing until Lydia makes up her mind."

Leo gave Janie a curious glance but he kept walking and

didn't say another word to her. Minutes later, he left—out the front door, not the back.

Janie's self-improvement campaign continued into the following week with calf roping, which old John was teaching her out in the corral. Since she could now loop the rope around a practice wooden cow with horns, she was progressing to livestock.

She followed John's careful instruction and tossed her loop over the head of the calf, but she'd forgotten to dig her heels in. The calf hadn't. He jerked her off her feet and proceeded to run around the ring like a wild thing, trying to get away from the human slithering after him at a breakneck pace.

Of course, Leo would drive up next to the corral in time to see John catch and throw the calf, leaving Janie covered in mud. She looked like a road disaster.

This time Leo didn't speak. He was too busy laughing. Janie couldn't speak, either, her mouth was full of mud. She gave both men a glare and stomped off toward the back door of the house, trailing mud and unspeakable stuff, fuming the whole while.

A bath and change of clothes improved her looks and her smell. She was resigned to finding Leo gone when she got out, so she didn't bother to dress up or put on makeup. She wandered out to the kitchen in jeans and a loose long-sleeved denim shirt, with her hair in a lopsided ponytail and her feet bare.

"You'll step on something sharp and cripple yourself," Hettie warned, turning from the counter where she was making rolls, her ample arms up the elbows in flour.

"I have tough feet," Janie protested with a warm smile. She went up and hugged Hettie hard from behind, loving the familiar smells of freshly washed cotton and flour that seemed to cling to her. Hettie had been around since Janie was six.

She couldn't imagine life without the gray-haired, blue-eyed treasure with her constantly disheveled hair and worried expression. "Oh, Hettie, what would we do without you?" she asked on a sigh, and closed her eyes.

"Get away, you pest," Hettie muttered, "I know what you're up to…Janie Brewster, I'll whack you!"

But Janie was already out of reach, dangling Hettie's apron from one hand, her green eyes dancing with mischief.

"You put that back on me or you'll get no rolls tonight!" Hettie raged at her.

"All right, all right, I was only kidding," Janie chuckled. She replaced the apron around Hettie's girth and was fastening it when she heard the door open behind her.

"You stop teaching her these tricks!" Hettie growled at the newcomer.

"Who, me?" Leo exclaimed with total innocence.

Janie's hands fumbled with the apron. Her heart ran wild. He hadn't left. She'd thought he was gone, and she hadn't bothered with her appearance. He was still here, and she looked like last year's roast!

"You'll drop that apron, Janie," Leo scolded playfully.

Janie glanced at him as she retied the apron. "You can talk," she chided. "I hear your housekeepers keep quitting because you untie aprons constantly! One kept a broom handle!"

"She broke it on my hard head," he said smugly. "What are you making, Hettie?"

"Rolls," she said. She glanced warily at Leo. "I can't make biscuits. Sorry."

He gave her a hard glare. "Just because I did something a little offbeat…"

"Carried that little chef right out of his restaurant, with him kicking and screaming all the way, I heard," Hettie mused, eyes twinkling.

"He said he could bake biscuits. I was only taking him home with me to let him prove it," Leo said belligerently.

"That's not what he thought," Hettie chuckled. "I hear he dropped the charges…?"

"Nervous little guy," Leo said, shaking his head. "He'd never have worked out, anyway." He gave her a long look. "You sure you can't bake a biscuit? Have you ever tried?"

"No, and I won't. I like working here," she said firmly.

He sighed. "Just checking." He peered over her shoulder fondly. "Rolls, huh? I can't remember when I've had a home-made roll."

"Tell Fred to invite you to supper," Hettie suggested.

He glanced at Janie. "Why can't she do it?"

Janie was tongue-tied. She couldn't think at all.

The lack of response from her dumbfounded Leo. To have Janie hesitate about inviting him for a meal was shocking. Leo scowled and just stared at her openly, which only made her more nervous and uncertain. She knew she looked terrible. Leo wanted a woman who could do ranch work and cook, but surely he wanted one who looked pretty, too. Right now, Janie could have qualified for the Frump of the Year award.

She bit her lower lip, hard, and looked as if she were about to cry.

"Hey," he said softly, in a tone he'd never used with her before, "what's wrong?"

"Have to let this rise," Hettie was murmuring after she'd covered the dough and washed her hands, oblivious to what was happening behind her. "Meanwhile I'm going to put another load of clothes in the washer, darlin'," she called to Janie over her shoulder.

The door into the dining room closed, but they didn't notice.

Leo moved closer to Janie, and suddenly his big, lean

hands were on her thin shoulders, resting heavily over the soft denim. They were warm and very strong.

Her breath caught in the back of her throat while she looked up into black eyes that weren't teasing or playful. They were intent, narrow, faintly glittering. There was no expression on his handsome face at all. He looked into her eyes as if he'd never seen them, or her, before—and she looked terrible!

"Come on," he coaxed. "Tell me what's wrong. If it's something I can fix, I will."

Her lips trembled. Surely, she could make up something, quick, before he moved away!

"I got hurt," she whispered in a shameful lie. "When the calf dragged me around the corral."

"Did you?" He was only half listening. His eyes were on her mouth. It was the prettiest little mouth, like a pink bow, full and soft, just barely parted over perfect, white teeth. He wondered if she'd been kissed, and how often. She never seemed to date, or at least, he didn't know about her boyfriends. He shouldn't be curious, either, but Marilee had hinted that Janie had more boyfriends than other local girls, that she was a real rounder.

Janie was melting. Her knees were weak. Any minute, she was going to be a little puddle of love looking up at his knees.

He felt her quiver under his hands, and his scowl grew darker. If she was as sophisticated as Marilee said she was, why was she trembling now? An experienced woman would be winding her arms around his neck already, offering her mouth, curving her body into his...

His fingers tightened involuntarily on her soft arms. "Come here," he said huskily, and tugged her right up against his tall, muscular body. Of all the Harts, he was the tallest, and the most powerfully built. Janie's breasts pressed into his diaphragm. She felt him tauten at the contact, felt his curiosity as he looked down into her wide, soft, dazed eyes. Her hands lightly touched his shirtfront, but hesitantly, as if it embarrassed her to touch him at all.

He let out a soft breath. His head was spinning with forbidden longings. Janie was barely twenty-one. She was the daughter of a man he did business with. She was off-limits. So why was he looking at her mouth and feeling his body swell sensuously at just the brush of her small breasts against him?

"Don't pick at my shirt," he said quietly. His voice was unusually deep and soft, its tone unfamiliar. "Flatten your hands on my chest."

She did that, slowly, as if she were just learning how to walk. Her hands were cold and nervous, but they warmed on his body. She stood very still, hoping against hope that he wasn't going to regain the senses she was certain he'd momentarily lost. She didn't even want to breathe, to do anything that would distract him. He seemed to be in a trance, and she was feeling dreams come true in the most unexpected and delightful way.

He smiled quizzically. "Don't you know how?"

Her lips were dry. She moistened them with just the tip of her tongue. He seemed to find that little movement fascinating. He watched her mouth almost hungrily. "How... to...do what?" she choked.

His hand went to her cheek and his thumb suddenly ran roughly over her lips, parting them in a whip of urgent, shocking emotion. "How to do this," he murmured as his head bent.

She saw the faint smile on his hard mouth as his lips parted. They brushed against hers in tiny little whispers of contact that weren't nearly enough to feed the hunger he was coaxing out of her.

Her nails curled into his shirt and he tensed. She felt

thick hair over the warm, hard muscles of his chest. Closer, she felt the hard, heavy thunder of his pulse there, under her searching hands.

"Nice," he whispered. His voice was taut now, like his body against her.

She felt his big hands slide down her waist to her hips while he was playing with her mouth in the most arousing way. She couldn't breathe. Did he know? Could he tell that she was shaking with desire?

Her lips parted more with every sensuous brush of his mouth against them. At the same time, his hands moved to her narrow hips and teased against her lower spine. She'd never felt such strange sensations. She felt her body swell, as if it had been stung all over by bees, but the sensation produced pleasure instead of pain.

He nibbled at her upper lip, feeling it quiver tentatively as his tongue slid under it and began to explore. One lean hand slid around to the base of her hips and slowly gathered them into his, in a lazy movement that made her suddenly aware of the changing contours of his body.

She gasped and pulled against his hand.

He lifted his head and searched her wide, shocked green eyes. "Plenty of boyfriends, hmm?" he murmured sarcastically, almost to himself.

"Boy…friends?" Her voice sounded as if she were being strangled.

His hand moved back to her waist, the other one moved to her round chin and his thumb tugged gently at her lower lip. "Leave it like this," he whispered. His mouth hovered over hers just as it parted, and she found herself going on tiptoe, leaning toward him, almost begging for his mouth to come down and cover hers.

But he was still nibbling at her upper lip, gently toying with it, until he tilted her chin and his teeth tugged softly at the lower lip. His mouth brushed roughly over hers, teaching it to follow, to plead, then to demand something more urgent, more thorough than this slow torment.

Her nails bit into his chest and she moaned.

As if he'd been waiting patiently for that tiny little sound, his arms swallowed her up whole and his eyes, when they met hers, glittered like candlelight from deep in a cave.

His hand was in her ponytail, ripping away the rubber band so that he could catch strands of it in his strong fingers and angle her face just where he wanted it.

"Maybe you are old enough…" he breathed just before his mouth plunged deeply into hers.

She tautened all over with heated pleasure. Her body arched against him, no longer protesting the sudden hardness of him against her. She reached up to hold him, to keep that tormenting, hungry mouth against her lips. It was every dream she'd ever dreamed, coming true. She could hardly believe it was happening here, in broad daylight, in the kitchen where she'd been trying so hard to learn to make things that would please him. But he seemed to be pleased, just the same. He groaned against her lips, and his arms were bruising now, as if he wasn't quite in control. That was exciting. She threw caution to the winds and opened her mouth deliberately under the crush of his, inviting him in.

She felt his tongue go deep into the soft darkness, and she shivered as his mouth devoured hers.

Only the sound of a door slamming penetrated the thick sensual fog that held them both in thrall.

Leo lifted his head, slowly, and looked down into a face he didn't recognize. Janie's green eyes were like wet emeralds in her flushed face. Her lips were swollen, soft, sensual. Her body was clinging to his. He had her off the floor in his hungry embrace, and his body was throbbing with desire.

He knew that she could feel him, that she knew he was

aroused. It was a secret thing, that only the two of them knew. It had to stay that way. He had to stop. This was wrong…!

He let go of her slowly, easing her back, while he sucked in a long, hard breath and shivered with a hunger he couldn't satisfy. He became aware of the rough grip he had on her upper arms and he relaxed it at once. He'd never meant to hurt her.

He fought for control, reciting multiplication tables silently in his mind until he felt his body unclench and relax.

It troubled him that he'd lost control so abruptly, and with a woman he should never have touched. He hadn't meant to touch her in the first place. He couldn't understand why he'd gone headfirst at her like that. He was usually cool with women, especially with Janie.

The way she was looking at him was disturbing. He was going to have a lot of explaining to do, and he didn't know how to begin. Janie was years too young for him, only his body didn't think so. Now he had to make his mind get himself out of this predicament.

"That shouldn't have happened," he said through his teeth.

She was hanging on every word, deaf to meanings, deaf to denials. Her body throbbed. "It's like the flu," she said, dazed, staring up at him. "It makes you…ache."

He shook her gently. "You're too young to have aches," he said flatly. "And I'm old enough to know better than to do something this stupid. Are you listening to me? This shouldn't have happened. I'm sorry."

Belatedly, she realized that he was backtracking. Of course he hadn't meant to kiss her. He'd made his opinion of her clear for years, and even if he liked kissing her, it didn't mean that he was ready to rush out and buy a ring. Quite the opposite.

She stepped away from him, her face still flushed, her eyes full of dreams she had to hide from him.

"I...I'm sorry, too," she stammered.

"Hell," he growled, ramming his hands into his pockets. "It was my fault. I started it."

She moved one shoulder. "No harm done." She cleared her throat and fought for inspiration. It came unexpectedly. Her eyes began to twinkle wickedly. "I have to take lessons when they're offered."

His eyebrows shot up. Had he heard her say that, or was he delusional?

"I'm not the prom queen," she pointed out. "Men aren't thick on the ground around here, except old bachelors who chew tobacco and don't bathe."

"I call that prejudice," he said, relaxing into humor.

"I'll bet you don't hang out with women who smell like dirty horses," she said.

He pursed his lips. Like hers, they were faintly swollen. "I don't know about that. The last time I saw you, I recall, you were neck-deep in mud and sh—"

"You can stop right there!" she interrupted, flushing.

His dark eyes studied her long hair, liking its thick waves and its light brown color. "Pity your name isn't Jeanie," he murmured. "Stephen Foster wrote a song about her hair."

She smiled. He liked her hair, at least. Maybe he liked her a little, too.

She was pretty when she smiled like that, he thought, observing her. "Do I get invited to supper?" he drawled, lost in that soft, hungry look she was giving him. "If you say yes, I might consider giving you a few more lessons. Beginner class only, of course," he added with a grin.

Chapter Two

Janie was sure she hadn't heard him say that, but he was still smiling. She smiled back. She felt pretty. No makeup, no shoes, disheveled—and Leo had kissed her anyway. She beamed. At least, she beamed until she remembered the Hart bread mania. Any of them would do anything for a biscuit. Did that extend to homemade rolls?

"You're looking suspicious," he pointed out.

"A man who would kidnap a poor little pastry chef might do anything for a homemade roll," she reminded him.

He sighed. "Hettie makes wonderful rolls," he had to admit.

"Oh, you!" She hit him gently and then laughed. He was impossible. "Okay, you can come to supper."

He beamed. "You're a nice girl."

Nice. Well, at least he liked her. It was a start. It didn't occur to her, then, that a man who was seriously interested in her wouldn't think of her as just "nice."

Hettie came back into the room, still oblivious to the undercurrents, and got out a plastic bowl. She filled it with English peas from the crisper. "All right, my girl, sit down here and shell these. You staying?" she asked Leo.

"She said I could," he told Hettie.

"Then you can go away while we get it cooked."

"I'll visit my bull. Fred's got him in the pasture."

Leo didn't say another word. But the look he gave Janie before he left the kitchen was positively wicked.

But if she thought the little interlude had made any permanent difference in her relationship with Leo, Janie was doomed to disappointment. He came to supper, but he spent the whole time talking genetic breeding with Fred, and although he was polite to Janie, she might as well have been on the moon.

He didn't stay long after supper, either, making his excuses and praising Hettie for her wonderful cooking. He smiled at Janie, but not the way he had when they were alone in the kitchen. It was as if he'd put the kisses out of his mind forever, and expected her to act as if he'd never touched her. It was disheartening. It was heartbreaking. It was just like old times, except that now Leo had kissed her and she wanted him to do it again. Judging by his attitude over supper, she had a better chance of landing a movie role.

She spent the next few weeks remembering Leo's hungry kisses and aching for more of them. When she wasn't daydreaming, she was practicing biscuit-making. Hettie muttered about the amount of flour she was going through.

"Janie, you're going to bankrupt us in the kitchen!" the older woman moaned when Janie's fifth batch of biscuits came out looking like skeet pigeons. "That's your second bag of flour today!"

Janie was glowering at her latest effort on the baking sheet. "Something's wrong, and I can't decide what. I mean, I put in salt and baking powder, just like the recipe said…"

Hettie picked up the empty flour bag and read the label. Her eyes twinkled. "Janie, darlin', you bought self-rising flour."

"Yes. So?" she asked obliviously.

"If it's self-rising, it already has the salt and baking powder in it, doesn't it?"

Janie burst out laughing. "So that's what I'm doing wrong! Hand me another bag of flour, could you?"

"This is the last one," Hettie said mournfully.

"No problem. I'll just drive to the store and get some more. Need anything?"

"Milk and eggs," Hettie said at once.

"We've got four chickens," Janie exclaimed, turning, "and you have to buy eggs?"

"The chickens are molting."

Janie smiled. "And when they molt, they don't lay. Sorry. I forgot. I'll be back in a jiffy," she added, peeling off her apron.

She paused just long enough to brush her hair out, leaving it long, and put on a little makeup. She thrust her arms into her nice fringed leather jacket, because it was seasonably cool outside as well as raining, and popped into her red sports car. You never could tell when you might run into Leo, because he frequently dashed into the supermarket for frozen biscuits and butter when he was between cooks.

Sure enough, as she started for the checkout counter with her milk, eggs and flour, she spotted Leo, head and shoulders above most of the men present. He was wearing that long brown Australian drover's coat he favored in wet weather, and he was smiling in a funny sort of way.

That was when Janie noticed his companion. He was bending down toward a pretty little brunette who was chattering away at his side. Janie frowned, because that dark wavy hair was familiar. And then she realized who it was. Leo was talking to Marilee Morgan!

She relaxed. Marilee was her friend. Surely, she was talking her up to Leo. She almost rushed forward to say hello, but what if she interrupted at a crucial moment? There was, after all, the annual Jacobsville Cattleman's Ball in two weeks, the Saturday before Thanksgiving. It was very likely that Marilee was dropping hints right and left that Janie would love Leo to escort her.

She chuckled to herself. She was lucky to have a friend like Marilee.

* * *

If Janie had known what Marilee was actually saying to Leo, she might have changed her mind about the other woman's friendship and a lot of other things.

"It was so nice of you to drive me to the store, Leo," Marilee was cooing at Leo as they walked out. "My wrist is really sore from that fall I took."

"No problem," he murmured with a smile.

"The Cattleman's Ball is week after next," Marilee added coyly. "I would really love to go, but nobody's asked me. I won't be able to drive by then, either, I'm sure. It was a bad sprain. They take almost as long as a broken bone to heal." She glanced up at him, weighing her chances. "Of course, Janie's told everybody that you're taking her. She said you're over there all the time now, that it's just a matter of time before you buy her a ring. Everybody knows."

He scowled fiercely. He'd only kissed Janie, he hadn't proposed marriage, for God's sake! Surely the girl wasn't going to get possessive because of a kiss? He hated gossip, especially about himself. Well, Janie could forget any invitations of that sort. He didn't like aggressive women who told lies around town. Not one bit!

"You can go with me," he told Marilee nonchalantly. "Despite what Janie told you, I am no woman's property, and I'm damned sure not booked for the dance!"

Marilee beamed. "Thanks, Leo!"

He shrugged. She was pretty and he liked her company. She wasn't one of those women who felt the need to constantly compete with men. He'd made his opinion about that pretty clear to Marilee in recent weeks. It occurred to him that Janie was suddenly trying to do just that, what with calf roping and ranch work and hard riding. Odd, when she'd never shown any such inclination before. But her self-assured talk about being his date for the ball set him off and stopped his mind from further reasoning about her sudden change of attitude.

He smiled down at Marilee. "Thanks for telling me about the gossip," he added. "Best way to curb it is to disprove it publicly."

"Of course it is. You mustn't blame Janie too much," she added with just the right amount of affection. "She's very young. Compared to me, I mean. If we hadn't been neighbors, we probably wouldn't be friends at all. She seems so…well, so juvenile at times, doesn't she?"

Leo frowned. He'd forgotten that Marilee was older than Janie. He thought back to those hard, hungry kisses he'd shared with Janie and could have cursed himself for his weakness. She was immature. She was building a whole affair on a kiss or two. Then he remembered something unexpectedly.

He glanced down at Marilee. "You said she had more boyfriends than anybody else in town."

Marilee cleared her throat. "Well, yes, *boy*friends. Not men friends, though," she added, covering her bases. It was hard to make Janie look juvenile if she was also a heartbreaking rounder.

Leo felt placated, God knew why. "There's a difference."

Marilee agreed. A tiny voice in her mind chided her for being so mean to her best friend, but Leo was a real hunk, and she was as infatuated with him as Janie was. All was fair in love and war, didn't they say? Besides, it was highly unlikely that Leo would ever ask Janie out—but, just in case, Marilee had planted a nice little suspicion in his mind to prevent that. She smiled as she walked beside him to his truck, dreaming of the first of many dances and being in Leo's arms. One day, she thought ecstatically, he might even want to marry her!

Janie went through two more bags of flour with attempts at biscuits that became better with each failed try. Finally, after several days' work, she had produced an edible batch that impressed even Hettie.

In between cooking, she was getting much better on horseback. Now, mounted on her black-and-white quarter horse, Blackie, she could cut out a calf and drive it into the makeshift corral used for doctoring sick animals. She could throw a calf, too, with something like professionalism, despite sore muscles and frequent bruises. She could rope, after a fashion, and she was riding better all the time. At least the chafing of her thighs against the saddle had stopped, and the muscles had acclimatized to the new stress being placed on them.

Saturday night loomed. It was only four days until the Cattleman's Ball, and she had a beautiful spaghetti-strapped lacy oyster-white dress to wear. It came to her ankles and was low-cut in front, leaving the creamy skin of her shoulders bare. There was a side-slit that went up her thigh, exposing her beautiful long legs. She paired the dress with white spiked high heels sporting ankle straps which she thought were extremely sexy, and she had a black velvet coat with a white silk lining to defend against the cold evening air. Now all she lacked was a date.

She'd expected Leo to ask her to the ball after those hungry kisses, despite his coolness later that day. But he hadn't been near the ranch since he'd had supper with her and her father. What made it even more peculiar was that he'd talked with her father out on the ranch several times. He just didn't come to the house. Janie assumed that he was regretting those hard kisses, and was afraid that she was taking him too seriously. He was avoiding her. He couldn't have made it plainer.

That made it a pretty good bet that he wasn't planning to take her to any Cattleman's Ball. She phoned Marilee in desperation.

The other woman sounded uneasy when she heard Janie's voice, and she was quick to ask why Janie had phoned.

"I saw you with Leo in the grocery store week before last," Janie began, "and I didn't interfere, because I was sure you were trying to talk him into taking me to the ball. But he didn't want to, did he?" she added sadly.

There was a sound like someone swallowing, on the other end of the phone. "Well, actually, no. I'm sorry." Marilee sounded as if she were strangling on the words.

"Don't feel bad," Janie said gently. "It's not your fault. You're my best friend in the whole world. I know you tried."

"Janie…"

"I had this beautiful white dress that I bought specially," Janie added on a sigh. "Well, that's that. Are you going?"

There was a tense pause. "Yes."

"Good! Anybody I know?"

"N…no," Marilee stammered.

"You have fun," Janie said.

"You…uh…aren't going, are you?" Marilee added.

Her friend certainly was acting funny, Janie thought. "No, I don't have a date," Janie chuckled. "There'll be other dances, I guess. Maybe Leo will ask me another time." After he's got over being afraid of me, she added silently. "If you see him," she said quickly, "you might mention that I can now cut out cattle and throw a calf. And I can make a biscuit that doesn't go through the floor when dropped!"

She was laughing, but Marilee didn't.

"I have to get to the hairdresser, Janie," Marilee said. "I'm really sorry…about the ball."

"Not your fault," Janie repeated. "Just have enough fun for both of us, okay?"

"Okay. See you."

The line went dead and Janie frowned. Something must be very wrong with Marilee. She wished she'd been more persistent and asked what was the matter. Well, she'd go over to Marilee's house after the dance to pump her for all the latest gossip, and then she could find out what was troubling her friend.

She put the ball to the back of her mind, despite the disappointment, and went out to greet her father as he rode in from the pasture with two of his men.

He swung out of the saddle at the barn and grinned at her. "Just the girl I wanted to see," he said at once. He pulled out his wallet. "I've got to have some more work gloves, just tore the last pair I had apart on barbed wire. How about going by the hardware store and get me another pair of those suede-palmed ones, extra large?"

"My pleasure," Janie said at once. Leo often went to the hardware store, and she might accidentally run into him there. "Be back in a jiffy!"

"Don't speed!" her father called to her.

She only chuckled, diving into her sports car. She remembered belatedly that she didn't have either purse or car keys, or her face fixed, and jumped right back out again to rectify those omissions.

Ten minutes later, she was parking her car in front of the Jacobsville Hardware Store. With a wildly beating heart, she noticed one of the black double-cabbed Hart Ranch trucks parked nearby. Leo! She was certain it was Leo!

With her heart pounding, she checked her makeup in the rearview mirror and tugged her hair gently away from her cheeks. She'd left it down today deliberately, remembering that Leo had something of a weakness for long hair. It was thick and clean, shining like a soft brown curtain. She was wearing a long beige skirt with riding boots, and a gold satin blouse. She looked pretty good, even if she did say so herself! Now if Leo would just notice her...

She walked into the hardware store with her breath catching in her throat as she anticipated Leo's big smile at her approach. He was the handsomest of the Hart brothers, and really, the most personable. He was kindness itself. She remembered his soft voice in her kitchen, asking what was wrong. Oh, to have that soft voice in her ear forever!

There was nobody at the counter. That wasn't unusual, the clerks were probably waiting on customers. She walked back to where the gloves were kept and suddenly heard Leo's deep voice on the other side of the high aisle, unseen.

"Don't forget to add that roll of hog wire to the order," he was telling one of the clerks.

"I won't forget," Joe Howland's pleasant voice replied. "Are you going to the Cattleman's Ball?" Joe added just as Janie was about to raise her voice and call to Leo over the aisle.

"I guess I am," Leo replied. "I didn't plan to, but a pretty friend needed a ride and I'm obliging."

Janie's heart skipped and fell flat. Leo already had a date? Who? She moved around the aisle and in sight of Leo and Joe. Leo had his back to her, but Joe noticed her and smiled.

"That friend wouldn't be Janie Brewster, by any chance?" Joe teased loudly.

The question made Leo unreasonably angry. "Listen, just because she caught the bouquet at Micah Steele's wedding is no reason to start linking her with me," he said shortly. "She may have a good family background, she may be easy on the eyes, she may even learn to cook someday—miracles still happen. But no matter what she does, or how well, she is never going to appeal to me as a woman!" he added. "Having her spreading ludicrous gossip about our relationship all over town isn't making her any more attractive to me, either. It's a dead turnoff!"

Janie felt a shock like an electric jolt go through her. She couldn't even move for the pain.

Joe, horrified, opened his mouth to speak.

Leo made a rough gesture with one lean hand, burning with pent-up anger. "She looks like the rough side of a corncob lately, anyway," Leo continued, warming to his subject. "The only thing she ever had going for her were her looks, and she's spent the last few weeks covered in mud or dust or bread flour. She's out all hours proving she can compete with any man on the place and she can't stop bragging about what a great catch she's made with me. She's already told half the town that I'm a kiss short of buying her an engagement ring. That is, when she isn't putting it around that I'm taking her to the Cattleman's Ball, when I haven't even damned well asked her! Well, she's got her eye on the wrong man. I don't want some half-baked kid with a figure like a boy and an ego the size of my boots! I wouldn't have Janie Brewster for a wife if she came complete with a stable of purebred Salers bulls, and that's saying something. She makes me sick to my stomach!"

Joe had gone pale and he was grimacing. Curious, Leo turned…and there was Janie Brewster, staring at him down the aisle with a face as tragic as if he'd just taken a whittling knife to her heart.

"Janie," he said slowly.

She took a deep, steadying breath and managed to drag her eyes away from his face. "Hi, Joe," she said with a wan little smile. Her voice sounded choked. She couldn't possibly look for gloves, she had to get away! "Just wanted to check and see if you'd gotten in that tack Dad ordered last week," she improvised.

"Not just yet, Janie," Joe told her in a gentle tone. "I'm real sorry."

"No problem. No problem at all. Thanks, Joe. Hello, Mr. Hart," she said, without really meeting Leo's eyes, and she even managed a smile through her tattered dignity. "Nice day out, isn't it? Looks like we might even get that rain we need so badly. See you."

She went out the door with her head high, as proudly as a conquering army, leaving Leo sick to his stomach for real.

"Why the hell didn't you say something?" Leo asked Joe furiously.

"Didn't know how," Joe replied miserably.

"How long had she been standing there?" Leo persisted.

"The whole time, Leo," came the dreaded reply. "She heard every word."

As if to punctuate the statement, from outside came the sudden raucous squeal of tires on pavement as Janie took off toward the highway in a burst of speed. She was driving her little sports car, and Leo's heart stopped as he realized how upset she was.

He jerked his cell phone out of his pocket and dialed the police department. "Is that Grier?" he said at once when the call was answered, recognizing Jacobsville's new assistant police chief's deep voice. "Listen, Janie Brewster just lit out of town like a scalded cat in her sports car. She's upset and it's my fault, but she could kill herself. Have you got somebody out on the Victoria road who could pull her over and give her a warning? Yeah. Thanks, Grier. I owe you one."

He hung up, cursing harshly under his breath. "She'll be spitting fire if anybody tells her I sent the police after her, but I can't let her get hurt."

"Thought she looked just a mite too calm when she walked out the door," Joe admitted. He glanced at Leo and grimaced. "No secret around town that she's been sweet on you for the past year or so."

"If she was, I've just cured her," Leo said, and felt his heart sink. "Call me when that order comes in, will you?"

"Sure thing."

Leo climbed into his truck and just sat there for a minute, getting his bearings. He could only imagine how Janie felt right now. What he'd said was cruel. He'd let his other irritations burst out as if Janie were to blame for them all. What Marilee had been telling him about Janie had finally bubbled over, that was all. She'd never done anything to hurt him before. Her only crime, if there was one, was thinking the moon rose and set on Leo Hart and taking too much for granted on the basis of one long kiss.

He laughed hollowly. Chances were good that she wouldn't be thinking it after this. Part of him couldn't help blaming her, because she'd gone around bragging about how he was going to marry her, and how lucky he was to have a girl like her in his life. Not to mention telling everybody he was taking her to the Cattleman's Ball.

But Janie had never been one to brag about her accomplishments, or chase men. The only time she'd tried to vamp Leo, in fact, had been in her own home, when her father was present. She'd never come on to him when they were alone, or away from her home. She'd been old-fashioned in her attitudes, probably due to the strict way she'd been raised. So why should she suddenly depart from a lifetime's habits and start spreading gossip about Leo all over Jacobsville? He remembered at least once when she'd stopped another woman from talking about a girl in trouble, adding that she hated gossip because it was like spreading poison.

He wiped his sweaty brow with the sleeve of his shirt and put his hat on the seat beside him. He hated what he'd said. Maybe he didn't want Janie to get any ideas about him in a serious way, but there would have been kinder methods of accomplishing it. He didn't think he was ever going to forget the look on her face when she heard what he was saying to Joe. It would haunt him forever.

Meanwhile, Janie was setting new speed records out on the Victoria Road. She'd already missed the turnoff that led back toward Jacobsville and her father's ranch. She was seething, hurting, miserable and confused. How could Leo think such things about her? She'd never told anybody how she felt about him, except Marilee, and she hadn't been spreading gossip. She hated gossip. Why did he know so little about her, when they'd known each other for years? What hurt the most was that he obviously believed those lies about her.

She wondered who could have told him such a thing. Her thoughts went at once to Marilee, but she chided herself for thinking ill of her only friend, her best friend. Certainly it had to be an enemy who'd been filling Leo's head full of lies. But…she didn't have any enemies that she knew of.

Tears were blurring her eyes. She knew she was going too fast. She should slow down before she wrecked the car or ran it into a fence. She was just thinking about that when she heard sirens and saw blue lights in her rearview mirror.

Great, she thought. Just what I need. I'm going to be arrested and I'll spend the night in the local jail….

She stopped and rolled down her window, trying unobtrusively to wipe away the tears while waiting for the uniformed officer to bend down and speak to her.

He came as a surprise. It wasn't a patrolman she knew, and she knew most of them by sight at least. This one had black eyes and thick black hair, which he wore in a ponytail. He had a no-nonsense look about him, and he was wearing a badge that denoted him as the assistant chief.

"Miss Brewster?" he asked quietly.

"Y…yes."

"I'm Cash Grier," he introduced himself. "I'm the new assistant police chief here."

"Nice to meet you," she said with a watery smile. "Sorry it has to be under these circumstances." She held out both wrists with a sigh. "Want to handcuff me?"

He pursed his lips and his black eyes twinkled unexpectedly. He didn't look like a man who knew what humor was. "Isn't that a little kinky for a conversation? What sort of men *are* you used to?"

She hesitated for just a second before she burst out laughing. He wasn't at all the man he appeared to be. She put her hands down.

"I was speeding," she reminded him.

"Yes, you were. But since you don't have a rap sheet, you can have a warning, just this once," he added firmly. "The speed limit is posted. It's fifty on all county roads."

She peered up at him. "This is a *county* road?" she emphasized, which meant that he was out of his enforcement area.

Nodding, he grinned. "And you're right, I don't have any jurisdiction out here, so that's why you're getting a warning and a smile." The smile faded. "In town, you'll get a ticket and a heavy scowl. Remember that."

"I will. Honest." She wiped at her eyes again. "I got a little upset, but I shouldn't have taken it out on the road. I'm sorry. I won't do it again."

"See that you don't." His dark eyes narrowed as if in memory. "Accidents are messy. Very messy."

"Thanks for being so nice."

He shrugged. "Everybody slips once in a while."

"That's exactly what I did…"

"I didn't mean you," he interrupted. His lean face took on a faintly dangerous cast. "I'm not nice. Not ever."

She was intimidated by that expression. "Oh."

He wagged a finger at her nose. "Don't speed."

She put a hand over her heart. "Never again. I promise."

He nodded, walked elegantly to his squad car and drove toward town. Janie sat quietly for a minute, getting herself back together. Then she started the car and went home, making up an apology for her father about his gloves without telling him the real reason she'd come home without them. He said he'd get a new pair the next day himself, no problem.

Janie cried herself to sleep in a miserable cocoon of shattered dreams.

As luck would have it, Harley Fowler, Cy Parks's foreman, came by in one of the ranch pickup trucks the very next morning and pulled up to the back door when he saw Janie walk out dressed for riding and wearing a broad-brimmed hat. Harley's boss Cy did business with Fred Brewster, and Harley was a frequent visitor to the ranch. He and Janie were friendly. They teased and played like two kids when they were together.

"I've been looking for you," Harley said with a grin as he paused just in front of her. "The Cattleman's Ball is Saturday night and I want to go, but I don't have a date. I know it's late to be asking, but how about going with me? Unless you've got a date or you're going with your dad…?" he added.

She grinned back. "I haven't got a date, and Dad's away on business and has to miss the ball this year. But I do have a pretty new dress that I'm dying to wear! I'd love to go with you, Harley!"

"Really?" His lean face lit up. He knew Janie was sweet on Leo Hart, but it was rumored that he was avoiding her like measles these days. Harley wasn't in love with Janie, but he genuinely liked her.

"Really," Janie replied. "What time will you pick me up?"

"About six-thirty," he said. "It doesn't start until seven, but I like to be on time."

"That makes two of us. I'll be ready. Thanks, Harley!"

"Thank you!" he said. "See you Saturday."

He was off in a cloud of dust, waving his hand out the window as he pulled out of the yard. Janie sighed with relief. She wanted nothing more in the world than to go to that dance and show Leo Hart how wrong he was about her chasing him. Harley was young and nice looking. She liked him. She would go and have a good time. Leo would be able to see for himself that he was off the endangered list, and he could make a safe bet that Janie would never go near him again without a weapon! As she considered it, she smiled coldly. Revenge was petty, but after the hurt she'd endured at Leo's hands, she felt entitled to a little of it. He was never going to forget this party. Never, as long as he lived.

Chapter Three

The annual Jacobsville Cattleman's Ball was one of the newer social events of the year. It took place the Saturday before Thanksgiving like clockwork. Every cattleman for miles around made it a point to attend, even if he avoided all other social events for the year. The Ballenger brothers, Calhoun and Justin, had just added another facility to their growing feedlot enterprise, and they looked prosperous with their wives in gala attire beside them. The Tremayne brothers, Connal, Evan, Harden, and Donald, and their wives were also in attendance, as were the Hart boys; well, Corrigan, Callaghan, Rey and Leo at least, and their wives. Simon and Tira didn't attend many local events except the brothers' annual Christmas party on the ranch.

Also at the ball were Micah Steele, Eb Scott, J. D. Langley, Emmett Deverell, Luke Craig, Guy Fenton, Ted Regan, Jobe Dodd, Tom Walker and their wives. The guest list read like a who's who of Jacobsville, and there were so many people that the organizers had rented the community center for it. There was a live country-western band, a buffet table that could have fed a platoon of starving men, and enough liquor to drown a herd of horses.

Leo had a highball. Since he hadn't done much drinking in recent years, his four brothers were giving him strange looks. He didn't notice. He was feeling so miserable that even a hangover would have been an improvement.

Beside him, Marilee was staring around the room with wide, wary eyes.

"Looking for somebody?" Leo asked absently.

"Yes," she replied. "Janie said she wasn't coming, but that isn't what your sister-in-law Tess just told me."

"What did she say?"

Marilee looked worried. "Harley Fowler told her he was bringing Janie."

"Harley?" Leo scowled. Harley Fowler was a courageous young man who'd actually backed up the town's infamous mercenaries—Eb Scott, Cy Parks and Micah Steele—when they helped law enforcement face down a gang of drug dealers the year before. Harley's name hadn't been coupled with any of the local belles, and he was only a working-class cowboy. Janie's father might be financially pressed at the moment, but his was a founding family of Jacobsville, and the family had plenty of prestige. Fred and his sister-in-law Lydia would be picky about who Janie married. Not, he thought firmly, that Janie was going to be marrying Harley....

"Harley's nice," Marilee murmured. "He's Cy Parks's head foreman now, and everybody says he's got what it takes to run a business of his own." What Marilee didn't add was that Harley had asked her out several times before his raid on the drug lord with the local mercenaries, and she'd turned him down flat. She'd thought he bragged and strutted a little too much, that he was too immature for her. She'd even told him so. It had made her a bitter enemy of his.

Now she was rather sorry that she hadn't given him a chance. He really was different these days, much more mature and very attractive. Not that Leo wasn't a dish. But she felt so guilty about Janie that she couldn't even enjoy his company, much less the party. If Janie showed up and saw her with Leo, she was going to know everything. It wasn't conducive to a happy evening at all.

"What's wrong?" Leo asked when he saw her expression.

"Janie's never going to get over it if she shows up and sees me with you," she replied honestly. "I didn't think how it would look…"

"I don't belong to anybody," Leo said angrily. "It's just as well to let Janie know that. So what if she does show up? Who cares?"

"I do," Marilee sighed.

Just as she spoke, Janie came in the door with a tall, good-looking, dark-haired man in a dark suit with a ruffled white shirt and black bow tie. Janie had just taken off her black velvet coat and hung it on the rack near the door. Under it, she was wearing a sexy white silk gown that fell softly down her slender figure to her shapely ankles. The spaghetti strips left her soft shoulders almost completely bare, and dipped low enough to draw any man's eyes. She was wearing her thick, light brown hair down. It reached almost to her waist in back in a beautiful, glossy display. She wore just enough makeup to enhance her face, and she was clinging to Harley's arm with obvious pleasure as they greeted the Ballengers and their wives.

Leo had forgotten how pretty Janie could look when she worked at it. Lately, he'd only seen her covered in mud and flour. Tonight, her figure drew eyes in that dress. He remembered the feel of her in his arms, the eager innocence of her mouth under his, and he suddenly felt uneasy at the way she was clinging to Harley's arm.

If he was uncomfortable, Marilee was even more so. She stood beside Leo and looked as if she hated herself. He took another long sip of his drink before he guided her toward Harley and Janie.

"No sense hiding, is there?" he asked belligerently.

Marilee sighed miserably. "No sense at all, I guess."

They moved forward together. Janie noticed them and her

eyes widened and darkened with pain for an instant. Leo's harsh monologue at the hardware store had been enough to wound her, but now she was seeing that she'd been shafted by her best friend, as well. Marilee said Janie didn't know her date, but all along, apparently, she'd planned to come with Leo. No wonder she'd been so curious about whether or not Janie was going to show up.

Everything suddenly made perfect sense. Marilee had filled Leo up with lies about Janie gossiping about him, so that she could get him herself. Janie felt like an utter fool. Her chin lifted, but she didn't smile. Her green eyes were like emerald shards as they met Marilee's.

"H…hi, Janie," Marilee stammered, forcing a smile. "You said you weren't coming tonight."

"I wasn't," Janie replied curtly. "But Harley was at a loose end and didn't have a date, so he asked me." She looked up at the tall, lean man beside her, who was some years younger than Leo, and she smiled at him with genuine affection even through her misery. "I haven't danced in years."

"You'll dance tonight, darlin'," Harley drawled, smiling warmly as he gripped her long fingers in his. He looked elegant in his dinner jacket, and there was a faint arrogance in his manner now that hadn't been apparent before. He glanced at Marilee and there was barely veiled contempt in the look.

Marilee swallowed hard and avoided his piercing gaze.

"I didn't know you could dance, Harley," Marilee murmured, embarrassed.

He actually ignored her, his narrow gaze going to Leo. "Nice turnout, isn't it?" he asked the older man.

"Nice," Leo said, but he didn't smile. "I haven't seen your boss tonight."

"The baby had a cold," Harley said. "He and Lisa don't leave him when he's sick." He looked down at Janie deliberately. "Considering how happy the two of them are, I guess marriage isn't such a bad vocation after all," he mused.

"For some, maybe," Leo said coldly. He was openly glaring at Harley.

"Let's get on the dance floor," Harley told Janie with a grin. "I'm anxious to try out that waltz pattern I've been learning."

"You'll excuse us, I'm sure," Janie told the woman who was supposed to be her best friend. Her eyes were icy as she realized how she'd been betrayed by Marilee's supposed "help" with Leo.

Marilee grimaced. "Oh, Janie," she groaned. "Let me explain...."

But Janie wasn't staying to listen to any halfhearted explanations. "Nice to see you, Marilee. You, too, Mr. Hart," she added with coldly formal emphasis, not quite meeting Leo's eyes. But she noted the quick firming of his chiseled lips with some satisfaction at the way she'd addressed him.

"Why do you call him Mr. Hart?" Harley asked as they moved away.

"He's much older than we are, Harley," she replied, just loudly enough for Leo to hear her and stiffen with irritation. "Almost another generation."

"I guess he is."

Leo took a big swallow of his drink and glared after them.

"She'll never speak to me again," Marilee said in a subdued tone.

He glared at her. "I'm not her personal property," he said flatly. "I never was. It isn't your fault that she's been gossiping and spreading lies all over town."

Marilee winced.

He turned his attention back to Janie, who was headed onto the dance floor with damned Harley. "I don't want her. What the hell do I care if she likes Harley?"

The music changed to a quick, throbbing Latin beat. Matt Caldwell and his wife, Leslie, were out on the dance floor already, making everybody else look like rank beginners. Everybody clapped to the rhythm until the very end, when the couple left the dance floor. Leo thought nobody could top that display until Harley walked to the bandleader, and the band suddenly broke into a Strauss waltz. That was when Harley and Janie took the floor. Then, even Matt and Leslie stood watching with admiration.

Leo stared at the couple as if he didn't recognize them. Involuntarily, he moved closer to the dance floor to watch. He'd never seen two people move like that to music besides Matt and Leslie.

The rhythm was sweet, and the music had a sweeping beauty that Janie mirrored with such grace that it was like watching ballet. Harley turned and Janie followed every nuance of movement, her steps matching his exactly. Her eyes were laughing, like her pretty mouth, as they whirled around the dance floor in perfect unison.

Harley was laughing, too, enjoying her skill as much as she enjoyed his. They looked breathless, happy—young.

Leo finished his drink, wishing he'd added more whiskey and less soda. His dark eyes narrowed as they followed the couple around the dance floor as they kept time to the music.

"Aren't they wonderful?" Marilee asked wistfully. "I don't guess you dance?"

He did. But he wasn't getting on that floor and making a fool of himself with Marilee, who had two left feet and the sense of rhythm of a possum.

"I don't dance much," Leo replied tersely.

She sighed. "It's just as well, I suppose. That would be a hard act to follow."

"Yes."

The music wound to a peak and suddenly ended, with

Janie draped down Harley's side like a bolt of satin. His mouth was almost touching hers, and Leo had to fight not to go onto the floor and throw a punch at the younger man.

He blinked, surprised by his unexpected reaction. Janie was nothing to him. Why should he care what she did? Hadn't she bragged to everyone that he was taking her to this very dance? Hadn't she made it sound as if they were involved?

Janie and Harley left the dance floor to furious, genuine applause. Even Matt Caldwell and Leslie congratulated them on the exquisite piece of dancing. Apparently, Harley had been taking lessons, but Janie seemed to be a natural.

But the evening was still young, as the Latin music started up again and another unexpected couple took the floor. It was Cash Grier, the new assistant police chief, with young Christabel Gaines in his arms. Only a few people knew that Christabel had been married to Texas Ranger Judd Dunn since she was sixteen—a marriage on paper, only, to keep herself and her invalid mother from losing their family ranch. But she was twenty-one now, and the marriage must have been annulled, because there she was with Cash Grier, like a blond flame in his arms as he spun her around to the throbbing rhythm and she matched her steps to his expert ones.

Unexpectedly, as the crowd clapped and kept time for them, handsome dark-eyed Judd Dunn himself turned up in evening dress with a spectacular redhead on his arm. Men's heads turned. The woman was a supermodel, internationally famous, who was involved at a film shoot out at Judd and Christabel's ranch. Gossip flew. Judd watched Christabel with Grier and glowered. The redhead said something to him, but he didn't appear to be listening. He watched the two dancers with a rigid posture and an expression more appropriate for a duel than a dance. Christabel ignored him.

"Who is that man with Christabel Gaines?" Marilee asked Leo.

"Cash Grier. He used to be a Texas Ranger some years ago. They say he was in government service as well."

Leo recalled that Grier had been working in San Antonio with the district attorney's office before he took the position of assistant police chief in Jacobsville. There was a lot of talk about Grier's mysterious past. The man was an enigma, and people walked wide around him in Jacobsville.

"He's dishy, isn't he? He dances a *paso doble* even better than Matt, imagine that!" Marilee said aloud. "Of course, Harley does a magnificent waltz. Who would ever have thought he'd turn out to be such a sexy, mature man…"

Leo turned on his heel and left Marilee standing by herself, stunned. He walked back to the drinks table with eyes that didn't really see. The dance floor had filled up again, this time with a slow dance. Harley was holding Janie far too close, and she was letting him. Leo remembered what he'd said about her in the hardware store, and her wounded expression, and he filled another glass with whiskey. This time he didn't add soda. He shouldn't have felt bad, of course. Janie shouldn't have been so possessive. She shouldn't have gossiped about him…

"Hi, Leo," his sister-in-law Tess said with a smile as she joined him, reaching for a clear soft drink.

"No booze, huh?" he asked with a grin, noting her choice.

"I don't want to set a bad example for my son," she teased, because she and Cag had a little boy now. "Actually, I can't hold liquor. But don't tell anybody," she added. "I'm the wife of a tough ex-Special Forces guy. I'm supposed to be a real hell-raiser."

He smiled genuinely. "You are," he teased. "A lesser woman could never have managed my big brother and an albino python all at once."

"Herman the python's living with his own mate these days," she reminded him with a grin, "and just between us, I don't really miss him!" She glanced toward her husband and sighed. "I'm one lucky woman."

"He's one lucky man." He took a sip of his drink and she frowned.

"Didn't you bring Marilee?" she asked.

He nodded. "Her wrist was still bothering her too much to drive, so I let her come with me. I've been chauffeuring her around ever since she sprained it."

Boy, men were dense, Tess was thinking. As if a woman couldn't drive with only one hand. She glanced past him at Marilee, who was standing by herself watching as a new rhythm began and Janie moved onto the floor with Harley Fowler. "I thought she was Janie's best friend," she mentioned absently. "You can never tell about people."

"What do you mean?"

She shrugged. "I overheard her telling someone that Janie had been spreading gossip about you and her all over town." She shook her head. "That's not true. Janie's so shy, it's hard for her to even talk to most men. I've never heard her gossip about anyone, even people she dislikes. I can't imagine why Marilee would tell lies about her."

"Janie told everybody I was bringing her to the ball," he insisted with a scowl.

"Marilee told people that Janie said that," Tess corrected. "You really don't know, do you? Marilee's crazy about you. She had to cut Janie out of the picture before she could get close to you. I guess she found the perfect way to do it."

Leo started to speak, but he hesitated. That couldn't be true.

Tess read his disbelief and just smiled. "You don't believe me, do you? It doesn't matter. You'll find out the truth sooner or later, whether you want to or not. I've got to find Cag. See you later!"

Leo watched her walk away with conflicting emotions. He

didn't want to believe——he *wouldn't* believe——that he'd been played for a sucker. He'd seen Janie trying to become a cattleman with his own eyes, trying to compete with him. He knew that she wanted him because she'd tried continually to tempt him when he went to visit her father. She flirted shamelessly with him. She'd melted in his arms, melted under the heat of his kisses. She hadn't made a single protest at the intimate way he'd held her. She felt possessive of him, and he couldn't really blame her, because it was his own lapse of self-control that had given her the idea that he wanted her. Maybe he did, physically, but Janie was a novice and he didn't seduce innocents. Her father was a business associate. It certainly wouldn't be good business to cut his own throat with Fred by making a casual lover of Janie.

He finished the whiskey and put the glass down. He felt light-headed. That was what came of drinking when he hadn't done it in a long time. This was stupid. He had to stop behaving like an idiot just because Fred Brewster's little girl had cut him dead in the receiving line and treated him like an old man. He forced himself to walk normally, but he almost tripped over Cag on the way.

His brother caught him by the shoulders. "Whoa, there," he said with a grin. "You're wobbling."

Leo pulled himself up. "That whiskey must be 200 proof," he said defensively.

"No. You're just not used to it. Leave your car here when it's time to go," he added firmly. "Tess and I will drop Marilee off and take you home. You're in no fit state to drive."

Leo sighed heavily. "I guess not. Stupid thing to do."

"What, drinking or helping Marilee stab Janie in the back?"

Leo's eyes narrowed on his older brother's lean, hard face. "Does Tess tell you everything?"

He shrugged. "We're married."

"If I ever get married," Leo told him, "my wife isn't going to tell anybody anything. She's going to keep her mouth shut."

"Not much danger of your getting married, with that attitude," Cag mused.

Leo squared his shoulders. "Marilee looks really great tonight," he pointed out.

"She looks pretty sick to me," Cag countered, eyeing the object of their conversation, who was standing alone against the opposite wall, trying to look invisible. "She should, too, after spreading that gossip around town about Janie chasing you."

"Janie did that, not Marilee," Leo said belligerently. "She didn't have any reason to make it sound like we were engaged, just because I kissed her."

Cag's eyebrows lifted. "You kissed her?"

"It wasn't much of a kiss," Leo muttered gruffly. "She's so green, it's pathetic!"

"She won't stay that way long around Harley," Cag chuckled. "He's no playboy, but women love him since he helped our local mercs take on that drug lord Manuel Lopez and won. I imagine he'll educate Janie."

Leo's dark eyes narrowed angrily. He hated the thought of Harley kissing her. He really should do something about that. He blinked, trying to focus his mind on the problem.

"Don't trip over the punch bowl," Cag cautioned dryly. "And for God's sake, don't try to dance. The gossips would have a field day for sure!"

"I could dance if I wanted to," Leo informed him.

Cag leaned down close to his brother's ear. "Don't 'want to.' Trust me." He turned and went back to Tess, smiling as he led her onto the dance floor.

Leo joined Marilee against the wall.

She glanced at him and grimaced. "I've just become the

Bubonic Plague," she said with a miserable sigh. "Joe How-land from the hardware store is here with his wife," she added uncomfortably. "He's telling people what you said to Janie and that I was responsible for her getting the rough side of your tongue."

He glanced down at her. "How is it your fault?"

She looked at her shoes instead of at him. She felt guilty and hurt and ashamed. "I sort of told Janie that you said you'd like her better if she could ride and rope and make biscuits, and stop dressing up all the time."

He stiffened. He felt the jolt all the way to his toes. "You told her that?"

"I did." She folded her arms over her breasts and stared toward Janie, who was dancing with Harley and apparently having a great time. "There's more," she added, steeling herself to admit it. "It wasn't exactly true that she was telling people you were taking her to this dance."

"Marilee, for God's sake! Why did you lie?" he demanded.

"She's just a kid, Leo," she murmured uneasily. "She doesn't know beans about men or real life, she's been protected and pampered, she's got money, she's pretty…." She moved restlessly. "I like you a lot. I'm older, more mature. I thought, if she was just out of the picture for a little bit, you…you might start to like me."

Now he understood the look on Janie's face when he'd made those accusations. Tess was right. Marilee had lied. She'd stabbed her best friend in the back, and he'd helped her do it. He felt terrible.

"You don't have to tell me what a rat I am," she continued, without looking up at him. "I must have been crazy to think Janie wouldn't eventually find out that I was lying about her." She managed to meet his angry eyes. "She never gossiped about you, Leo. She wanted you to take her to this party so much that it was all she talked about for weeks. But she never told anybody you were going to. She thought I was helping her by hinting that she'd like you to ask her." She laughed coldly. "She was the best friend I ever had, and I've stabbed her in the back. She'll never speak to me again after tonight, and I deserve whatever I get. For what it's worth, I'm really sorry."

Leo was still trying to adjust to the truth. He could talk himself blue in the face, but Janie would never listen to him now. He was going to be about as welcome as a fly at her house from now on, especially if Fred found out what Leo had said to and about her. It would damage their friendship. It had already killed whatever feeling Janie had for him. He knew that without the wounded, angry glances she sent his way from time to time.

"You said you didn't want her chasing you," Marilee reminded him weakly, trying to find one good thing to say.

"No danger of that from now on, is there?" he agreed, biting off the words.

"None at all. So a little good came out of it."

He looked down at her with barely contained anger. "How could you do that to her?"

"I don't even know." She sighed raggedly. "I must have been temporarily out of my mind." She moved away from the wall. "I wonder if you'd mind driving me home? I…I really don't want to stay any longer."

"I can't drive. Cag's taking us home."

"You can't drive? Why?" she exclaimed.

"I think the polite way of saying it is that I'm stinking drunk," he said with glittery eyes blazing down at her.

She grimaced. No need to ask why he'd gotten that way. "Sorry," she said inadequately.

"You're sorry. I'm sorry. It doesn't change anything." He looked toward Janie, conscious of new and painful regrets. It all made sense now, her self-improvement campaign. She'd been dragged through mud, thrown from horses, bruised and battered in a valiant effort to become what she thought Leo wanted her to be.

He winced. "She could have killed herself," he said huskily. "She hadn't been on a horse in ages or worked around cattle." He looked down at Marilee with a black scowl. "Didn't you realize that?"

"I wasn't thinking at the time," Marilee replied. "I've always worked around the ranch, because I had to. I never thought of Janie being in any danger. But I guess she was, at that. At least she didn't get hurt."

"That's what you think," Leo muttered, remembering how she'd looked at the hardware store.

Marilee shrugged and suddenly burst into tears. She dashed toward the ladies' room to hide them.

At the same time, Harley left Janie at the buffet table and went toward the rest rooms himself.

Leo didn't even think. He walked straight up to Janie and caught her by the hand, pulling her along with him.

"What do you think you're doing?" she raged. "Let go of me!"

He ignored her. He led her right out the side door and onto the stone patio surrounded by towering plants that, in spring, were glorious in blossom. He pulled the glass door closed behind him and moved Janie off behind one of the plants.

"I want to talk to you," he began, trying to get his muddled mind to work.

She pulled against his hands. "I don't want to talk to you!" she snapped. "You go right back in there to your date, Leo Hart! You brought Marilee, not me!"

"I want to tell you…" he tried again.

She aimed a kick at his shin that almost connected.

He sidestepped, overbalancing her so that she fell heavily against him. She felt good in his arms, warm, delicate and sweetly scented. His breath caught at the feel of her soft skin under his hands where the dress was low-cut in back.

"Harley will…be missing me!" she choked.

"Damn Harley," he murmured huskily and the words went into her mouth as he bent and took it hungrily.

His arms swallowed her, warm under the dark evening suit, where her hands rested just at his rib cage. His mouth was ardent, insistent, on her parted lips.

He forced them apart, nipping the upper one with his teeth while his hands explored the softness of her skin. He was getting drunk on her perfume. He felt himself going taut as he registered the hunger he was feeling to get her even closer. It wasn't enough….

His hands went to her hips and jerked them hard into the thrust of his big body, so that she could feel how aroused he was.

She stiffened and then tried to twist away, frantic at the weakness he was making her feel. He couldn't do this. She couldn't let him do it. He was only making a point, showing her that she couldn't resist him. He didn't even like her anymore. He'd brought her best friend to the most talked-about event in town!

"You…let me go!" she sobbed, tearing her mouth from his. "I hate you, Leo Hart!"

He was barely able to breathe, much less think, but he wasn't letting go. His eyes glittered down at her. "You don't hate me," he denied. "You want me. You tremble every time I get within a foot of you. It's so noticeable a blind man couldn't mistake it." He pulled her close, watching her face as her thighs touched his. "A woman's passion arouses a man's," he whispered roughly. "You made me want you."

"You said I made you sick," she replied, her voice choking on the word.

"You do." His lips touched her ear. "When a man is this

aroused, and can't satisfy the hunger, it makes him sick," he said huskily, with faint insolence. He dragged her hips against his roughly. "Feel that? You've got me so hot I can't even think…!" Leo broke off abruptly as Janie stomped on his foot.

"Does that help?" she asked while he was hobbling on the foot her spiked heel hadn't gone into.

She moved back from him, shaking with desire and anger, while he cursed roundly and without inhibition.

"That's what you get for making nasty remarks to women!" she said furiously. "You don't want me! You said so! You want Marilee. That's why you're taking her around with you. Remember me? I'm that gossiping pest who runs after you everywhere. Except that I'll never do it again, you can bet your life on that! I wouldn't have you on ice cream!"

He stood uneasily on both feet, glaring at her. "Sure you would," he said with a venomous smile. His eyes glittered like a diamondback uncoiling. "Just now, I could have had you in the rosebushes. You'd have done anything I wanted."

He was right. That was what hurt the most. She pushed back her disheveled hair with a trembling hand. "Not anymore," she said, feeling sick. "Not when I know what you really think of me."

"Harley brought you," he said coldly. "He's a boy playing at being a man."

"He's closer to my age than you are, Mr. Hart!" she shot back.

His face hardened and he took a quick step toward her.

"That's what you've said from the start," she reminded him, near tears. "I'm just a kid, you said. I'm just a kid with a crush, just your business associate's pesky daughter."

He'd said that. He must have been out of his mind. Looking at her now, with that painful maturity in her face, he couldn't believe he'd said any such thing. She was all woman. And she was with Harley. Damn Harley!

"Don't worry, I won't tell Dad that you tried to seduce me on the patio with your new girlfriend standing right inside the room," she assured him. "But if you ever touch me again, I'll cripple you, so help me God!"

She whirled and jerked open the patio door, slamming it behind her as she moved through the crowd toward the buffet table.

Leo stood alone in the cold darkness with a sore foot, wondering why he hadn't kept his mouth shut. If a bad situation could get worse, it just had.

Chapter Four

Janie and Harley were back on the dance floor by the time Leo made his way inside, favoring his sore foot.

Marilee was standing at the buffet table, looking as miserable as he felt.

"Harley just gave me hell," she murmured tightly as he joined her. "He said I was lower than a snake's belly, and it would serve me right if Janie never spoke to me again." She looked up at him with red-rimmed eyes. "Do you think your brother would mind dropping us off now? He could come right back…"

"I'll ask him," Leo said, sounding absolutely fed up.

He found Cag talking to Corrigan and Rey at the buffet table. Their wives were in another circle, talking to each other.

"Could you run Marilee home now and drop me off on the way back?" he asked Cag in a subdued tone.

Corrigan gaped at him. "You've never left a dance until the band packed up."

Leo sighed. "There's a first time for everything."

The women joined them. Cag tugged Tess close. "I have to run Leo and Marilee home."

Tess's eyebrows went up. "Now? Why so early?"

Leo glared. His brothers cleared their throats.

"Never mind," Cag said quickly. "I won't be a minute…"

"Rey and I would be glad to do it…" Meredith volunteered, with a nod from her husband.

"No need," Dorie said with a smile, cuddling close to her husband. "Corrigan can run Leo and Marilee home and come right back. Can't you, sweetheart?" she added.

"Sure I can," he agreed, lost in her pretty eyes.

"But you two don't usually leave until the band does, either," Leo pointed out. "You'll miss most of the rest of the dance if you drive us."

Corrigan pursed his lips. "Oh, we've done our dancing for the night. Haven't we, sweetheart?" he prompted.

Dorie's eyes twinkled. She nodded. "Indeed we have! I'll just catch up on talk until he comes back. We can have the last dance together. Don't give it a thought, Leo."

Leo was feeling the liquor more with every passing minute, but he was feeling all sorts of undercurrents. The women looked positively gleeful. His brothers were exchanging strange looks.

Corrigan looked past Leo to Cag and Rey. "You can all come by our house after the dance," he promised.

"What for?" Leo wanted to know, frowning suspiciously.

Corrigan hesitated and Cag scowled.

Rey cleared his throat. "Bull problems," he said finally, with a straight face. "Corrigan's advising me."

"He's advising me, too," Cag said with a grin. "He's advising both of us."

All three of them looked guilty as hell. "I know more about bulls than Corrigan does," Leo pointed out. "Why don't you ask me?"

"Because you're in a hurry to go home," Corrigan improvised. "Let's go."

Leo went to get Marilee. She said a subdued, hurried goodbye to Cag and Rey and then their wives. Leo waited patiently, vaguely aware that Cag and Rey were standing apart, talking in hushed whispers. They were both staring at Leo.

As Marilee joined him, Leo began to get the idea. Corrigan had sacrificed dancing so that he could pump Leo for gossip and report back to the others. They knew he was drinking, which he never did, and they'd probably seen him hobble back into the room. Then he'd wanted to leave early. It didn't take a mind reader to put all that together. Something had happened, and his brothers—not to mention their wives—couldn't wait to find out what. He glared at Corrigan, but his brother only grinned.

"Let's go, Marilee," Leo said, catching her by the arm.

She gave one last, hopeful glance at Janie, but was pointedly ignored. She followed along with Leo until the music muted to a whisper behind them.

When Marilee had been dropped off, and they were alone in the car, Corrigan glanced toward his brother with mischievous silvery eyes and pursed his lips.

"You're limping."

Leo huffed. "You try walking normally when some crazy woman's tried to put her heel through your damned boot!"

"Marilee stepped on you?" Corrigan said much too carelessly.

"Janie stepped on me, on purpose!"

"What were you doing to her at the time?"

Leo actually flushed. It was visible in the streetlight they stopped under waiting for a red light to change on the highway.

"Well!" Corrigan exclaimed with a knowing expression.

"She started it," he defended himself angrily. "All these months, she's been dressing to the hilt and waylaying me every time I went to see her father. She damned near seduced me on the cooking table in her kitchen last month, and then she goes and gets on her high horse because I said a few little things I shouldn't have when she was eavesdropping!"

"You said a lot of little things," his brother corrected.

"And from what I hear, she left town in a dangerous rush and had to be slowed down by our new assistant chief. In fact, you called and asked him to do it. Good thinking."

"Who told you that?" Leo demanded.

Corrigan grinned. "Our new assistant chief."

"Grier can keep his nose out of my business or I'll punch it for him!"

"He's got problems of his own, or didn't you notice him step outside with Judd Dunn just before we left?" Corrigan whistled softly. "Christabel may think she's her own woman, but Judd doesn't act like any disinterested husband I ever saw."

"He's got a world famous model on his arm," Leo pointed out.

"It didn't make a speck of difference once he saw Christabel on that dance floor with Grier. He was ready to make a scene right there." He glanced at Leo. "And *he* wasn't drinking," he emphasized.

"I am not jealous of Janie Brewster," Leo told him firmly.

"Tell that to Harley. He had to be persuaded not to go after you when Janie came back inside in tears," Corrigan added, letting slip what he'd overheard.

That made it worse. "Harley can mind his own damned business, too!"

"He is. He likes Janie."

"Janie's not going to fall for some wet-behind-the-ears would-be world-saver," Leo raged.

"He's kind to her. He teases her and picks at her. He treats her like a princess." He gave his brother a wry glance. "I'll bet he wouldn't try to seduce her in the rosebushes."

"I didn't! Anyway, there weren't any damned rosebushes out there."

"How do you know that?"

Leo sighed heavily. "Because if there had been, I'd be wearing them."

Corrigan chuckled. Having had his own problems with the course of true love, he could sympathize with his brother. Sadly, Leo had never been in love. He'd had crushes, he'd had brief liaisons, but there had never been a woman who could stand him on his ear. Corrigan was as fascinated as their brothers with the sudden turn of events. Leo had tolerated Janie Brewster, been amused by her, but he'd never been involved enough to start a fight with her, much less sink two large whiskeys when he hardly even touched beer.

"She's got a temper, fancy that?" Corrigan drawled.

Leo sighed. "Marilee was telling lies," he murmured. "She said Janie had started all sorts of gossip about us. I'd kissed her, and liked it, and I was feeling trapped. I thought the kiss gave her ideas. And all the time... Damn!" he ground out. "Tess knew. She told me that Marilee had made up the stories, and I wouldn't listen."

"Tess is sharp as a tack," his older brother remarked.

"I'm as dull as a used nail," Leo replied. "I don't even know when a woman is chasing me. I thought Janie was. And all the time, it was her best friend Marilee." He shook his head. "Janie said I was the most conceited man she ever met. Maybe I am." He glanced out the window at the silhouettes of buildings they passed in the dark. "She likes Harley. That would have been funny a few months ago, but he keeps impressive company these days."

"Harley's matured. Janie has, too. I thought she handled herself with dignity tonight, when she saw you with Marilee." He chuckled. "Tira would have emptied the punch bowl over her head," he mused, remembering his redheaded sister-in-law's temper.

"Simon would have been outraged," he added. "He hates scenes. You're a lot like him," he said unexpectedly, glancing at the younger man. "You can cut up, but you're as somber as a judge when you're not around us. Especially since we've all married."

"I'm lonely," Leo said simply. "I've had the house to myself since Rey married Meredith and moved out, almost a year ago. Mrs. Lewis retired. I've got no biscuits, no company…"

"You've got Marilee," he was reminded.

"Marilee sprained her wrist. She's needed me to drive her places," Leo said drowsily.

"Marilee could drive with one hand. I drove with a broken arm once."

Leo didn't respond. They were driving up to the main ranch house, into the driveway that made a semicircle around the front steps. The security lights were on, so was the porch light. But even with lights on in the front rooms of the sprawling brick house, it looked empty.

"You could come and stay with any of us, whenever you wanted to," Corrigan reminded him. "We only live a few miles apart."

"You've all got families. Children. Well, except Meredith and Rey."

"They're not in a hurry. Rey's the youngest. The rest of us are feeling our ages a bit more."

"Hell," Leo growled, "you're only two years older than me."

"You're thirty-five," he was reminded. "I'll be thirty-eight in a couple of months."

"You don't look it."

"Dorie and the babies keep me young," Corrigan admitted with a warm smile. "Marriage isn't as bad as you think it is. You have someone to cook for you, a companion to share your sorrows when the world hits you in the head, and your triumphs when you punch back. Not to mention having a warm bed at night."

Leo opened the door but hesitated. "I don't want to get married."

Corrigan's pale eyes narrowed. "Dorie was just a little younger than Janie when I said the same thing to her. I mistook her for an experienced woman, made a very heavy pass, and then said some insulting things to her when she pulled back at the last minute. I sent her running for the nearest bus, and my pride stopped me from carrying her right back off it again. She went away. It was eight long years before she came home, before I was able to start over with her." His face hardened. "You know what those years were like for me."

Leo did. It was painful even to recall them. "You never told me why she left."

Corrigan rested his arm over the steering wheel. "She left because I behaved like an idiot." He glanced at his brother. "I don't give a damn what Marilee's told you about Janie, she isn't any more experienced than Dorie was. Don't follow in my footsteps."

Leo wouldn't meet the older man's eyes. "Janie's a kid."

"She'll grow up. She's making a nice start, already."

Leo brushed back his thick, unruly hair. "I was way out of line with her tonight. She said she never wanted to see me again."

"Give her time."

"I don't care if she doesn't want to see me," Leo said belligerently. "What the hell do I want with a mud-covered little tomboy, anyway? She can't even cook!"

"Neither can Tira," Corrigan pointed out. "But she's a knockout in an evening gown. So is our Janie, even if she isn't as pretty as Marilee."

Leo shrugged. "Marilee's lost a good friend."

"She has. Janie won't ever trust her again, even if she can forgive her someday."

Leo glanced back at his older brother. "Isn't it amazing how easy it is to screw up your whole life in a few unguarded minutes?"

"That's life, *compadre*. I've got to go. You going to be okay?"

Leo nodded. "Thanks for the ride." He glowered at Corrigan. "I guess you're in a hurry to get back, right?"

Corrigan's eyes twinkled. "I don't want to miss the last dance!"

Or the chance to tell his brothers everything that had happened. But, what the hell, they were family.

"Drive safely," Leo told Corrigan as he closed the car door.

"I always do." Corrigan threw up his hand and drove away.

Leo disarmed the alarm system and unlocked the front door, pausing to relock it and rearm the system. He'd been the victim of a mugging last October in Houston, and it had been Rey's new wife, Meredith, who had saved him from no worse than a concussion. But now he knew what it was to be a victim of violent crime, and he was much more cautious than he'd ever been before.

He tossed his keys on his chest of drawers and took off his jacket and shoes. Before he could manage the rest, he passed out on his own bed.

Janie Brewster was very quiet on the way home. Harley understood why. He and Janie weren't an item, but he hated seeing a woman cry. He'd wanted, very badly, to punch Leo Hart for that.

"You should have let me hit him, Janie," he remarked thoughtfully.

She gave him a sad little smile. "There's been enough gossip already, although I appreciate the thought."

"He was drinking pretty heavily," Harley added. "I noticed that one of his brothers took him and Marilee home early. Nice of him to find a designated driver, in that condition. He looked as if he was barely able to walk without staggering."

Janie had seen them leave, with mixed emotions. She turned her small evening bag in her lap. "I didn't know he drank hard liquor at all."

"He doesn't," Harley replied. "Eb Scott said that he'd never known Leo to take anything harder than a beer in company." He glanced at her. "That must have been some mixer you had with him."

"He'd been drinking before we argued," she replied. She looked out the darkened window. "Odd that Marilee left with him."

"You didn't see the women snub her, I guess," he murmured. "Served her right, I thought." His eyes narrowed angrily as he made the turn that led to her father's ranch. "It's low to stab a friend in the back like that. Whatever her feelings for Hart, she should have put your feelings first."

"I thought you liked her, Harley."

He stiffened. "I asked her out once, and she laughed."

"What?"

He stared straight ahead at the road, the center of which was lit by the powerful headlights of the truck he was driving. "She thought it was hilarious that I had the nerve to ask her to go on a date. She said I was too immature."

Ouch, she thought. A man like Harley would have too much pride to ever go near a woman who'd dented his ego that badly.

He let out a breath. "The hell of it is, she was right," he conceded with a wry smile. "I had my head in the clouds, bragging about my mercenary training. Then I went up against Lopez with Eb and Cy and Micah." He grimaced. "I didn't have a clue."

"We heard that it was a firefight."

He nodded. His eyes were haunted. "My only experience of combat was movies and television." His lean hands gripped the wheel hard. "The real thing is less…comfortable. And that's all I'll say."

"Thank you for taking me to the ball," she said, changing the subject because he'd looked so tormented.

His face relaxing, he glanced at her. "It was my pleasure. I'm not ready to settle down, but I like you. Anytime you're at a loose end, we can see a movie or get a burger."

She chuckled. "I feel the same way. Thanks."

He pursed his lips and gave her a teasing glance. "We could even go dancing."

"I liked waltzing."

"I want to learn those Latin dances, like Caldwell and Grier." He whistled. "Imagine Grier doing Latin dances! Even Caldwell stood back and stared."

"Mr. Grier is a conundrum," she murmured. "Not the man he seems, on the surface."

"How would you know?" he asked.

She cleared her throat. "He stopped me for speeding out on the Victoria road."

"Good for him. You drive too fast."

"Don't you start!"

He frowned. "What was he doing out there? He doesn't have jurisdiction outside Jacobsville."

"I don't know. But he's very pleasant."

He hesitated. "There's some, shall we say, unsavory gossip about him around town," he told her.

"Unsavory, how?" she asked, curious.

"It's probably just talk."

"Harley!"

He slowed for a turn. "They say he was a government assassin at one point in his life."

She whistled softly. "You're kidding!"

He glanced at her. "When I was in the Rangers, I flew overseas with a guy who was dressed all in black, armed to the teeth. He didn't say a word to the rest of us. I learned later that he was brought over for a very select assignment with the British commandos."

"What has that got to do with Grier?"

"That's just the thing. I think it *was* Grier."

She felt cold chills running up her arms.

"It was several years ago," he reiterated, "and I didn't get a close look, but sometimes you can tell a man just by the way he walks, the way he carries himself."

"You shouldn't tell anybody," she murmured, uneasy, because she liked Grier.

"I never would," Harley assured her. "I told my boss, but nobody else. Grier isn't the sort of man you'd ever gossip about, even if half the things they tell are true."

"There's more?" she exclaimed.

He chuckled. "He was in the Middle East helping pinpoint the laser-guided bombs, he broke up a spy ring in Manhattan as a company agent, he fought with the freedom fighters in Afghanistan, he foiled an assassination attempt against one of our own leaders under the nose of the agency assigned to protect them…you name it, he's done it. Including a stint with the Texas Rangers and a long career in law enforcement between overseas work."

"A very interesting man," she mused.

"And intimidating to our local law enforcement guys. Interesting that Judd Dunn isn't afraid of him."

"He's protective of Christabel," Janie told him. "She's sweet. She was in my high school graduating class."

"Judd's too old for her," Harley drawled. "He's about Leo Hart's age, isn't he, and she's just a few months older than you."

He was insinuating that Leo was too old for her. He was probably right, but it hurt to hear someone say it. Nor was she going to admit something else she knew about Christabel, that Judd had married the girl when she was just sixteen so that she wouldn't lose her home. Christabel was twenty-one and Judd had become her worst enemy.

"Sorry," Harley said when he noticed her brooding expression.

"About what?" she asked, diverted.

"I guess you think I meant Leo Hart's too old for you."

"He is," she said flatly.

He looked as if he meant to say more, but the sad expression on her face stopped him. He pulled into her driveway and didn't say another word until he stopped the truck at her front door.

"I know how you feel about the guy, Janie," he said then. "But you can want something too much. Hart isn't a marrying man, even if his brothers were. He's a bad risk."

She turned to face him, her eyes wide and eloquent. "I've told myself that a hundred times. Maybe it will sink in."

He grimaced. He traced a pattern on her cheek with a lean forefinger. "For what it's worth, I'm no stranger to unreturned feelings." He grimaced. "Maybe some of us just don't have the knack for romance."

"Speak for yourself," she said haughtily. "I have the makings of a Don Juanette, as Leo Hart is about to discover!"

He tapped her cheek gently. "Stop that. Running wild won't change anything, except to make you more miserable than you are."

She drew in a long breath. "You're right, of course. Oh, Harley, why can't we make people love us back?"

"Wish I knew," he said. He leaned forward and kissed her lightly on the lips. "I had fun. I'm sorry you didn't."

She smiled. "I did have fun. At least I didn't end up at the ball by myself, or with Dad, to face Leo and Marilee."

He nodded, understanding. "Where is your dad?"

"Denver," she replied on a sigh. "He's trying to interest a combine in investing in the ranch, but you can't tell anybody."

He scowled. "I didn't realize things were that bad."

She nodded. "They're pretty bad. Losing his prize bull was a huge financial blow. If Leo hadn't loaned him that breeding bull, I don't know what we'd have done. At least he likes Dad," she added softly.

It was Harley's opinion that he liked Fred Brewster's daughter, too, or he wouldn't have been putting away whiskey like that tonight. But he didn't say it.

"Can I help?" he asked instead.

She smiled at him. "You're so sweet, Harley. Thanks. But there's not much we can do without a huge grubstake. So," she added heavily, "I'm going to give up school and get a job."

"Janie!"

"College is expensive," she said simply. "Dad can't really afford it right now, and I'm not going to ask him to try. There's a job going at Shea's…"

"You can't work at Shea's!" Harley exclaimed. "Janie, it's a roadhouse! They serve liquor, and most nights there's a fight."

"They serve pizza and sandwiches, as well, and that's what the job entails," she replied. "I can handle it."

It disturbed Harley to think of an innocent, sweet girl like Janie in that environment. "There are openings at fast-food joints in town," he said.

"You don't get good tips at fast-food joints. Stop while you're ahead, Harley, you won't change my mind," she said gently.

"If you take the job, I'll stop in and check on you from time to time," he promised.

"You're a sweetheart, Harley," she said, and meant it. She kissed him on the cheek, smiled, and got out of the cab. "Thanks for taking me to the ball!"

"No sweat, Cinderella," he said with a grin. "I enjoyed it, too. Good night!"

"Good night," she called back.

She went inside slowly, locking the door behind her. Her steps dragging, she felt ten years older. It had been a real bust of an evening all around. She thought about Leo Hart and she hoped he had the king of hangovers the next morning!

The next day, Janie approached the manager of Shea's, a nice, personable man named Jed Duncan, about the job.

He read over her résumé while she sat in a leather chair across from his desk and bit her fingernails.

"Two years of college," he mused. "Impressive." His dark eyes met hers over the pages. "And you want to work in a bar?"

"Let me level with you," she said earnestly. "We're in financial trouble. My father can't afford to send me back to school, and I won't stand by and let him sink without trying to help. This job doesn't pay much, but the tips are great, from what Debbie Connor told me."

Debbie was her predecessor, and had told her about the job in the first place. Be honest with Jed, she'd advised, and lay it on the line about money. So Janie did.

He nodded slowly, studying her. "The tips are great," he agreed. "But the customers can get rowdy. Forgive me for being blunt, Miss Brewster, but you've had a sheltered upbringing. I have to keep a bouncer here now, ever since Calhoun Ballenger had it out with a customer over his ward—now his wife—and busted up the place. Not that Calhoun wasn't in the right," he added quickly. "But it became obvious that hot tempers and liquor don't mix, and you can't run a roadhouse on good intentions."

She swallowed. "I can get used to anything, Mr. Duncan. I would really like this job."

"Can you cook?"

She grinned. "Two months ago, I couldn't. But I can now. I can even make biscuits!"

He chuckled. "Okay, then, you should be able to make a pizza. We'll agree that you can work for two weeks and we'll see how it goes. You'll waitress and do some cooking. If you can cope, I'll let you stay. If not, or if you don't like the work, we'll call it quits. That suit you?"

She nodded. "It suits me very well. Thank you!"

"Does your father know about this?" he added.

She flushed. "He will, when he gets home from Denver. I don't hide things from him."

"It's not likely that you'll be able to hide this job from him," he mused with a chuckle. "A lot of our patrons do business with him. I wouldn't like to make more enemies than I already have."

"He won't mind," she assured him with a smile. She crossed her fingers silently.

"Then come along and I'll acquaint you with the job," Jed said, moving around the desk. "Welcome aboard, Miss Brewster."

She smiled. "Thanks!"

Chapter Five

Fred Brewster came home from Denver discouraged. "I couldn't get anybody interested," he told Janie as he flopped down in his favorite easy chair in the living room. "Everybody's got money problems, and the market is down. It's a bad time to fish for partners."

Janie sat down on the sofa across from him. "I got a job."

He just stared at her for a minute, as if he didn't hear her. "You what?"

"I got a job," she said, and smiled at him. "I'll make good money in tips. I start tonight."

"Where?" he asked.

"A restaurant," she lied. "You can even come and eat there, and I'll serve you. You won't have to tip me, either!"

"Janie," he groaned. "I wanted you to go back and finish your degree."

She leaned forward. "Dad, let's be honest. You can't afford college right now, and if I went, it would have to be on work-study. Let me do this," she implored. "I'm young and strong and I don't mind working. You'll pull out of this, Dad, I know you will!" she added gently. "Everybody has bad times. This is ours."

He scowled. "It hurts my pride…"

She knelt at his feet and leaned her arms over his thin, bony knees. "You're my dad," she said. "I love you. Your problems are my problems. You'll come up with an angle that will get us out of this. I don't have a single doubt."

Those beautiful eyes that were so like his late wife's weakened his resolve. He smiled and touched her hair gently. "You're like your mother."

"Thanks!"

He chuckled. "Okay. Do your waitress bit for a few weeks and I'll double my efforts on getting us out of hock. But no late hours," he emphasized. "I want you home by midnight, period."

That might be a problem. But why bother him with complications right now?

"We'll see how it goes," she said easily, getting to her feet. She planted a kiss on his forehead. "I'd better get you some lunch!"

She dashed into the kitchen before he could ask any more questions about her new employment.

But she wasn't so lucky with Hettie. "I don't like the idea of you working in a bar," she told Janie firmly.

"*Shhhh!*" Janie cautioned, glancing toward the open kitchen door. "Don't let Dad hear you!"

Hettie grimaced. "Child, you'll end up in a brawl, sure as God made little green apples!"

"I will not. I'm going to waitress and make pizzas and sandwiches, not get in fights."

Hettie wasn't convinced. "Put men and liquor together, and you get a fight every time."

"Mr. Duncan has a bouncer," she confided. "I'll be fine."

"Mr. Hart won't like it," she replied.

"Nothing I do is any of Leo Hart's business anymore," Janie said with a glare. "After the things he's said about me, his opinion wouldn't get him a cup of coffee around here!"

"What sort of things?" Hettie wanted to know.

She rubbed her hands over the sudden chill of her arms. "That I'm a lying, gossiping, man-chaser who can't leave him alone," she said miserably. "He was talking about me to

Joe Howland in the hardware store last week. I heard every horrible word."

Hettie winced. She knew how Janie felt about the last of the unmarried Hart brothers. "Oh, baby. I'm so sorry!"

"Marilee lied," she added sadly. "My best friend! She was telling me what to do to make Leo notice me, and all the time she was finding ways to cut me out of his life. She was actually at the ball with Leo. He took her..." She swallowed hard and turned to the task at hand. Brooding was not going to help her situation. "Want a sandwich, Hettie?"

"No, darlin', I'm fine," the older woman told her. She hugged Janie warmly. "Life's tangles work themselves out if you just give them enough time," she said, and went away to let that bit of homespun philosophy sink in.

Janie was unconvinced. Her tangles were bad ones. Maybe her new job would keep Leo out of her thoughts. At least she'd never have to worry about running into him at Shea's, she told herself. After Saturday night, he was probably off hard liquor for life.

By Saturday night, Janie had four days of work under her belt and she was getting used to the routine. Shea's opened at lunchtime and closed at eleven. Shea's served pizza and sandwiches and chips, as well as any sort of liquor a customer could ask for. Janie often had to serve drinks in between cooking chores. She got to recognize some of the customers on sight, but she didn't make a habit of speaking to them. She didn't want any trouble.

Her father had, inevitably, found out about her nocturnal activities. Saturday morning, he'd been raging at her for lying to him.

"I do work in a restaurant," she'd defended herself. "It's just sort of in a bar."

"You work in a bar, period!" he returned, furious. "I want you to quit, right now!"

It was now or never, she told herself, as she faced him bravely. "No," she replied quietly. "I'm not giving notice. Mr. Duncan said I could work two weeks and see if I could handle it, and that's just what I'm going to do. And don't you dare talk to him behind my back, Dad," she told him.

He looked tormented. "Girl, this isn't necessary!"

"It is, and not only because we need the money," she'd replied. "I need to feel independent."

He hadn't considered that angle. She was determined, and Duncan did have a good bouncer, a huge man called, predictably, Tiny. "We'll see," he'd said finally.

Janie had won her first adult argument with her parent. She felt good about it.

Harley showed up two of her five nights on the job, just to check things out. He was back again tonight. She grinned at him as she served him pizza and beer.

"How's it going?" he asked.

She looked around at the bare wood floors, the no-frills surroundings, the simple wooden tables and chairs and the long counter at which most of the customers—male customers—sat. There were two game machines and a jukebox. There were ceiling fans to circulate the heat, and to cool the place in summer. There was a huge dance floor, where people could dance to live music on Friday and Saturday night. The band was playing now, lazy Western tunes, and a couple was circling the dance floor alone.

"I really like it here," she told Harley with a smile. "I feel as if I'm standing on my own two feet for the first time in my life." She leaned closer. "And the tips are really nice!"

He chuckled. "Okay. No more arguments from me." He glanced toward Tiny, a huge man with tattoos on both arms and a bald head, who'd taken an immediate liking to Janie. He was reassuringly close whenever she spoke to customers or served food and drinks.

"Isn't he a doll?" Janie asked, smiling toward Tiny, who smiled back a little hesitantly, as if he were afraid his face might crack.

"That's not a question you should ask a man, Janie," he teased.

Grinning, she flipped her bar cloth at him, and went back to work.

Leo went looking for Fred Brewster after lunch on Monday. He'd been out of town at a convention, and he'd lost touch with his friend.

Fred was in his study, balancing figures that didn't want to be balanced. He looked up as Hettie showed Leo in.

"Hello, stranger," Fred said with a grin. "Sit down. Want some coffee? Hettie, how about…!"

"No need to shout, Mr. Fred, it's already dripping," she interrupted him with a chuckle. "I'll bring it in when it's done."

"Cake, too!" he called.

There was a grumble.

"She thinks I eat too many sweets," Fred told Leo. "Maybe I do. How was the convention?"

"It was pretty good," Leo told him. "There's a lot of talk about beef exports to Japan and improved labeling of beef to show country of origin. Some discussion of artificial additives," he confided with a chuckle. "You can guess where that came from."

"J. D. Langley and the Tremayne brothers."

"Got it in one guess." Leo tossed his white Stetson into a nearby chair and sat down in the one beside it. He ran a hand through his thick gold-streaked brown hair and his dark eyes pinned Fred. "But aside from the convention, I've heard some rumors that bother me," he said, feeling his way.

"Oh?" Fred put aside his keyboard mouse and sat back. He'd heard about Janie's job, he thought, groaning inwardly. He drew in a long breath. "What rumors?" he asked innocently.

Leo leaned forward, his crossed arms on his knees. "That you're looking for partners here."

"Oh. That." Fred cleared his throat and looked past Leo. "Just a few little setbacks…"

"Why didn't you come to me?" Leo persisted, scowling. "I'd loan you anything you needed on the strength of your signature. You know that."

Fred swallowed. "I do…know that. But I wouldn't dare. Under the circumstances." He avoided Leo's piercing stare.

"What circumstances?" Leo asked with resignation, when he realized that he was going to have to pry every scrap of information out of his friend.

"Janie."

Leo's breath expelled in a rush. He'd wondered if Fred knew about the friction between the two of them. It was apparent that he did. "I see."

Fred glanced at him and winced. "She won't hear your name mentioned," he said apologetically. "I couldn't go to you behind her back, and she'd find out anyway, sooner or later. Jacobsville is a small town."

"She wouldn't be likely to find out when she's away at college," Leo assured him. "She has gone back, hasn't she?"

There was going to be an explosion. Fred knew it without saying a word. "Uh, Leo, she hasn't gone back, exactly."

His eyebrows lifted. "She's not here. I asked Hettie. She flushed and almost dragged me in here without saying anything except Janie wasn't around. I assumed she'd gone back to school."

"No. She's, uh, got a job, Leo. A good job," he added, trying to reassure himself. "She likes it very much."

"Doing what, for God's sake?" Leo demanded. "She has no skills to speak of!"

"She's cooking. At a restaurant."

Leo felt his forehead. "No fever," he murmured to himself. It was a well-known fact that Janie could burn water in a pan. He pinned Fred with his eyes. "Would you like to repeat that?"

"She's cooking. She can cook," he added belligerently at Leo's frank astonishment. "Hettie spent two months with her in the kitchen. She can even make…" he started to say "biscuits" and thought better of it "…pizza."

Leo whistled softly. "Fred, I didn't know things were that bad. I'm sorry."

"The bull dying was nobody's fault," Fred said heavily. "But I used money I hoped to recoup to buy him, and there was no insurance. Very few small ranchers could take a loss like that and remain standing. He was a champion's offspring."

"I know that. I'd help, if you'd let me," Leo said earnestly.

"I appreciate it. But I can't."

There was a long, pregnant pause. "Janie told you about what happened at the ball, I suppose," Leo added curtly.

"No. She hasn't said a single word about that," Fred replied. He frowned. "Why?" He understood, belatedly, Leo's concerned stare. "She did tell me about what happened in the hardware store," he added slowly. "There's more?"

Leo glanced away. "There was some unpleasantness at the ball, as well. We had a major fight." He studied his big hands. "I've made some serious mistakes lately. I believed some gossip about Janie that I should never have credited. I know better now, but it's too late. She won't let me close enough to apologize."

That was news. "When did you see her?" Fred asked, playing for time.

"In town at the bank Friday," he said. "She snubbed me." He smiled faintly. It had actually hurt when she'd given him a harsh glare, followed by complete oblivion to his presence. "First time that's happened to me in my life."

"Janie isn't usually rude," Fred tried to justify her behavior. "Maybe it's just the new job…"

"It's what I said to her, Fred," the younger man replied heavily. "I really hurt her. Looking back, I don't know why I ever believed what I was told."

Fred was reading between the lines. "Marilee can be very convincing, Janie said. And she had a case on you."

"It wasn't mutual," Leo said surprisingly. "I didn't realize what was going on. Then she told me all these things Janie was telling people…" He stopped and cursed harshly. "I thought I could see through lies. I guess I'm more naive than I thought I was."

"Any man can be taken in," Fred reassured him. "It was just bad luck. Janie never said a word about you in public. She's shy, although you might not realize it. She'd never throw herself at a man. Well, not for real," he amended with a faint smile. "She did dress up and flirt with you. She told Hettie it was the hardest thing she'd ever done in her life, and she agonized over it for days afterward. Not the mark of a sophisticated woman, is it?"

Leo understood then how far he'd fallen. No wonder she'd been so upset when she overheard him running down her aggressive behavior. "No," he replied. "I wish I'd seen through it." He smiled wryly. "I don't like aggressive, sophisticated women," he confessed. "Call it a fatal flaw. I liked Janie the way she was."

"Harmless?" Fred mused.

Leo flushed. "I wouldn't say that."

"Wouldn't you?" Fred leaned back in his chair, smiling at the younger man's confusion. "I've sheltered Janie too much. I wanted her to have a smooth, easy path through life. But I did her no favors. She's not a dress-up doll, Leo, she's a woman. She needs to learn independence, self-sufficiency. She has a temper, and she's learning to use that, too. Last week, she stood up to me for the first time and told me what she was going to do." He chuckled. "I must confess, it was pretty shocking to realize that my daughter was a woman."

"She's going around with Harley," Leo said curtly.

"Why shouldn't she? Harley's a good man—young, but steady and dependable. He, uh, did go up against armed men and held his own, you know."

Leo did know. It made him furious to know. He didn't hang out with professional soldiers. He'd been in the service, and briefly in combat, but he'd never fought drug dealers and been written up in newspapers as a local hero.

Fred deduced all that from the look on Leo's lean face. "It's not like you think," he added. "She and Harley are friends. Just friends."

"Do I care?" came the impassioned reply. He grabbed up his Stetson and got to his feet. He hesitated, turning back to Fred. "I won't insist, but Janie would never have to know if I took an interest in the ranch," he added firmly.

Fred was tempted. He sighed and stood up, too. "I've worked double shifts for years, trying to keep it solvent. I've survived bad markets, drought, unseasonable cold. But this is the worst it's ever been. I could lose the property so easily."

"Then don't take the risk," Leo insisted. "I can loan you what it takes to get you back in the black. And I promise you, Janie will never know. It will be between the two of us. Don't lose the ranch out of pride, Fred. It's been in your family for generations."

Fred grimaced. "Leo…"

The younger man leaned both hands on the desk and impaled Fred with dark eyes. "Let me help!"

Fred studied the determination, the genuine concern in

that piercing stare. "It would have to be a secret," he said, weakening.

Leo's eyes softened. "It will be. You have my word. Blake Kemp's our family attorney. I'll make an appointment. We can sit down with him and work out the details."

Fred had to bite down hard on his lower lip to keep the brightness in his eyes in check. "You can't possibly know how much..." He choked.

Leo held up a hand, embarrassed by his friend's emotion. "I'm filthy rich," he said curtly. "What good is money if you can't use it to help out friends? You'd do the same for me in a heartbeat if our positions were reversed."

Fred swallowed noticeably. "That goes without saying." He drew in a shaky breath. "Thanks," he bit off.

"You're welcome." Leo slanted his hat across his eyes. "I'll phone you. By the way, which restaurant is Janie working at?" he added. "I might stop by for lunch one day."

"That wouldn't be a good idea just yet," Fred said, feeling guilty because Leo still didn't know what was going on.

Leo considered that. "You could be right," he had to agree. "I'll let it ride for a few days, then. Until she cools down a little, at least." He grinned. "She's got a hell of a temper, Fred. Who'd have guessed?"

Fred chuckled. "She's full of surprises lately."

"That she is. I'll be in touch."

Leo was gone and Fred let the emotion out. He hadn't realized how much his family ranch meant to him until he was faced with the horrible prospect of losing it. Now, it would pass to Janie and her family, her children. God bless Leo Hart for being a friend when he needed one so desperately. He grabbed at a tissue and wiped his eyes. Life was good. Life was very good!

Fred was still up when Janie got home from work. She was tired. It had been a long night. She stopped in the kitchen to say good-night to Hettie before she joined her father in his study.

"Hettie said Leo came by," she said without her usual greeting. She looked worried. "Why?"

"He wanted to check on his bull," he lied without meeting her eyes.

She hesitated. "Did he…ask about me?"

"Yes," he said. "I told him you had a job working in a restaurant."

She stared at her feet. "Did you tell him which one?"

He looked anxious. "No."

She met his eyes. "You don't have to worry, Dad. It's none of Leo Hart's business where I work, or whatever else I do."

"You're still angry," he noted. "I understand. But he wants to make peace."

She swallowed, hearing all over again his voice taunting her, baiting her. She clenched both hands at her sides. "He wants to bury the hatchet? Good. I know exactly where to bury it."

"Now, daughter, he's not a bad man."

"Of course he's not. He just doesn't like me," she bit off. "You can't blame him, not when he's got Marilee."

He winced. "I didn't think. You lost your only friend."

"Some friend," she scoffed. "She's gone to spend the holidays in Colorado," she added smugly. "A rushed trip, I heard."

"I imagine she's too ashamed to walk down the main street right now," her father replied. "People have been talking about her, and that's no lie. But she's not really a bad woman, Janie. She just made a mistake. People do."

"You don't," she said unexpectedly, and smiled at him. "You're the only person in the world who wouldn't stab me in the back."

He flushed. Guilt overwhelmed him. What would she say

when she knew that he was going to let Leo Hart buy into the ranch, and behind her back? It was for a good cause, so that she could eventually inherit her birthright, but he felt suddenly like a traitor. He could only imagine how she'd look at him if she ever found out....

"Why are you brooding?" she teased. "You need to put away those books and go to bed."

He stared at the columns that wouldn't balance and thought about having enough money to fix fences, repair the barn, buy extra feed for the winter, buy replacement heifers, afford medicine for his sick cattle and veterinarian's fees. The temptation was just too much for him. He couldn't let the ranch go to strangers.

"Do you ever think about down the road," Fred murmured, "when your children grow up and take over the ranch?"

She blinked. "Well, yes, sometimes," she confessed. "It's a wonderful legacy," she added with a soft smile. "We go back such a long way in Jacobsville. It was one of your great-uncles who was the first foreman of the Jacobs ranch properties when the founder of our town came here and bought cattle, after the Civil War. This ranch was really an offshoot of that one," she added. "There's so much history here!"

Fred swallowed. "Too much to let the ranch go down the tube, or end up in the hands of strangers, like the Jacobs place did." He shook his head. "That was sad, to see Shelby and Ty thrown off their own property. That ranch had been in their family over a hundred years."

"It wasn't much of a ranch anymore," she reminded him. "More of a horse farm. But I understand what you mean. I'm glad we'll have the ranch to hand down to our descendants." She gave him a long look. "You aren't thinking of giving it up without a fight?"

"Heavens, no!"

She relaxed. "Sorry. But the way you were talking..."

"I'd do almost anything to keep it in the family," Fred assured her. "You, uh, wouldn't have a problem with me taking on a partner or an investor?"

"Of course not," she assured him. "So you found someone in Colorado after all?" she added excitedly. "Somebody who's willing to back us?"

"Yes," he lied, "but I didn't hear until today."

"That's just great!" she exclaimed.

He gave her a narrow look. "I'm glad you think so. Then you can give up that job and go back to college…"

"No."

His eyebrows went up. "But, Janie…"

"Dad, even with an investor, we still have the day-to-day operation of the ranch to maintain," she reminded him gently. "How about groceries? Utilities? How about cattle feed and horse feed and salt blocks and fencing?"

He sighed. "You're right, of course. I'll need the investment for the big things."

"I like my job," she added. "I really do."

"It's a bad place on the weekends," he worried.

"Tiny likes me," she assured him. "And Harley comes in at least two or three times a week, mostly on Fridays and Saturdays, to make sure I'm doing all right. I feel as safe at Shea's as I do right here with you."

"It's not that I mind you working," he said, trying to explain.

"I know that. You're just worried that I might get in over my head. Tiny doesn't let anybody have too much to drink before he makes them leave. Mr. Duncan is emphatic about not having drunks on the place."

Fred sighed. "I know when I'm licked. I may show up for pizza one Saturday night, though."

She grinned. "You'd be welcome! I could show you off to my customers."

"Leo wanted to know where you were working," he said abruptly. "He wanted to come by and see you."

Her face tautened. "I don't want to see him."

"So I heard. He was, uh, pretty vocal about the way you snubbed him."

She tossed back her hair. "He deserved it. I'm nobody's doormat. He isn't going to walk all over me and get away with it!"

"He won't like you working at Shea's, no matter what you think."

"Why do you care?" she asked suspiciously.

He couldn't tell her that Leo might renege on the loan if he knew Fred was letting her work in such a dive. He felt guilty as sin for not coming clean. But he was so afraid of losing the ranch. It was Janie's inheritance. He had to do everything he could to keep it solvent.

"He's my friend," he said finally.

"I used to think he was mine, too," she replied. "But friends don't talk about each other the way he was talking about me. As if I'd ever gossip about him!"

"I think he knows that now, Janie."

She forced the anger to the back of her mind. "I guess if he knew what I was doing, he'd faint. He doesn't think I can cook at all."

"I did tell him you had a cooking job," he confided.

Her eyes lit up. "You did? What did he say?"

"He was…surprised."

"He was astonished," she translated.

"It bothered him that you snubbed him. He said he felt really bad about the things he said, that you overheard. He, uh, told me about the fight you had at the ball, too."

Her face colored. "What did he tell you?"

"That you'd had a bad argument. Seemed to tickle him that you had a temper," he added with a chuckle.

"He'll find out I have a temper if he comes near me again."
She turned. "I'm going to bed, Dad. You sleep good."

"You, too, sweetheart. Good night."

He watched her walk away with a silent sigh of relief. So far, he thought, so good.

Chapter Six

The following Wednesday, Leo met with Blake Kemp and Fred Brewster in Kemp's office, to draw up the instrument of partnership.

"I'll never be able to thank you enough for this, Leo," Fred said as they finished a rough draft of the agreement.

"You'd have done it for me," Leo said simply. "How long will it take until those papers are ready to sign?" he asked Kemp.

"We'll have them by Monday," Kemp assured him.

"I'll make an appointment with your receptionist on the way out," Leo said, rising. "Thanks, Blake."

The attorney shook his outstretched hand, and then Fred's. "All in a day's work. I wish most of my business was concluded this easily, and amiably," he added wryly.

Leo checked his watch. "Why don't we go out to Shea's and have a beer and some pizza, Fred?" he asked the other man, who, curiously, seemed paler.

Fred was scrambling for a reason that Leo couldn't go to Shea's. "Well, because, uh, because Hettie made chili!" he remembered suddenly. "So why don't you come home and eat with me? We've got Mexican corn bread to go with it!"

Leo hesitated. "That does sound pretty good," he had to admit. Then he remembered. Janie would be there. He was uncomfortable with the idea of rushing in on her unexpectedly, especially in light of recent circumstances. He was still a little embarrassed about his own behavior. He searched for a reason to refuse, and found one. "Oh, for Pete's sake, I almost forgot!" he added, slapping his forehead. "I'm supposed to have supper with Cag and Tess tonight. We're going in together on two new Santa Gertrudis bulls. How could I have forgotten…got to run, Fred, or I'll never make it on time!"

"Sure, of course," Fred said, and looked relieved. "Have a good time!"

Leo chuckled. "I get to play with my nephew. That's fun, all right. I like kids."

"You never seemed the type," Fred had to admit.

"I'm not talking about having any of my own right away," Leo assured him. "I don't want to get married. But I like all my nephews, not to mention my niece."

Fred only smiled.

"Thanks for the offer of supper, anyway," he told the older man with a smile. "Sorry I can't come."

Fred relaxed. "That's okay, Leo. More for me," he teased. "Well, I'll go home and have my chili. Thanks again. If I can ever do anything for you, anything at all, you only have to ask."

Leo smiled. "I know that, Fred. See you."

They parted in the parking lot. Leo got in his double-cabbed pickup and gunned the engine.

Fred got into his own truck and relaxed. At least, he thought, he didn't have to face Leo's indignation today. With luck, Leo might never realize what was going on.

Leo, honest to the core, phoned Cag and caged an invitation to supper to discuss the two new bulls the brothers were buying. But he had some time before he was due at his brother's house. He brooded over Fred's dead bull, and Christabel's, and he began to wonder. He had a bull from that same lot, a new lineage of Salers bulls that came from a Victoria breeder. Two related bulls dying in a month's time seemed just a bit too much for coincidence. He picked up the phone and called information.

Cag and Tess were still like newlyweds, Leo noted as he carried their toddler around the living room after supper, grinning from ear to ear as the little boy, barely a year old, smiled up at him and tried to grab his nose. They sat close together on the sofa and seemed to radiate love. They were watching him with equal interest.

"You do that like a natural," Cag teased.

Leo shifted the little boy. "Lots of practice," he chuckled. "Simon's two boys, then Corrigan's boy and their new girl, and now your son." He lifted an eyebrow. "Rey and Meredith are finally expecting, too, I hear."

"They are," Cag said with a sigh. He eyed his brother mischievously. "When are you planning to throw in the towel and join up?"

"Me? Never," Leo said confidently. "I've got a big house to myself, all the women I can attract, no responsibilities and plenty of little kids to spoil as they grow." He gave them an innocent glance. "Why should I want to tie myself down?"

"Just a thought," Cag replied. "You'll soon get tired of going all the way to town every morning for a fresh biscuit." Cag handed the baby back to Tess.

"I'm thinking of taking a cooking course," Leo remarked. Cag roared.

"I could cook if I wanted to!" Leo said indignantly.

Tess didn't speak, but her eyes did.

Leo stuffed his hands in his pockets. "Well, I don't really want to," he conceded. "And it is a long way to town. But I can manage." He sprawled in an easy chair. "There's something I want to talk to you about—besides our new bulls."

"What?" Cag asked, sensing concern.

"Fred's big Salers bull that died mysteriously," Leo said. "Christabel and Judd Dunn lost one, too, a young bull."

"Judd says it died of bloat."

"I saw the carcass, he didn't. He thinks Christabel made it up, God knows why. He wouldn't even come down from Victoria to take a look at it. It wasn't bloat. But she didn't call a vet out, and they didn't find any marks on Fred's bull." He sighed. "Cag, I've done a little checking. The bulls are related. The young herd sire of these bulls died recently as well, and the only champion Salers bull left that's still walking is our two-year-old bull that I loaned to Fred, although it's not related to the dead ones."

Cag sat up straight, scowling. "You're kidding."

Leo shook his head. "It's suspicious, isn't it?"

"You might talk to Jack Handley in Victoria, the rancher we bought our bull from."

"I did." He leaned forward intently. "Handley said he fired two men earlier this year for stealing from him. They're brothers, John and Jack Clark. One of them is a thief, the other has a reputation for vengeance that boggles the mind. When one former employer fired Jack Clark, he lost his prize bull and all four young bulls he'd got from it. No apparent cause of death. Handley checked and found a pattern of theft and retribution with those brothers going back two years. At least four employers reported similar problems with theft and firing. There's a pattern of bull deaths, too. The brothers were suspects in a recent case in Victoria, but there was never enough evidence to convict anyone. Until now, I don't imagine anyone's connected the dots."

"How the hell do they keep getting away with it?" Cag wanted to know.

"There's no proof. And they're brawlers," Leo said. "They intimidate people."

"They wouldn't intimidate us," Cag remarked.

"They wouldn't. But do you see the common thread here? Handley crossed the brothers. He had a new, expensive Salers bull that he bred to some heifers, and he sold all the young bulls this year, except for his seed bull. His seed bull, and all its offspring, which isn't many, have died. Christabel Gaines's young bull was one of Handley's, like Fred's. And Jack Clark was fired by Judd Dunn for stealing, too."

Cag was scowling. "Where are the brothers now?"

"I asked Handley. He says John Clark is working on a ranch near Victoria. We know that Jack, the one with a reputation for getting even, is right here in Jacobsville, driving a cattle truck for Duke Wright," Leo said. "I called Wright and told him what I know. He's going to keep an eye on the man. I called Judd Dunn, too, but he was too preoccupied to listen. He's smitten with that redheaded supermodel who's in the movie they're making on Christabel's ranch—Tippy Moore, the 'Georgia Firefly.'"

"He'll land hard, if I make my guess," Cag said. "She's playing. He isn't."

"He's married, too," Leo said curtly. "Something he doesn't seem to remember."

"He only married Christabel because she was going to lose the ranch after her father beat her nearly to death in a drunken rage. Her mother was an invalid. No way could the two of them have kept it solvent," Cag added. "That's not a real marriage. I'm sure he's already looked into annulling it when she turns twenty-one."

"She was twenty-one this month," Leo said. "Poor kid. She's got a real case on him, and she's fairly plain except for those soulful brown eyes and a nice figure. She couldn't compete with the Georgia Firefly."

"So ask yourself what does a supermodel worth millions want with a little bitty Texas Ranger?" Cag grinned.

Tess gave him a speaking look. "As a happily married woman, I can tell you that if I wasn't hung up on you, Judd Dunn would make my mouth water."

Cag whistled.

Leo shrugged. "Whatever. But I think we should keep a close eye on our Salers bull, as well as Wright's new cattle-truck driver. Handley says Clark likes to drink, so it wouldn't hurt to keep an eye out at Shea's, as well."

Cag frowned thoughtfully. "You might have a word with Janie…"

"Janie?"

"Janie Brewster," his brother said impatiently. "Tell her what the man looks like and have her watch him if he ever shows up out there."

Leo stared at his brother. "Will you make sense? Why would Janie be at Shea's roadhouse in the first place?"

Realization dawned. Cag looked stunned, and then uncomfortable.

Tess grimaced. "He doesn't know. I guess you'd better tell him."

"Tell me what?" Leo grumbled.

"Well, it's like this," Cag said. "Janie's been working at Shea's for a couple of weeks…"

"She's working in a bar?" Leo exploded violently.

Cag winced. "Now, Leo, she's a grown woman," he began calmly.

"She's barely twenty-one!" he continued, unabashed. "She's got no business working around drunks! What the hell is Fred thinking, to let her get a job in a place like that?"

Cag sighed. "Talk is that Fred's in the hole and can hardly make ends meet," he told Leo. "I guess Janie insisted on helping out."

Leo got to his feet and grabbed up his white Stetson, his lips in a thin line, his dark eyes sparking.

"Don't go over there and start trouble," Cag warned. "Don't embarrass the girl with her boss!"

Leo didn't answer him. He kept walking. His footsteps, quick and hard, described the temper he was in. He even slammed the door on the way out, without realizing he had.

Cag looked at Tess worriedly as Leo's car careened down the driveway. "Should I warn her?" he asked Tess.

She nodded. "At least she'll be prepared."

Cag thought privately that it was unlikely that anybody could prepare for Leo in a temper, but he picked up the phone just the same.

Shea's wasn't crowded when Leo jerked to a stop in the parking lot. He walked into the roadhouse with blood in his eye. Three men at a table near the door stopped talking when they saw him enter. Apparently they thought he looked dangerous.

Janie was thinking the same thing. She'd assured Cag that she wasn't afraid of Leo, but it was a little different when the man was walking toward her with his eyes narrow and his lips compressed like that.

He stopped at the counter. He noted her long apron, her hands with a dusting of flour, a pencil behind her ear. She looked busy. There were three cowboys at the counter drinking beers and apparently waiting for pizzas. A teenage boy was pulling a pizza on a long paddle out of a big oven behind her.

"Get your things," he told Janie in a tone he hadn't used with her since she was ten and had gotten into a truck with a cowboy who offered her a trip to the visiting carnival. He'd busted up that cowboy pretty bad, and for reasons Janie only learned later. She'd had a very close call. Leo had saved her. But she didn't need saving right now.

She lifted her chin and glared at him. The night of the ball came back to her vividly. "How's your foot?" she asked with sarcasm.

"My foot is fine. Get your things," he repeated curtly.

"I work here."

"Not anymore."

She crossed her arms. "You planning to carry me out kicking and screaming? Because that's the only way I'm leaving."

"Suits me." He started around the counter.

She picked up a pitcher of beer and dumped the contents on him. "Now you listen to me…Leo!"

The beer didn't even slow him down. He had her up in his arms and he turned, carrying her toward the door. She was kicking and screaming for all she was worth.

That attracted Tiny, the bouncer. He was usually on the job by six, but he'd arrived late today. To give him credit, the minute he saw Janie, he turned and went toward the big man bullying her.

He stepped in front of Leo. "Put her down, Leo," he drawled.

"You tell him, Tiny!" Janie sputtered.

"I'm taking her home where she'll be safe," Leo replied. He knew Tiny. The man was sweet-natured, but about a beer short of a six-pack on intelligence. He was also as big as a house. It didn't hurt to be polite. "She shouldn't be working in a bar."

"It isn't a bar," Tiny said reasonably. "It's a roadhouse. It's a nice roadhouse. Mr. Duncan don't allow no drunks. You put Miss Janie down, Leo, or I'll have to hit you."

"He'll do it," Janie warned. "I've seen him do it. He's hit men even bigger than you. Haven't you, Tiny?" she encouraged.

"I sure have, Miss Janie."

Leo wasn't backing down. He glared at Tiny. "I said," he replied, his voice dangerously soft, "I'm taking her home."

"I don't think she wants to go, Mr. Hart," came a new source of interference from the doorway behind him.

He swung around with Janie in his big arms. It was Harley Fowler, leaning against the doorjamb, looking intimidating. It would have been a joke a year ago. The new Harley made it look good.

"You tell him, Harley!" Janie said enthusiastically.

"You keep still," Leo told her angrily. "You've got no business working in a rough joint like this!"

"You have no right to tell me where I can work," Janie shot right back, red-faced and furious. "Won't Marilee mind that you're here pestering me?" she added viciously.

His cheeks went red. "I haven't seen Marilee in two weeks. I don't give a damn if I never see her again, either."

That was news. Janie looked as interested as Harley seemed to.

Tiny was still hovering. "I said, put her down," he persisted.

"Do you really think you can take on Tiny and me both?" Harley asked softly.

Leo was getting mad. His face tautened. "I don't know about Tiny," he said honestly, putting Janie back on her feet without taking his eyes off Harley. "But you're a piece of cake, son."

As he said it, he stepped forward and threw a quick punch that Harley wasn't expecting. With his mouth open, Harley tumbled backward over a table. Leo glared at Janie.

"You want this job, keep it," he said, ice-cold except for the glitter in those dark eyes. "But if you get slugged during a brawl or hassled by amorous drunks, don't come crying to me!"

"As…as if I ever…would!" she stammered, shocked by his behavior.

He turned around and stalked out the door without giving Harley a single glance.

Janie rushed to Harley and helped him back to his feet. "Oh, Harley, are you hurt?" she asked miserably.

He rubbed his jaw. "Only my pride, darlin'," he murmured with a rough chuckle. "Damn, that man can throw a punch! I wasn't really expecting him to do it." His eyes twinkled. "I guess you're a little more important to him than any of us realized."

She flushed. "He's just trying to run my life."

Tiny came over and inspected Harley's jaw. "Gonna have a bruise, Mr. Fowler," he said politely.

Harley grinned. He was a good sport, and he knew a jealous man when he saw one. Leo had wanted to deck him at the ball over Janie, but he'd restrained himself. Now, maybe, he felt vindicated. But Harley wished there had been a gentler way of doing it. His jaw was really sore.

"The beast," Janie muttered. "Come on, Harley, I'll clean you up in the bathroom before it gets crowded. Okay, guys, fun's over. Drink your beer and eat your pizzas."

"Yes, mother," one of the men drawled.

She gave him a wicked grin and led Harley to the back. She was not going to admit the thrill it had given her that Leo was worried about her job, or that people thought he was jealous of Harley. But she felt it all the way to her bones.

Leo was lucky not to get arrested for speeding on his way to Fred's house. He had the sports car flat-out on the four lane that turned onto the Victoria road, and he burned rubber when he left the tarmac and turned into Fred's graveled driveway.

Fred heard him coming and knew without a doubt what was wrong.

He stood on the porch with his hands in his jean pockets as he studied the darkening sky behind Leo, who was already out of the car and headed for the porch. His Stetson was pulled down right over his eyes, cocked as they said in cowboy vernacular, and Fred had never seen Leo look so much like a Hart. The brothers had a reputation for being tough customers. Leo looked it right now.

"I want her out of that damned bar," Leo told Fred flatly, without even a conventional greeting. "You can consider it a term of the loan, if you like, but you get her home."

Fred grimaced. "I did try to talk her out of it, when I found out where she was working," he said in his own defense. "Leo, she stood right up to me and said she was old enough to make her own decisions. What do I say to that? She's twenty-one and she told me she wasn't giving up her job."

Leo cursed furiously.

"What happened to your shirt?" Fred asked suddenly. He leaned closer and made a face. "Man, you reek of beer!"

"Of course I do! Your daughter baptized me in front of a crowd of cowboys with a whole pitcher of the damned stuff!" Leo said indignantly.

Fred's eyes opened wide. "Janie? My Janie?"

Leo looked disgusted. "She flung the pitcher at me. And then she set the bouncer on me and appealed to Harley Fowler for aid."

"Why did she need aid?" Fred asked hesitantly.

"Oh, she was kicking and screaming, and they thought she was in trouble, I guess."

"Kicking…?"

Leo's lips compressed. "All right, if you have to know, I tried to carry her out of the bar and bring her home. She resisted."

Fred whistled. "I'd say she resisted." He was trying very hard not to laugh. He looked at Leo's clenched fists. One, the right one, was bleeding. "Hit somebody, did you?"

"Harley," he returned uncomfortably. "Well, he shouldn't have interfered! He doesn't own Janie, she's not his private stock. If he were any sort of a man, he'd have insisted that she go home right then. Instead, he stands there calmly ordering me to put her down. Ordering me. Hell! He's lucky it was only one punch!"

"Oh, boy," Fred said, burying his face in his hand. Gossip was going to run for a month on this mixer.

"It wasn't my fault," Leo argued, waving his hands. "I went in there to save her from being insulted and harassed by drunk men, and look at the thanks I get? Drenched in beer, threatened by ogres, giggled at…"

"Who giggled?"

Leo shifted. "This little brunette who was sitting with one of the Tremayne brothers' cowboys."

Fred cleared his throat. He didn't dare laugh. "I guess it was a sight to see."

Grimacing, Leo flexed his hand. "Damned near broke my fingers on Harley's jaw. He needs to learn to keep his mouth shut. Just because he's not afraid of drug lords, he shouldn't think he can take me on and win."

"I'm sure he knows that now, Leo."

Leo took a deep breath. "You tell her I said she's going to give up that job, one way or the other!"

"I'll tell her." It won't matter though, he thought privately. Janie was more than likely to dig her heels in big time after Leo's visit to Shea's.

Leo gave him a long, hard stare. "I'm not mean with money, I don't begrudge you that loan. But I'm not kidding around with you, Fred. Janie's got no business in Shea's, even with a bouncer on duty. It's a rough place. I've been there on nights when the bouncer didn't have time for a cup of coffee, and there's been at least one shooting. It's dangerous. Even more dangerous right now."

Something in the younger man's tone made Fred uneasy. "Why?"

"Fred, you don't breathe a word of this, even to Janie, understand?"

Fred nodded, curious.

Leo told him what he'd learned from Handley about the Clark brothers, and the loss of the related Salers bulls.

Fred's jaw flew open. "You think my bull was killed deliberately?"

"Yes, I do," Leo admitted solemnly. "I'm sorry to tell you that, because I can't prove it and neither can you. Clark is shrewd. He's never been caught in the act. If you can't prove it, you can't prosecute."

Fred let out an angry breath. "Of all the damned mean, low things to do!"

"I agree, and it's why I'm putting two men over here to watch my bull," he added firmly. "No sorry cattle-killer is going to murder my bull and get away with it. I'm having video cameras installed, too. If he comes near that bull, I'll have his hide in jail!"

Fred chuckled. "Don't I wish he'd try," he said thoughtfully.

"So do I, but I don't hold out a lot of hope," Leo returned. He moved his shoulders restlessly. The muscles were stretched, probably from Janie's violent squirming. He remembered without wanting to the feel of her soft breasts pressed hard against his chest, and he ached.

"Uh, about Janie," Fred continued worriedly.

Leo stared at him without speaking.

"Okay," the older man said wearily. "I'll try to talk some sense into her." He pursed his lips and peered up at Leo. "Of course, she could be a lot of help where she is right now," he murmured thoughtfully. "With the Clark man roaming around loose, that is. She could keep an eye on him if he comes into Shea's. If he's a drinking man, that's the only joint around that sells liquor by the drink."

"She doesn't know what he looks like," Leo said.

"Can't you find out and tell her?"

Leo sighed. "I don't like her being in the line of fire."

"Neither do I." Fred gave the other man a curious scrutiny. "You and Harley and I could arrange to drop in from time to time, just to keep an eye on her."

"She'll have to ask Harley. I won't."

"You're thinking about it, aren't you?" Fred persisted.

Leo was. His eyes narrowed. "My brothers could drop in occasionally, and so could our ranch hands. The Tremaynes would help us out. I know Harden. I'll talk to him. And most of our cowhands go into Shea's on the weekend. I'll talk to our cattle foreman."

"I know Cy Parks and Eb Scott," Fred told him. "They'd help, too."

Leo perked up. With so many willing spies, Janie would be looked after constantly, and she'd never know it. He smiled.

"It's a good idea, isn't it?"

Leo glared at him. "You just don't want to have to make Janie quit that job. You're scared of her, aren't you? What's the matter, think she'd try to drown you in cheap beer, too?"

Fred burst out laughing. "You have to admit, it's a shock to think of Janie throwing beer at anybody."

"I guess it is, at that," Leo seconded, remembering how shy Janie had been. It was only after Marilee had caused so much trouble with her lies that Leo had considered Janie's lack of aggression.

In the past, that was, he amended, because he'd never seen such aggression as he'd encountered in little Janie Brewster just an hour ago.

He shook his head. "It was all I could do not to get thrown on the floor. She's a handful when she's mad. I don't think I've ever seen her lose her temper before."

"There's a lot about her you don't know," Fred said enigmatically.

"Okay, she can stay," Leo said at once. "But I'll find out what Clark looks like. I'll get a picture if I can manage it. Maybe Grier at the police station would have an idea. He's sweet on Christabel Gaines, and she lost a bull to this dude, so he might be willing to assist."

"Don't get Judd Dunn mad," Fred warned.

Leo shrugged. "He's too stuck on his pretty model to care much about Christabel right now, or Grier, either. I don't want any more bulls killed, and I want that man out of the way before he really hurts somebody."

"Have you talked to his boss?"

"Duke Wright didn't have a clue that his new truck driver was such an unsavory character," Leo said, "and he was keen to fire him on the spot. I persuaded him not to. He needs to be where we can watch him. If he puts a foot wrong, we can put him away. I love animals," Leo said in an uncharacteristically tender mood. "Especially bulls. The kind we keep are gentle creatures. They follow us around like big dogs and eat out of our hands." His face hardened visibly. "A man who could cold-bloodedly kill an animal like that could kill a man just as easily. I want Clark out of here. Whatever it takes. But Janie's going to be watched, all the time she's working," Leo added firmly. "Nobody's going to hurt her."

Fred looked at the other man, sensing emotions under the surface that Leo might not even realize were there.

"Thanks, Leo," he said.

The younger man squared his shoulders and shrugged. "I've got to go home and change my shirt." He looked down at himself and smiled ruefully. "Damn. I may never drink another beer."

"It tastes better than it wears," Fred said, deadpan.

Leo gave him a haughty look and went home.

Chapter Seven

Leo stopped by Cash Grier's office at the police station in Jacobsville, catching the new assistant chief of police on his lunch hour.

"Come on in," Grier invited. He indicated his big desk, which contained a scattering of white boxes with metal handles. "Like Chinese food? That's moo goo gai pan, that's sweet-and-sour pork, and that's fried rice. Help yourself to a plate."

"Thanks, but I had barbecue at Barbara's Café," Leo replied, sitting down. He noted with little surprise that the man was adept with chopsticks. "I saw Toshiro Mifune catch flies with those things in one of the 'Samurai Trilogy' films," he commented.

Grier chuckled. "Don't believe everything you see, and only half of what you hear," he replied. He gave Leo a dark-eyed appraisal over his paper plate. "You're here about Clark, I guess."

Leo's eyebrows jumped.

"Oh, I'm psychic," Grier told him straight-faced. "I learned that when I was in the CIA knocking off enemy government agents from black helicopters with a sniper kit."

Leo didn't say a word.

Grier just shook his head. "You wouldn't believe the stuff I've done, to hear people talk."

"You're mysterious," Leo commented. "You keep to yourself."

Grier shrugged. "I have to. I don't want people to notice the aliens spying on me." He leaned forward confidentially. "You see them, too, don't you?" he asked in a hushed tone.

Leo began to get it. He started laughing and was secretly relieved when Grier joined him. The other man leaned back in his chair, with his booted feet propped on his desk. He was as fit as Leo, probably in even better condition, if the muscles outlined under that uniform shirt were any indication. Grier was said to move like lightning, although Leo had never seen him fight. The man was an enigma, with his black hair in a rawhide ponytail and his scarred face giving away nothing—unless he wanted it to.

"That's more like it," Grier said as he finished his lunch. "I thought I'd move to a small town and fit in." He smiled wryly. "But people are all the same. Only the scenery changes."

"It was the same for Cy Parks when he first moved here," Leo commented.

Grier gave him a narrow look. "Are you asking a question?"

"Making a comment," Leo told him. "One of our local guys was in the military during a conflict a few years back, in a special forces unit," he added deliberately, recounting something Cy Parks had told him about Harley Fowler. "He saw you on a plane, out of uniform and armed to the teeth."

Grier began to nod. "It's a small world, isn't it?" he asked pleasantly. He put down his plate and the chopsticks with deliberate preciseness. "I did a stint with military intelligence. And with a few…government agencies." He met Leo's curious eyes. "How far has that gossip traveled?"

"It got to Cy Parks and stopped abruptly," Leo replied, recalling what Cy had said to Harley about loose lips. "Jacobsville is a small town. We consider people who live here family, whether or not we're related to them. Gossip isn't encouraged."

Grier was surprised. He actually smiled. "If you asked Parks, or Steele, or Scott why they moved here," he said after a minute, "I imagine you'd learn that what they wanted most was an end to sitting with their backs to the wall and sleeping armed."

"Isn't that why you're here?" Leo wanted to know.

Grier met his eyes levelly. "I don't really know why I'm here, or if I can stay here," he said honestly. "I think I might eventually fit in. I'm going to give it a good try for six months," he added, "no matter how many rubber-necked ya-hoos stand outside my office trying to hear every damned word I say!" he raised his voice.

There were sudden, sharp footfalls and the sound of scurrying.

Leo chuckled. Grier hadn't even looked at the door when he raised his voice. He shrugged and smiled sheepishly. "I don't have eyes in the back of my head, but I love to keep people guessing about what I know."

"I think that may be part of the problem," Leo advised.

"Well, it doesn't hurt to keep your senses honed. Now. What do you want to know about Clark?"

"I'd like some way to get a photo of him," Leo confessed. "A friend of mine is working at Shea's. I'm going to ask her if she'll keep an eye on who he talks to, what he does, if he comes in there. She'll need to know what he looks like."

Grier sobered at once. "That's dangerous," he said. "Clark's brother almost killed a man he suspected of spying on him, up in Victoria. He made some threats, too."

Leo frowned. "Why are guys like that on the streets?"

"You can't shoot people or even lock them up without due process here in the States," Grier said with a wistful smile. "Pity."

"Listen, do they give you real bullets to go with that gun?" Leo asked, indicating the .45 caliber automatic in a shoul-der holster that the man was wearing.

"I haven't shot anybody in months," Grier assured him.
"I was a cyber crime specialist in the D.A.'s office San Antonio. I didn't really beat up that guy I was accused of ha-
rassing, I just told him I'd keep flies off him if he didn't level
with me about his boss's illegal money laundering. I had access to his computerized financial records," he added with a
twinkle in his dark eyes.

"I heard about that," Leo chuckled. "Apparently you used
some access codes that weren't in the book."

"They let me off with a warning. When they checked my
ID, I still had my old 'company' card."

Leo just shook his head. He couldn't imagine Grier being
in trouble for very long. He knew too much. "All that spe-
cialized background, and you're handing out speeding tickets in Jacobsville, Texas."

"Don't knock it. Nobody's shot at me since I've been
here." He got up and opened his filing cabinet with a key. "I
have to keep it locked," he explained. "I have copies of doc-
uments about alien technology in here." He glanced at Leo
to see if he was buying it and grinned. "Did you read that
book by the Air Force guy who discovered night vision at a
flying saucer crash?" He turned back to the files. "Hell, I
should write a book. With what I know, governments might
topple." He hesitated, frowned, with a file folder in his hand.
"Our government might topple!"

"Clark?" Leo prompted.

"Clark. Right." He took a paper from the file, replaced it,
closed the cabinet and locked it again. "Here. You don't have
a clue where this photo came from, and I never saw you."

Leo was looking at a photograph of two men, obviously
brothers, in, of all things, a newspaper clipping. Incredibly,
they'd been honored with a good citizen award in another Texas
town for getting a herd of escaped cattle out of the path of traffic and back into a fenced pasture with broken electric fencing.

"Neat trick," Grier said. "They cut the wire to steal the cattle, and then were seen rounding them up. Everybody thought they were saving the cattle. They had a tractor trailer truck just down the road and told people they were truck drivers who saw the cattle out and stopped to help." He laughed wholeheartedly. "Can you believe it?"

"Can you copy this for me?"

"That's a copy of the original. You can have it," Grier told him. "I've got two more."

"You were expecting trouble, I gather," Leo continued.

"Two expensive bulls in less than a month, both from the same herd sire, is a little too much coincidence even for me," Grier said as he sat back down. "When I heard Clark was working for Duke Wright, I put two and two together."

"There's no proof," Leo said.

"Not yet. We'll give him a little time and see if he'll oblige us by hanging himself." He laced his lean, strong hands together on the desk in front of him. "But you warn your friend not to be obvious. These are dangerous men."

"I'll tell her."

"And stop knocking men over tables in Shea's. It's outside the city limits, so I can't arrest you. But I can have the sheriff pick you up for brawling," Grier said abruptly, and he was serious. "You can't abduct women in plain sight of the public."

"I wasn't abducting her, I was trying to save her!"

"From what?"

"Fistfights!"

Grier lost it. He got up from his desk. "Get out," he invited through helpless laughter. "I have real work to do here."

"If Harley Fowler said I hit him without provocation, he's lying," Leo continued doggedly. "He never should have ordered me to put her down, and leave my hands free to hit him!"

"You should just tell the woman how you feel," Grier advised. "It's simpler." He glanced at Leo's swollen hand. "And less painful."

Leo didn't really know how he felt. That was the problem. He gave Grier a sardonic look and left.

He worried about letting Janie get involved, even from the sidelines, with Clark. Of course, the man might not even come near Shea's. He might buy a bottle and drink on the ranch, in the bunkhouse. But it wasn't a long shot to think he might frequent Shea's if he wanted company while he drank.

He disliked anything that might threaten Janie, and he didn't understand why he hated Harley all of a sudden. But she was in a great position to notice a man without being obvious, and for everyone's sake, Clark had to be watched. A man who would kill helpless animals was capable of worse.

He went looking for her Sunday afternoon, in a misting rain. She wasn't at home. Fred said that she was out, in the cold rain no less, wandering around the pecan trees in her raincoat. Brooding, was how Fred put it. Leo climbed back into his pickup and went after her.

Janie was oblivious to the sound of an approaching truck. She had her hands in her pockets, her eyes on the ground ahead of her, lost in thought.

It had been a revelation that Leo was concerned about her working at Shea's, and it had secretly thrilled her that he tried to make her quit. But he'd washed his hands of her when she wouldn't leave willingly, and he'd hurt her feelings with his comment that she shouldn't complain if she got in trouble. She didn't know what to make of his odd behavior. He'd given her a hard time, thanks to Marilee. But she hadn't been chasing him lately, so she couldn't understand why he was so bossy about her life. And she did feel guilty that he'd slugged poor Harley, who was only trying to help her.

The truck was almost on top of her before she finally heard the engine and jumped to the side of the ranch trail.

Leo pulled up and leaned over to open the passenger door. "Get in before you drown out there," he said.

She hesitated. She wasn't sure if it was safe to get that close to him.

He grimaced. "I'm not armed and dangerous," he drawled. "I just want to talk."

She moved closer to the open door. "You're in a very strange mood lately," she commented. "Maybe the lack of biscuits in your life has affected your mind."

Both eyebrows went up under his hat.

She flushed, thinking she'd been too forward. But she got into the truck and closed the door, removing the hood of her raincoat from her long, damp hair.

"You'll catch cold," he murmured, turning up the heat.

"It's not that wet, and I've got a lined raincoat."

He drove down the road without speaking, made a turn, and ended up in a field on the Hart ranch, a place where they could be completely alone. He put the truck in park, cut off the engine, and leaned back against his door to study her from under the wide brim of his Stetson. "Your father says you won't give up the job."

"He's right," she replied, ready to do battle.

His fingers tapped rhythmically on the steering wheel. "I've been talking to Grier," he began.

"Now listen here, you can't have me arrested because I won't quit my job!" she interrupted.

He held up a big, lean hand. "Not about that," he corrected. "We've got a man in town who may be involved in some cattle losses. I want you to look at this picture and tell me if you've ever seen him in Shea's."

He took the newspaper clipping out of his shirt pocket, unfolded it, and handed it to her.

She took it gingerly and studied the two faces surrounded by columns of newsprint. "I don't know the man on the left," she replied. "But the one on the right comes in Saturday nights and drinks straight whiskey," she said uneasily. "He's loud and foul-mouthed, and Tiny had to ask him to leave last night."

Leo's face tightened. "He's vindictive," he told her.

"I'll say he is," she agreed at once. "When Tiny went out to get into his car, all his tires were slashed."

That was disturbing. "Did he report it to the sheriff?"

"He did," she replied. "They're going to look into it, but I don't know how they'll prove anything."

Leo traced an absent pattern on the seat behind her head. They were silent while the rain slowly increased, the sound of it loud on the hood and cab of the truck. "The man we're watching is Jack Clark," he told her, "the man you recognize in that photo." He took it back from her, refolded it, and replaced it in his pocket. "If he comes back in, we'd like you to see who he talks to. Don't be obvious about it. Tell Tiny to let it slide about his tires, I'll see that they're replaced."

"That's nice of you," she replied.

He shrugged. "He's protective of you. I like that."

His eyes were narrow and dark and very intent on her face. She felt nervous with him all at once and folded her hands in her lap to try and keep him from noticing. It was like another world, closed up with him in a truck in a rainstorm. It outmatched her most fervent dreams of close contact.

"What sort of cattle deaths do you suspect him of?" she asked curiously.

"Your father's bull, for one."

Her intake of breath was audible. "Why would he kill Dad's bull?" she wanted to know.

"It was one of the offspring of a bull he killed in Victoria. He worked for the owner, who fired him. Apparently his idea of proper revenge is far-reaching."

"He's nuts!" she exclaimed.

He nodded. "That's why you have to be careful if he comes back in. Don't antagonize him. Don't stare at him. Don't be obvious when you look at him." He sighed angrily. "I hate the whole idea of having you that close to a lunatic. I should have decked Tiny as well as Fowler and carried you out of there anyway."

His level, penetrating gaze made her heart race. "I'm not your responsibility," she challenged.

"Aren't you?" His dark eyes slid over her from head to toe. His head tilted back at a faintly arrogant angle.

She swallowed. He looked much more formidable now than he had at Shea's. "I should go," she began.

He leaned forward abruptly, caught her under the arms, and pulled her on top of him. He was sprawled over the front seat, with one long, powerful leg braced against the passenger floorboard and the other on the seat. Janie landed squarely between his denim-clad legs, pressed intimately to him.

"Leo!" she exclaimed, horribly embarrassed at the intimate proximity and trying to get up.

He looped an arm around her waist and held her there, studying her flushed face with almost clinical scrutiny. "If you keep moving like that, you're going to discover the major difference between men and women in a vivid way, any minute."

She stilled at once. She knew what he meant. She'd felt that difference with appalling starkness at the ball. In fact, she was already feeling it again. She looked at him and her face colored violently.

"I told you," he replied, pursing his lips as he surveyed the damage. "My, my, didn't we know that men are easily aroused when we're lying full length on top of them?" he drawled. "We do now, don't we?"

She hit his shoulder, trying to hold on to her dignity as well as her temper. "You let go of me!"

"Spoilsport," he chided. He shifted her so that her head fell onto his shoulder and he could look down into her wide, startled eyes. "Relax," he coaxed. "What are you so afraid of?"

She swallowed. The closeness was like a drug. She felt swollen. Her legs trembled inside the powerful cage his legs made for them. Her breasts were hard against his chest, and they felt uncomfortably tight as well.

He looked down at them with keen insight, even moving her back slightly so that he could see the hard tips pressing against his shirt.

"You stop...looking at that!" she exclaimed without thinking.

He lifted an eyebrow and his smile was worldly. "A man likes to know that he's making an impression," he said outrageously.

She bit her lower lip, still blushing. "You're making too much of an impression already," she choked.

He leaned close and brushed his mouth lazily over her parted lips. "My body likes you," he whispered huskily. "It's making very emphatic statements about what it wants to do."

"You need...to speak...firmly to it," she said. She was trying to sound adult and firm, but her voice shook. It was hard to think, with his mouth hovering like that.

"It doesn't listen to reason," he murmured. He nibbled tenderly at her upper lip, parting it insistently from its companion. His free hand came up to tease around the corners of her mouth and down her chin to the opening her v-necked blouse made inside her raincoat.

His mouth worked on her lips while his hands freed her from the raincoat and slowly, absently, from her blouse as well. She was hardly aware of it. His mouth was doing impossibly erotic things to her lips, and one of his lean, strong hands was inside her blouse, teasing around the lacy edges of her brassiere.

The whole time, one long, powerful leg was sliding against the inside of her thigh, in a way so arousing that she didn't care what he did to her, as long as he didn't try to get up.

Her hands had worked their way into his thick, soft hair, and she was lifting up, trying to get closer to those slow, maddening fingers that were brushing against the soft flesh inside her bra. She'd never dreamed that a man could arouse her so quickly with nothing more invasive than a light brushing stroke of his hand. But she was on fire with hunger, need, aching need, to have him thrust those fingers down inside her frilly bra and close on her breast. It was torture to have him tease her like this. He was watching her face, too, watching the hunger grow with a dark arrogance that was going to make her squirm later in memory.

Right now, of course, she didn't care how he looked at her. If he would just slide that hand…down a…couple of… inches!

She was squirming in another way now, twisting her body ardently, pushing up against his stroking fingers while his mouth nibbled and nipped at her parted lips and his warm breath went into her mouth.

The rain was falling harder. It banged on the hood, and on top of the cab, with tempestuous fury. Inside, Janie could hear the tormented sound of her own breathing, feel her heartbeat shaking her madly, while Leo's practiced caresses grew slower and lazier on her taut body.

"Will you…please…!" she sputtered, gripping his arms.

"Will I please, what?" he whispered into her mouth.

"T…t…touch me!" she cried.

He nipped her upper lip ardently. "Touch you where?" he tormented.

Tears of frustration stung her eyes as they opened, meeting his. "You…know…where!"

He lifted his head. His face was taut, his eyes dark and glittery. He watched her eyes as his hand slowly moved down to where she ached to have it. She ground her teeth together to keep from crying out when she felt that big, warm, strong hand curl around her breast.

She actually shuddered, hiding her face in his throat as the tiny culmination racked her slender body and made it helpless.

"You are," he breathed, "the most surprising little treasure…"

His mouth searched for hers and suddenly ravished it while his hand moved on her soft flesh, molding it, tracing it, exploring it, in a hot, explosive silence. He kissed her until her mouth felt bruised and then she felt his hand move again, lifting free of her blouse, around to her back, unhooking the bra.

She didn't mind. She lifted up to help him free the catch. She looked up at him with wild, unsatisfied longing, shivering with reaction to the force of the desire he was teaching her.

"It will change everything," he whispered as he began to move the fabric away from her body. "You know that."

"Yes." She shivered.

Both hands slid against her rib cage, carrying the fabric up with them until he uncovered her firm, tip-tilted little breasts. He looked at them with pure pleasure and delight. His thumbs edged out and traced the wide, soft nipples until they drew into hard, dusky peaks. His mouth ached to taste them.

She shifted urgently in his arms, feeling him turn toward her, feeling his leg insinuate itself even more intimately against her. He looked into her dazed eyes as his hand pressed hard against the lowest part of her spine and moved her right in against the fierce arousal she'd only sensed before.

She gasped, but he didn't relent. If anything, he brought her even closer, so that he was pressed intimately to her and the sensations exploded like sensual fire in her limbs.

"Leo!" she cried out, shivering.

"You turn me on so hard that I can't even think," he ground out as he bent to her open mouth. "I didn't mean for this to happen, Janie," he groaned into her mouth as he turned her under him on the seat and pressed his hips down roughly against hers. "Feel me," he whispered. "Feel me wanting you!"

She was lost, helpless, utterly without hope. She clung to him with no thought for her virtue or the future. She was drowning in the most delicious erotic pleasure she'd ever dreamed of experiencing. She could feel him, feel the rough, thrusting rhythm of his big body as he buffeted her against the seat. Something hit her arm. She was twisted in his embrace, and one leg was almost bent backward as he crushed her under him. Any minute, limbs were going to start breaking, she thought, and even that didn't matter. She wanted him…! She didn't realize she'd said it aloud until she heard his voice, deep and strained.

"I want you, too," he whispered back.

She felt his hand between them, working at her jeans. His hand was unfastening them. She felt it, warm and strong, against her belly. It was sliding down. She moved to make it easier for him, her mouth savage under the devouring pressure of his lips…

Leo heard the loud roar of an approaching engine in his last lucid second before he went in over his head. He froze against Janie's warm, welcoming body. His head lifted. He could barely breathe.

He looked down into her wide, misty eyes. It only then occurred to him that they were cramped together on the seat, his body completely covering hers, her bra and blouse crumpled at her collarbone, her jeans halfway down over her hips.

"What the hell are we doing?!" he burst out, shocked.

"You mean you don't know?" she gasped with unconscious humor.

He looked at the windows, so fogged up that nothing was visible outside them. He looked down at Janie, lying drowsy and submissive under the heavy crush of him.

He drew his hand away from her jeans and whipped onto his back so that he could help her sit up. He slid back into his own seat, watching her fumble her clothes back on while he listened, shell-shocked, to the loud tone of a horn from the other vehicle.

Janie was a mess. Her lips were swollen. Her cheeks were flushed. Her clothes were wrinkled beyond belief. Her hair stood out all around from the pressure of his hands in it.

He was rumpled, too, his hair as much as hers. His hat was on the floorboard somewhere, streaked with water from her raincoat and dirt from the floor mats. His shirt had obvious finger marks and lipstick stains on it.

He just stared at her for a long moment while the other vehicle came to a stop beside his truck. He couldn't see anything. All the windows were thickly fogged. Absently, he dug in the side pocket of the door for the red rag he always carried. He wiped the fog from the driver's window and scowled as he saw his brother Cag sitting in another ranch truck, with Tess beside him. They were trying not to stare and failing miserably!

Chapter Eight

Belatedly, Leo rolled the window down and glared at his brother and sister-in-law. "Well?" he asked belligerently.

"We just wondered if you were all right," Cag said, clearing his throat and trying very hard not to look at Janie. "The truck was sitting out here in the middle of nowhere, but we didn't see anybody inside."

"That's right," Tess said at once. "We didn't see anybody. At all. Or anything."

"Not anything." Cag nodded vigorously.

"I was showing Janie a photo of the Clark man," Leo said curtly. He pulled it out of his pocket. It was crumpled and slightly torn. He glared at it, trying to straighten it. "See?"

Cag cleared his throat and averted his eyes. "You, uh, should have taken it out of your pocket before you showed it to her… I'm going!"

Cag powered his window up with a knowing grin and gunned the engine, taking off in a spray of mud. Leo let his own window back up with flattened lips.

Janie was turned away from him, her shoulders shaking. Odd little noises that she was trying to smother kept slipping out. She was about to burst trying not to laugh.

He leaned back against the seat and threw the clipping at her.

"It's not my fault," she protested. "I was sitting here minding my own business when you got amorous."

He pursed his swollen lips and gave her a look that would have melted butter. "Amorous. That's a good word for it."

She was coming down from the heights and feeling self-conscious. She picked up the clipping and handed it back to him, belatedly noticing his white Stetson at her feet. She picked it up, too, and grimaced. "Your poor hat."

He took it from her and tossed it into the small back seat of the double cab. "It will clean," he said impatiently.

She folded her hands in her lap, toying with the streaked raincoat that she'd propped over her legs.

"Marilee caused a lot of trouble between us," he said after a minute, surprising her into meeting his somber gaze. "I'm sorry about that."

"You mean I don't really make you sick?" she asked in a thin voice.

He winced. "I was furious about what I thought you'd done," he confessed. "It was a lie, Janie, like all the other terrible things I said. I'm sorry for every one of them, if it does any good."

She toyed with a button on her raincoat and stared out the window at the rain. It did help, but she couldn't stop wondering if he hadn't meant it. Maybe guilt brought the apology out of him, rather than any real remorse. She knew he didn't like hurting people.

A long sigh came from the other side of the pickup. "I'll drive you back home," he said after a minute, and put the truck in gear. "Fasten your seat belt, honey."

The endearment made her feel warm all over, but she didn't let it show. She didn't really trust Leo Hart.

He turned back onto the main road. "Fred and I are going to mob you with company at Shea's," he said conversationally. "Between us, we know most of the ranchers around Jacobsville. You can ask Harley to keep dropping in from time to time, and Fred and I will talk to the others."

She gave him a quick glance. "Harley's jaw was really bruised."

His eyes darkened. "He had no business interfering. You don't belong to damned Harley!"

She didn't know what to say. That sounded very much like jealousy. It couldn't be, of course.

His dark eyes glanced off hers. "Do you sit around in parked trucks with him and let him take your blouse off?" he asked suddenly, furiously.

"I do *not!*" she exploded.

He calmed down at once. He shifted in the seat, still uncomfortable from the keen hunger she'd kindled in his powerful body. "Okay."

Her long fingers clenched on the fabric of the coat. "You have no right to be jealous of me!" she accused angrily.

"After what we just did?" he asked pleasantly. "In your dreams, Janie."

"I don't belong to you, either," she persisted.

"You almost did," he replied, chuckling softly. "You have no idea what a close call that was. Cag and Tess saved you."

"Excuse me?"

He gave her a rueful glance. "Janie, I had your jeans half off, or have you forgotten already?"

"Leo!"

"I'm not sure I could have stopped," he continued, slowing to make a turn. "And you were no damned help at all," he added with affectionate irony, "twisting your hips against me and begging me not to stop."

She gasped. Her face went scarlet. "Of all the blatant…!"

"That's how it was, all right," he agreed. "Blatant. For the record, when a man gets that hard, it's time to call a halt any way you can, before you get in over your head. I can tell you haven't had much practice at it, but now is a good time to listen to advice."

"I don't need advice!"

"Like hell you don't. Once I got my mouth on your soft belly, you'd never have been able to make me stop."

She stared at him with slowly dawning realization. She remembered the hot, exquisite pleasure of his mouth on her breasts. She could only imagine how it would feel to let him kiss her there, on her hips, on her long legs....

"You know far too much about women," she gritted.

"You know absolutely nothing about men," he countered. He smiled helplessly. "I love it. You were in over your head the minute I touched you with intent. You'd have let me do anything I wanted." He whistled softly. "You can't imagine how I felt, knowing that. You were the sweetest candy I've ever had."

He was confounding her. She didn't know what to make of the remarks. He'd been standoffish, insulting, offensive and furious with her. Now he'd done a complete about-face. He was acting more like a lover than a big brother.

His dark eyes cut around sideways and sized up her expression. "Do you think things can just go back to the way they were before?" he asked softly. "I remember telling you that it was going to change everything."

She swallowed. "I remember."

"It already has. I look at you and get aroused, all over again," he said bluntly. "It will only get worse."

Her face flamed. "I will not have an affair with you."

"Great. I'm glad to know you have that much self-control. You can teach it to me."

"I won't get in a truck with you again," she muttered.

"I'll bring the car next time," he said agreeably. "Of course, we'll have to open both doors. I'll never be able to stretch out in the front seat the way I did in the cab of this truck."

Her fingers clenched on the raincoat. "That won't happen again."

"It will if I touch you."

She glared at him. "You listen here…!"

He pulled the truck onto a dirt road that led through one of Fred's pastures, threw it out of gear, switched off the engine and reached for Janie with an economy of motion that left her gasping.

He had her over his lap, and his mouth hit hers with the force of a gust of wind. He burrowed into her parted lips while one lean hand went to her spine, grinding her into the fierce arousal that just the touch of her had provoked.

"Feel that?" he muttered against her lips. "Now try to stop me."

She went under in a daze of pleasure. She couldn't even pretend to protest, not even when his big hand found her breast and caressed it hungrily right through the cloth of her blouse.

Her arms went around his neck. She lifted closer, shivering, as she felt the aching hunger of his body echo in her own. She moaned helplessly.

"Of all the stupid things I've done lately…" He groaned, too, his big arms wrapping her up tight as the kiss went on and on and on.

He moved out from under the steering wheel and shifted her until she was straddling his hips, her belly lying against his aroused body so blatantly that she should have been shocked. She wasn't. He felt familiar to her, beloved to her. She wanted him. Her body yielded submissively to the insistent pressure of both his hands on her hips, dragging them against his in a fever of desire.

The approaching roar of a truck engine for the second time in less than an hour brought his head up. He looked down into Janie's heated face, at the position they were in. His dazed eyes went out the windshield in time to see Fred's old pickup coming down the long pasture road about a quarter mile ahead of them.

He let out a word Janie had only heard Tiny use during heated arguments with patrons, and abruptly put her back in her own seat, pausing to forcefully strap her into her seat belt.

She felt shaky all over. Her eyes met his and then went involuntarily to what she'd felt so starkly against her hungry body. She flushed.

"Next time you'll get a better look," he said harshly. "I wish I could explain to you how it feels."

She wrapped her arms around her body. "I know…how it feels," she whispered unsteadily. "I ache all over."

The bad temper left him at once. He scowled as he watched her, half-oblivious to Fred's rapid approach. He couldn't take his eyes off her. She was delicious.

She managed to meet his wide, shocked eyes. "I'm sorry."

"For what?" he asked huskily. "You went in headfirst, just like I did."

She searched his eyes hungrily. Her body was on fire for him. "If you used something…" she said absently.

He actually flushed. He got back under the steering wheel and avoided looking at her. He couldn't believe what she was saying.

Fred roared up beside them and pulled onto the hard ground to let his window down.

"Rain's stopped," he told Leo. "I thought I'd run over to Eb Scott's place and have a talk with him about getting his cowboys to frequent Shea's at night."

"Good idea," Leo said, still flushed and disheveled.

Fred wisely didn't look too closely at either of them, but he had a pretty good idea of what he'd interrupted. "I won't be long, sweetheart," he told Janie.

"Okay, Dad. Be careful," she said in a husky voice.

He nodded, grinned, and took off.

Leo started the engine. He was still trying to get his breath. He stared at the dirt path ahead instead of at Janie. "I could use something," he said after a minute. "But lovemaking is addictive, Janie. One time would be a beginning, not a cure, do you understand?"

She shook her head, embarrassed now that her blood was cooling.

He reached out and caught one of her cold hands in his, intertwining their fingers. "You can't imagine how flattered I am," he said quietly. "You're a virgin, and you'd give yourself to me…"

She swallowed hard. "Please. Don't."

His hand contracted. "I'll drive you home. If you weren't working next Saturday, we could take in a movie and have dinner somewhere."

Her heart jumped up into her throat. "M…me?"

He looked down at her with the beginnings of possession. "You could wear that lacy white thing you wore to the ball," he added softly. "I like your shoulders bare. You have beautiful skin." His eyes fell to her bodice and darkened. "Beautiful breasts, too, with nice nipples…"

"Leo Hart!" she exclaimed, horrified.

He leaned over and kissed her hungrily. "I'll let you look at me next time," he whispered passionately. "Then you won't be so embarrassed when we compare notes."

She thought of seeing him without clothes and her whole face colored.

"I know what I said, but…" she protested.

He stopped the truck, bent, and kissed her again with breathless tenderness. "You've known me half your life, Janie," he said, and he was serious. He searched her worried eyes. "Am I the kind of man who takes advantage of a green girl?"

She was worried, too. "No," she had to admit.

His breathing was uneven as he studied her flushed face. "I never would," he agreed. "You were special to me even before I kissed you the first time, in your own kitchen." His head bent again. His mouth trailed across hers in soft, biting little kisses that made her moan. "But now, after the taste of you I've just had, I'm going to be your shadow. You don't even realize what's happened, do you?"

"You want me," she said huskily.

His teeth nibbled her upper lip. "It's a little more complicated than sex." He kissed her again, hard, and lifted his head with flattering reluctance. "Look up addiction in the dictionary," he mused. "It's an eye-opener."

"Addiction?"

His nose brushed hers. "Do you remember how you moaned when I put my hands inside your blouse?"

She swallowed. "Yes."

"Now think how it would feel if I'd put my mouth on your breast, right over the nipple."

She shivered.

He nodded slowly. "Next time," he promised, his voice taut and hungry. "You have that to look forward to. Meanwhile, you keep your eyes and ears open, and don't do anything at work that gives Clark a hint that you're watching him," he added firmly.

"I'll be careful," she promised unsteadily.

His eyes were possessive on her soft face. "If he touches you, I'll kill him."

It sounded like a joke. It wasn't. She'd never seen that look in a man's eyes before. In fact, the way he was watching her was a little scary.

His big hand slid under her nape and brought her mouth just under his. "You belong to me, Janie," he whispered as his head moved down. "Your first man is going to be me. Believe it!"

The kiss was as arousing as it was tender, but it didn't last long. He forced himself to let her go, to move away. He started the truck again, put it in gear, and went back down the farm road. But his hand reached for hers involuntarily, his fingers curling into hers, as if he couldn't bear to lose contact with her. She didn't know it, but he'd reached a decision in those few seconds. There was no going back now.

Jack Clark did show up in the bar, on the following Friday night.

Janie hadn't told any of the people she worked with about him, feeling that any mention of what she knew about him might jeopardize her safety.

But she did keep a close eye on him. The man was rangy and uncouth. He sat alone at a corner table, looking around as if he expected trouble and was impatient for it to arrive.

A cowboy from Cy Parks's spread, one of Harley Fowler's men, walked to the counter and sat down, ordering a beer and a pizza.

"Hey, Miss Janie," he said with a grin that showed a missing front tooth. "Harley said to tell you he'd be in soon to see you."

"That's sweet of him," she said with a grin. "I'll just put your order in, Ned."

She scribbled the order on a slip of green paper and put it up on the long string for Nick, the teenage cook, with a clothespin.

"Where's my damned whiskey?" Clark shouted. "I been sitting here five minutes waiting for it!"

Janie winced as Nick glanced at her and shrugged, indicating the pizza list he was far behind on. He'd taken the order and got busy all of a sudden. Tiny was nowhere in sight. He was probably out back having a cigarette. Nick was up to his elbows in dough and pizza sauce. Janie had to get Clark's order, there was nobody else to do it.

She got down a shot glass, poured whiskey into it, and put it on one of the small serving trays.

She took it to Clark's table and forced a smile to her lips. "Here you are, sir," she said, placing the shot glass in front of him. "I'm sorry it took so long."

Clark glared up at her from watery blue eyes. "Don't let that happen again. I don't like to be kept waiting."

"Yes, sir," she agreed.

She turned away, but he caught her apron strings and jerked her back. She caught her breath as his hand slid to the ones tied at her waist.

"You're kind of cute. Why don't you sit on my lap and help me drink this?" he drawled.

He was already half-lit, she surmised. She would have refused him the whiskey, if Tiny had been close by, despite the trouble he'd already caused. But now she was caught and she didn't know how to get away. All her worst fears were coming to haunt her.

"I have to get that man's drink," she pointed to Harley's cowboy. "I'll come right back, okay?"

"That boy can get his drink."

"He's making pizza," she protested. "Please."

That was a mistake. He liked it when women begged. He smiled at her. It wasn't a pleasant smile. "I said, come here!"

He jerked her down on his thin, bony legs and she screamed.

In a flash, two cowboys were on their feet and heading toward Clark, both of them dangerous looking.

"Well, looky, looky, you've got guardian angels in cowboy boots!" Clark chuckled. He stood up, dragging Janie with him. "Stay back," he warned, catching her hair in its braid. "Or else." He slapped her, hard, across the face, making her cry out, and his hand went into his pocket and came out with a knife. He flicked it and a blade appeared. He caught her around the shoulders from behind and brandished the knife. "Stay back, boys," he said again. "Or I'll cut her!"

The knife pressed against her throat. She was shaking. She remembered all the nice self-defense moves she'd ever learned in her life from watching television or listening to her father talk. Now, she knew how useless they were. Clark would cut her throat if those men tried to help her. She had visions of him dragging her outside and assaulting her. He could do anything. There was nobody around to stop him. These cowboys weren't going to rush him and risk her life. If only Leo were here!

She was vaguely aware of Nick sliding out of sight toward the telephones. If he could just call the sheriff, the police, anybody!

Her hands went to Clark's wrist, trying to get him to release the press of the blade.

"You're hurting," she choked.

"Really?" He pressed harder.

Janie felt his arm cutting off the blood to her head. Then she remembered something she'd heard of a female victim doing during an attack. If she fainted, he might turn her loose.

"Can't...breathe..." she gasped, and closed her eyes. He might drop her if she sagged, he might cut her throat. She could die. But they'd get him. That would almost be worth it....

She let her body sag just as she heard a shout from the doorway. She pretended to lose consciousness. In the next few hectic seconds, Clark threw her to the floor so hard that she hit right on her elbow and her head, and groaned aloud with the pain of impact.

At the same moment, Leo Hart and Harley Fowler exploded into the room from the front door and went right for Clark, knife and all. They'd been in the parking lot, talking about Janie's situation, and had come running when they heard the commotion.

Harley aimed a kick at the knife and knocked it out of Clark's hands, but Clark was good with his feet, too. He landed a roundhouse kick in Harley's stomach and put him over a table. Leo slugged him, but he twisted around, got Leo's arm behind him and sent him over a table, too.

The two cowboys held back, aware of Leo's size and Harley's capability, and the fact that Clark had easily put both of them down.

There was a sudden silence. Janie dragged herself into a sitting position in time to watch Cash Grier come through the doorway and approach Clark.

Clark dived for the knife, rolled, and got to his feet. He lunged at Grier with the blade. The assistant police chief waited patiently for the attack, and he smiled. It was the coldest, most dangerous smile Janie had ever seen in her life.

Clark lunged confidently. Grier moved so fast that he was like a blur.

Seconds later, the knife was in Grier's hand. He threw it, slamming it into the wall next to the counter so deep that it would take Tiny quite some time, after the brawl, to pull it out again. He turned back to Clark even as the knife hit, fell into a relaxed stance, and waited.

Clark rushed him, tipsy and furious at the way the older man had taken his knife away. Grier easily sidestepped the intended punch, did a spinning heel kick that would have made Chuck Norris proud, and proceeded to beat the living hell out of the man with lightning punches and kicks that quickly put him on the floor, breathless and drained of will. It was over in less than three minutes. Clark held his ribs and groaned. Grier stood over him, not even breathing hard, his hand going to the handcuffs on his belt. He didn't even look winded.

Leo had picked himself up and rushed to Janie, propping her against his chest while she nursed her elbow.

"Is it broken?" he asked worriedly.

She shook her head. "Just bruised. Is my mouth bleeding?" she asked, still dazed from the confrontation.

He nodded. His face was white. He cursed his own helplessness. Between them, he and Harley should have been able to wipe the floor with Clark. He pulled out a white linen handkerchief and mopped up the bleeding lip and the cut on her cheek from Clark's nails. A big, bad bruise was already coming out on the left side of her face.

By now, Grier had Clark against a wall with a minimum of fuss. He spread the man's legs with a quick movement of his booted feet and nimbly cuffed him.

"I'll need a willing volunteer to see the magistrate and file a complaint," Grier asked.

"Right here," Harley said, wiping his mouth with a handkerchief. "I expect Mr. Hart will do the same."

"You bet," Leo agreed. "But I've got to get Janie home first."

"No rush," Grier said, with Clark by the neck. "Harley, you know where magistrate Burr Wiley lives, don't you? I'm taking Clark by there now."

"Yes, sir, I do, I'll drive right over there and swear out a complaint so you can hold that…gentleman," Harley agreed, substituting for the word he really meant to use. "Janie, you going to be okay?" he added worriedly.

She was wobbly, but she got to her feet, with Leo's support. "Sure," she said. She managed a smile. "I'll be fine."

"I'll get you!" Clark raged at Janie and Leo. "I'll get both of you!"

"Not right away," Grier said comfortably. "I'll have the judge set bail as high as it's possible to put it, and we'll see how many assault charges we can press."

"Count on me for two of them!" Janie volunteered fearlessly, wincing as her jaw protested.

"But not tonight," Leo said, curling his arm around her. "Come on, honey," he said gently. "I'll take you home."

They followed Grier with his prisoner and Harley out the door and over to Leo's big double-cabbed pickup truck.

He put her inside gently and moved around to the driver's seat. She noticed then, for the first time, that he was in working clothes.

"You must have come right from work," she commented.

"We were moving livestock to a new pasture," he replied. "One of the bulls got out and we had to chase him through the brush. Doesn't it show?" he added with a nod toward his scarred batwing chaps and his muddy boots. "I meant to be here an hour ago. Harley and I arrived together. Just in the nick of time, too."

"Two of Cy Parks's guys were at the counter," she said, "but when Clark threatened to cut me, they were afraid to rush him."

He caught her hand in his and held it tight, his eyes going to the blood on her face, her blouse, her forearm. She was going to have a bruise on her pretty face. The sight of those marks made him furious.

"I'll be all right, thanks to all of you," she managed to say.

"We weren't a hell of a lot of help," he said with a rueful smile. "Even Harley didn't fare well. Clark must have a military background of some sort. But he was no match for Grier." He shook his head. "It was like watching a martial arts movie. I never even saw Grier move."

She studied him while he started the truck and put their seat belts on. "Did he hurt you?"

"Hurt my pride," he replied, smiling gently. "I've never been put across a table so fast."

"At least you tried," she pointed out. "Thank you."

"I should never have let you stay in there," he said. "It's my fault."

"It was my choice."

He kissed her eyelids shut. "My poor baby," he said softly. "I'm not taking you to your father in this condition," he added firmly, noting the blood on her blouse and face. "I'll take you home with me and clean you up, first. We'll phone him and tell him there was a little trouble and you'll be late."

"Okay," she said. "But he's no wimp."

"I know that." He put the truck in gear. "Humor me. I want to make sure you're all right."

"I'm fine," she argued, but then she smiled. "You can clean me up, anyway."

He pursed his lips and smiled wickedly. "Best offer I've had all night," he replied as he pulled out of the parking lot.

Chapter Nine

The house was quiet, deserted. The only light was the one in the living room. Leo led Janie down the hall to his own big bedroom, closed the door firmly, and led her into his spacious blue-tiled bathroom.

The towels were luxurious, sea-blue and white-striped blue towels, facecloths and hand towels. There were soaps of all sorts, a huge heated towel rack, and a whirlpool bath.

He tugged her to the medicine cabinet and turned her so that he could see her face. "You've got a bad scratch here," he remarked. He tilted her chin up, and found another smaller cut on the side of her throat, thankfully not close enough to an artery to have done much damage.

His hands went to her blouse. She caught them.

"It's all right," he said gently.

She let go.

He unfastened the blouse and tossed it onto the floor, looking her over for other marks. He found a nasty bruise on her shoulder that was just coming out. He unfastened the bra and let it fall, too, ignoring her efforts to catch it. There was a bruise right on her breast, where Clark had held her in front of him.

"The bastard," he exclaimed, furious, as he touched the bruise.

"He got a few bruises, too, from Grier," she said, trying to comfort him. He looked devastated.

"He'd have gotten more from me, if I hadn't walked right into that punch," he said with self-contempt. "I can't remember the last time I took a stupid hit like that."

She reached up and touched his lean face gently. "It's all right, Leo."

He looked down at her bare breasts and his eyes narrowed hotly. "I don't like that bruise."

"I got a worse one when my horse threw me last month," she told him. "It will heal."

"It's in a bad place."

She smiled. "So was the other one."

He unzipped her jeans and she panicked.

He didn't take any notice. He bent and removed her shoes and socks and then stripped the jeans off her. She was wearing little lacy white briefs and his hands lingered on them.

"Leo!" she screeched.

He grimaced. "I knew it was going to be a fight all the way, and you're in no condition for another one." He unbraided her hair and let it tangle down her shoulders. He turned and started the shower.

"I can do this!" she began.

His hands were already stripping off the briefs. He stopped with his hands on her waist and looked at her with barely contained passion. "I thought you'd be in a class of your own," he said huskily. "You're a knockout, baby." He lifted her and stood her up in the shower, putting a washcloth in her hand before he closed the sliding glass door. "I'll get your things in the wash."

She was too shell-shocked to ask if he knew how to use a washing machine. *Well, you fool,* she told herself, *you stood there like a statue and let him take your clothes off and stare at you! What are you complaining about?*

She bathed and used the shampoo on the shelf in the shower stall, scrubbing until she felt less tainted by Clark's filthy touch.

She turned off the shower and climbed out, wrapping herself in one of the sea-blue towels. It was soft and huge, big enough for Leo, who was a giant of a man. It swallowed her up whole.

Before she could wonder what she was going to do about something to wear, he opened the door and walked right in with a black velvet robe.

"Here," he said, jerking the towel away from her and holding out the robe.

She scurried into it, red-faced and embarrassed.

He drew her back against him and she realized that she wasn't the only one who'd just had a shower. He was wearing a robe, too. But his was open, and the only thing under it was a pair of black silk boxer shorts that left his powerful legs bare. His chest was broad and covered with thick, curling hair. He turned her until she was facing him, and his eyes were slow and curious.

"You'll have bruises. Right now, I want to treat those cuts with antibiotic cream. Then we'll dry your hair and brush it out." He smiled. "It's long and thick and glossy. I love your hair."

She smiled shyly. "It takes a lot of drying."

"I'm not in a hurry. Neither are you. I phoned your dad and told him as little as I could get away with."

"Was he worried?"

He lifted an eyebrow as he dug in the cabinet for the antibiotic cream. "About your virtue, maybe," he teased. "He thinks I've got you here so I can make love to you."

She felt breathless. "Have you?" she asked daringly.

He turned back to her with the cream in one big hand. His eyes went over her like hands. "If you want it, yes. But it's up to you."

That was a little surprising. She stood docilely while he applied the cream to her cuts and then put it away. He hooked a hair dryer to a plug on the wall and linked his fingers through her thick light brown hair while he blew it dry. There was something very intimate about standing so close to him while he dried her hair. She thought she'd never get over the delight of it, as long as she lived. Every time she washed her hair from now on, she'd feel Leo's big hands against her scalp. She smiled, her head back, her eyes closed blissfully.

"Don't go to sleep," he teased as he put the hair dryer down. "I'm not."

She felt his lips in her hair at the same moment she felt his hands go down over her shoulders and into the gap left by the robe.

If she'd been able to protest, that would have been the time to do it. But she hesitated, entranced by the feel of his hands so blatantly invading the robe, smoothing down over her high, taut breasts as if he had every right to touch her intimately whenever he felt like it.

Seconds later, the robe was gone, she was turned against him, his robe was on the floor, and she was experiencing her first adult embrace without clothing.

She whimpered at the fierce pleasure of feeling his bare, hair-roughened chest against her naked breasts. Her nails bit into the huge muscles of his upper arms as she sucked in a harsh breath and tried to stay on her feet.

"You like that, do you?" he whispered at her lips. "I know something that's even more exciting."

He picked her up in his arms and started kissing her hungrily. She responded with no thought of denying him whatever he wanted.

He carried her to the bed, paused to whip the covers and the pillows out of the way, and placed her at the center of it. His hands went to the waistband of his boxer shorts, but he hesitated, grinding his teeth together as he looked at her nudity with aching need.

He managed to control his first impulse, which was to strip and bury himself in her. He eased onto the bed beside her, his chest pressing her down into the mattress while his mouth opened on her soft lips and pressed them wide apart.

"I've ached for this," he ground out, moving his hands from her breasts down her hips to the soft inside of her thighs. "I've never wanted anything so much!"

She tried to speak, but one of his hands invaded her in the most intimate touch she'd ever experienced. Her eyes flew open and she gaped up at him.

"You're old enough, Janie," he whispered, moving his hand just enough to make her tense. "And I've waited as long as I can."

As he spoke, he touched her delicately and when she protested, he eased down to cover her mouth with his. His fingers traced her, probed, explored her until she began to whimper and move with him. It was incredible. She was lying here, naked, in his bed, letting him explore her body as if it belonged to him. And she was…enjoying it. Glorying in it. Her back arched and she moaned as he found a pressure and a rhythm that lifted her off the bed on a wave of pleasure.

One of his long, powerful legs hooked over one of hers. She felt him at her hip, aroused and not hiding it. Through the thin silk, she was as aware of him as if he'd been naked.

"Touch me," he groaned. "Don't make me do it all. Help me."

She didn't understand what he wanted. Her hands went to his chest and began to draw through the thick hair there.

"No, baby," he whispered into her mouth. He caught one of her hands and tugged it down to the shorts he was wearing. "Don't be afraid. It's all right."

He coaxed her hand onto that part of him that was blatantly male. She gasped. He lifted his head and looked into her eyes, but he wouldn't let her hand withdraw. He spread her fingers against him, grimacing as the waves of pleasure hit him and closed his eyes on a shudder.

His reaction fascinated her. She knew so little. "Does it…hurt?"

"What?" he asked huskily. "Your hand, or what it's doing?"

"Both. Either."

He pressed her hand closer, looking down. "Look," he whispered, coaxing her eyes to follow his. It was intimate. But not intimate enough for him.

"Don't panic, baby," he whispered, levering onto his back. He ripped off the shorts and tossed them onto the carpet. He rolled onto his side and caught one of her hands, insistent now, drawing it to him.

She made a sound as she looked, for the first time, at an aroused male without a thing to conceal him except her hand.

"Don't be embarrassed," he whispered roughly. "I wouldn't want any other woman to see me like this."

"You wouldn't?"

He shook his head. It was difficult not to lose control. But he eased her fingers back to him and held them there. "I'm vulnerable."

Her eyes brightened. "Oh." She hadn't considered that he was as helpless as she was to resist the pleasure of what they were doing.

His own hand went back to her body. He touched her, as she was touching him, and he smiled at her fascination.

She couldn't believe it was happening at all. She stared up at him with all her untried longings in her eyes, on her rapt face. She belonged to him. He belonged to her. It was incredible.

"Are you going to?" she whispered.

He kissed her eyelids lazily. "Going to what?"

"Take me," she whispered back.

He chuckled, deep in his throat. "What a primitive description. It's a mutual thing, you know. Wouldn't you take me, as well?"

Her eyes widened. "I suppose I would," she conceded. She stiffened and shivered. "Oh!"

His eyes darkened. There was no more humor on his face as his touch became slowly invasive. "Will you let me satisfy you?" he asked.

"I don't...understand."

"I know. That's what makes it so delicious." He bent slowly, but not to her mouth. His lips hovered just above her wide nipple. "This is the most beautiful thing I've ever done with a woman," he whispered. His lips parted. "I want nothing, except to please you."

His mouth went down over the taut nipple in a slow, exquisite motion that eventually all but swallowed her breast. She felt his tongue moving against the nipple, felt the faint suction of his mouth. All the while, his hand was becoming more insistent, and far more intimate, on her body. He felt her acceptance, even as she opened her legs for him and began to moan rhythmically with every movement of his hands.

"Yes," he whispered against her breast when he felt the pulsing of her body. "Let me, baby." He lifted his head and looked down into her eyes as she moaned piteously.

She was pulsating. She felt her body clench. She was slowly drifting up into a glorious, rhythmic heat that filled her veins, her arteries, the very cells of her body with exquisite pleasure. She'd never dreamed there was such pleasure.

"Janie, touch me, here," he whispered unsteadily.

She felt his hand curling around her fingers, teaching her, insistent, his breath jerky and violent as he twisted against her.

"Baby," he choked, kissing her hungrily. "Baby, baby!"

He moved, his big body levering slowly between her long legs. He knelt over her, his eyes wild, his body shuddering, powerfully male, and she looked up at him with total submission, still shivering from the taste of pleasure he'd already given her. It would be explosive, ecstatic. She could barely breathe for the anticipation. She was lost. He was going to have her now. She loved him. She was going to give herself. There was nothing that could stop them, nothing in all the world!

"Mr. Hart! Oh, Mr. Hart! Are you in here?"

Leo stiffened, his body kneeling between her thighs, his powerful hands clenching on them. He looked blindly down into her wide, dazed eyes. He shuddered violently and his eyes closed on a harsh muffled curse.

He threw himself onto the bed beside her, on his belly. He couldn't stop shaking. He gasped at a jerky breath and clutched the sheet beside his head as he fought for control.

"Mr. Hart!" the voice came again.

He suddenly remembered that he hadn't locked the bedroom door, and the cowboy didn't know that he wasn't alone. Even as he thought it, he heard the doorknob turn. "Open that door...and you're fired!" he shouted hoarsely. Beside him, Janie actually gasped as she belatedly realized what was about to happen.

The doorknob was released at once. "Sorry, sir, but I need you to come out here and look at this bull. I think there's something wrong with him, Mr. Hart! We got him loaded into one of the trailers and put him in the barn, but..."

"Call the vet!" he shouted. "I'll be there directly!"

"Yes, sir!"

Footsteps went back down the carpeted hall. Leo lifted his head. Beside him, Janie looked as shattered as he felt. Tears were swimming in her eyes.

He groaned softly, and pulled her to him, gently. "It's all

right," he whispered, kissing her eyelids shut. "Don't cry, baby. Nothing happened."

"Nothing!" she choked.

His hands smoothed down the long line of her back. "Almost nothing," he murmured dryly.

She was horrified, not only at her own behavior, but at what had almost happened. "If he hadn't called to you," she began in a high-pitched whisper.

His hands tangled in her long hair and he brought her mouth under his, tenderly. He nibbled her upper lip. "Yes, I know," he replied gently. "But he did." He pulled away from her and got to his feet, stretching hugely, facing her. He watched her try not to look at him with amused indulgence. But eventually, she couldn't resist it. Her eyes were huge, shocked...delighted.

"Now, when we compare notes, you'll have ammunition," he teased.

She flushed and averted her eyes, belatedly noticing that she wasn't wearing clothes, either. She tugged the sheet up over her breasts, but it was difficult to feel regrets when she looked at him.

He was smiling. His eyes were soft, tender. He looked down at what he could see of her body above the sheet with pride, loving the faint love marks on her breasts that his mouth had made.

"Greenhorn," he chided at her scarlet blush. "Well, you know a lot more about men now than you did this morning, don't you?"

She swallowed hard. Her eyes slid down him. She didn't look away, but she was very flushed, and not only because of what she was seeing. Her body throbbed in the most delicious way.

"I think I'd better take you home. Now," he added with a rueful chuckle. "From this point on, it only gets worse."

He was still passionately aroused. He wondered if she realized what it meant. He chuckled at her lack of comprehension. "I could have you three times and I'd still be like this," he said huskily. "I'm not easily satisfied."

She shivered as she looked at him, her body yielded, submissive.

"You want to, don't you?" he asked quietly, reading her expression. "So do I. More than you know. But we're not going that far together tonight. You've had enough trauma for a Friday night."

He caught her hand and pulled her up, free of the sheet and open to his eyes as he led her back into the bathroom. He turned on the shower and climbed in with her, bathing both of them quickly and efficiently, to her raging embarrassment.

He dried her and then himself before he put his shorts back on and left her to get her things. He'd washed them while she was in the shower the first time and put them in the dryer. They were clean and sweet-smelling, and the bloodstains were gone.

But when she went to take them from him, he shook his head. "One of the perks," he said softly. "I get to dress you."

And he did, completely. Then he led her to the dresser, and ran his own brush through her long, soft hair, easing it back from her face. The look in his eyes was new, fascinating, incomprehensible. She looked back at him with awe.

"Now you know something about what sex feels like, even though you're still very much a virgin," he said matter-of-factly. "And you won't be afraid of the real thing anymore, when it happens, will you?"

She shook her head, dazed.

He put the brush down and framed her face in his big, lean hands. He wasn't smiling. "You belong to me now," he said huskily. "I belong to you. Don't agonize over what you let me do to you tonight. It's as natural as breathing. Don't lie awake feeling shame or embarrassment. You saw me as helpless as I saw you. There won't be any jokes about it, any gossiping about it. I'll never tell another living soul what you let me do."

She relaxed. She hadn't really known what to expect. But he sounded more solemn than he'd ever been. He was looking at her with a strange expression.

"Are you sorry?" she asked in a hushed whisper.

"No," he replied quietly. "It was unavoidable. I was afraid for you tonight. I couldn't stop Clark. Neither could Harley. Until Grier walked in, I thought you'd had it. What happened in here was a symptom of the fear, that's all. I wanted to hold you, make you part of me." He drew in a shaky breath and actually shivered. "I wanted to go right inside you, Janie," he whispered bluntly. "But we'll save that pleasure for the right time and place. This isn't it."

She colored and averted her eyes.

He turned her face back to his. "Meanwhile," he said slowly, searching her eyes, "we'll have no more secrets, of any kind, between us."

She stood quietly against him, watching his face. "Nobody's seen me without my clothes since I was a little kid," she whispered, as if it was a fearful secret.

"Not that many women have seen me without mine," he replied unexpectedly. He smiled tenderly.

Her eyebrows arched.

"Shocked?" he mused, moving away to pull clothes out of his closet and socks out of his drawers. He sat down to pull on the socks, glancing at her wryly. "I'm not a playboy. I'm not without experience, but there was always a limit I wouldn't cross with women I only knew slightly. It gives people power over you when they know intimate things about you."

"Yes," she said, moving to sit beside him on the bed, with her hands folded in her lap. "Thanks."

"For what?"

She smiled. "For making it feel all right. That I...let you touch me that way, I mean."

He finished pulling on his socks and tilted her face up to his. He kissed her softly. "I won't ever touch another woman like that," he whispered into her mouth. "It would be like committing adultery, after what we did on this bed."

Her heart flew up into the clouds. Her wide, fascinated eyes searched his. "Really?"

He chuckled. "Are you anxious to rush out and experiment with another man?"

She shook her head.

"Why?"

She smiled shyly. "It would be like committing adultery," she repeated what he'd said.

He stood up and looked down at her with possession. "It was a near thing," he murmured. "I don't know whether to punch that cowboy or give him a raise for interrupting us. I lost it, in those last few seconds. I couldn't have stopped."

"Neither could I." She lifted her mouth for his soft kiss. She searched his eyes, remembering what he'd told her. "But the books say a man can only do it once," she blurted out, "and then he has to rest."

He laughed softly. "I know. But a handful of men can go all night. I'm one of them."

"Oh!"

He pulled up his slacks and fastened them before he shouldered into a knit shirt. He turned back to her, smoothing his disheveled hair. "I was contemplating even much more explosive pleasures when someone started shouting my name."

This was interesting. "More explosive pleasures?" she prompted.

He drew her up against him and held her close. "What we did and what we didn't do, is the difference between licking an ice-cream cone and eating a banana split," he teased. "What you had was only a small taste of what we can have together."

"Wow," she said softly.

"Wow," he echoed, bending to kiss her hungrily. He sighed into her mouth. "I was almost willing to risk getting you pregnant, I was so far gone." He lifted his head and looked at her. "How do you feel about kids, Janie?"

"I love children," she said honestly. "How about you?"

"Me too. I'm beginning to rethink my position on having them." His lean hand touched her belly. "You've got nice wide hips," he commented, testing them.

She felt odd. Her body seemed to contract. She searched his eyes because she didn't understand what was happening to her.

"You can tell Shea's you're through," he said abruptly. "I'm not risking you again. If we can't keep Clark in jail for the foreseeable future, we have to make plans to keep you safe."

Her lips parted. She'd all but forgotten her horrible experience. She touched her throat and felt again the prick of the knife. "You said he was vindictive."

"He'll have to get through me," he said. "And with a gun, I'm every bit his equal," he added.

She reached up and touched his hard mouth. "I don't want you to get hurt."

"I don't want you to get hurt," he seconded. His face twisted. "Baby, you are the very breath in my body," he whispered, and reached for her.

She felt boneless as he kissed her with such passion and fire that she trembled.

"I wish I didn't have to take you home," he groaned at her lips. "I want to make love to you completely. I want to lie against you and over you, and inside you!"

She moaned at his mouth as it became deep and insistent, devouring her parted lips.

He was shivering. He had to drag his mouth away from hers. He looked shattered. He touched her long hair with a hand that had a faint tremor. "Amazing," he whispered gruffly. "That I couldn't see it, before it happened."

"See what?" she asked drowsily.

His eyes fell to her swollen, parted lips. "Never mind," he whispered. He bent and kissed her with breathless tenderness. "I'm taking you home. Then I'll see about my bull. Tomorrow morning, I'll come and get you and we'll see about swearing out more warrants against Clark."

"You don't think Clark will get out on bond?" she asked worriedly.

"Not if Grier can prevent it." He reached for his truck keys and took her by the arm. "We'll go out the back," he said. "I don't want anyone to know you were here with me tonight. It wouldn't look good, even under the circumstances."

"Don't worry, nobody will know," she assured him.

The next morning, Fred Brewster came into the dining room looking like a thunderstorm.

"What were you doing in Leo Hart's bedroom last night when you were supposed to be working, Janie?" he asked bluntly.

She gaped at him with her mouth open. He was furious.

"How in the world…?" she exclaimed.

"One of the Harts' cowboys went to get him about a sick bull. He saw Leo sneaking you out the back door!" He scowled and leaned closer. "And what the hell happened to your face? Leo said you had a troublesome customer and he was bringing you home! What the hell's going on, Janie?"

She was scrambling for an answer that wouldn't get her in even more trouble when they heard a pickup truck roar up the driveway and stop at the back door. A minute later there was a hard rap, and the door opened by itself.

Leo came in, wearing dressy boots and slacks, a white shirt with a tie, and a sports coat. His white Stetson had been cleaned and looked as if it had never been introduced to a muddy truck mat. He took off the hat and tossed it onto the counter, moving past Fred to look at Janie's face.

"Damn!" he muttered, turning her cheek so that the violet bruise was very noticeable. "I didn't realize he hit you that hard, baby!"

"Hit her?!" Fred burst out. "Who hit her, and what was she doing in your bedroom last night?!"

Leo turned toward him, his face contemplative, his dark eyes quiet and somber. "Did she tell you?" he asked.

"I never!" Janie burst out, flushing.

"One of your cowboys mentioned it to one of my cowboys," Fred began.

Leo's eyes flashed fire. "He'll be drawing his pay at the end of the day. Nobody, but nobody, tells tales about Janie!"

Father and daughter exchanged puzzled glances.

"Why are you so shocked?" he asked her, when he saw her face. "Do you think I take women to my house, ever?"

She hadn't considered that. Her lips parted on a shocked breath.

He glanced at Fred, who was still unconvinced. "All right, you might as well know it all. Jack Clark made a pass at her in Shea's and when she protested, he pulled a knife on her." He waited for that to sink in, and for Fred to sit down, hard, before he continued. "Harley and I got there about the same time and heard yelling. We went inside to find Janie with a knife at her throat. We rushed Clark, but he put both of us over a table. Janie's co-worker had phoned the sheriff, but none of the deputies were within quick reach, so they radioed Grier and he took Clark down and put him in jail." He grimaced, looking at Janie's face. "She was covered with blood and so upset that she could hardly stand. I couldn't bring myself to take her home in that condition, so I took her home with me and cleaned her up and calmed her down first."

Fred caught Janie's hand in his and held it hard. "Oh, daughter, I'm sorry!"

"It's okay. We were trying to spare you, that's all," she faltered.

Leo pulled a cell phone from his pocket, dialed a number, and got his foreman. "You tell Carl Turley that he's fired. You get him the hell out of there before I get home, or he'll need first aid to get off the ranch. Yes. Yes." His face was frightening. "It was true. Clark's in jail now, on assault charges. Of course nothing was going on, and you can repeat that, with my blessing! Just get Turley out of there! Right."

He hung up and put the phone away. He was vibrating with suppressed fury, that one of his own men would gossip about him and Janie, under the circumstances. "So much for gossip," he gritted.

"Thanks, Leo," Fred said tersely. "And I'm sorry I jumped to the wrong conclusion. It's just that, normally, a man wouldn't take a woman home with him late at night unless he was…well…"

"…planning to seduce her?" Leo said for him. He looked at Janie and his eyes darkened.

She flushed.

"Yes," Fred admitted uncomfortably.

Leo's dark eyes began to twinkle as they wandered over Janie like loving hands. "Would this be a bad time to tell you that I have every intention of seducing her at some future time?"

Chapter Ten

Fred looked as if he'd swallowed a chicken, whole. He flushed, trying to forget that Leo had loaned him the money to save his ranch, thinking only of his daughter's welfare. "Now, look here, Leo…" he began.

Leo chuckled. "I was teasing. She's perfectly safe with me, Fred," he replied. He caught Janie's hand and tugged her to her feet. "We have to go see the magistrate about warrants," he said, sobering. "I want him to see these bruises on her face," he added coldly. "I don't think we'll have any problem with assault charges."

Janie moved closer to Leo. He made her feel safe, protected. He bent toward her, his whole expression one of utter tenderness. Belatedly, Fred began to understand what he was seeing. Leo's face, to him, was an open book. He was shocked. At the same time, he realized that Janie didn't understand what was going on. Probably she thought he was being brotherly.

"Don't you want breakfast first?" Fred offered, trying to get his bearings again.

For the first time, Leo seemed to notice the table. His hand, holding Janie's, contracted involuntarily. Bacon, scrambled eggs, and…biscuits? Biscuits! He scowled, letting go of Janie's fingers to approach the bread basket. He reached down, expecting a concretelike substance, remembering that he and Rey had secretly sailed some of Janie's earlier efforts at biscuit-making over the target range for each other and used them for skeet targets. But these weren't hard. They were flaky, delicate. He opened one. It was soft inside. It smelled delicious.

He was barely aware of sitting down, dragging Janie's plate under his hands. He buttered a biscuit and put strawberry jam on it. He bit into it and sighed with pure ecstasy.

"I forgot about the biscuits," Janie told her father worriedly.

Fred glanced at their guest and grimaced. "Maybe we should have saved it for a surprise."

Leo was sighing, his eyes closed as he chewed.

"We'll never get to the magistrate's now," Janie thought aloud.

"He'll run out of biscuits in about ten minutes, at that rate," Fred said with a grin.

"I'll get another plate. We can split the eggs and bacon," Janie told her father, inwardly beaming with pride at Leo's obvious enjoyment of her efforts. Now, finally, the difficulty of learning to cook seemed worth every minute.

Leo went right on chewing, oblivious to movement around him.

The last biscuit was gone with a wistful sigh when he became aware of his two companions again.

"Who made the biscuits?" Leo asked Janie.

She grimaced. "I did."

"But you can't cook, honey," he said gently, trying to soften the accusation.

"Marilee said you didn't like me because I couldn't make biscuits or cook anything edible," she confessed without looking at him. "So I learned how."

He caught her fingers tightly in his. "She lied. But those were wonderful biscuits," he said. "Flaky and soft inside, delicately browned. Absolutely delicious."

She smiled shyly. "I can make them anytime you like."

He was looking at her with pure possession. "Every morning," he coaxed. "I'll stop by for coffee. If Fred doesn't mind," he added belatedly.

Fred chuckled. "Fred doesn't mind," he murmured dryly.

Leo scowled. "You look like a cat with a mouse."

Fred shrugged. "Just a stray thought. Nothing to worry about."

Leo held the older man's reluctant gaze and understood the odd statement. He nodded slowly. He smiled sheepishly as he realized that Fred wasn't blind at all.

Fred got up. "Well, I've got cattle to move. How's your bull, by the way?" he added abruptly, worried.

"Colic," Leo said with a cool smile. "Easily treated and nothing to get upset over."

"I'm glad. I had visions of you losing yours to Clark as well."

"He isn't from the same herd as yours was, Fred," Leo told him. "But even so, I think we'll manage to keep Clark penned up for a while. Which reminds me," he added, glancing at Janie. "We'd better get going."

"Okay. I'll just get the breakfast things cleared away first."

Leo sat and watched her work with a smitten expression on his face. Fred didn't linger. He knew a hooked fish when he saw one.

They swore out warrants and presented them to the sheriff. Clark had already been transferred to the county lockup, after a trip to the hospital emergency room the night before, and Leo and Janie stopped in to see Grier at the police station.

Grier had just finished talking to the mayor, a pleasant older man named Tarleton Connor, newly elected to his position. Connor and Grier had a mutual cousin, as did Grier and Chet Blake, the police chief. Chet was out of town on police business, so Grier was nominally in charge of things.

"Have a seat," Grier invited, his eyes narrow and angry on Janie's bruised face. "If it's any consolation, Miss Brewster, Clark's got bruised ribs and a black eye."

She smiled. It was uncomfortable, because it irritated the bruise. "Thanks, Mr. Grier," she said with genuine appreciation.

"That goes double for me," Leo told him. "He put Harley and me over a table so fast it's embarrassing to admit it."

"Why?" Grier asked, sitting down behind his desk. "The man was a martial artist," he elaborated. "He had a studio up in Victoria for a while, until the authorities realized that he was teaching killing techniques to ex-cons."

Leo's jaw fell.

Grier shrugged. "He was the equivalent of a black belt, too. Harley's not bad, but he needs a lot more training from Eb Scott before he could take on Clark." He pursed his lips and his eyes twinkled as he studied Leo's expression. "Feel better now?"

Leo chuckled. "Yes. Thanks."

Grier glanced at Janie's curious expression. "Men don't like to be overpowered by other men. It's a guy thing," he explained.

"Anybody ever overpower you?" Leo asked curiously.

"Judd Dunn almost did, once. But then, I taught him everything he knows."

"You know a lot," Janie said. "I never saw anybody move that fast."

"I was taught by a guy up in Tarrant County," Grier told her with a smile. "He's on television every week. Plays a Texas Ranger."

Janie gasped.

"Nice guy," Grier added. "And a hell of a martial artist."

Leo was watching him with a twinkle in his own eyes. "I did think the spinning heel kick looked familiar."

Grier smiled. He sat up. "About Clark," he added. "His brother came to see him at the county lockup this morning and got the bad news. With only one charge so far, Harley's, he's only got a misdemeanor…"

"We took out a warrant for aggravated assault and battery," Leo interrupted. "Janie had a knife at her throat just before you walked in."

"So I was told." Grier's dark eyes narrowed on Janie's throat. The nick was red and noticeable this morning. "An inch deeper and we'd be visiting you at the funeral home this morning."

"I know," Janie replied.

"You kept your head," he said with a smile. "It probably saved your life."

"Can you keep Clark in jail?" she asked worriedly.

"I'll ask Judge Barnett to set bail as high as he can. But Clark's brother isn't going to settle for a public defender. He said he'd get Jack the best attorney he could find, and he'd pay for it." He shrugged. "God knows what he'll pay for it with," he added coldly. "John Clark owes everybody, up to and including his boss. So does our local Clark brother."

"He may have to have a public defender."

"We'll see. But meanwhile, he's out of everybody's way, and he'll stay put."

"What about his brother?" Leo wanted to know. "Is Janie in any danger?"

Grier shook his head. "John Clark went back to Victoria after he saw his brother. I had him followed, by one of my off-duty guys, just to make sure he really left. But I'd keep my eyes open, if I were you, just the same. These boys are bad news."

"We'll do that," Leo said.

* * *

He drove Janie back to his own ranch and took her around with him while he checked on the various projects he'd initiated. He pulled up at the barn and told her to stay in the truck.

She was curious until she remembered that he'd fired the man who'd interrupted them the night before. She was glad about the interruption, in retrospect, but uneasy about the gossip that man had started about her and Leo.

He was back in less than five minutes, his face hard, his eyes blazing. He got into the truck and glanced at her, forcibly wiping the anger out of his expression.

"He's gone," he told her gently. "Quit without his check," he added with a rueful smile. "I guess Charles told him what I said." He shrugged. "He wasn't much of a cowboy, at that, if he couldn't tell colic from bloat."

She reached out and put her nervous fingers over his big hand on the steering wheel. He flinched and she jerked her hand back.

"No!" He caught her fingers in his and held them tight. "I'm sorry," he said at once, scowling. "You've never touched me voluntarily before. It surprised me. I like it," he added, smiling.

She was flushed and nervous. "Oh. Okay." She smiled shyly.

He searched her eyes with his for so long that her heart began to race. His face tautened. "This won't do," he said in a husky, deep tone. He started the truck with a violent motion and drove back the way they'd come, turning onto a rutted path that led into the woods and, far beyond, to a pasture. But he stopped the truck halfway to the pasture, threw it out of gear, and cut off the engine.

He had Janie out of her seat belt and into his big arms in seconds, and his hungry mouth was on her lips before she could react.

She didn't have any instincts for self-preservation left. She melted into his aroused body, not even protesting the intimate way he was pressing her hips against his. Her arms curled around his neck and she kissed him back with enthusiasm.

She felt his hands going under her blouse, against her breasts. That felt wonderful. It was perfectly all right, because she belonged to him.

He lifted his mouth from hers, breathing hard, and watched her eyes while his hands caressed her. She winced and he caught his breath.

"I'm sorry!" he said at once, soothing the bruise he'd forgotten about. "I didn't mean to hurt you," he whispered.

She reached up to kiss his eyelids shut, feeling the shock that ran through him at the soft caress. His hands moved to her waist and rested there while he held his breath, waiting. She felt the hunger in him, like a living thing. Delighted by his unexpected submission to her mouth, she kissed his face softly, tenderly, drawing her lips over his thick eyebrows, his eyelids, his cheeks and nose and chin. They moved to his strong throat and lingered in the pulsating hollow.

One lean hand went between them to the buttons of his cotton shirt. He unfastened them quickly, jerking the fabric out of her way, inviting her mouth inside.

Her hands spread on the thick mat of hair that covered the warm, strong muscles of his chest. Her mouth touched it, lightly, and then not lightly. She moved to where his heart beat roughly, and then over the flat male nipple that was a counterpart to her own. But the reaction she got when she put her mouth over it was shocking.

He groaned so harshly that she was sure she'd hurt him. She drew back, surprising a look of anguish on his lean face.

"Leo?" she whispered uneasily.

"It arouses me," he ground out, then he shivered.

She didn't know what to do next. He looked as if he ached to have her repeat the caress, but his body was as taut as a rope against her.

"You'll have to tell me what to do," she faltered. "I don't want to make it worse."

"Whatever I do is going to shock you speechless," he choked out. "But, what the hell…!"

He dragged her face back to his nipple and pressed it there, hard. "You know what I want."

She did, at some level. Her mouth eased down against him with a soft, gentle suction that lifted him back against the seat with a harsh little cry of pleasure. His hands at the back of her head were rough and insistent. She gave in and did what he was silently asking her for. She felt him shudder and gasp, his body vibrating as if it was overwhelmed by pleasure. He bit off a harsh word and trembled violently for a few seconds before he turned her mouth away from him and pressed her unblemished cheek against his chest. His hands in her hair trembled as they caressed her scalp. His heartbeat was raging under her mouth.

He fought to breathe normally. "Wow," he whispered unsteadily.

Her fingers tangled in the thick hair under them. "Did you really like it?" she whispered back.

He actually laughed, a little unsteadily. "Didn't you feel what was happening to me?"

"You were shaking."

"Yes. I was, wasn't I? Just the way you were shaking last night when I touched you…"

Her cheek slid back onto his shoulder so that she could look up into his soft eyes. "I didn't know a man would be sensitive, there, like a woman is."

He bent and drew his lips over her eyelids. "I'm sensitive, all right." His lips moved over her mouth and pressed there hungrily. "It isn't enough, Janie. I've got to have you. All the way."

"Right now?" she stammered.

He lifted his head and looked down at her in his arms. He was solemn, unsmiling, as he met her wide eyes. His body was still vibrating with unsatisfied desire. Deliberately, he drew her hips closer against his and let her feel him there.

She didn't protest. If anything, her body melted even closer.

One lean hand went to her belly and rested there, between them, while he searched her eyes. "I want...to make you pregnant," he said in a rough whisper.

Her lips fell open. She stared at him, not knowing what to say.

He looked worried. "I've never wanted that with a woman," he continued, as if he was discussing the weather. His fingers moved lightly on her body. "Not with anyone."

He was saying something profound. She hadn't believed it at first, but the expression on his face was hard to explain away.

"My father would shoot you," she managed to say weakly.

"My brothers would shoot me, too," he agreed, nodding.

She was frowning. She didn't understand.

He bent and kissed her, with an odd tenderness. He laughed to himself. "Just my luck," he breathed against her lips, "to get mixed up with a virgin who can cook."

"We aren't mixed up," she began.

His hand contracted against the base of her spine, grinding her into him, and one eyebrow went up over a worldly smile as she blushed.

She cleared her throat. "We aren't very mixed up," she corrected.

He nibbled at her upper lip. "I look at you and get turned on so hard I can hardly walk around without bending over double. I touch you and I hurt all over. I dream of you every single night of my life and wake up vibrating." He lifted his head and looked down into her misty eyes. He wasn't smiling. He wasn't kidding. "Never like this, Janie. Either we have each other, or we stop it, right now."

Her fingers touched his face lovingly. "You can do whatever you like to me," she whispered unsteadily.

His jaw tautened. "Anything?"

She nodded. She loved him with all her heart.

His eyes closed. His arms brought her gently against him, and his mouth buried itself in her throat, pressing there hot and hard for a few aching seconds. Then he dragged in a harsh breath and sat up, putting her back in her seat and fastening her seat belt.

He didn't look at her as he fastened his own belt and started the truck. She sat beside him as he pulled out onto the highway, a little surprised that he didn't turn into the road that led to his house. She'd expected him to take her there. She swallowed hard, remembering the way they'd pleasured each other on his big bed the night before, remembering the look of his powerful body without clothes. She flushed with anticipated delight. She was out of her mind. Her father was going to kill her. She looked at Leo with an ache that curled her toes up inside her shoes, and didn't care if he did. Some things were worth dying for.

Leo drove right into town and pulled into a parking spot in front of the drugstore. Right, she thought nervously, he was going inside to buy…protection…for what they were going to do. He wanted a child, though, he'd said. She flushed as he got out of the truck and came around to open her door.

He had to unfasten her seat belt first. She didn't even have the presence of mind to accomplish that.

He helped her out of the truck and looked down at her with an expression she couldn't decipher. He touched her cheek gently, and then her hair, and her soft mouth. His eyes were full of turmoil.

He tugged her away from the truck and closed her door, leading her to the sidewalk with one small hand tightly held in his fingers.

She started toward the drugstore.

"Wrong way, sweetheart," he said tenderly, and led her right into a jewelry store.

The clerk was talking to another clerk, but he came forward, smiling, when they entered the shop.

"May I help you find something?" he asked Leo.

"Yes," Leo said somberly. "We want to look at wedding bands."

Janie felt all the blood draining out of her face. It felt numb. She hoped she wasn't going to pass out.

Leo's hand tightened around her fingers, and slowly linked them together as he positioned her in front of the case that held engagement rings and wedding rings.

The clerk took out the tray that Leo indicated. Leo looked down at Janie with quiet, tender eyes.

"You can have anything you want," he said huskily, and he wasn't talking solely of rings.

She met his searching gaze with tears glistening on her lashes. He bent and kissed the wetness away.

The clerk averted his eyes. It was like peering through a private window. He couldn't remember ever seeing such an expression on a man's face before.

"Look at the rings, Janie," Leo said gently.

She managed to focus on them belatedly. She didn't care about flashy things, like huge diamonds. She was a country girl, for all her sophistication. Her eyes kept coming back to a set of rings that had a grape leaf pattern. The wedding band was wide, yellow gold with a white gold rim, the pattern embossed on the gold surface. The matching engagement ring had a diamond, but not a flashy one, and it contained the same grape leaf pattern on its circumference

"I like this one," she said finally, touching it.

There was a matching masculine-looking wedding band. She looked up at Leo.

He smiled. "Do you want me to wear one, too?" he teased.

Her eyes were breathless with love. She couldn't manage words. She only nodded.

He turned his attention back to the clerk. "We'll take all three," he said.

"They'll need to be sized. Let me get my measuring rod," the clerk said with a big grin. The rings were expensive, fourteen karat, and that diamond was the highest quality the store sold. The commission was going to be tasty.

"It isn't too expensive?" Janie worried.

Leo bent and kissed the tip of her nose. "They're going to last a long time," he told her. "They're not too expensive."

She couldn't believe what was happening. She wanted to tell him so, but the clerk came back and they were immediately involved in having their fingers sized and the paperwork filled out.

Leo produced a gold card and paid for them while Janie looked on, still shell-shocked.

Leo held her hand tight when they went back to the truck. "Next stop, city hall," he murmured dryly. "Rather, the fire station—they take the license applications when city hall is closed. I forgot it was Saturday." He lifted both eyebrows at her stunned expression. "Might as well get it all done in one day. Which reminds me." He pulled out his cell phone after he'd put her in the truck and phoned the office of the doctors Coltrain. While Janie listened, spellbound, he made an appointment for blood tests for that afternoon. The doctors Coltrain had a Saturday clinic.

He hung up and slipped the phone back into his pocket with a grin. "Marriage license next, blood tests later, and about next Wednesday, we'll have a nice and quiet small wedding followed by," he added huskily, "one hell of a long passionate wedding night."

She caught her breath at the passion in his eyes. "Leo, are you sure?" she wanted to know.

He dragged her into his arms and kissed her so hungrily that a familiar couple walking past the truck actually stared amusedly at them for a few seconds before hurrying on past.

"I'm sorry, baby. I can't…wait…any longer," he ground out into her eager mouth. "It's marriage or I'm leaving the state!" He lifted his head, and his eyes were tortured. He could barely breathe. "Oh, God, I want you, Janie!"

She felt the tremor in his big body. She understood what he felt, because it was the same with her. She drew in a slow breath. It was desire. She thought, maybe, there was some affection as well, but he was dying to have her, and that was what prompted marriage plans. He'd said often enough that he was never going to get married.

He saw all those thoughts in her eyes, even through the most painful desire he'd ever known. "I'll make you glad you said yes," he told her gruffly. "I won't ever cheat on you, or hurt you. I'll take care of you all my life. All of yours."

It was enough, she thought, to take a chance on. "All right," she said tenderly. She reached up and touched his hard, swollen mouth. "I'll marry you."

It was profound, to hear her say it. He caught his breath at the raging arousal the words produced in his already-tortured body. He groaned as he pressed his mouth hard into the palm of her hand.

She wasn't confident enough to tease him about his desire for her. But it pleased her that he was, at least, fiercely hungry for her in that way, if no other.

He caught her close and fought for control. "We'd better go and get a marriage license," he bit off. "We've already given Evan and Anna Tremayne an eyeful."

"What?" she asked drowsily.

"They were walking past when I kissed you," he said with a rueful smile.

"They've been married for years," she pointed out.

He rubbed his nose against hers. "Wait until we've been married for years," he whispered. "We'll still be fogging up windows in parked trucks."

"Think so?" she asked, smiling.

"Wait and see."

He let go of her, with obvious reluctance, and moved back under the steering wheel. "Here we go."

They applied for the marriage license, had the blood tests, and then went to round up their families to tell them the news.

Janie's aunt Lydia had gone to Europe over the holidays on an impromptu sightseeing trip, Fred Brewster told them when they gave him the news. "She'll be livid if she misses the wedding," he said worriedly.

"She can be here for the first christening," Leo said with a grin at Janie's blush. "You can bring Hettie with you, and come over to the ranch for supper tomorrow night," he added, amused at Fred's lack of surprise at the announcement. "I've invited my brothers to supper and phoned Barbara to have it catered. I wanted to break the news to all of them at once."

"Hettie won't be surprised," Fred told them, tongue-in-cheek. "But she'll enjoy a night out. We'll be along about six."

"Fine," Leo said, and didn't offer to leave Janie at home. He waited until she changed into a royal-blue pantsuit with a beige top, and carried her with him to the ranch.

He did chores and paperwork with Janie right beside him, although he didn't touch her.

"A man only has so much self-control," he told her with

a wistful sigh. "So we'll keep our hands off each other, until the wedding. Fair enough?"

She grinned at him. "Fair enough!"

He took her home after they had supper at a local restaurant. "I'd love to have taken you up to Houston for a night on the town," he said when he walked her to her door. "But not with your face like that." He touched it somberly. "Here in Jacobsville, everybody already knows what happened out at Shea's last night. In Houston, people might think I did this, or allowed it to happen." He bent and kissed the painful bruise. "Nobody will ever hurt you again as long as I live," he swore huskily.

She closed her eyes, savoring the soft touch of his mouth. "Are you sure you want to marry me?" she asked.

"I'm sure. I'll be along about ten-thirty," he added.

She looked up at him, puzzled. "Ten-thirty?"

He nodded. "Church," he said with a wicked grin. "We have to set a good example for the kids."

She laughed, delighted. "Okay."

"See you in the morning, pretty girl," he said, and brushed his mouth lightly over hers before he bounded back down the steps to his car and drove off with a wave of his hand.

Fred was amazed that Leo did take her to church, and then came back to the house with her for a lunch of cold cuts. He and Fred talked cattle while Janie lounged at Leo's side, still astounded at the unexpected turn of events. Fred couldn't be happier about the upcoming nuptials. He was amused that Hettie had the weekend off and didn't know what had happened. She had a shock coming when she arrived later in the day.

Leo took Janie with him when he went home, approving her choice of a silky beige dress and matching high heels, pearls in her ears and around her throat, and her hair long and luxurious down her back.

"Your brothers will be surprised," Janie said worriedly on the way there.

Leo lifted an eyebrow. "After the Cattleman's Ball? Probably not," he said. Then he told her about Corrigan offering to drive him home so that he could pump him for information to report back to the others.

"You were very intoxicated," she recalled, embarrassed when she recalled the fierce argument they'd had.

"I'd just found out that Marilee had lied about you," he confided. "And seeing you with damned Harley didn't help."

"You were jealous," she realized.

"Murderously jealous," he confessed at once. "That only got worse, when you took the job at Shea's." He glanced at her. "I'm not having you work there any longer. I don't care what compromises I have to make to get you to agree."

She smiled to herself. "Oh, I don't mind quitting," she confessed. "I'll have enough to do at the ranch, after we're married, getting settled in."

"Let's try not to talk about that right now, okay?"

She stared at him, worriedly. "Are you getting cold feet?" she asked.

"I'll tell you what I'm getting," he said, turning dark eyes to hers. And he did tell her, bluntly, and starkly. He nodded curtly at her scarlet flush and directed his attention back at the road. "Just for the record, the word 'marriage' reminds me of the words 'wedding night,' and I go nuts."

She whistled softly.

"So let's think about food and coffee and my brothers and try not to start something noticeable," he added in a deep tone. "Because all three of them are going to be looking for obvious signs and they'll laugh the place down if they see any."

"We can recite multiplication tables together," she agreed.

He glanced at her with narrow eyes. "Great idea," he

replied sarcastically. "That reminds me of rabbits, and guess what rabbits remind me of?"

"I know the Gettysburg Address by heart," she countered. "I'll teach it to you."

"That will put me to sleep."

"I'll make biscuits for supper."

He sat up straight. "Biscuits? For supper? To go with Barbara's nice barbecue, potato salad and apple pie. Now that's an idea that just makes my mouth water! And here I am poking along!" He pushed down on the accelerator. "Honey, you just said the magic word!"

She chuckled to herself. Marriage, she thought, was going to be a real adventure.

Chapter Eleven

Not only did Corrigan, Rey, and Cag show up for supper with their wives, Dorie, Meredith and Tess, but Simon and Tira came all the way from Austin on a chartered jet. Janie had just taken off her apron after producing a large pan of biscuits, adding them to the deliciously spread table that Barbara and her assistant had arranged before they left.

All four couples arrived together, the others having picked up Simon and Tira at the Jacobsville airport on the way.

Leo and Janie met them at the door. Leo looked unprepared.

"All of you?" he exclaimed.

Simon shrugged. "I didn't believe them," he said, pointing at the other three brothers. "I had to come see for myself."

"We didn't believe him, either," Rey agreed, pointing at Leo.

They all looked at Janie, who moved closer to Leo and blushed.

"If she's pregnant, you're dead," Cag told Leo pointedly when he saw the look on Janie's face. He leaned closer before Leo could recover enough to protest. "Have you been beating her?"

"She is most certainly not pregnant!" Leo said, offended. "And you four ought to know that I have never hit a woman in my life!"

"But he hit the guy who did this to me," Janie said with pride, smiling up at him as she curled her fingers into his big ones.

"Not very effectively, I'm afraid," Leo confessed.

"That's just because the guy had a black belt," Janie said, defending Leo. "Nobody but our assistant police chief had the experience to bring him down."

"Yes, I know Grier," Simon said solemnly. "He's something of a legend in law enforcement circles, even in Austin."

"He has alien artifacts in his filing cabinet, and he was a government assassin," Janie volunteered with a straight face.

Everybody stared at her.

"He was kidding!" Leo chuckled.

She grinned at him. He wrinkled his nose at her. They exchanged looks that made the others suddenly observant. All at once, they became serious.

"We can do wedding invitations if we e-mail them tonight," Cag said offhand. He pulled a list from his pocket. "This is a list of the people we need to invite."

"I can get the symphony orchestra to play," Rey said, nodding. "I've got their conductor's home phone number in my pocket computer." He pulled it out.

"We can buy the gown online and have it overnighted here from Neiman-Marcus in Dallas," Corrigan volunteered. "All we need is her dress size. What are you, a size ten?"

Janie balked visibly, but nodded. "Here comes her father," Dorie said enthusiastically, noting the new arrival.

"I'll e-mail the announcement to the newspaper," Tess said. "They have a Tuesday edition, we can just make it. We'll need a photo."

There was a flash. Tira changed the setting on her digital camera. "How's this?" She asked, showing it to Tess and Meredith.

"Great!" Meredith said. "We can use Leo's computer to

download it and e-mail it straight to the paper, so they'll have it first thing tomorrow. We can e-mail it to the local television station as well. Come on!"

"Wait for me! I'll write the announcement," Dorie called to Corrigan, following along behind the women.

"Hey!" Janie exclaimed.

"What?" Tira asked, hesitating. "Oh, yes, the reception. It can be held here. But the cake! We need a caterer!"

"Cag can call the caterer," Simon volunteered his brother.

"It's my wedding!" Janie protested.

"Of course it is, dear," Tira said soothingly. "Let's go, girls."

The women vanished into Leo's study. The men went into a huddle. Janie's father and Hettie came in the open door, looking shell-shocked.

"Never mind them," Leo said, drawing Janie to meet her parent and her housekeeper. "They're taking care of the arrangements," he added, waving his hand in the general direction of his brothers and sisters-in-law. "Apparently, it's going to be a big wedding, with a formal gown and caterers and newspaper coverage." He grinned. "You can come, of course."

Janie hit him. "We were going to have a nice, quiet little wedding!"

"You go tell them what you want, honey," he told Janie. "Just don't expect them to listen."

Hettie started giggling. Janie glared at her.

"You don't remember, do you?" the housekeeper asked Janie. "Leo helped them do the same thing to Dorie, and Tira, and Tess, and even Meredith. It's payback time. They're getting even."

"I'm afraid so," Leo told Janie with a smug grin. "But look at the bright side, you can just sit back and relax and not have to worry about a single detail."

"But, my dress…" she protested.

He patted her on the shoulder. "They have wonderful taste," he assured her.

Fred was grinning from ear to ear. He never would have believed one man could move so fast, but he'd seen the way Leo looked at Janie just the morning before. It was no surprise to him that a wedding was forthcoming. He knew a man who was head over heels when he saw one.

By the end of the evening, Janie had approved the wedding gown, provided the statistics and details of her family background and education, and climbed into the car with Leo to let him take her home.

"The rings will be ready Tuesday, they promised," he told her at her father's door. He smiled tenderly. "You'll be a beautiful bride."

"I can't believe it," she said softly, searching his lean face.

He drew her close. "Wednesday night, you'll believe it," he said huskily, and bent to kiss her with obvious restraint. "Now, good night!"

He walked to the car. She drifted inside, wrapped in dreams.

It was a honey of a society wedding. For something so hastily concocted, especially with Christmas approaching, it went off perfectly. Even the rings were ready on time, the dress arrived by special overnight delivery, the blood tests and marriage license were promptly produced, the minister engaged, press coverage assured, the caterer on time—nothing, absolutely nothing, went wrong.

Janie stood beside Leo at the Hart ranch at a makeshift arch latticed with pink and white roses while they spoke their vows. Janie had a veil, because Leo had insisted. And after the last words of the marriage ceremony were spoken, he lifted the veil from Janie's soft eyes and looked at her with smoldering possession. He bent and kissed her tenderly, his lips barely brushing hers. She had a yellowing bruise on one cheek and she was careful to keep that side away from the camera, but Leo didn't seem to notice the blemish.

"You are the most beautiful bride who ever spoke her vows," he whispered as he kissed her. "And I will cherish you until they lay me down in the dark!"

She reached up and kissed him back, triggering a burst of enthusiastic ardor that he was only able to curb belatedly. He drew away from her, smiling sheepishly at their audience, caught her hand, and led her back to the house through a shower of rice.

The brothers were on the job even then. The press was delicately prompted to leave after the cake and punch were consumed, the symphony orchestra was coaxed to load their instruments. The guests were delicately led to the door and thanked. Then the brothers carried their wives away in a flurry of good wishes and, at last, the newlyweds were alone, in their own home.

Leo looked at Janie with eyes that made her heart race. "Alone," he whispered, approaching her slowly, "at last."

He bent and lifted her, tenderly, and carried her down the hall to the bedroom. He locked the door. He took the phone off the hook. He closed the curtains. He came back to her, where she stood, a little apprehensive, just inside the closed door.

"I'm not going to hurt you," he said softly. "You're a priceless treasure. I'm going to be slow, and tender, and I'm going to give you all the time you need. Don't be afraid of me."

"I'm not, really," she said huskily, watching him divest her of the veil and the hairpins that held her elaborate coiffure in place with sprigs of lily of the valley. "But you want me so much," she tried to explain. "What if I can't satisfy you?"

He laughed. "You underestimate yourself."

"Are you sure?"

He turned her around so that he could undo the delicate hooks and snaps of her gown. "I'm sure."

She let him strip her down to her lacy camisole, white stockings and lacy white garter belt, her eyes feeding on the delighted expression that claimed his lean face.

"Beautiful," he said huskily. "I love you in white lace."

"You're not bad in a morning coat," she teased, liking the vested gray ceremonial rig he was wearing.

"How am I without it?" he teased.

"Let's find out." She unbuttoned his coat and then the vest under it. He obligingly stripped them off for her, along with his tie, and left the shirt buttons to her hands. "You've got cuff links," she murmured, trying to release them.

"I'll do it." He moved to the chest of drawers and put his cuff links in a small box, along with his pocket change and keys. He paused to remove his shirt and slacks, shoes and socks before he came back to her, in silky gray boxer shorts like the ones he'd worn the night they were almost intimate.

"You are...magnificent," she whispered, running her hands over his chest.

"You have no idea how magnificent, yet." He unsnapped the shorts and let them fall, coaxing her eyes to him. He shivered at the expression on her face, because he was far more potent than he'd been the one time she'd looked at him like this.

While she was gaping, he unfastened the camisole with a delicate flick of his fingers and unhooked the garter belt. He stripped the whole of it down her slender body and tipped her back onto the bed while he pulled the stockings off with the remainder of her clothing.

He pulled back the cover and tossed the pillows off to the side before he arranged her on the crisp white sheets and stood over her, vibrating with desire, his eyes eating her nude body, from her taut nipples to the visible trembling of her long, parted legs.

She watched him come down to her with faint apprehension that suddenly vanished when he pressed his open mouth down, hard, right on her soft belly.

He'd never touched her like that, and in the next few feverish minutes, she went from shock to greater shock as he displayed his knowledge of women.

"No, you can't, you can't!" she sobbed, but he was, he did, he had!

She arched up toward his mouth with tears of tortured ecstasy raining down her cheeks in a firestorm of sensation, sobbing as the pleasure stretched her tight as a rope under the warm, expert motions of his lips.

She gasped as the wave began to hit her. Her eyes opened, and his face was there, his body suddenly right over hers, his hips thrusting down. She felt him, and then looked and saw him, even as she felt the small stabbing pain of his invasion. The sight of what was happening numbed the pain, and then it was gone all together as he shifted roughly, dragging his hips against hers as he enforced his possession of her innocence.

Her nails bit into his long back as he moved on her, insisting, demanding. His face, above her, was strained, intent.

"Am I hurting you?" he ground out.

"N...no!" she gasped, lifting toward him, her eyes wide, shocked, fascinated.

He looked down, lifting himself so that he could watch her body absorb him. "Look," he coaxed through his teeth. "Look, Janie. Look at us."

She glanced down and her breath caught at the intimate sight that met her eyes. She gasped.

"And we've barely begun," he breathed, shifting suddenly, fiercely, against her.

She sobbed, shivering.

He did it again, watching her face, assessing her reaction. "I can feel you, all around me, like a soft, warm glove," he whispered, his lips compressing as pleasure shot through him with every deepening motion of his hips. "Take me, baby. Take me inside you. Take all of me. Make me scream, baby," he murmured.

She was out of her mind with the pleasure he was giving her. She writhed under him, arching her hips, pushing against him, watching his face. She shifted and he groaned harshly. She laughed, through her own torment, and suddenly cried out as the pleasure became more and more unbearable. Her hands went between them, in a fever of desire.

"Yes," he moaned as he felt her trembling touch. "Yes. Oh…God…baby…do it, do it! Do it!"

She was going to die. She opened her eyes and looked at him, feeling her body pulse as he shortened and deepened his movements, watching her with his mouth compressed, his eyes feverish.

"Do it…harder," she choked.

He groaned in anguish and his hips ground into hers suddenly, his hands catching her wrists and slamming them over her head as he moved fiercely above her, his eyes holding hers prisoner as his body enforced its possession violently.

She felt her body strain to accommodate him and in the last few mad seconds, she wondered if she would be able to…

He blurred in her sight. She was shaking. Her whole body rippled in a shuddering parody of convulsions, whipping against his while her mouth opened, gasping at air, and her voice uttered sounds she'd never heard from it in her entire life.

"Get it," he groaned. "Yes. Get it…!"

He cried out and then his body, too, began to shudder rhythmically. A sound like a harsh sob tore from his throat.

He groaned endlessly as his body shivered into completion. Seconds, minutes, hours, an eternity of pleasure later, he collapsed on her.

They both shivered in the aftermath. She felt tears on her face, in her mouth. She couldn't breathe. Her body ached, even inside, and when she moved, she felt pleasure stab her in the most secret places, where she could still feel him.

She sobbed, her nails biting into the hands pinning her wrists.

He lifted his head. "Look at me," he whispered, and when she did, he began to move again.

She sobbed harder, her legs parting, her hips lifting for him, her whole body shivering in a maelstrom of unbelievable delight.

"I can go again, right now," he whispered huskily, holding her eyes. "Can you? Or will it hurt?"

"I can't…feel pain," she whimpered. Her eyes closed on a shiver and then opened again, right into his. "Oh, please," she whispered brokenly. "Please, please…!"

He began to move, very slowly. "I love watching you," he whispered breathlessly. "Your face is beautiful, like this. Your body…" He looked down at it, watching its sensuous movements in response to his own. "I could eat you with a spoon right now, Mrs. Hart," he added shakily. "You are every dream of perfection that I've ever had."

"And you…are mine," she whispered. She lifted up to him, initiating the rhythm, whimpering softly as the pleasure began to climb all over again. "I love you…so much," she sobbed.

His body clenched. He groaned, arched, his face going into her throat as his body took over from his mind and buffeted her violently.

She went over the edge almost at once, holding on for dear life while he took what he wanted from her. It was feverish, ardent, overwhelming. She thought she might faint from the ecstasy when it throbbed into endless satiation. He went with her, every second of the way. She felt him when his body gave up the pleasure he sought, felt the rigor, heard the helpless throb of his voice at her ear when he shuddered and then relaxed completely.

She held him close, drinking in the intimate sound and feel and scent of his big body over hers in the damp bed. It had been a long, wild loving. She'd never imagined, even in their most passionate encounters, that lovemaking would be like this.

She told him so, in shy whispers.

He didn't answer her. He was still, and quiet, for such a long time that she became worried.

"Are you all right?" she whispered at his ear. Over her, she could hear and feel the beat of his heart as it slowly calmed.

His head lifted, very slowly. He looked into her wide eyes. "I lost consciousness for a few seconds," he said quietly. He touched her lower lip, swollen from the fierce pressure of his mouth just at the last. "I thought…I might die, trying to get deep enough to satisfy us both."

She flushed.

He put his finger over her lips. He wasn't smiling. He moved deliberately, letting her feel him. "You aren't on the Pill," he said. "And I was too hot to even think of any sort of birth control. Janie," he added, hesitantly, "I think I made you pregnant."

Her eyes searched his. "You said you wanted to," she reminded him in a whisper.

"I do. But it should have been your choice, too," he continued, sounding worried.

She traced his long, elegant nose and smiled with delicious exhaustion. "Did you hear me shouting, Leo, stop and run to the pharmacy to buy protection!"

He laughed despite the gravity of the situation. "Was that about the time I was yelling, 'get it, baby'?"

She hit his chest, flushed, and then laughed.

"You did, too, didn't you?" he asked with a smug grin. "So did I. Repeatedly." He groaned as he moved slowly away from her and flopped onto his back, stretching his sore muscles. "Damn, I'm sore! And I told you I could go all night, didn't I?"

She sat up, torn between shock and amusement as she met his playful eyes. "Sore? Men get sore?"

"When they go at it like that, they do," he replied sardonically. "What a wedding night," he said, whistling through his lips as he studied her nude body appreciatively. "If they gave medals, you could have two."

Her eyebrows arched. "Really? I was…I was all right?"

He tugged her down to him. "Women have egos, too, don't they?" he asked tenderly. He pushed her damp hair away from her cheeks and mouth. "You were delicious. I've never enjoyed a woman so much."

"I didn't know anything at all."

He brought her head down and kissed her eyelids. "It isn't a matter of knowledge."

She searched his eyes. "You had enough of that for both of us," she murmured.

"Bodies in the dark," he said, making it sound unimportant. "I wanted to have you in the light, Janie," he said solemnly. "I wanted to look at you while I was taking you."

"That's a sexist remark," she teased.

"You took me as well," he conceded. He touched her mouth with a long forefinger. "I've never seen anything so beautiful," he whispered, and sounded breathless. "Your face, your body…" His face clenched. "And the pleasure." His eyes closed and he shivered. "I've never known anything like it." His eyes opened again. "It was love," he whispered to her, scowling. "Making love. Really making love."

Her breath caught in her throat. She traced his sideburn to his ear. "Yes."

"Do you know what I'm trying to tell you?" he asked quietly.

She looked down into his eyes and saw it there. Her heart jumped into her throat. "You're telling me that you love me," she said.

He nodded. "I love you. I knew it when Clark assaulted you, and I went at him. It hurt my pride that I couldn't make him beg for forgiveness. I cleaned you up and dried your hair, and knew that I loved you, all at once. It was a very small step from there to a wedding ring." He brought hers to his lips and kissed it tenderly. "I couldn't bear the thought of losing you. Not after that."

She smiled dreamily. "I loved you two years ago, when you brought me a wilted old daisy you'd picked out in the meadow, and teased me about it being a bouquet. You didn't know it, but to me, it was."

"I've given you a hard time," he told her, with obvious regret. "I'm sorry."

She leaned down and kissed him tenderly. "You made up for it." She moved her breasts gently against his chest. "I really can go all night," she whispered. "When you've recovered, I'll show you."

He chuckled under the soft press of her mouth, and his big arms swallowed her. "When *you're* recovered, I'll let you. I love you, Mrs. Hart. I love you with all my heart."

"I love you with all mine." She kissed him again, and thought how dreams did, sometimes, actually come true.

A week later, they celebrated their first Christmas together at a family party, to which Janie's father, aunt Lydia and Hettie were also invited. After kissing her with exquisite tenderness beneath the mistletoe, Leo gave Janie an emerald necklace, to match her eyes he said, and she gave him an expensive pocket watch, with his name and hers engraved inside the case.

On New Year's Eve, the family gathered with other families at the Jacobsville Civic Center for the first annual celebration. A live band played favorites and couples danced on the polished wood floor. Calhoun Ballenger had mused aloud that since Jacobsville's economy was based on cattle and agriculture, they should drop a pair of horns instead of a ball to mark the new year. He was red-faced at the celebration, when the city fathers took him seriously and did that very thing.

While Leo and Janie stood close together on the patio of the second floor ballroom to watch the neon set of longhorns go down to the count, a surprising flurry of snow came tumbling from the sky to dust the heads of the crowd.

"It's snowing!" Janie exclaimed, holding out a hand to catch the fluffy precipitation. "But it never snows in Jacobsville! Well, almost never."

Leo caught her close as the horns went to the bottom of the courthouse tower across the street and bent to her mouth, smiling. "One more wish come true," he teased, because he knew how much she loved snow. "Happy New Year, my darling," he whispered.

"Happy New Year," she whispered back, and met his kiss with loving enthusiasm, to the amused glances of the other guests. They were, after all, newlyweds.

The new year came and soon brought with it unexpected tragedy. John Clark went back to Victoria to get his jailed brother a famous attorney, but he didn't have any money. So he tried to rob a bank to get the money. He was caught in the act by a security guard and a Texas Ranger who was working on a case locally. Judd Dunn was one of the two men who exchanged shots with Clark in front of the Victoria Bank and Trust. Clark missed. Judd and the security guard didn't. Ballistics tests were required to pinpoint who fired the fatal bullet.

Jack Clark, still in jail in Victoria, was let out long enough to attend his brother's funeral in Victoria. He escaped from the kindly sheriff's deputy who was bringing him back in only handcuffs instead of handcuffs and leg chains. After all, Jack Clark had been so docile and polite, and even cried at his brother's grave. The deputy was rewarded for his compassion by being knocked over the head twice with the butt of his own .38 caliber service revolver and left for dead in a driving rain in the grass next to the Victoria road. Later that day, his squad car was found deserted a few miles outside Victoria.

It was the talk of the town for several days, and Leo and Janie stayed close to home, because they knew Clark had scores to settle all around Jacobsville. They were in their own little world, filled with love. They barely heard all the buzz and gossip. But what they did hear was about Tippy Moore and Cash Grier.

"Tippy's not Grier's sort," Janie murmured sleepily. They didn't do a lot of sleeping at night, even now. She cuddled up in her husband's lap and nuzzled close. "He needs someone who is gentle and sweet. Not a harpy."

He wrapped her up close and kissed the top of her head. "What would you know about harpies?" he teased. "You're the sweetest single human being I've ever known."

She smiled.

"Well, except for me, of course," he added.

"Leo Hart!" she exclaimed, drawing back.

"You said I was sweet," he murmured, bending his head. "You said it at least six times. You were clawing my back raw at the time, and swearing that you were never going to live through what I was doing to you…"

She tugged his head down and kissed him hungrily. "You're sweet, all right," she whispered raggedly. "Do it again…!"

He groaned. They were never going to make it to the bed. But the doors were locked…what the hell.

An hour later, he carried her down the hall to their bedroom and tucked her up next to him, exhausted and still smiling.

"At least," he said wearily, "Hopefully Clark will go to prison for a long, long time when he's caught. He won't be in a position to threaten you again."

"Or you." She curled closer. "Did I tell you that Marilee phoned me yesterday?"

He stiffened. "No."

She smiled. "It's okay. She only wanted to apologize. She's going to Europe to visit her grandmother in London. I told her to have a nice trip."

"London's almost far enough away."

She sighed, wrapping her arms around him. "Be generous. She'll never know what it is to be as happy as we are."

"Who will?" he teased, but the look he gave her was serious. He touched her hair, watching her succumb to sleep.

He lay awake for a long time, his eyes intent on her slender, sleeping body. She made wonderful biscuits, she could shoot a shotgun, she made love like a fairy. He wondered what he'd ever done in his life to deserve her.

"Dreams," she whispered, shocking him.

"What, honey?"

She nuzzled her face into his throat and melted into him. "Dreams come true," she whispered, falling asleep again.

He touched her lips with his and smoothed back her long hair. "Yes, my darling," he whispered with a long, sweet smile. "Dreams come true."

* * * * *

Turn the page for a preview
of New York Times bestselling author
Diana Palmer's
newest hardcover for HQN Books

BEFORE SUNRISE

Available this July at your favorite book outlet

Chapter One

THE CROWD WAS DENSE, but he stood out. He was taller than most of the other spectators and looked elegant in his expensive, tailored gray-vested suit. He had a lean, dark face, faintly scarred, with large, almond-shaped black eyes and short eyelashes. His mouth was wide and thin-lipped, his chin stubbornly jutted. His thick, jet-black hair was gathered into a neat ponytail that fell almost to his waist in back. Several other men in the stands wore their hair that way. But they were white. Cortez was Comanche. He had the background to wear the unconventional hairstyle. On him, it looked sensual and wild and even a little dangerous.

Another ponytailed man, a redhead with a receding hairline and thick glasses, grinned and gave him the victory sign. Cortez shrugged, unimpressed, and turned his attention toward the graduation ceremonies. He was here against his will and the last thing he felt like was being friendly. If he'd followed his instincts, he'd still be in Washington going over a backlog of federal cases he was due to prosecute in court.

The dean of the university was announcing the names of the graduates. He'd reached the Ks, and on the program, Phoebe Margaret Keller was the second name under that heading.

It was a beautiful spring day at the University of Tennessee at Knoxville, so the commencement ceremony was being held outside. Phoebe was recognizable by the long platinum blond braid trailing the back of her dark gown as she accepted her diploma with one hand and shook hands with the dean with the other. She moved past the podium and switched her tassel to the other side of her cap. Cortez could see the grin from where he was standing.

He'd met Phoebe a year earlier, while he was investigating some environmental sabotage in Charleston, South Carolina. Phoebe, an anthropology major, had helped him track down a toxic waste site. He'd found her more than attractive, despite her tomboyish appearance, but time and work pressure had been against them. He'd promised to come and see her graduate, and here he was. But the age difference was still pretty formidable, because he was thirty-six and she was twenty-three. He did know Phoebe's aunt Derrie, from having worked with her during the Kane Lombard pollution case. If he needed a reason for showing up at the graduation, Phoebe was Derrie's late brother's child and he was almost a friend of the family.

The dean's voice droned on, and graduate after graduate accepted a diploma. In no time at all, the exercises were over and whoops of joy and congratulations rang in the clear Tennessee air.

No longer drawing attention as the exuberant crowd moved toward the graduates, Cortez hung back, watching. His black eyes narrowed as a thought occurred to him. Phoebe wasn't one for crowds. Like himself, she was a loner. If she was going to work her way around the people to find her aunt Derrie, she'd do it away from the crowd. So he started looking for alternate routes from the stadium to the parking lot. Minutes later, he found her, easing around the side of the building, almost losing her balance as she struggled with the too-long gown, muttering to herself about people who couldn't measure people properly for gowns.

"Still talking to yourself, I see," he mused, leaning against the wall with his arms folded across his chest.

She looked up and saw him. With no time to prepare, her delight swept over her even features with a radiance that took his breath. Her pale blue eyes sparkled and her mouth, devoid of lipstick, opened on a sharply indrawn breath.

"Cortez!" she exclaimed.

She looked as if she'd run straight into his arms with the least invitation, and he smiled indulgently as he gave it to her. He levered away from the wall and opened his arms.

She went into them without any hesitation whatsoever, nestling close as he enfolded her tightly.

"You came," she murmured happily into his shoulder.

"I said I would," he reminded her. He chuckled at her unbridled enthusiasm. One lean hand tilted up her chin so that he could search her eyes. "Four years of hard work paid off, I see."

"So it did. I'm a graduate," she said, grinning.

"Certifiable," he agreed. His gaze fell to her soft pink mouth and darkened. He wanted to bend those few inches and kiss her, but there were too many reasons why he shouldn't. His hand was on her upper arm and, because he was fighting his instincts so hard, his grip began to tighten.

She tugged against his hold. "You're crushing me," she protested gently.

"Sorry." He let her go with an apologetic smile. "That training at Quantico dies hard," he added on a light note, alluding to his service with the FBI.

"No kiss, huh?" she chided with a loud sigh, searching his dark eyes.

One eye narrowed amusedly. "You're an anthropology major. Tell me why I won't kiss you," he challenged.

"Native Americans," she began smugly, "especially Native American men, rarely show their feelings in public. Kissing me in a crowd would be as distasteful to you as undressing in front of it."

His eyes softened as they searched her face. "Whoever taught you anthropology did a very good job."

She sighed. "Too good. What am I going to use it for in Charleston? I'll end up teaching..."

"No, you won't," he corrected. "One of the reasons I came was to tell you about a job opportunity."

Her eyes widened, brightened. "A job?"

"In D.C.," he added. "Interested?"

"Am I ever!" A movement caught her eye. "Oh, there's Aunt Derrie!" she said, and called to her aunt. "Aunt Derrie! Look, I graduated, I have proof!" She held up her diploma as she ran to hug her aunt and then shake hands with U.S. Senator Clayton Seymour, who'd been her aunt's boss for years before they became engaged.

"We're both very happy for you," Derrie said warmly. "Hi, Cortez!" she beamed. "You know Clayton, don't you?"

"Not directly," Cortez said, but he shook hands anyway.

Clayton's firm lips tugged into a smile. "I've heard a lot about you from my brother-in-law, Kane Lombard. He and my sister Nikki wanted to come today, but their twins were sick. If you're going to be in town tonight, we'd love to have you join us for supper," he told Cortez. "We're taking Phoebe out for a graduation celebration."

"I wish I had time," he said quietly. "I have to go back tonight."

"Of course. Then we'll see you again sometime, in D.C.," Derrie said, puzzled by the strong vibes she sensed between her niece and Cortez.

"I've got something to discuss with Phoebe," he said, turning to Derrie and Clayton. "I need to borrow her for an hour or so."

"Go right ahead," Derrie said. "We'll go back to the hotel and have coffee and pie and rest until about six. Then we'll pick you up for supper, Phoebe."

"Thanks," she said. "Oh, my cap and gown…!" She stripped it off, along with her hat, and handed them to Derrie.

"Wait, Phoebe, weren't the honor graduates invited to a luncheon at the dean's house?" Derrie protested suddenly.

Phoebe didn't hesitate. "They'll never miss me," she said, and waved as she joined Cortez.

"An honor graduate, too," he mused as they walked back through the crowd toward his rental car. "Why doesn't that surprise me?"

"Anthropology is my life," she said simply, pausing to exchange congratulations with one of her friends on the way. She was so happy that she was walking on air.

"Nice touch, Phoebe," the girl's companion murmured with a dry glance at Cortez as they moved along, "bringing your anthropology homework along to graduation."

"Bill!" the girl cried, hitting him.

Phoebe had to stifle a giggle. Cortez wasn't smiling. On the other hand, he didn't explode, either. He gave Phoebe a stern look.

"Sorry," she murmured. "It's sort of a squirrelly day."

He shrugged. "No need to apologize. I remember what it's like on graduation day."

"Your degree would be in law, right?"

He nodded.

"Did your family come to your graduation?" she asked curiously.

He didn't answer her. It was a deliberate snub, and it should have made her uncomfortable, but she never held back with him.

"Another case of instant foot-in-mouth disease," she said immediately. "And I thought I was cured!"

He chuckled reluctantly. "You're as incorrigible as I remember you."

"I'm amazed that you did remember me, or that you took the trouble to find out when and where I was graduating so that you could be here," she said. "I couldn't send you an invitation," she added sheepishly, "because I didn't have your address. I didn't really expect you, either. We only spent an hour or two together last year."

"They were memorable ones. I don't like women very much," he said as they reached the unobtrusive rental car, a gray American-made car of recent vintage. He turned and looked down at her solemnly. "In fact," he added evenly, "I don't like being in public display very much."

She lifted both eyebrows. "Then why are you here?"

He stuck his hands deep into his pockets. "Because I like you," he said. His dark eyes narrowed. "And I don't want to."

"Thanks a lot!" she said, exasperated.

He stared at her. "I like honesty in a relationship."

"Are we having one?" she asked innocently. "I didn't notice."

His mouth pulled down at one corner. "If we were, you'd know," he said softly. "But I came because I promised that I would. And the offer of the job opportunity is genuine. Although," he added, "it's rather an unorthodox one."

"I'm not being asked to take over the archives at the Smithsonian, then? What a disappointment!"

Laughter bubbled out of his throat. "Funny girl." He opened the passenger door with exaggerated patience and he smiled faintly. "You bubble, don't you?" he remarked. "I've never known anyone so animated."

"Yes, well, that's because you're suffering from sensory deprivation resulting from too much time spent with your long nose stuck in law books. Dull, dry, boring things."

"The law is not boring," he returned.

"It depends which side you're sitting on." She frowned. "This job you're telling me about wouldn't have to do with anything legal, would it? Because I only had one course in government and a few hours of history, but..."

"I don't need a law clerk," he returned.

"Then what do you need?"

"You wouldn't be working for me," he corrected. "I have ties to a group that fights for sovereignty for the Native American tribes. They have a staff of attorneys. I thought you might fit in very well, with your background in anthropology. I've pulled some strings to get you an interview."

She didn't speak for a minute. "I think you're forgetting something. My major is anthropology. Most of it is forensic anthropology. Bones."

He glanced at her. "You wouldn't be doing that for them."

"What would I be doing?"

"It's a desk job," he admitted. "But a good one."

"I appreciate your thinking of me," she said carefully. "But I can't give up fieldwork. That's why I've applied at the Smithsonian for a position with the anthropology section."

He was quiet for a long moment. "Do you know how indigenous people feel about archaeology? We don't like having people dig up our sacred sites and our relatives, however old they are."

"I just graduated," she reminded him. "Of course I do. But there's a lot more to archaeology than digging up skeletons!"

His eyes were cold. "And it doesn't stop you from wanting to get a job doing something that resembles grave-digging?"

She gasped. "It is not grave-digging! For heaven's sake…"

He held up a hand. "We can agree to disagree, Phoebe," he told her. "You won't change my mind any more than I'll change yours. I'm sorry about the job, though. You'd have been an asset to them."

She unbent a little. "Thanks for recommending me, but I don't want a desk job. Besides, I may go on to graduate school after I've had a few months to get over the past four years. They've been pretty hectic."

"Yes, I remember."

"Why did you recommend me for that job? There must be

a line of people who'd love to have it—people better qualified than I am."

He turned his head and looked directly into her eyes.
There was something that he wasn't telling her, something
deep inside him.

"Maybe I'm lonely," he said shortly. "There aren't many
people who aren't afraid to come close to me these days."

"Does that matter? You don't like people close," she said.

She searched his arrogant profile. There were new lines
in that lean face, lines she hadn't seen last year, despite the
solemnity of the time they'd spent together. "Something's
upset you," she said out of the blue. "Or you're worried about
something."

Both dark eyebrows went up. "I beg your pardon?" he asked
curtly.

The hauteur went right over her head. "Not something to
do with work, either," she continued, reasoning aloud. "It's
something very personal…"

"Stop right there," he said shortly. "I invited you out to talk
about a job, not about my private life."

"Ah. A closed door. Intriguing." She stared at him. "Not
a woman?"

"You're the only woman in my life."

She laughed unexpectedly. "That's a good one."

"I'm not kidding. I don't have affairs or relationships."
He glanced at her as he merged into traffic again and
turned at the next corner. "I might make an exception for
you, but don't get your hopes up. A man has his reputation
to consider."

She grinned. "I'll remember that you said that."

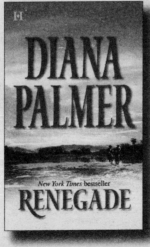

If you enjoyed what you just read,
then we've got an offer you can't resist!

Take 2 bestselling novels FREE!
Plus get a FREE surprise gift!

Clip this page and mail it to MIRA®

IN U.S.A.
3010 Walden Ave.
P.O. Box 1867
Buffalo, N.Y. 14240-1867

IN CANADA
P.O. Box 609
Fort Erie, Ontario
L2A 5X3

YES! Please send me 2 free MIRA® novels and my free surprise gift. After receiving them, if I don't wish to receive anymore, I can return the shipping statement marked cancel. If I don't cancel, I will receive 4 brand-new novels every month, before they're available in stores! In the U.S.A., bill me at the bargain price of $4.99 plus 25¢ shipping and handling per book and applicable sales tax, if any*. In Canada, bill me at the bargain price of $5.49 plus 25¢ shipping and handling per book and applicable taxes**. That's the complete price and a savings of over 20% off the cover prices—what a great deal! I understand that accepting the 2 free books and gift places me under no obligation ever to buy any books. I can always return a shipment and cancel at any time. Even if I never buy another The Best of the Best™ book, the 2 free books and gift are mine to keep forever.

185 MDN DZ7J
385 MDN DZ7K

Name _____ (PLEASE PRINT) _____

Address _____ Apt.# _____

City _____ State/Prov. _____ Zip/Postal Code _____

*Not valid to current The Best of the Best™, Mira®,
suspense and romance subscribers.*

*Want to try two free books from another series?
Call 1-800-873-8635 or visit www.morefreebooks.com.*

* Terms and prices subject to change without notice. Sales tax applicable in N.Y.
** Canadian residents will be charged applicable provincial taxes and GST.
All orders subject to approval. Offer limited to one per household.
® and ™are registered trademarks owned and used by the trademark owner and or its licensee.

BOB04R